THE FIFTH
RULE OF TEN

ALSO BY GAY HENDRICKS AND TINKER LINDSAY

The First Rule of Ten

The Second Rule of Ten

The Broken Rules of Ten

The Third Rule of Ten

The Fourth Rule of Ten

All of the above are available at your local bookstore,
or may be ordered by visiting:

Hay House UK: www.hayhouse.co.uk
Hay House USA: www.hayhouse.com®
Hay House Australia: www.hayhouse.com.au
Hay House South Africa: www.hayhouse.co.za
Hay House India: www.hayhouse.co.in

THE FIFTH RULE OF TEN

A TENZING NORBU MYSTERY

GAY HENDRICKS & TINKER LINDSAY

HAY HOUSE

Carlsbad, California • New York City • London
Sydney •Johannesburg • Vancouver • New Delhi

First published and distributed in the United Kingdom by:
Hay House UK Ltd, Astley House, 33 Notting Hill Gate, London W11 3JQ
Tel: +44 (0)20 3675 2450; Fax: +44 (0)20 3675 2451; www.hayhouse.co.uk

Published and distributed in the United States of America by:
Hay House Inc., PO Box 5100, Carlsbad, CA 92018-5100
Tel: (1) 760 431 7695 or (800) 654 5126
Fax: (1) 760 431 6948 or (800) 650 5115; www.hayhouse.com

Published and distributed in Australia by:
Hay House Australia Ltd, 18/36 Ralph St, Alexandria NSW 2015
Tel: (61) 2 9669 4299; Fax: (61) 2 9669 4144; www.hayhouse.com.au

Published and distributed in the Republic of South Africa by:
Hay House SA (Pty) Ltd, PO Box 990, Witkoppen 2068
info@hayhouse.co.za; www.hayhouse.co.za

Published and distributed in India by:
Hay House Publishers India, Muskaan Complex, Plot No.3, B-2,
Vasant Kunj, New Delhi 110 070
Tel: (91) 11 4176 1620; Fax: (91) 11 4176 1630; www.hayhouse.co.in

Distributed in Canada by:
Raincoast Books, 2440 Viking Way, Richmond, B.C. V6V 1N2
Tel: (1) 604 448 7100; Fax: (1) 604 270 7161; www.raincoast.com

Copyright © 2016 by Gay Hendricks and Tinker Lindsay

Cover design: Charles McStravick • Interior design: Pamela Homan

A catalogue record for this book is available from the British Library.

ISBN: 978-1-78180-568-8

CHAPTER 1

My heart was a fist, pounding against its cage of ribs.

Let me out, let me out, let me out.

Easy, Ten. There's enough oxygen, especially out here on the deck. All those trees? That's their only job, to make oxygen.

I would never take breathing for granted again. I'd always assumed it was automatic. And it was.

Until the day came when it wasn't.

I fumbled for the only weapon that made sense, given the circumstances.

A pen.

CHAPTER 2

I pulled the yellow legal pad close, a flickering candle my only source of light, unless you counted the sickle of moon. My hand glided across the paper.

```
                           Topanga Canyon, Calif.
                    June 2, Year of the Wooden Horse

    Geshe Lobsang and Geshe Yeshe
    Dorje Yidam Monastery
    Dharamshala, India

    Venerable brothers,

    I will never mail this letter.
    You will never read it.
    But my mind has become my enemy. Once
again, I turn to you for clarity.
    I am alone on my deck overlooking the
gloomy canyon and you are somewhere far
above, hurtling closer with every hour. You
come to offer wisdom, to affirm your lifelong
commitment to the Buddha's teachings.
    And so, of course, my pen brings me to the
subject I most want to avoid. Commitment.
    Commitment has always seemed risky to me,
a notion that can serve right action, but also
its reverse. Here they call such a thing a
double-edged sword. But to me, commitment is
more like our ceremonial phurba, the dagger
```

with its three blades. Triple-edged, like the Buddha's teachings on the three potential responses of the mind: Attraction. Aversion. Neutrality.

I am once again pinned between the first two.

Yeshe and Lobsang, you know this about me. You saw me plunge into our Gelugpa tradition as a child, when we were novices at Dorje Yidam. I was so fervent, so sure. We all were, remember? We took refuge in the Three Jewels and vowed to keep the Five Precepts.

A decade later you watched the teenage me flee from the monastery as if my life depended on it.

I did the same with the Los Angeles Police Department. At my academy graduation I made a solemn commitment to protect and serve. No LAPD rookie was more dedicated. No homicide detective put in longer hours. And then, one day, I was done. I had to get out. I was suffocating.

You have always accepted this contradiction in me: How deeply I'm drawn to the idea of commitment. How fiercely I push against it.

And of course I know, at least intellectually, that somewhere in between the pull and push is a third choice. Equanimity. The middle way. I long for it, for the supple strength of the willow; roots grounded in the Buddha's teaching, trunk sturdy yet flexible, branches bending and swaying through sunshine and storm. A man like that feels compassion for all, touches and tastes spacious liberation while staying true to his commitments. A man like that is worthy of trust.

I feel so very far from that man, as I sit here in the darkness.

Be specific, Ten.

Okay. The truth: I am suffering from a painful case of commitment backlash.

Julie is amazing. Smart. Funny. Strong. Vulnerable. She's creative, and self-reliant, and her lovemaking is passionate and inventive. (I would apologize for that detail, Lobsang, but as I said before, you will never read this.) There are moments I feel like the most fortunate man in the world, when I am awash in gratitude.

And then there are times like tonight, when I didn't so much wake up as claw my way to the surface of consciousness. When her warm body, usually a source of comfort, smothered me to the point of suffocation. I had to practice great restraint not to shove her away as I leapt out of bed, gasping.

How can I tell her this? That at times my skin burns with unease, as if she were toxic? How could she possibly understand such a thing when I don't understand it myself? And yet I must tell her, because I also know how secrets destroy.

The thought of losing her forever stops my heart. The thought of staying with her forever stops my breath.

I can hear you, Yeshe: *Tenzing, this is not about Julie. This is an ancient karmic resistance, the bitter fruit of many lifetimes of suffering and ignorance . . .*

Maybe so. But I'd very much like to be done with this particular hindrance in this particular lifetime. My friend Jean likes to say the first step toward solution is admitting the problem. It worked for her with drugs and alcohol. Maybe it will work for me with love.

I admit it. I'm terrified of making this commitment. And I'm equally terrified of being a man who cannot commit, of living and dying alone, not to mention coming back for another maddening round of this particular struggle.

There is more to admit: this particular turmoil is like an emotional vise, squeezing out other pockets of darkness. Blank places where memories should be. The gnawing sense that I am both chasing and being chased by a ghost. I don't want to bolt again.

I feel the need to set myself another guideline. To write down a new rule, so that maybe I can actually live it. Just to be clear, this is not an expectation—I've been easing up on those, with some success—but more a deep intention: *May I be mindful both making and keeping commitments that they be springboards to liberation, instead of suffering, for all sentient beings.*

Including this one.

Huh. My jaw no longer feels clamped to the point of breaking. The in-and-out breaths are easier. Even the horizon is now streaked with rose and gold. Across the canyon, the dark mist dissolves and a lone star winks at me.

Your plane grows nearer.

I can't wait to see you.

Ten

CHAPTER 3

Kim's body, normally stiff, was rigid as a plank. She reached for her pierced right eyebrow. Her finger and thumb found the metal stud and twisted it back and forth like a stubborn key.

Why was she here in my house? In my office? I had given her two weeks off. Yeshe and Lobsang were landing at LAX with their Buddhist entourage in a few hours, and whether I persuaded them to actually sleep here or not, they'd be in and out of my tiny abode. The thought of adding my odd assistant to a fiancée, dog, cat, and herd of monks made my head want to explode.

"I brought you something, Mr. Norbu." Kim rummaged through her backpack and produced a photograph. "I keep it in the drawer next to my bed. I look at it every night before I go to sleep."

For a young woman whose fashion choices included enough body piercings to repair a steel bridge and a short, spiky Mohawk that was weapons-grade stiff, she remained strangely formal with me. Kim's doctors claimed that she placed somewhere toward the middle on the autism spectrum, but I found her quirks to be no more extreme than most people's—she just displayed hers more publicly.

I tried to keep my voice gentle. "I'm sorry, why are you . . . ?"

"This is my brother. This is Bobby." Kim handed me the three-by-five photo. "Our last Christmas together. Bobby was nine and I was four."

Bobby. Kim's missing brother.

The colors were faded, the emulsion cracked from prolonged exposure to sunlight and scrutiny. The two children were in pajamas. His were mottled green and gray, a camouflage print, while Kim wore festive red-and-white stripes.

Bobby had a protective arm around his younger sister, and he aimed a slight scowl at the camera. His other hand clutched a toy rifle. A green plastic helmet, far too big for his head, tipped low across his brow.

The young Kim's hair was light brown, feather soft, and shaped like a bowl, a far cry from her current crown of black thorns. She stared straight ahead with a blank look, her arms stiff, her hands curled into half fists. I recognized the ramrod stance: she adopted it three mornings a week when she reported here for work and awaited her daily assignments.

"He took me on adventures," Kim said. "He always shared his food with me. We both liked Cheetos the best."

"Cheetos?"

"They are puffy and cheesy and bright orange. They are delicious. Shall I buy you some?"

"Maybe not," I said.

I glanced at my watch. Julie would be back any minute. "Kim, I'm happy to see this photograph, but . . ."

"I never felt scared when I was with Bobby." Kim's voice rose as she took back the picture and held it close to her eyes as if searching for clues. "I loved that Christmas, at least the morning part. Bobby got a G.I. Joe footlocker, and I got a Cut and Style Barbie with detachable hair. I still have it. It is the only Barbie I ever got."

She set the photo on my desk, an abrupt move.

"Kim . . ."

"But I also hated that Christmas because my mother and father started shouting at each other when we were eating our dinner, macaroni and cheese and peas and carrots, and the next morning . . ." Kim blinked. "Mr. Norbu, my mouth wants to stop talking." She blinked again, twice. "Now my stomach is starting to hurt."

I waited. Kim's therapist had given her two specific behaviors for dealing with her heightened response to the world. Whenever she felt overwhelmed, he suggested she first express a truth about her response that was unarguable: "My mouth wants to stop talking," for example. And second, he advised her to feel what was happening with her body.

I'd come to appreciate these two techniques myself as almost foolproof tools for safe passage through situations fraught with emotion.

"I may have to cry, Mr. Norbu."

"I understand," I said. "Please, cry if you want to." Allowing Kim to feel her feelings was the quickest route to the other side of turmoil.

Kim stood frowning, her vision turning inward. Then her face cleared. She nodded twice. "Yes. I am okay now."

I gestured to the picture. "Why did you bring me this, Kim?"

She stared, as if it were obvious. "You said you would help me find him. For my birthday present. You promised, remember?"

I scoured my brain. Yes, there had been a moment, a few weeks back. She'd mentioned that her birthday was coming up.

"What do you want for your birthday?" I'd asked.

"Bobby," she'd answered. "All I want is Bobby."

"I'll help you," I'd replied. "As soon as I have time. I promise."

And then I'd gotten the e-mail from Yeshe and Lobsang, and everything else flew from my head.

My stomach tightened up a notch. "When is it again? Your birthday?"

"This Thursday, Mr. Norbu. I told you before." A series of tics rippled across her face. Her fingers twitched.

Today was Monday. I calculated rapidly. My friends would need at least one day to rest and recover from the brutally long journey from Dharamshala, and probably

another to prepare for the sand mandala ceremony. This just might work.

"Okay, Kim. Here's what I can do. I can work on finding Bobby for a couple of days. I may not find him, but I'll try my hardest."

Kim's face smoothed. "Thank you, Mr. Norbu. I knew you would keep your promise."

I grabbed a legal pad from the desk and flipped past the predawn letter to Yeshe and Lobsang, the one where I pledged to keep my commitments. A small sigh escaped. That was the problem with setting a new intention: it was invariably, immediately put to the test.

"Can you tell me what happened that morning, the morning after Christmas?"

"My father took my brother and drove away. I never saw Bobby or my father again."

"What about your mother? Did she keep in touch with them?"

"She told me they were gone. Gone for good." Kim's mouth twisted. "But Bobby leaving wasn't good for me, was it, Mr. Norbu?"

"No. No, it wasn't."

"I kept asking her about him until my mother said if I bothered her one more time about Bobby, she would be gone for good, too. So I stopped."

"What does she say now?"

Kim swallowed hard. I waited. Tank had wandered over to my desk area. He moved to Kim's legs and nudged at one ankle. Kim scooped 17 pounds of Persian blue into her arms and hugged him close. Normally Tank would not tolerate such impertinence, but for Kim he made an exception, as if he sensed her need.

His dense animal nature seemed to calm her. "My mother is dead, Mr. Norbu. Cancer, five years ago. I did try one more time to find out about Bobby, right before she died, but she told me to let sleeping dogs lie. Why would she say that?

She never let me have a dog. She hated them. Just like she hated everything else. My mother was a very angry person."

Julie and I needed to leave for the airport within the hour. But pushing Kim harder would only shut her down, and I needed to learn what I could. I took my cue from Tank, who lay still in her arms.

Another minute passed.

"I tried to find Bobby on Facebook, Mr. Norbu," Kim said. "That was after I Googled him. As 'Bobby,' and also as 'Robert.'" She again reached up to the small metal post bisecting one eyebrow and twisted it between her thumb and forefinger. "I looked at five hundred and thirty-six pictures before I gave up. And anyway I have no idea what he looks like now or where he lives. There are thousands of Robert Smiths, dead and alive."

"Wait a minute. Robert *Smith*? I thought your last name was Nordquist?"

"My mother changed our name back to Nordquist after my father left with Bobby. She said my father could take his name and shove it where the sun does not shine."

Robert Nordquist was a relatively unique name. Robert Smith was going to be an absolute nightmare to track down, unless I could narrow the field.

"Do you remember Bobby's date of birth by any chance?"

"Not exactly. I know he was born the same month as me."

I wrote down: Bobby Smith. Born sometime in June.

Two days was looking a little optimistic.

Kim leaned over to set Tank on the floor. Halfway there he executed a flying-squirrel leap and landed a few feet away with a decisive *thud*. He strolled off, as if leaving was his idea all along.

Like his owner, Tank was obsessed with maintaining at least the illusion of control.

Tank entered the kitchen to reconnoiter the food bowl situation. Julie's voice sing-songed through the screen door. "We're ho-ome!"

I tapped the photograph. "May I keep this for a few days?"

Kim nodded. Her metal tongue stud click-clicked against her teeth, another nervous "tell."

"Do you think you will be able to find him?" Kim asked.

"I hope so. I'll do my absolute best."

In the kitchen Julie unhooked a wheezing Homer from his leash, a semicircle of pink protruding from his mouth. Homer's tongue was a permanent pennant announcing his inner state of bulldog being, in this case, hot, tired, and thirsty. He collapsed, panting.

Unlike Homer, Julie seemed energized by the exercise. The front of her T-shirt was marked with two triangles of dampness, one just above her breasts, the other lower down. My body took note.

Kim and Julie zippered past each other, Julie taking care not to brush against any part of Kim's body. She was impeccable about respecting Kim's need for a physical safety zone.

"Hey," I called out.

Julie waved over her shoulder and continued into our bedroom. In a moment the shower started up. I moved to the living-room windows and glanced outside. As I watched, Kim climbed on her bicycle. She had somehow crammed her helmet onto the bed of spikes, and she pedaled sturdily down the driveway toward Topanga Canyon Road and out of sight.

Why had I just agreed to this? Two days was not a lot of time, and I was rusty. I hadn't taken on a single missing-person's case in almost a year. The last misper case had almost gotten me killed.

I studied the photograph of Kim and had my answer. Four years old. I could only imagine what had happened to her in the intervening decades, an only child with an anxiety disorder, an angry mother, and without her older sibling as protector.

I crossed the living room and shimmied past the bookcase, which was bulging to the point of overflow since Julie had added her poetry and short story anthologies, plus an

extensive cookbook collection. In desperation I'd switched to using a Kindle.

I slipped behind the five-paneled screen that delineated my meditation alcove. It was very cramped since I'd moved the partition closer to the wall, adding space to the living room and subtracting it from my place of refuge.

I stood before the makeshift altar. My discarded red monk's robe served as a cloth covering, camouflaging the old suitcase I'd lugged from Dharamshala when I arrived here 16 years ago. I suppose I could have just bought a low table from IKEA and been done with it, but this way I was always reminded of my roots, and my hybrid nature.

Over time I'd added mementos of the ensuing time in California—feathers, stones, a misshapen bullet. They balanced the sacred spiritual aids of my previous world: a string of carved sandalwood beads; a photograph of His Holiness the 14th Dalai Lama; a small stone statue of the Buddha. The silk *thangka* of the Wheel of Life hung behind the altar, overseeing all.

Today I would summon an ancient protector. I placed the photograph of Kim and her brother Bobby next to a delicate Green Tara carved out of jade.

I took a step back, closed my eyes, and prostrated three times, chanting: *Om tare tuttare ture soha. Om tare tuttare ture soha. Om tare tuttare ture soha.*

I prostrate to the Liberator, mother of all victorious ones.

With any luck the goddess of compassion would step down from her lotus throne and bring me guidance so that I could keep my commitment to Kim. Quickly.

I quieted my senses to hear Green Tara's reply.

What I heard was Homer slopping up water from his bowl in the kitchen.

Welcome to my overpopulated world. The house was maybe 1,200 square feet. Divided by four, that gave us each . . .

I didn't want to think about it.

"We'd better go, Jules," I called out to the bedroom, my voice maybe a little sharper than necessary. "We don't want to be late."

CHAPTER 4

The mahogany steering wheel felt warm and smooth in my hands. I downshifted onto the Sepulveda exit and we slowed to a crawl, surrounded by limos and airport vans following the signs to LAX. The drive had been quiet, both Julie and I absorbed in our own thoughts.

A pair of policemen waved us straight through the security checkpoint. No terrorist in his right mind would drive a bright yellow 1965 Shelby Mustang en route to committing subversive acts.

We began the slow loop, avoiding the impulsive swerves of taxis and hotel transportation buses until I could pull into Lot 4, just beyond the Tom Bradley International Terminal.

"Ten?"

Julie's voice was high, like a child's. In an instant, my own throat tightened. She'd been so subdued on the way here. Had she felt my aversion this morning, once again vaulting me out of bed before dawn? Was she going to ask me about it? It wouldn't be the first time she'd zeroed in on my shadows.

"What happens if they don't like me?"

Relief flooded my body. I wasn't ready for the other conversation. Not yet. "They'll love you," I replied. "Anyway, it's not about Yeshe and Lobsang liking you. It's about them liking me when I'm around you. Don't worry. I'm the one in their crosshairs."

The machine spat out a ticket.

In moments I had squeezed the Mustang between two identical black Lincoln Town Cars. Their bumpers displayed the charmingly antiquated California Livery license plates, a

title better suited to an earlier time, when people traveled in horse-drawn carriages and arrived with their own retinues. The state was finally going to stop issuing livery plates, and I mourned their passing, as I did snail mail and phone booths. Julie says I was born in the wrong century.

She was already out of the car. She stretched, bending her waist from side to side.

Early this morning I'd stroked her awake, her skin silk beneath my hands. The writing had calmed me, and I'd managed to crawl back into bed before she stirred. As if nothing had happened. As if everything was fine.

Inside the terminal, a phalanx of limo drivers in black three-piece suits scanned the arrivals area, handwritten placards positioned at their chests like tactical shields. A steady dribble of travelers trudged past, finally released from Customs and Immigration, surely one of the *bardo* realms of purgatory. Some lugged wheelies, others pushed carts piled high with their life's attachments. Even the children's faces were painted with exhaustion.

I double-checked Yeshe's e-mail and located an electronic arrivals board overhead. The split-flap display shuffled through departure cities and times with confusing speed.

Flip. Flip. There it was—the Delhi-Frankfurt Flight.

"Their plane just landed."

Julie grimaced. "My stomach is in knots. I think it's nerves."

"Take a deep breath," I said, and I did the same, though in my case excitement was the culprit.

We moved to the flecked gray concrete wall overlooking the flecked gray concrete ramp. It was crowded, everyone jockeying for the best look, as if at a sporting event. One toddler in her mother's arms clutched a pair of Mylar welcome-home balloons. Her bowl-shaped haircut reminded me of Kim's as a girl. A few paparazzi, bodies bristling with cameras, scoured the passengers below with eager eyes, on the lookout for money shots. All around us smartphones announced texted progress reports with a *ding*.

Mine was stubbornly silent.

Suddenly the back of my neck tingled, a whispered warning hinting of hidden danger.

Someone was watching me.

"Yeshe said the temple was sending a van and driver," I said, covering, as I scanned the crowd around us carefully. Nothing hooked my vision. I tried to dismiss the feeling as a false alarm. But my ears were now pricked like a dog's.

A large flat-screen monitor occupied a blue Plexiglas divider on the far side of the welcome lobby. Rotating images promoted optimistic slices of diversity in America. The looped series culminated in a robed goddess of copper and steel, rising from New York Harbor. In case anyone missed the point, every few minutes the words *Welcome to the United States of America* flashed.

"I wonder what their story is." Julie pointed. A cluster of young people moved up the ramp, their own huddled mass. It was hard to tell their genders. All their heads were loosely wrapped in white shawls, and all wore caftan-like robes of different hues. Their complexions ranged from darkish to fair, but their eyes uniformly gleamed with the pure light of the converted.

I referred to the arrivals board.

"London, I think."

The back of my neck prickled a second time.

I spun, but no one was paying me any mind. The little girl with the bowl cut hurtled past, silver balloons bouncing above her like giddy satellites.

"Papa! Papa!" A soldier in khaki uniform and peaked cap dropped to one knee, his arms outstretched. His wife reached his side, and he rose with his daughter still clinging. The couple embraced, and he set his military cap on his daughter's head, tucked between them. It tipped low over her eyes.

The London group flowed to one side of the family reunion and on out the glass doors as if they were a single

organism. I filed the image away. I was still on high alert, and something about their robes . . .

My phone buzzed: *Blocked Caller,* the screen read. Joy flooded my body.

"Hey! Welcome to Los Angeles!" I answered. Faint sounds throbbed in my ear.

"Hram hram hram." A low chant, barely audible.

"Hello? Yeshe? Is that you?"

"Hram hram hram hram." The monotone delivery intensified in volume. *"HRAM HRAM HRAM HRAM."*

"I'm sorry. Who is this calling?"

The chanting abruptly cut off. "We're here," a voice whispered. Then, nothing.

A hand grasped my arm and my insides cartwheeled.

"Well, well, well. Lama Tenzing Norbu. I told Adina this morning I was sure I'd find you here."

I whirled, my heart hammering.

It had been 14 years, but I knew him in an instant. His hair had turned completely gray, but it flowed back from his forehead in the same thick stream, and the laugh lines were etched deeper, but they fanned out from the same blue-green eyes. At almost 70, Dr. Eric Leonard still radiated *karuna*—compassion.

"Dr. Leonard, hello." I managed a smile, though I was shaken by the phone call. It wasn't like Yeshe and Lobsang to play practical jokes.

"Call me Eric, please. My goodness, you are a sight for sore eyes, Ten. How long has it been?"

"Too long," I tugged Julie over. "Jules, this is Eric Leonard. I lived in his basement when I first moved to California to teach at the temple. I told you about him, right?"

"Of course," Julie said. She turned to Eric. "You're his Yoda."

"His Yoda?" He looked puzzled.

"You changed Ten's life. Not to mention mine. I would never have met Ten if you hadn't asked him that million-dollar question."

"'Lama Tenzing, ask your heart. What does it truly long for?'" I quoted.

"See?" Julie said. "Totally Yoda thing to say."

I completed the introduction. "Eric, this is Julie Forsythe. Julie's brother-in-law Bill Bohannon was my partner in Robbery/Homicide. Bill's married to Julie's half sister Martha, and Julie and I met when Martha set us up . . ." I was babbling. I closed my mouth.

Eric directed his next words at Julie. "Ten would have figured things out eventually. To this day, I've never met a wiser or more reluctant Buddhist lama. Believe me, the only man Ten revered back then was Arthur Conan Doyle."

He glanced at Julie's left hand, where a small silver and turquoise ring winked. "Are you two . . . ?"

"Engaged," Julie said. "A bit stalled, actually." She tossed me a look, but I wasn't catching. "We can't seem to get it together to pick an actual date. How does anyone survive the wedding insanity?" To my ears, her laugh was a little forced.

I jumped in. "What about you?" I said to Eric. "Still youth advisor at Ganden Gyatso?" Eric and his wife Adina had been temple stalwarts.

"Oh, yes. Youth advisor, chairman of the board, planner of monk tours, and apparently chauffeur. At least for this afternoon. We had a little crisis arise with the volunteer driver." Eric shook his head. "Poor Danny. I tried to warn him. Karma ripens around these tours, big time. In Danny's case, it ripened for him before the monks even landed. He broke his ankle over the weekend trying to be the next Tony Hawk."

I must have looked baffled.

"Skateboarding," Julie said. She often served as my cultural translator.

"Ten?" Eric's kind eyes took me in. "I heard about your father's death. That must have been confusing for you, and hard. But perhaps also liberating?"

"You always were good at reading situations," I said, and left it at that.

"So what are you up to these days? Still a card-carrying member of the LAPD?"

"I'm on my own, now. A private investigator."

"I see. Freelance. Do a lot of driving around, do you?"

"Driving around . . . ?"

I saw what he was doing.

"Ahh. You need a driver."

"I'm afraid so. I'd do it, but I have wall-to-wall clients most days, otherwise . . ."

"I'd love to," I said, but reality hijacked my excitement before it had time to take hold. A hot flare of anger followed. This is why you should never promise anyone anything.

Eric read my face like a chart.

"You'd love to, but?"

"But, I just committed to a job, at least for the next two days. I'm sorry."

Julie's body had sprung to attention, like Homer when one of us opened the refrigerator door.

"I'll do it," she said. "I'm going out of my mind waiting for the lawyers to finish up lawyering so I can start scouting for restaurant sites." She motioned vaguely, as if hoping to conjure up a restaurant right here in the terminal.

"Julie's a professional chef," I explained to Eric. I turned to Julie. "Are you sure you should?"

"Think about it. It's perfect, Ten. You get a break from having Homer and me underfoot, and I get to have a purpose. Other than 'future bride,' I mean." She turned to Eric. "I swear to God, if my sister drags me to one more bridal boutique I'm going to punch her in the nose. Talk about karma ripening." Her face clouded. "Oh God, is it okay that I'm a woman?"

"I'll check, but I don't see why that would cause a problem," Eric said, amused. "Times have changed since Tenzing was a novice."

"And it's for how long?" Julie already had her phone calendar out.

"Eleven days. A week here plus four days in Ojai. The tour culminates in a full moon celebration, location as yet to be determined, on the twelfth. We're treating this as a kind of pilot fund-raising program. Very last minute. If it proves successful, we'll bring a group back next year for a longer tour."

"Do you think they'd mind if Homer rode shotgun? He's very enlightened for a bulldog."

I was feeling distinctly left out, even though I was the one doing the leaving.

"So this is great," I said, keeping my voice light. "Julie can chauffeur the first few days. Then I can take over."

Eric's eyes crinkled, missing nothing. "Just to be clear, you'll both be ferrying five Tibetan lamas in a rented Ford eight-passenger Econoline to and from different venues around Los Angeles. They'll also need to shop for food and supplies. They largely do their own cooking."

"Dumplings. Excellent," Julie said. "About time I added Tibetan *momos* to my repertoire."

I opened my mouth. Closed it. My discomfort had everything to do with my own internal state and nothing to do with hers. I would unpack my puzzling resistance later.

"I see them," Eric said.

Chapter 5

Two figures wrapped in maroon robes made steady progress up the ramp. Yeshe and Lobsang. Here. In Los Angeles. My heart swelled so quickly it hurt.

I waved, but they were focused on balancing their carts, piled high with duffel bags, suitcases, and several bulky boxes encased in airport plastic. As usual, my friends' primary purpose was maintaining equanimity, or in this case equilibrium.

"Which one's which?" Julie asked. "No, wait. Don't tell me, I want to guess. Lobsang's the stocky one with the scowl, and Yeshe's right behind him, the gangly guy with the sweet smile."

"Right on both counts," I said, my voice rough with feeling.

Two more monks appeared behind them. They hurried up the ramp to Lobsang and Yeshe and took over the cart pushing. I didn't know either. They were too young to have been at the monastery when I was.

"That first fellow there, the boy in front, is one of Rinpoche's protégés, Wangdue Chodak," Eric said. "Wangdue is quite the scholar."

"Wang-due Cho-dak." Julie rolled the syllables in her mouth. "Unusual."

"Not if you're Tibetan," I said. "Families don't pass along surnames like over here. Parents name their kids for objects. Sometimes simple things, like a flower or a day of the week. But more often for certain . . ." I reached for the right term. "Elements. You know, positive traits."

"So no last names?" Julie said.

"Nope. Take me. Tenzing means 'holder of the teachings,' and Norbu means 'jewel.' Or Yeshe, that translates as 'wise,' and Lobsang equals 'noble minded.' I guess the idea is to encourage right action from birth."

"That's very cool," Julie said.

"Also very confusing. Every Tibetan is named some combination of a limited number of elements. Plus, they're reversible. There are probably five thousand Wangdue Chodaks and another five thousand Chodak Wangdues."

Eric laughed. "I never really thought about it that way. Like a world inhabited by John Does and Doe Johns."

"Yup," I said. "Talk about a nightmare if a Tibetan goes missing."

Eric looked at me strangely. Our paths had gone in such different directions.

"Here comes one more," Julie said.

"The ritual master for the tour," Eric said. "Venerable Geshe Lharampa Sonam Chophel."

I was startled. "Lama Sonam?" I caught Julie's eye. "He was my personal tutor, back in the day. He was very kind to me."

Sonam. *Merit.* Chophel. *Flourishing of the Dharma.* Lama Sonam was well named.

I squinted, troubled by his appearance. Sonam was only in his midfifties, but his posture was bent and he walked with a slight shuffle. His left hand trembled, fingers rubbing against thumb with the telltale palsy of a neurological disorder.

So he was mortal. I did not want to know that. I cleared my throat. "I had no idea he was coming. Though he speaks English fluently, so it makes sense."

For a moment I felt light-headed, my past on a collision course with my present. Privately I kept both worlds alive. But publicly, the need for separation was strong. East and west. Inner and outer. Light and dark. Then and now.

My love life and my spiritual one.

Ahh. I had located the source of my resistance to the idea of Julie as their tour driver.

Welcome to the Divided States of Ten.

I circled and dodged bystanders, making my way to the head of the ramp. I arrived just as they reached the top.

"*Tashi deley*, Lama Tenzing!" Yeshe's beam was contagious, and passengers all around him smiled through their fatigue.

"*Tashi deley, tashi deley.*" The Tibetan salutation reverberated between the three of us, more blessing than greeting. *Tashi deley—I honor the greatness within you.*

I hugged Lobsang first and then pulled Yeshe into a gruff embrace. They were so much more than ambassadors from my past. They were my brothers and the keepers of my soul.

"You are here, indeed," I said to Yeshe after finally releasing him. "But next time, leave out the weird chanting, okay?"

Yeshe looked puzzled.

"Your phone call to me," I said. "From customs."

He shook his head. "I not call. Calling not allowed."

"Then who . . . ?"

But Yeshe, eyes twinkling, gestured behind me. "Look," he said.

My beaming fiancée had cornered Lobsang. This should be interesting.

"Lobsang? I'm Julie." She paused, uncertain how to proceed.

Lobsang pulled a white *khata* from a small duffel bag. His motions formal, he draped the narrow scarf of white silk around Julie's neck.

"*Tashi deley.*"

"Oh. It's beautiful!" Julie moved as if to hug him. Lobsang stepped back, completely flustered.

"Sorry, is that . . ." Now Julie's cheeks were flushed. "I'm just . . . I'm very happy to finally meet you, Lobsang."

"*Too je che,*" he said stiffly. "Tank you."

"I'm going to be your driver," she added before moving on to Yeshe, leaving Lobsang mystified.

He'd get used to it.

As I turned to Geshe Sonam, my body started to vibrate, as if someone had struck a bell, deep in my chest. After so many years of spiritual practice, Geshe Sonam's internal state had grown very pure. Just being near him activated a kind of delicious thrum in my veins. I closed my eyes for a moment, letting the sweet sparks travel through my body. I reached for the Tibetan word.

Bde-ba. Bliss. As powerful as any chemically induced high, and for some, just as addictive. The Buddha warns us not to pay *bde-ba* too much mind, lest we get caught in its pleasurable, carbonated web. But for this instant, I let the current flow.

"Geshe Sonam," I said. "I am so very honored that you are here. Welcome." I bowed.

"No ceremony, Tenzing!" Sonam replied. "We are in America now, yes?"

"Yes," I said. And with that, I finally knew it to be true.

The two younger monks stood to the side, guarding the carts. The first was built like a fire hydrant, strong and squat. His small ears jutted from his squarish head like little shutters.

I asked him his name, the Tibetan vowels a little stale on my tongue. *"Khedrand ming gangyin?"*

He answered in English. "My name Thoknay Jampa. But here in US I think I will be called TJ. Okay?"

"Sounds good, TJ."

Julie stepped next to me, and TJ pointed to her scarf.

"Khata, very good!" He showed us a similar scarf, tucked inside his robe. "See? His Holiness bless this! Very special! Very special!" He was a little overeager, like a puppy.

The fifth member of the group stood quietly, the final unknown in this equation.

"Lama Wangdue," I said. *"Tashi deley."* I honor the greatness within you.

Wangdue appeared to be even younger than TJ, barely 20, with burnished walnut skin and deep-set eyes. His nose, like mine, was more aquiline than was typical with Tibetans, but he had our trademark high cheekbones.

He was studying me just as closely.

"You are Tenzing Norbu," he said, his pronunciation thick, but understandable.

"Yes."

"You are no longer monk."

"No, I am no longer a monk."

"Police?"

"No. No longer a policeman either. I'm a private investigator. A detective."

TJ had been eavesdropping, and he broke in. "Yeshe tell us! Monk detective! Like TV show! I download on iPad! Very good!"

I nodded, clueless. I still didn't own a flat screen, though Julie had been pushing for one.

"You keep people safe, Tenzing Norbu?" Wangdue asked.

Odd question.

I shrugged. "Safe enough, I guess."

He seemed to relax at this. But his eyes remained unfocused, as if trying to make something out, past the words.

Together, we wheeled the heavy carts out into the harsh glare.

CHAPTER 6

The white Econoline with its Buddhist cargo, Eric at the wheel, zigzagged east onto the 105. We followed easily.

Once we'd connected onto the 110 North, Julie shot me a look. "Want to tell me about this convenient new job of yours?"

"Hardly convenient. More a matter of bad timing." I explained the situation with Kim and her missing brother, leaving nothing out.

"You think two days will do it?" Julie's voice was skeptical.

"Absolutely," I said, with more confidence than I felt.

We zipped through downtown and merged onto the Hollywood Freeway. The afternoon traffic was surprisingly light, and soon we were exiting onto Hollywood Boulevard, turning right on Bronson and right again on Franklin. A spectacular peach-streaked sky announced sunset. The hills served as a radiant backdrop to the iconic letters of the Hollywood sign.

Two quick lefts, and we finally landed on West Live Oak Drive and pulled into the driveway.

"Are you kidding me?" Julie asked.

"I know."

The Leonard's three-story Mediterranean house was exactly as breathtaking as I remembered, although the faded pinkish stucco was now terra cotta red. Built in the thirties and set high on a hillside, the site offered unobstructed views from downtown all the way to the ocean, depending on where you stood. Someone famous once lived here, but I could never remember his name.

Adina Leonard flew out of the front door, the dark hair of my memory transformed into a pure white mane that tumbled down her back. Her hair ignited in the setting sun.

She moved from monk to monk like a hummingbird, pausing in flight as if to sip each one's nectar. I waited. Finally she turned to Julie and me, a question in her eyes. Then recognition dawned.

"Ten!" She clasped my shoulders and planted a kiss on my forehead. "How's that tender heart of yours doing?"

She switched her attention to Julie. Her eyes were like twin lasers. She nodded.

"Yes," she said. "I can see this working."

"Adina," Eric called. "Can you show everyone where they're going?"

Adina moved away, her hair a snowy cape.

"Whoa," Julie said. "She's intense."

"We were all in love with her."

We grabbed a couple of boxes and walked through the front door.

"Up or down?" Julie said.

"Down."

She followed me down a flight of stairs.

"This is where you lived?" Julie sounded incredulous.

"Sort of," I said. "They've made some changes."

My tiny bedroom with a half bathroom had adjoined a storage area. Now we were looking at a graceful rotunda connecting to a wide-open, rectangular-shaped room. It was like entering a giant keyhole.

Two wrought-iron twin beds, a daybed, and two small air mattresses took up the right half.

Yeshe trotted over to relieve Julie of her box.

"Oh look! A dormitory!" I motioned to the beds. "You should feel right at home."

I followed Yeshe to the far wall, and we added our cartons to the growing stack.

"What did you bring, half of India?" I teased. "What happened to austerity?"

Yeshe laughed, and for a moment we both enjoyed the ease that comes with lifelong friendship. It seemed like the right time to ask.

"*Neg chareng tansong,*" I said, plucking the words from my memory bank.

"English, please," Yeshe said. "I need learn better."

"I missed you."

"Ah. But now no need, yes?"

"Come stay with me," I said. "You and Lobsang both. My place is small, but I have a couch and I'm sure I can borrow Eric's air mattress."

Yeshe's eyes softened even more. "Tenzing, is not . . ." He gestured to the group. "We come here, but we not stop being monks in monastery. We make our practice, like always." He patted my arm. "Lobsang and I with you every day. We with you in India, and we with you right now."

"All right, well, will you at least come see my house? How about dinner tomorrow?"

"Yes. We come," Yeshe said. His eyes twinkled. "All of us."

Lobsang was standing with Sonam and Eric in a sitting area that seemed to double as a breakfast nook. In the morning, I knew, light would pour through the round leadglass windows, portholes into a sea of sunshine. I headed over, as Yeshe joined Julie in the well-stocked kitchenette. They opened and closed drawers until they had uncovered a large copper pot and a ladle. A bowl of fresh fruit and avocados sat to one side of a granite counter. Adina had added a blue pitcher bursting with sunflowers.

The Leonards were such good people. Why had I let life create such distance between us? I took a seat at the round kitchen table, enjoying the bustle.

Yeshe soon had a big pot of water boiling. He unearthed a plastic baggie of loose black tea from his duffel.

"You made it through customs with that?" Julie said. "I'm surprised you didn't land in jail."

"Nobody look. Nobody ask." Yeshe dumped a handful of loose tea in the pot, and soon the downstairs filled with its smoky fragrance. "Good to be monk sometimes."

"I go unpack," Lobsang announced. He nodded to me. "You come."

I claimed the edge of the daybed. Lobsang quickly organized clothing: a few pairs of socks and shoes, boxers, and three sets each of the Tibetan monk's daily uniform—burgundy, wraparound, cap sleeve *dhonka*; matching cotton underskirt; and the large rectangular *zhen* robe used as a top layer of draping.

"You still use zhen, Tenzing?" Lobsang asked, his hands busy.

I pictured the red cloth over my home altar. "Every day," I said.

"*Hanh.*" Lobsang narrowed his eyes, but I held his gaze with the innocence of the somewhat truthful.

TJ and Wangdue sat cross-legged on the twin beds in front of matching iPads.

"Dr. Eric, you have password?" TJ called out.

Eric came over and tapped onto TJ's screen. Stamp-size images bloomed.

I elbowed Lobsang. "Excuse me, iPads? What kind of crazy libertarian monastery are you running over there?"

Lobsang grunted, his favorite mode of deflection.

"*Chreng thini hachang gaposong,*" I said. *Your presence brings me happiness.*

"Brothers, it is late," Sonam announced to the room, stifling a yawn. "Tea, bread, and then I am thinking sleep, yes? Come, come to the kitchen, everyone!"

Yeshe and Julie doled out mugs of sweet tea. Julie caught my eye. I shook my head. With or without yak butter, Yeshe's tea had always been strong enough to stop a freight train.

The mass of memories was starting to close in on me. I needed a moment alone.

I climbed the two flights of stairs to the Leonards' living room but there was no escaping the past—the room was

exactly as it had been when I lived here. The furniture was a blend of Balinese and midcentury modern. Persian miniatures and Japanese prints took up most of the wall space. A circular standing gong occupied the far corner of the room, its leather-topped mallet hanging to one side. My hand itched to raise the mallet and let loose a reverberating summons.

Though to what, I no longer knew.

When I lived with Adina and Eric, they'd hosted fundraising events in this room. Microfinance, reproductive justice, clean water, endangered species—no need was too small, no plight too distant. Adina had never had a career but she was a passionate connector of people and causes, always with the goal of raising the world's consciousness.

I slid the plate glass door sideways and stepped outside. Their deck overlooked a dark expanse of rugged terrain. In fact, I'd gotten the idea to build my own deck from theirs.

I leaned against the railing. Griffith Park seemed to stretch for miles, untamed space in the midst of civilized sprawl.

An owl hooted, somewhere to my left. A second answered, a higher-pitched response. The air was fresh, although my lungs couldn't seem to take much in.

"That's Bronson Canyon." Eric moved to my side. "A pair of owls built a nest there recently. I hear them every night now." He leaned against the railing. "I love standing out here. It helps remind me that I am part of the natural world. A mammal, first and foremost."

The blade of moon was barely visible.

"June moon," I said.

"Five days down, twenty-five to go," Eric said.

"What do you mean?"

Eric's eyes widened. "You really have pulled away, haven't you? I'm talking about *Saka Dawa*."

"Oh. Right." Named for the Saka star, Saka Dawa was a monthlong celebration commemorating the Buddha's birth, enlightenment, and death. Kind of like Christmas, Easter, and a dash of Halloween, all rolled into one. The full moon

that fell during this month, Saka Dawa Duchen, was the most potent day of an already potent month.

And I had forgotten about all of it, completely.

"I hope you're coming to the temple, at least. For the *puja* this Thursday, I mean," Eric said.

"Yes. Of course." Yeshe and Lobsang had already wrangled a promise out of me to attend their initial event—a temple fund-raiser organized, of course, by Adina. Fine by me, as long as I was there to observe, not participate. Not my world, not anymore.

The thought saddened me.

A coyote cackled, the sound both gleeful and ominous.

"This is nice. Just like the old days," Eric said.

"I know. I was remembering all the fund-raisers Adina used to host here."

"Still does," he said. "Though she spends a lot of her time online now. Virtual outreach—the future of global connectivity. Adina's a big believer in using whatever works. She's off to a gathering later tonight, the sacred feminine. I think. I can't keep up. Her practice puts everyone else's to shame." He laughed. "Sorry, that didn't come out right."

"No, I get it. I've always admired Adina's commitment."

"Amazing woman. When we found out we couldn't conceive, she barely skipped a beat. She says she thinks of all the people she helps as her children."

What if that happened to Julie and me? The evening suddenly seemed stale and close. Was there no fresh air anywhere in this city?

"Ten? You seem . . ." Eric changed course. "Listen, I'm here. If you ever need anything."

"I know that. Thank you."

I turned away from the dark canyon.

"It's getting late," I said. "I should get Julie."

Heading home, the traffic was light. I pictured the scene back at the house. Tank would play hard to get. He often stayed out of sight when Julie and I returned after being gone for a while, long enough, say, to miss a meal. He liked to

make sure we both understood that Tank, and only Tank, chose when and how to forgo his food. Homer, in contrast, would be flattened on the floor by the kitchen door, morose and desperate to go out.

"Homer'll be fine," Julie said, reading my mind. "He's got a cast-iron bladder."

I was ready for the day to be done. As much as I loved the idea of Yeshe and Lobsang staying with me, the reality would have been daunting. I don't do well when tugged in too many directions. And Julie was right about my needing more personal space.

"I invited everyone for dinner tomorrow night," I said.

"How funny. So did I."

I touched the back of Julie's hand. She turned it over and we interlaced fingers as I steered one-handed through the darkness.

This is what family feels like.

Out of nowhere the image of the soldier embracing his wife and child at the airport popped into my head. How they held on to each other. The way he placed his military hat on his daughter's head. The way it fell over her eyes.

An insight streaked across my mind, a comet trailing truth.

Of course.

Green Tara had come through after all. I knew how to find Kim's brother, Bobby. The answer traced back to their childhood.

It usually does.

CHAPTER 7

I paused at the head of the driveway to check my pulse. One hundred and thirty-two beats per minute. Good. I'd run long and hard this morning. Then I checked the mailbox, also a habit, though delivery was in the afternoon.

A single white envelope lay inside. My name and address were block-printed by hand in blue ink. No return address. No stamp.

It was probably another irrigation reminder from our die-hard environmentalist neighbor. She'd taken to leaving helpful drought-related fliers in all our mailboxes. The last one recommended soaker hoses for slow-dripping any live oaks on our properties.

I jogged slowly up the graveled lane. Inside the house I tossed the unopened envelope next to the stack of unpaid bills on my desk. My work was also suffering a drought. Sorry, soaker hoses were not in the budget.

It was so quiet. Julie and Homer were long gone. My cat and I were alone. The silence was both welcome and unnerving. I'd grown used to the little sounds of a shared life. Tank and I generated a lot less noise, but we also generated less warmth.

Not to say that I didn't relish the rare opportunity to take all the time I needed for a full set of yoga stretches on the deck, without Homer sniffing and licking at my face; or to enjoy a full hour of uninterrupted meditation with only the distant call of mourning doves to visit the silence; or to sprint the perimeter of Topanga State Park, muscles screaming, fully alone with my thoughts.

I seem to be blessed, or maybe it's cursed, with a constitution that craves solitude. I require doses of deep stillness or I start losing an essential piece of who or what I am. I realized I'd been missing myself—had been for a while.

I peeled off my running clothes, showered, and ran an unnecessary brush over my cropped black hair. My reflection looked the same as always. Vaguely Asian, as Bill liked to say. Julie thought I was ridiculously handsome, but then she would. I saw a pleasant-enough-looking man, but one whose nature was tinged with a sadness he could never completely access or erase.

"Cheer up," I said, and faked a smile.

Tank wandered in to investigate.

"Just me, buddy. Talking to myself."

I dressed quickly. Jeans. White T-shirt. Flip-flops. Moving to the kitchen, I poured a mug of coffee. Julie had tracked down Peruvian beans untreated by poisons and untainted by child laborers. The taste was slightly acidic, but as she liked to remind me, it was a small price to pay. I carried the mug to my office—a workstation set at an angle in the far corner of the living room.

I may have the best commute in Los Angeles.

I put in a call to Kim. As I waited, I picked up the photograph of her and Bobby. If last night's hunch was correct, the green helmet on Bobby's head wasn't plastic, and it wasn't a toy. It was real. And it was way too large for him because it probably belonged to his father.

"Hello, this is Kim speaking."

"It's Ten. I have a question. Was your father ever in the military? The army, maybe?"

"I do not know, Mr. Norbu," she said. Her tongue stud tap-tapped against her teeth, a personal Morse code indicating distress. "I am sorry. Is it important?"

"Not to worry. What's your father's first name?"

"Oh," she said. "Dave."

"Dave Smith. That's your father's name." Oh, man. Couldn't someone on that side of the family have tried

for something even slightly unusual? Wangdue Smith, for example?

"My mother always called him That Fucking Asshole Dave, Mr. Norbu. But you can probably disregard everything but the Dave part." She coughed softly.

I was stunned.

"Kim, did you just make . . . ?"

"Yes, Mr. Norbu. I made a joke." She coughed again, or maybe that was how she laughed. I'd never heard her do either before. "I have to go now Mr. Norbu." And she hung up.

I stared at the phone. Kim moved through her life as if every action was a discrete occurrence, with its own specific lifespan, usually brief. Once its time was up, it was up. She was remarkably efficient, and one of the hardest workers I'd ever come across. But for me, her fascinating oddness was maybe her strongest draw. Like the view from my deck, she never presented the same face twice.

I did some calculating. If Kim was 4 in the picture, and she was 26 now, that meant the picture was taken in 1992. Which meant Bobby was born in 1983, although that didn't mean Dave Smith was no longer in the service. Soldiers on leave got their wives pregnant all the time.

The helmet was olive green and looked well worn, as if it had served active time. I suspected it was army, but just in case, I'd make the parameters of my Google search nice and wide.

I typed *Army/Navy Military Helmets, 1960–1985* into the search bar, pressed enter, and let the engine do its thing. A dozen or more links appeared, but they seemed weirdly unrelated to my quest. Mostly they sent me to *Veterans Affairs*. I tried Google Images. The pictures that popped up were equally random—a minor-league football poster, a medal of merit. I did find one helmet, but it looked nothing like mine. I went back to the earlier links and started to scroll and open my way down the list.

This time I got lucky, on an eBay link to collectible military gear, of all things. I found a visual match almost immediately.

I was looking at a U.S. Army–issue steel pot helmet liner, dull green, and minus its camouflage covering. I dug deeper into the Internet now that my helmet had a name. The steel pot liner was first issued to ground troops during the Second World War and was used up until the mid 1980s, when the Kevlar helmet, or K-pot liner, replaced it. I assumed Dave was too young for Korea, and the helmet was too old for Bosnia. That put Kim and Bobby's father squarely in the blood-soaked fields and jungles of Vietnam.

The Vietnam War. According to many, one of America's most damaging examples of misdirected commitment. Its veterans were still paying with their wounded psyches. As a rookie patrol officer I'd encountered dozens of them passed out on Skid Row, victims of untreated post-traumatic stress disorder. Kim and her mother were probably far better off without Dave Smith in their lives.

Okay. I had a lead. Now I could fritter away hours I didn't have, or I could lean on my friend Bill. What else were ex-partners still on the force for?

Happily, Bill was in his office, and he was answering his phone.

"Hey, Norbu. Don't tell me. You and Julie are ready to tie the knot."

"All in good time."

"Yeah, well, we both know *good time* doesn't stand a chance against *Martha time*. She's back on the warpath, lining up potential venues. You'd think we were talking about a fucking inaugural ball, though given what these assholes want to charge, I'm sure it will cost you more. You got a job yet?"

"Not exactly." I was glad to hear Bill's teasing tone. Last year, when he and Martha were separated, there was little to joke about. But he came to his senses and came back home,

and now they'd been meeting with a counselor. Their marriage was healing daily.

"Well, I'm sure you didn't call me out of the goodness of your heart. What gives?"

"I'm trying to trace a Vietnam vet, name of Dave Smith. Actually, I'm looking for his son, Bobby Smith, but first things first. The thing is, my military contacts presently consist of a bunch of vagrants on Third and Main and a lesbian FBI agent who only answers my call when it's code orange and above. Can you help a partner out?"

"I might know a guy," Bill said.

"I thought you might."

"I had a John Doe last year. Homeless dude, shot himself in Tellefson Park. Only ID was a dog tag in his pocket, everything rubbed off but the last three numbers of his social. Dave ID'd him in less than a day."

"Dave?"

"Yeah, his name's also Dave. Dave Brown."

"Of course it is."

Bill read off contact information and I jotted it down. "He works out of Phoenix. Runs the Benefits Department, Western division. You could also try the L.A. branch office but they're worse than useless. Dave's your best bet. Tell him you got his name from me."

"Thanks."

"How's the Kumbaya fest going?"

"Excuse me?"

"Isn't this the week you're saving Tibet?"

"Right. It's going well. Everyone got here safe and sound. You guys should come to the temple this Thursday. Bring the girls. They're celebrating Buddha's birthday."

"Just what I need. More birthday parties."

"You can meet my two oldest friends."

"Just what I need, more monks."

I waited.

"Ah, hell, it's time Lola and Maude got exposed to their Uncle Ten's sordid past. God knows we all got 'em, right?" His laugh was a little hollow.

"How's everything going with that?"

"It's going. I got therapists and counselors up the wazoo, but it's going."

Bill and Martha's marital crisis had been precipitated by the unwelcome discovery last July that he'd had an affair two decades ago while stationed in Bosnia. An illegitimate son, Sasha, was the result. When Sasha suddenly dropped out of sight, his mother, Mila, and grandmother Irena showed up to ask Bill for help. The ensuing clash of commitments had left everyone, myself included, bruised and shaken. The drama took all of us to a dark and dangerous place. People died, and I was changed, but not necessarily in a good way.

I shook off the chill of bad memories.

"So I'll see you then?"

"Just promise me you won't be up on the stage levitating or something."

"I promise. And thanks for the army contact, Bill. I owe you."

"Actually, now that I have you on the line, I got something I want to run by you."

"Something exciting?" My pulse quickened, a reflexive instinct.

"Not sure about exciting, but definitely weird. A couple of locals from Beachwood Canyon were hiking up in Griffith Park this morning, and they got seriously spooked. The front desk routed their call to me, for lack of a better idea."

"What do you mean, spooked?"

"Freaked out. I sent Sully and Mack to take a look. Apparently they take this hike every day, and they swear on a stack of bibles the fucking thing must have showed up overnight."

"*What* showed up?" Bill loved to draw these stories out, just to get to me.

"Dead body," he said. "Or I should say, the insinuation of a dead body. The actual body was nowhere to be found."

"Somebody moved it?"

"The hikers say no. Not nearby, anyway. They looked."

"A dead body but no corpse, just an insinuation? Bill, what are you talking about?"

"I'm getting to that. Somebody left a coroner's outline, right where the dirt path turns into asphalt. Life-size. Couple of gang tags next to it, as well."

"Sounds more like vandalism than homicide."

"I would agree. Except these taggers didn't use spray cans, and they didn't use paint."

Dread pricked my forearms. "Go on."

"Fuckers used blood."

CHAPTER 8

Bill said he'd report back to me once he had more information on this art project from hell. I knew what he was doing. He was trying to get me back in the saddle. But I wasn't going to let the mystery fire up my cylinders the way it would have not that long ago.

It had nothing to do with me.

I moved outside to the deck and let the midday sun warm my arms and face.

I slammed the railing with one fist.

Who was I trying to fool? I hadn't felt remotely challenged by anything in months, ever since I'd returned from that frenzied trip to Bosnia-Herzegovina. I'd actively sought out calmer cases, the PI version of misdemeanors as opposed to felonies; deadbeat dads and insurance-claim scammers, the staple diet of most private detectives. But lately even these small, dull jobs had dried up. And lately I couldn't shake off the feeling that I might never earn enough again, with or without a fire in my belly.

In the canyon, a topcoat of green riffled, live oak and eucalyptus leaves stroked into motion by a warm breeze blowing in from the ocean. The air tasted stale, and the light suddenly seemed to dim.

A wave of dizziness blindsided me. My mouth filled with an acrid mixture of bile and panic. I bent in two, head below my knees, until the nausea passed.

What was going on with me?

I hustled inside and dialed Phoenix. Distraction was the obvious solution.

"Veterans Affairs, Dave Brown speaking." His voice was hoarse, as if filtered through dust.

I told him my dilemma.

"Tried your local office?"

"Bill Bohannon suggested you might be more efficient."

"He's got that right." He hacked out a laugh, which led to a bout of wheezing. "Worthless asswipes, most of 'em. Gimme what you got. I'll see what I can do."

"It's not much. The father's name is David Smith. Probably served sometime between 1965 and 1972, I'm guessing in Vietnam or maybe Cambodia. He lived in California for at least a decade afterward. All I know is he was army. Thanks, I'll be here all day."

"Who said anything about all day? Lemme put you on hold for a few minutes. Think you can hold on to your horses that long?"

Tinny music filled my ear. Tank wandered over, and I stroked the thin silk that papered his ears.

"Found the fucker," Dave rasped. "Corporal David Smith. Believe it or not, only Dave Smith over there during that time frame. What are the odds? Looks like he lives in San Diego. What's your e-mail address?"

I gave it to him.

"Nailed it, by the way. Smith was stationed in Danang in '69 and '70. Almost identical time as me. Never ran into him, though. Same hell, different hole I guess."

My e-mail pinged.

"Got it. You're fast."

"I have my ways. I sent a recent address, plus a home phone, though these days who the fuck knows what anyone uses to communicate? He's been cashing in his disability benefit checks since he moved to that address, and if he'd moved again, believe me, he would have let us know."

"And if he died?"

"He's alive. I can't guarantee what kind of shape he's in, but he's definitely alive."

"What's the disability?"

"Can't tell. Could be anything from tinnitus to the big C. Maybe his lungs are for shit, like mine. We were all practically mainlining Agent Orange over there. Why—does it matter?"

"Not really. I just prefer to know who I'm dealing with."

"Don't we all, pal, don't we all."

Chapter 9

I called the number, newly energized, and proceeded to sit through nine or ten rings. Just as I was about to quit, someone picked up.

"Not interested, asshole. Don't call here again," a voice growled before I got out a word. *Click*.

My work number comes up as *unknown caller*, for obvious reasons. A private detective hunting down a lead doesn't want to broadcast the fact. Unfortunately, that means some people assume you're a different kind of hunter, a hungry salesman robo-calling unsuspecting victims.

I dialed again. This time, he didn't answer at all.

Now what?

Tank chose this moment to butt my calf with his head. I checked the time. It was well past noon.

"Sorry. I lost track." But my cat had disappeared.

I found Tank hovering by his food dish. When your live-in fiancée is a trained chef, meals magically appear at their proper times. But today we were just a couple of bachelors, on our own.

I took full advantage. Don't get me wrong, I'd never eaten better or healthier food in my life than with Julie as our in-house cook, and my trim waistline proved it. But Julie wasn't here today, was she?

"Dessert first, my friend," I said.

I treated Tank to a bowl of fresh-squeezed tuna juice, straight from the can. Julie worried about the mercury, but Tank did love it so.

"Don't get used to this," I told him.

As he lapped up the fishy nectar, I made myself the biggest, gooiest peanut-butter-and-honey sandwich this side of the Himalayas, adding a layer of sliced bananas for good measure. I washed the whole thing down with a glass of cold milk and licked the sticky overflow from my fingers and plate. Sometimes a man's gotta do what a man's gotta do.

Tank's bowl, too, was tongued clean. I forked in a half can of organic beef and chicken, vegetables included, no grains or additives allowed, so my conscience wouldn't prick.

"Party's over. Eat your meat and veggies," I said to Tank.

I forced down a farmer's market carrot for the same reason and got back to work.

The stubborn corporal still wasn't answering his phone, and no recording or service clicked on to accept my message.

I Googled Smith's address. He lived in the City Heights section of San Diego, just east of midcity. The address was close to University Avenue, but the actual building lay like an afterthought on a side street, a cul-de-sac off the main thoroughfare that looked about as necessary to the neighborhood's survival as the appendix was to the human body.

I called Julie.

"Hey, Yeshe and I were just talking about you." I heard a bell clang.

"Where are you?"

"Trader Joe's. For the third time. I need to seriously school these guys in the art of making a list." She lowered her voice. "You should see them shopping. It's hilarious."

I felt a pang. "I thought everyone would be resting today."

"Nope. Full speed ahead with this crew. They've been up for hours. How about you? I've been picturing you sitting in the kitchen in your underwear guzzling beer and scooping out peanut butter with your bare hands."

"Witch," I said.

"Not that yoghurt, Yeshe," I heard, "get the Greek one."

I was missing a lot. Already.

"Okay, I'm back. So, what time should we plan on dinner tonight?"

Once again, I regretted my promise to Kim. But a deal was a deal. I described the situation to Julie. "I think I have to go see this guy. If I leave right now, I can get there before dark. Hopefully wrap things up tonight."

Julie hesitated. So far, neither of us was getting exactly what we wanted. "Okay, I guess. We'll move it to tomorrow." Then, as she did so well, she rallied. "Hey, so Yeshe's been showing me how to make *khapsay* for the puja ceremony."

"Khapsay? I love khapsay." The traditional fried-dough recipe had traveled, along with the slow-moving stream of fleeing monks, across the mountainous border into India from Lhasa and was always a huge hit with the younger monks at Dorje Yidam.

"Yeah, we've fried, like, a ton. I'm covered in grease, but Yeshe's still worried there won't be enough. He's like a Buddhist Jewish mother."

I know that, I thought. *He's my best friend.*

I said, "Can you put him on the phone, please?"

"*Tashi deley,* Tenzing. It is beautiful day today, yes? How you doing? You fine?"

"I'm so sorry I'm not there."

"Julie explain. Is good you help find your friend's brother. Is good to keep promise! We having fun!"

Clearly.

"What do you think of Julie?"

Like Bill, Yeshe loved to keep me hanging. But Yeshe used gaps in time to make me aware of my attachment to outcomes. I released the breath I'd been holding.

"Yeshe?"

"I am thinking," he said. And then, "I see why you want grow old with her. Julie is your . . . what is word? Same?"

"Equal?"

"Just so. Equal."

A part of me regretted asking.

CHAPTER 10

The squat structure of grayish wood was slapped onto a narrower building of brick and glass like a mistake. The sidewalk in front was punctured with skinny half-dead trees and bordered with sparse grass struggling to stay alive. I parked my beater car, a dusty Dodge Neon, in front. We fit right in.

I retrieved the Smith & Wesson AirLite from the glove box and slipped it into my Windbreaker pocket. I had brought it along, just in case. Ex-vets could be a jumpy lot.

It had been a while since I'd carried. I'd forgotten how right it felt to be armed and on the hunt.

Outside, the air smelled slightly moldy. I stretched numb muscles and thought longingly of the ocean, only a few miles away. The sun lay low in the sky, but even a bath of late gold light couldn't raise the spirits of this housing project.

The front door was jammed open with a cinder block. I stepped inside. The entryway reeked of stale vomit, fresh urine, and chronic hopelessness. As I waited for the elevator, I scanned the community board, papered with 3" by 5" handwritten cards offering dubious housecleaning services or inquiring after cheap rooms.

Someone had tacked up an incongruous flier promoting "realized teacher, enlightened wallah, and perfect embodiment of compassion, Maha Mudra." Another siren of spirituality—California was full of them.

The female figure was indistinct, as if standing behind a drop cloth of gauze. She gazed downward, long black tresses obscuring much of her face, scarlet lips and dark eyes mysterious behind a curtain of hair and filtered light. A red bindi marked her third eye with a confetti-size disc just above the

THE FIFTH RULE OF TEN

brows. I was pretty sure *maha mudra* was a term used by Buddhists as well as Hindus. Either way, it had a nice ring to it.

Still no elevator, so I took the stairs to the second floor. Apartment 216 was on the right-hand side, facing away from the street. The doorbell was an open wound plastered over with torn-off pieces of masking tape. I took the hint and knocked, but not before stepping to one side of the door—an ex-cop's instinct when confronting an ex-soldier.

No one answered. Given what I already knew about David Smith's social skills, I wasn't deterred. I upgraded from knocking to pounding.

"Shut the fuck up!" someone yelled from behind a door farther along the corridor.

I took a short break and then resumed my hammering.

A dead bolt scraped and the door opened a crack, a thick chain still in place. I sidled partially into view.

"Who th'hell are you? Go away." Bad breath wafted in sulfurous fumes from a mouth full of untended teeth.

"I'm the one who's been calling. I'm not here to sell," I said. "I'm here to buy."

The door closed.

Inhale. Exhale. Inhale . . .

He released the safety chain and opened the door, revealing a gloomy cave within. I stepped inside.

Dave Smith was a rheumy-eyed wreck of a man. His cheeks and chin were covered with patchy gray stubble and his mouth leaked at the corners. A piece of twine held up stained khakis. His sleeveless undershirt was the dull color that Julie insists comes with cheap laundry soap and the refusal to wash whites separately. I glanced down. You can tell a lot about a person from his shoes. His were black leather, thick and clunky, like cop shoes. His left foot was at least one size larger than his right.

I switched to breathing through my mouth, trying to be unobtrusive, though a part of me felt repelled.

At the police academy, we were taught to sympathize with our less-fortunate fellows, but never to empathize. Empathy could get into your bones. Empathy could break you.

But empathy is also a close relative of compassion, and both are central tenets of Buddhism. And at the monastery, we were taught to cultivate empathy, not avoid it. Sympathy might be a safe response, but empathy was a powerful spiritual tool.

I felt past my resistance toward the collection of smells and disappointments before me, the mass of unhealed sores and unaddressed rage. I allowed this fallen soldier's pain to be a reflection of my own. I wore his wounded skin, for just a moment.

Tashi deley, I thought: I honor the greatness within you.

He straightened his shoulders and hitched his pants, as if he sensed the change in my attitude.

"Corporal Smith," I said. "I appreciate you letting me come inside."

He waved at a couple of worn wingback chairs, their upholstered arms shiny and frayed with age. The blinds were drawn and the room murky, although a thin slot of light underlined the windowsills, hinting at a brighter world outside. I sank into one dank armchair. Hopefully the stuffing wasn't colonized by carpet beetles or worse.

My eyes adjusted.

The entire apartment was no bigger than a few hundred square feet. Brown wall-to-wall carpeting turned into yellowish linoleum floor tiles in the kitchen area and bathroom. I couldn't see into the bedroom, nor did I wish to.

"Want water or something? I'm outta beer."

"I'm fine, thank you."

Dave walked to the other chair, his gait rolling, as if crossing a ship's pitching deck. He lowered himself into a sitting position. One pant leg hitched up, and I saw a metal pylon where an ankle should be. That explained the bigger shoe. I had found his disability, at least the most visible one.

He caught me looking. "Didn't lose the leg in 'Nam. Lost it over here. Type 2 diabetes. Goddamn Agent Orange, the gift that keeps on giving." He tugged his pant cuff over the prosthesis. "Why are you here?" he asked.

"My name is Tenzing Norbu. I'm a private detective, and I'm hoping you can connect me with your son Robert, or Bobby."

He stared at the brown carpet.

This wasn't an interrogation, but I let the silence build between us anyway. He'd talk when it got to be too much. People almost always did.

"Haven't spoken to him in years," he finally said. "Not since the day he turned eighteen. Outta here like a bat outta hell and that was that."

"I'm sorry," I said.

"Yeah, well, it's my own fucking fault. I wouldn't want me for a father either. Why're you looking for him?"

I didn't feel comfortable bringing Kim into this discussion.

"It's a work matter," I said. "I've been hired to locate his whereabouts. Do you have any idea where he might have gone?"

"Not a clue," he said. "But if you do run across him, tell him his old man's still a loser, and proud of it."

"And he hasn't been in touch since?"

"You callin' me a liar?"

"No. I was just hoping that you might . . ."

"You sure you don't want some water or something?"

"No, that's not . . ."

He limped into the kitchen. He returned with an AR-15 pointed straight at my heart.

"Easy," I said.

"My ex sent you, didn't she?" Dave may have had one gimpy leg, but both gun hands seemed to work just fine. "She turned our two kids against me. And now she's after my money? Well fuck that bitch. And fuck you."

His left hand slid back the charging handle and freed it with a *snick*. He'd chambered a deadly round. How ironic—a

deadbeat dad I wasn't even looking for was about to shoot me for finding him.

My outsides froze, but my inner ironist kept right on going.

At least this is California. At least he only has 10 rounds at point-blank range to hit the bull's-eye.

Speaking of eyes, his were rheumy, but also, I now saw, clouded, offering a possible reprieve. I was counting on cataracts. If I was wrong, I was dead. My right hand inched into my right pocket. My fingers found wood. I clasped the walnut grip. The feel of the snub nose calmed me. I could shoot him through my pocket, if it came to that.

"Corporal Smith, your ex-wife passed away three years ago," I said. "But you're right about one thing. I wasn't telling you the full truth."

His eyes narrowed. He licked his lips.

"I'm doing this for your daughter, for Kim."

"Kim?" He seemed confused. "Why?"

"Because Kim works for me, and I've come to care deeply about her. Because she asked me for help. Because she deserves to see her big brother again."

His grip wavered.

"I made a commitment to her to find him, a commitment I plan on keeping. Don't do something you'll regret, Corporal. I'm not your enemy."

"Well, shit." He lowered his weapon and sat heavily. He stood the rifle next to his chair.

"Sure you don't want to engage the safety?"

"No need," he said. "Empty"

I let go of the AirLite's trigger.

"Story of my life," he added, to no one in particular.

Near-death experiences, even those based on false assumptions, take their toll on the body. Sweat beaded my upper lip and my throat was parched, but no way was I asking for water. The airless room was suddenly intolerable. I stood. "Well, if there isn't anything else." I held out my

hand. "Thanks anyway, Corporal Smith." After a moment, he shook it.

As he limped me to the door, a thought hit me.

"You say your son left on his birthday? So that would mean June . . . ?"

"Thirteenth. Bobby was born under a bad sign—Friday the thirteenth, 1986. June, like you said. Both my childr—" he said, shut the thought down, and ushered me out. He was done.

The carpet in the dark corridor was sticky underfoot. Behind me, the dead bolt engaged with a click of finality.

Or not.

Before I reached the stairwell I heard Dave's door open again.

"Try the navy."

"The navy?"

"Yeah. After he ran off, I found a computer printout in his bedroom about that naval air station up there at Lemoore. Bobby always did like playing soldiers." Dave shrugged. "Of course, once he figured out his old man was army, he switched to navy. Kid was obsessed with fighter planes in high school, 'Rough Raiders,' shit like that. All he wanted was to see them Super Hornets in action. He begged me to take him to one of their air shows."

"And did you?"

"Nah. I was much too busy messing up my life. That air show was the last damn thing he threw in my face."

Chapter 11

Could it be that easy?

With over a decade to reinvent his life, Bobby Smith had a big head start. Statistics were not on my side. He could be anywhere, doing just about anything. He could be dead. But I now had a date of birth, a strong hunch, and Green Tara as part of my arsenal. I knew something about reinvention as a young man, about pursuing a lifelong dream once you were free to do so.

Ask your heart. What does it truly long for?

All it took was one Yoda. Hopefully Bobby had encountered his own. But either way, if I were the 18-year-old Bobby sick to death of my chaotic life and self-destructive, self-pitying father, I knew what I'd have done. I'd have taken a direct route to a sanctuary of order, one that also held the key to my hoped-for future.

I'd have enlisted in the navy, with the goal of becoming a fighter pilot. Chosen the way of commitment.

Back in the car, I grabbed my phone and fired up my digital Dr. Watson, also known as Dr. Google. I scouted and researched, letting intuition take the lead, and soon entered the previously unknown, at least to me, world of the Lemoore Naval Air Station. Training facility of elite military aviators. Home of numerous strike fighter squadrons. If I was right, Bobby would be familiar to these men and women. If I was lucky, he might even have become a member of a squadron, a pilot of his own Super Hornet, and commander of his destiny.

If not, I could always drive home and begin the search anew, using his birth date as a starting point.

It was too late in the day to drive to Lemoore and apply my Tibetan charm in person. In any case, this quest of mine was more a matter of sentiment than protocol. I needed to find a way to circumvent the front office of the Naval Station if I was going to get anywhere.

My thumbs wheeled and tapped the phone screen, pulled by an invisible magnet deeper and deeper into the world of FA-18s, of fleet air defense and fighter escorts.

I tapped and read, tapped and read, scrolling through aviation history, skimming chains of command, until my eye snagged on the words *family members*. My thumbs paused.

The title OMBUDSMAN dominated the page. I had no idea what an ombudsman was. It sounded like some sort of meditative garden gnome. But if the ombudsman's domain included family members, he or she was for me.

Lemoore Naval Station's ombudsman had a name— Mpingo Draper—and a telephone number with a 559 area code. I didn't hesitate—this was definitely the kind of call a person could make after hours.

"Hell-lo!" Warm, female, almost certainly African-American.

"Ms. Draper?"

"Honey, it's Mpingo, and just so you know, I'm too old, too black, and too set in my ways to answer to *Mizz*. How can I help you? And make it snappy, I got marinara sauce cooking."

"My name is Tenzing Norbu. I'm a private detective, and I've been on a crazy chase all day trying to find a missing sibling. Eventually, it's led me to you."

"Well shoot, now you got my attention."

"How long have you been ombudsman, err, woman for the naval station?"

"Man suits me fine. Since 1998. Why?"

"That's great. So, I'm guessing you've probably gotten to know quite a few pilots over the years . . . ?"

"Son, you need to spit it out. I could die at any moment."

"Have you ever run across a navy pilot by the name of Bobby Smith? He's in his late twenties—he'll be thirty come June thirteenth, to be specific."

The long pause caused my heart to speed up.

"Why?"

"My client Kim Nordquist is his younger sister. She wants very much to find him."

"Kim Nordquist, you say?"

"That's correct."

Another silence, a brief one. "Well, what do you know? Cheeto's got a baby sister."

"Sorry, Cheeto?"

"That's what his squadron calls him. That man eats so many Cheetos he bleeds bright orange."

I had to make sure I wasn't misunderstanding.

"Are you saying Bobby Smith is actually stationed in Lemoore?"

"That's what I'm saying. And so we're clear, it's Lieutenant Robert Smith of the Fighting-14 Tophatters. He's an instructor—part of the training program—not to mention slot pilot for the F/A-18 air shows. The boy can flat-out fly. This is Cheeto's second fleet tour, but first time here. He and his family live on post."

"He's married?"

"Oh, yes. To Ramona. Their daughter Kimmy's in Kindergarten. She's sharp as a tack. Already speaks two languages."

"Kimmy . . ."

"Long for Kim. He told me once she was named for his little sister. That's how I knew you weren't blowing smoke."

I fist-pumped the air. I had found Kim's brother. He was alive, and he was well.

"You want me to tell him, have him surprise his baby sister with a call?"

"I think I'd better talk to him first," I said. "Kim, too."

"How about I have him call you. This number good?"

"Please."

"What do you want me to say?"

"Just tell him it's a family matter to do with his sister."

"You got it. And son, just so you know, I'm keeping you on file."

"Is that bad?"

She chuckled. "We're dealing with a chronic runaway right now. Captain's daughter. Brittany's back home at the moment. As of today. But her poor daddy's blood pressure didn't get the memo. I might need your help down the road."

Her breathing grew quiet, over the line.

"You know," Mpingo said, "usually the calls I get are full of woe. This one's son is selling painkillers in Fresno. That one's daughter wants to drop out of high school. Someone's husband got caught messing with someone else's wife. But this call . . ."

"I know," I said. "This is one of the good calls."

"I'll let Bobby know," Mpingo said. "You take care now."

The San Diego sky had grown dark, streetlamps blinking on without my noticing. I couldn't see Dave Smith's windows from here, but I imagined him sitting in his shadowed cave, too weighed down with disappointment to get up and switch on the lights.

Maybe that would change. I didn't blame Bobby for cutting and running. But once one piece of a family triangle shifted, other pieces sometimes followed, like choreographed dancers reconfiguring. Impossible rifts found a way to heal. What was shattered became whole. All it took was the willingness to soften one's obstinate commitment to "never" and allow enough room for "maybe someday."

Sometimes my job felt thankless. But not tonight.

My cell phone broke into song—a chorus of women announcing sweetly that they were going to a chapel to get married. The chapel of love, apparently, to the snapping of fingers and in three-part harmony.

Julie had been messing with my ringtone again. I'd figure out the proper retaliation later.

"Yes?"

"This is Lieutenant Robert Smith. I understand you want to talk to me about something?"

"I do." I allowed myself one in-and-out breath, and a nod to Green Tara. *Om tare tuttare ture soha.* "Lieutenant Smith, I have reason to believe my employee, Kim, is your younger sister. She's wanted to find you for a very long time."

Nothing.

"Lieutenant Smith?"

"That's impossible," he said. "Kim is dead."

"Thankfully, that's not true. She goes by your mother's maiden name. Kim Nordquist. She's twenty-five years old. Like you, she was born in June. Also like you, she loves to eat Cheetos."

"But the old man said they both . . ." He cleared his throat. "Does this mean . . . is my mother still . . ."

"I'm sorry," I said. "Your mother died of cancer three years ago. But Kim is very much alive. She lives in Los Angeles. She works as my assistant."

He expelled a rush of air. "Is she . . . is she okay? I mean, is she . . . normal?"

I thought about my answer. "Well, that depends on your definition of normal. She's certainly unique, but she functions just fine."

"I can't wrap my brain around this," Bobby said. "I'm sorry, who did you say you were again?"

"I didn't. My name is Tenzing Norbu. I'm an ex-cop. Now I work as a private investigator."

"And you're sure. You're sure she didn't die in a car wreck eleven years ago."

"I'm sure."

"This is just . . . thank you. Thank you. You have no idea what this means to me."

I pictured Kim, finger and thumb working her eyebrow stud as she examined her brother's faded nine-year-old face every night, searching for something, anything that might lead her to his life.

"Actually, I think I do."

CHAPTER 12

I arrived home three hours later in a state of euphoria mingled with exhaustion. I had stopped only once, for gas and a 12-ounce bag of trail mix. The snack was now blockading my digestive system like pebbled rubble.

Bobby and I had agreed that I would talk to Kim first, and he would await her call. I wasn't sure how Kim would initially react. Good news can trigger at least as much anxiety as bad. But knowing Kim, she would wade through whatever fears got stirred up and eventually reach the other shore, the one that included having a family again.

Julie had left the deck light on, and it cast a halo of light onto the slatted wood. Inside, the kitchen smelled faintly of fried dough. A small plate of khapsay sat on the counter. I unwrapped the plastic covering. The curled rectangles, crisp and dusted with sugar, catapulted me back to another time and place. I took a piece and let it soften in my mouth.

Tank wandered in.

"*Tashi deley*, Tank," I said. "That's Tibetan for 'life is pretty good tonight.'"

I removed my shoes and tiptoed into the bedroom, Tank at my heels. Homer emitted soft snores from his dog bed. His nasal passages had to be no wider than swizzle sticks.

The sheets stirred as Julie turned over, but the weariness that suddenly hit me made the idea of talking unimaginable. I could barely remember the correct sequence of turns to my ancient combination lock, and I stashed my gun and ammunition in the closet safe with one eye closed. As I moved to the bathroom to brush the khapsay sugar off my teeth, those

ridiculous brides-to-be burst into song. *"Goin' to the chapel and we're gonna get . . ."*

Shit. I'd left my phone in my Windbreaker pocket. I hustled to the closet to silence their bragging. They were never going to be lonely again. Good for them.

"Call you right back," I whispered into the phone and disconnected. I checked Julie. She was good at faking sleep. But not that good.

"You are so caught," I said. Julie threw back her head and laughed, her face flooding with color. I love that about her. She laughs like she means it.

"Your face," was all she said.

"I love you. Go back to sleep."

I walked outside to the deck and checked caller ID, but I already knew who it was.

The rest of Los Angeles had long since packed it in, but Mike Koenigs was just getting started. Mike was born with one hand on a mouse, the other on a keyboard. I wouldn't be surprised if his sinews were composed of fiber-optic cable. He maintained the hours of a desert rat, sleeping by day, cyber-tracking by night. I'd kept him out of hacker-jail as a teenager. These days he could buy and sell me many times over legally hacking for high-end companies. But we'd stayed friends, and Mike had helped me out of more than one jam since I'd left the force.

He wouldn't have called for no reason.

The cool air felt good on my skin. The canyon was still, the city asleep.

"Yo."

"It's me," I said, my voice low. "This better be good."

"Hey, boss. Sorry about the time. So, I just got a hit on something pretty interesting." Excitement laced his voice.

Mike was one of the mellowest guys I knew. I blamed both excess weed and excess brain cells—with so much RAM packed between his ears there was little room left for agitation. For him to exhibit this degree of enthusiasm meant he'd discovered something significant.

"I'm listening," I said.

"So, you remember that dark web server from last year, the one those asshole traffickers used? N, D, R, S . . ."

"Indra's Net?"

"So you say. But yeah, that's the one."

"What about it."

"It's baaa-aaack."

Icy worms crawled up my spine. "Are you certain?"

"'Fraid so. I imbedded an alert system on my hard drive after the network shut down, just in case. And sure enough, sucker's come back to life. Reincarnation is a beautiful thing, my man."

"Can you tell who's behind it? Who's using it?"

"Not who's behind it, that would make me the NSA. But affirmative on the users. They all seem pretty benign, as far as I can tell. Not like the old crowd. It's mostly a social streaming network connected to chat rooms for well-meaning airheads. Yay for world peace, worship the goddess within, don't eat bacon or vaccinate your kids, like that. So far, anyway. Still, you never know. Those were some nasty fuckers. I'd hate to think they were up and running again."

So did I. NDRSNT was a dark strand of the worst kind of commerce, a supplier of human victims I'd thought was gone for good.

"Anyway, I'm on it, boss."

A second wave of exhaustion sucked me under. I couldn't get warm. I tucked in closer to Julie and lay there, chilled to the bone. Lay awake for what seemed like hours, haunted by the hollow eyes of trafficked children.

When sleep finally came, an unwelcome guest clung to its back.

I am lying facedown.

Dark.

Much too dark.

I sweep the cold floor with my palms. The surface is rough, like cement. This place feels familiar. Should I be afraid?

Someone else is here. I push to my knees. A woman.

Julie? Is that you?

But I know it isn't.

Valerie? No. Not my mother either.

I stand and face her. The woman is tall, much taller than I am. I can barely make her out through the veil that covers her from head to toe. She is silent. She holds a baby in her arms. Also silent.

I have a lamp in my right hand. I walk closer.

The baby looks at me. For a moment, the baby is me.

Give him to me, I say, though my mouth makes no sound.

She places the baby on the cold concrete. He is just an infant but he stands like a little man, one arm pointing upward, the other pointing to the earth.

Shakyamuni, I say. Liberator.

He begins to pulsate with light.

I hold out my hands. They are dark green. Webbed, like a frog's. Now ferns grow from the fingers, reaching and curling toward the baby boy.

This is the spirit world of lucid wisdom. Beyond life and beyond death. I have been here before.

The infant Buddha scatters like sand.

I am running out of time.

Lead me. Show me.

I am hurled to another place. The tower. The answers are here. I step inside.

Something is different.

I can almost see.

I start up the steep, spiral staircase. I will make it to the top. I have to.

I climb to the second level. A window. I look outside. My mother, Valerie, is there. One hand waves at me. The other holds a silver goblet full of red fluid.

"Don't," I say. But she cannot hear me. She lifts the chalice to her lips.

I need to hurry. I stumble on the circular stairs. My palm lands on the rough wall. The wall pushes back. It moves closer.

Closer. The round interior winds inward, squeezing and pressing. It bandages me in stone, a deadly tourniquet.

I can't breathe.

Tenzing.

That voice again. Low, clear, neutral. Neither male nor female. Its dense presence is inside the walls, wrapping me in its arms. Like a lover. Like a python.

I can't breathe.

Tenzing. Let go. Give over to me. It is better that way.

I don't want to die.

The voice is tender: You belong to me.

No.

You belong to me. And I belong to you.

No!

Don't you know that you can only find freedom when you commit absolutely?

I don't want to commit. I don't want to die.

I can't breathe.

CHAPTER 13

I struggled awake. Sunlight poured into the bedroom.
The sheets were damp.

Julie stood in the doorway. She moved to the bed and touched my back. "Baby, you're soaked." She shifted her hand to my forehead. Her fingers felt cool against my skin. "Are you all right?"

"Sorry," I said. "I can't . . ."

I rolled out of bed and hurried into the kitchen. I pushed through the screen door and almost fell as a thick body hurtled past me and onto the deck. Homer lowered his head and waggled his tail, waiting for me to finish the game.

"Not now, Homer!" He cringed. I felt terrible. "Sorry. Sorry." My skin felt too tight for my body and my chest hurt.

Julie stepped next to me. "Ten?"

"Just a bad dream," I said.

"The tower dream again?"

"Yes."

"Want to talk about it?"

"Not really. Not now, anyway." I attempted a smile. I did not want to go back inside that tower.

Julie slipped her arms around my waist from behind. She rested her cheek against my back. "You were making these little gasping sounds."

Her arms tightened. Panic closed in again. I twisted around in her arms. I wanted to push her off, but settled for pulling away. Just a little.

"I'm fine. I really am."

Julie let go. "Okay, well, I need to go. See you at dinner. Homer? Come!" She crossed to the van, lifted Homer inside, and just like that, they were gone.

I berated myself, which only made things worse. I tried calling Julie, but she wasn't answering.

I climbed the wooden steps to my deck and leaned against the railing. Topanga Canyon might be bathed in gold but the air hung thick as a shroud, or so my lungs claimed. I was caught in the fused waltz of mood and perception.

What finally shifted things was the sight of Kim pedaling slowly up the drive.

The Buddha says everything exists in a state of transition. Nothing stays put, positive or negative. We do our best to cling to the good and to reject the bad, but no matter how hard we try, both will inevitably arise. And both will just as inevitably disburse. Right now I was grateful for the disbursement part.

"Kim!" I called. She froze, her helmet half-off. "I have good news."

CHAPTER 14

Kim had all coping mechanisms working full bore, but her eyes were as bright as I'd ever seen them.

"Do you want some privacy?" I asked. "I can leave."

"No, Mr. Norbu. I would like you to stay."

She waited, knees jiggling, phone at her ear. I had made a pot of hot tea, and we sat across from each other at the kitchen table, the smoky perfume of Lapsang Souchong rising from our mugs.

Kim's face changed.

"Bobby? Hello. This is Kim. Your sister." A small smile spread as she listened. Such smiles were rare. "I know. I know. You did? You named her Kim?" She listened some more. "He is right here. I will tell him."

Kim lowered her cell phone and met my eyes.

"My brother says thank you. He would like me to come to his house for a visit. Bobby has a daughter. He calls her Kimmy."

"Great idea," I said. "Take all the time you need."

As Kim and her brother worked out details, I moved to the pile of bills on my desk. It was well past the first of the month. I couldn't put off reality any longer.

I logged on, brought up my Excel spreadsheets, and forced myself to look. My Julius Rosen emergency fund—guilt money my wealthy, now-deceased client had willed me after endangering my life—was healthy. Ish. That is to say, the total was in the low five figures, but I had earmarked the bulk of it for our wedding.

It was my other, working account, the one I used to pay bills, which caused the heart palpitations. I'd had very little income since January, and for months I had been dipping into my savings to make up the difference.

The stab of shame was unexpected. I tried to trace its origin. Was it because I was almost broke? That hadn't stopped me in the past. When I left the force, or rather asked them to lay me off, I had also made what Bill and Martha thought was an insane decision, to forgo unemployment checks. But for me, taking that money was as good as saying to the universe that I couldn't or wouldn't thrive on my own. Experience had proved me right, at least at first. I'd followed my intuition, and again and again, intuitive leaps led to high-paying clients. Success bred success. Good fortune followed trust.

What had changed?

I had.

I had lost the ability to trust in myself. I had stopped inviting the river to carry me wherever it flowed. I wasn't moving, but neither had I climbed out onto the bank. At least that would have been a conscious decision. No, I was stuck in the rush of water, clutching a rooted branch, too stubborn or scared to unclench my fist.

Something in my present life had thrown a switch in my brain, and I no longer felt free to just go with the flow, willy-nilly.

Listen to yourself, Ten. *Go with the flow. Willy-nilly.* Who even talked that way?

My mother did, that's who. Great. Now my dead mother had co-opted my voice.

Kim appeared by my desk.

"I am leaving now," she said. "Do you need anything?"

A return to easeful intention would be nice.

"No thanks, Kim. Just enjoy. Happy birthday."

Kim's body rocked back and forth, tiny jerks of motion. "Mr. Norbu?"

"Yes, Kim."

"My arms want to hug you, but my mind won't let me do it."

"Then let this be a virtual hug, Kim." I formed a circle with my arms, clasped my forearms, and squeezed. She did the same, and I swear I felt her embrace.

I wrote checks for the pile of outstanding invoices, tucked them into envelopes, and sealed and stamped them. No electronic banking for me, not with Mike as a friend.

He'd installed both anti-virus and anti-malware programs on my computer, but still. His tales of identity theft were enough to make me want to use an abacus and pay people in cowrie shells.

Once again, I was short several hundred dollars, even with Julie insisting on contributing her half of the expenses. And that, too, made me feel bad. She'd moved here to be with me, giving up her lucrative chef's job in Chicago. Like me, she'd joined the freelance world, at least until her restaurant got funded. The private catering jobs were only occasional and not very lucrative. So also like me, she'd been dipping into her savings to make up the difference.

At least we both had savings to draw on. I should have been grateful. Instead, I was anxious.

And fed up, after sentencing myself to this professional *bardo*, this ring of tedium, leeched of color and joy. I was good at this kind of job. I just wasn't great at it. I didn't hate what I was doing. I just didn't love it. I got paid, but never that well. My experience so far of the year of the wooden horse? Boring. Boring. Boring.

Until today. Today was different. I had reconnected Kim and her long-lost brother, and the act had brought joy to all three of us. Four, if you counted Mpingo. And five, once I told Julie. I'd followed a hunch, and the result was effortless. Why was I fighting this obvious ability of mine? What was I resisting?

You know.

But I didn't know. I could analyze and rationalize all I wanted, but I still didn't know.

My eyes drifted to the envelope from yesterday, still lying on my desk, still unopened. I sighed. Better see what my well-meaning neighbor had in mind.

I opened the flap. No letter inside, but something smaller. I tipped the envelope and shook out the contents. A pink business card fell onto the desk. I picked it up.

Not a business card. A driver's license, and it belonged to no one I knew.

"Knock-knock! It's me! Martha!"

What was she doing here?

"Julie's not here," I called.

Martha said nothing.

I let the flare of irritation subside. I needed to ground myself, in case Martha was in a karma-ripening mood. I set the license on my desk to check out later.

Martha was pouring herself the last of the coffee. She lifted her mug.

"Sorry, should I make more?"

I waved her off.

"I won't stay long. I know you're working."

I didn't tell her otherwise. We sat across from each other at the kitchen table.

Martha was nine years older than Julie, which put her at forty-three now. The past year had added lines to her face and subtracted pounds from her frame. She had done something new to her hair—I didn't remember it being that blonde—but it suited her.

"I like your hair," I said, and she fluffed it with one hand. "How are the twins?"

"Relentless."

"I can imagine."

Martha had left her job as a court reporter to concentrate on raising the twins full time. I don't know how she did it—one afternoon of babysitting Maude and Lola put me in a coma for a week. But Martha had German in her DNA and she ran her family like a well-oiled panzer tank. Her energy level was such that whatever her job, she'd always required side projects to keep the spark plugs firing.

For the first few years of motherhood, her top priority had been changing my status from "single" to "in a relationship." Now . . .

She rummaged in her purse and pulled out several color printouts and three typewritten pages, stapled together.

My heart sank.

"I brought these venues for you both to look over. My favorite so far is the Terranea Resort, on the coast of Palos Verdes, but it's booked until next fall, so . . ."

"Martha."

"There's also the Japanese garden downtown, you're okay with Japan, it's China that you hate, right? But you have to use their caterer, and I just can't see Julie going for that. Now Saddle Back Ranch in Malibu is probably the closest thing to local, but again, fully booked for months . . ."

"MARTHA."

"What?"

"Does Julie know you've been doing this research?"

Martha had the good graces to blush. "Not exactly."

"Because as I'm sure you know, she and I still haven't decided on a date."

"I do know that," she said.

I waited.

"I'm sorry." She looked miserable.

"I don't understand," I said. "Why the rush? What is causing this pressure, this discomfort in you?"

"I just . . . I want to make sure it happens," she said. "I feel like once you and Julie get married, you know, then that means Bill and I will . . ."

"Stay married?"

Martha nodded, her eyes welling.

I walked around the table and touched her shoulder. "Hey. Look at me."

She did.

"Healing takes time, Martha."

She sniffed. "I know, I know."

"The thing is, for some of us, so does choosing a wedding date." I passed her a paper towel and she blew her nose.

"You're a good friend," she said. She neatly folded the printouts and tucked them into her purse. Her hand paused at the stapled pages. "Can I leave these, at least?"

I picked them up and leafed through columns of names and addresses. A few I knew, cops, mostly. The majority I didn't.

I turned back to page one. "'Julie's guest list,'" I read out loud. I raised my eyebrows at Martha.

"Bill and I eloped," Martha said, after a moment. "I never got to . . ." Her voice trailed off at the look on my face.

I hurried her out the door before I made her cry again.

"Don't forget to make your own list," she called over her shoulder. "It's all about the head count!" She climbed into their latest family car, a Mazda minivan, and drove away, her good humor restored.

The guest list lay on the table like an accusation.

Martha and Julie had a huge blended family that extended from Chicago to Germany and points beyond. Everyone had managed to stay on pretty good terms with everyone else, generating a seemingly endless supply of friendly and communicative siblings, stepsiblings, and cousins. Add to that the fact that Julie attracted friends like ripe mangoes attract fruit flies, and you had a very, very long guest list.

I had a cat, two monks, and a cyber-geek who probably didn't even own a tie.

Mother? Dead.

Father? Also dead.

Other family . . . ?

A rush of blackness attacked inside my eyelids. My blood swam and I had to sit down before I passed out. I jammed my palms against my eyes until the dark flood receded.

Enough.

I walked straight to my desk and picked up the phone. I still remembered his number, after all these years.

"This is Dr. Eric Leonard," I heard. "I can't come to the phone right now, so please leave your number, and I'll get back to you just as soon as I can."

"Dr. Leonard," I said. "Eric." My heart was still pounding. "This is Tenzing. I'd really like to talk with you. Officially, I mean. I'm drowning. I need help."

I let go of the branch.

CHAPTER 15

I had done it. The relief was immediate, as a rush of energy followed this simple act of commitment. I sat back and enjoyed the newfound spaciousness inside.

My eyes drifted to the odd gift left in my mailbox this morning, and I picked up the stranger's driving license. *DRIVING LICENCE*, I should say, for that was what the block letters across the top stated. Below them was the Euro flag, dark blue with a circle of bright yellow stars, the initials *UK* in the center.

I studied the image of a young man. White. Reddish stringy hair, long scythe of a nose, and a glum smudge of goatee like a taunt. Full, almost feminine mouth. He'd be handsome if he weren't so sullen. He pouted at the camera as if resenting its existence. Or maybe it was his own life he hated. His identical ghost to the right, though smaller in size, was just as surly. In between the scowling twins, an official stamp of some sort.

Who was he?

Surname *PURDHAM-COOTE* with the suffix *III*. First name, *COLIN*. Below the names, a date—23-04-94, and the word *LONDON*. So Colin Purdham-Coote III was 20 and was either born or lived in London. I'm not a certified private investigator for nothing.

Next to the numbers *4a* and *4b*, I further deduced when he'd gotten his license, April 30, three years ago, and when it would expire, April 29, seven years from now. Next to *4c* was a set of initials that meant nothing to me. The license number itself, *5*, was a long series of letters and digits I would decipher later if necessary.

His signature was an angry, illegible scrawl.

Underneath his irate autograph, a London address.

And finally, across the bottom, a string of code after the number *9*: *AM*, *A1*, *A2*, *B1*, *B*, *C1*, and so on.

I flipped it over. How thoughtful of them. To the left, a list explaining the numbered information on the front. To the right, a chart of the same coded letters, complete with illustrations, showing when and what kind of vehicles this particular young man could and could not drive.

But not a single clue as to why the 20-year-old Colin Purdham-Coote III was no longer in possession of his driving license, and I was.

This called for a cold beer.

I opened the refrigerator door and foraged. Julie had mentioned there was still some leftover pad thai. There it was, front and center. I set it on the counter. I moved condiment jars and Tupperware containers like chess pieces until I found a bottle of Goose Island Matilda hiding like a beautiful Belgian pawn. It was mine to capture, and I took it.

I poured straight down the middle of a widemouthed glass goblet, let the amber liquid foam up, and waited for the foam to settle. Pour. Foam. Settle. Pour. Foam. Settle. I love how mindfulness can be applied to any action. After five minutes the bottle was empty and the glass was full. I set the goblet aside to breathe.

I refreshed Tank's water dish. He still had food in his bowl. He was sprawled in a patch of sun on the driveway, a mound of fur on a rug of light.

Sometimes I would wait for half an hour before drinking a Trappist-brewed ale, so the flavor could fully bloom. This was not one of those times.

I carried the beer and noodles outside, toasted the cloudless sky, and took my first swallow. There is nothing else on this planet like the first swallow of cold Belgian pale ale on a hot day—that moment when the smooth snap of hops meets the warm tongue and the scent strikes your nostrils, yeasty and alive.

I hadn't eaten much today and the alcohol soon initiated a light, pleasant buzz that traveled through my arteries like a stream of humming bees. I opened the pad thai container and forked cold rice noodles into my mouth—any more buzz and I'd need a nap. The bean sprouts were still crunchy, and the sesame oil, fresh-chopped cilantro, and red pepper flakes added just the right amount of counter punch to the malty ale. I alternated solids and liquids so I could end the meal with a final mouthful of beer.

Tank brushed up against my right calf. I positioned the top of my foot tight against his soft belly. Using my foot as a kind of human winch, I arched and released his spine a few times. Cat calisthenics.

I considered calling Julie again, but even if I left now to join my friends, I'd have to turn right back around and come home. I had three hours until the entourage arrived. Subtract an hour to shower and meditate, and I still had enough to make a start.

"Okay, Mr. Purdham-Coote," I said. "Let's find out who you are."

I don't know if people realize how much they expose through social media. It's like offering anyone who wants to snoop a free and anonymous peek into their private diaries, their most embarrassing moments, their underwear drawer, and their garbage can, all at once and without the mess. There's a street term in Los Angeles for the knuckle and neck tattoos popular with gang members: job killers, they're called. The same title could apply to a certain class of Twitter, Facebook, Tumblr, or Instagram post. I see these snapshots of bloodshot leers, half-clothed bodies, bongs in the background, and I want to say, "Fellow travelers, I know this seems like a good idea, but there will come a time when you want someone to hire you."

I'm only 33 years old, and very new to the technology, but even I know better.

Colin Purdham-Coote had just such an awkward array of visual missteps, at least up until about six months ago,

though even his tackiest pictures included ties and blue blazers. His drink of choice appeared to be tequila, with a chaser of hash oil from a water pipe.

Digging deeper, I discovered that this entitled young man had gone to a very expensive and academically rigorous school in central London called Westminster and was now at the even more expensive and academically rigorous university called Cambridge.

He may have breathed the rarified air of aristocracy, learned to wield a cricket bat, and recited Shakespeare onstage, but from his posts you would conclude that his major sport was Partying, and his major subject Complaining.

Then something changed. Sometime late last year he posted a couple of pictures where he was clear-eyed and smiling. His hair was still long, but clean and shiny. In one photo, he stood shoulder to shoulder with another young man, untagged by name but equally radiant. Of Indian descent, as swarthy as Colin was fair. He'd slung one arm over Colin's shoulder. He wore a gold ring on his middle finger, a thick band with an imbedded stone. I enlarged the image, zooming in on the ring. An amber cat's-eye filled the screen.

They were like pepper and salt. Maybe they were mates, maybe lovers, I couldn't tell. But Colin was transformed. And then he was gone. I scrolled and cross-scrolled, checked all the sites, but he had simply stopped posting. No more technological footprint.

I moved back to the license.

His address was 63 Eaton Square, SW1—like his school, right in the heart of London. I Googled the address. Unless he'd managed between hits of hashish to invent the next Facebook, Colin was still living at home—a seven-bedroom Georgian town house that screamed *wealthy parents*.

Where there's a Third, there's a Second. A couple of searches and clicks revealed that indeed, Colin Two was a very successful financier and a bona fide blue blood. Also entitled. Literally. He was a baron, like his father, the original Colin, before him.

In the past, unearthing information was done with binoculars and door-to-doors, visits to libraries to access microfiche for archived newspaper articles. There was a tactile element to investigation. Today might be less hands-on than the past, but there's a lot to be said for the speed of online research.

I soon dug up a flattering feature in the *Financial Times* from five years ago. I took a moment to study the photograph—a man and woman in black tie and gown facing forward, their posture formal, like a museum portrait from another time. Behind them, flanked by mounted stag heads, was a huge fireplace, the kind you could roast a boar in, no problem.

A ruddy Lord Purdham-Coote, his hairline receding along with his chin, towered next to a waifish blonde with skin like parchment paper. Apparently papa had genetically received and passed along to his son the wispy reddish hair and narrow hook of a nose.

I scanned the article.

Actually, everything about Lord Purdham-Coote II was hereditary: his slot at Queens' College, Cambridge; his managerial position at the Bank of England; his title of Baron; his wealth. I was willing to bet the stags were hand-me-downs as well.

Were lords even listed?

I tried London information. Lo and behold and tallyho, a British recording, the voice female and formal, recited an actual telephone number for Colin and Winifred Purdham-Coote, Number 63, Eaton Square.

I did the math. Two o'clock here made it ten o'clock in London.

What would Sherlock do?

Sherlock would take the plunge. Politely.

I dialed the number.

"Yeesss?"

"Lord Purdham-Coote?"

"Yeesss?" Somehow he managed to make one benign syllable sound like three condescending ones.

"My name is Tenzing Norbu. I'm calling from Los Angeles. I apologize for calling so late, but I seem to have your son Colin's driving license in my possession. It was delivered to my mailbox anonymously. I thought you should know."

"How extraordinary," he said after a pause. "Are you quite certain, young man?" His tone already maddened me. I was starting to understand Junior's need for tequila and bongs.

"Fairly certain. Birth date April twenty-fourth, 1994?"

"Darling," I heard, "there's a young man here name of Nor-gay, says he's a friend of Collie's. From Los Angeles, of all places."

"Norbu, actually, and I'm not . . ." but Purdham-Coote was deep in conversation with Celia or Arabella or Queen Victoria, or whatever her name was.

Breathe, Tenzing. You need this man's help.

"Can we call you back, Mr. Norgay?"

"Bu. Nor-bu. Sure." I gave him my number.

"Does tomorrow suit? We need to talk to our son first, naturally."

"Tomorrow is fine."

Talk about a whole load of nothing. Still, even that was something.

A small window of unstructured time remained. I visualized my immediate future. Some stretches, 20 minutes on my cushion counting breaths and allowing thoughts, and maybe even a Tank-length nap. Somehow, the simple act of calling Eric had invited spaciousness back into my life, at least for the moment.

I moved to the deck and stood, feet shoulder-width apart and firm on the warm redwood planks. I allowed a slow in-breath to descend into my belly, swelling its edges like a balloon. I exhaled fully.

One conscious breath and I already felt like a new man.

As a novice lama at Dorje Yidam, I would often find myself struggling—with memorization of the chants, with the finer points of debate. Sonam would gently remind me, "You will never find ease or success, Lama Tenzing, except through the gate of breathing."

Keeping the knees soft, I inhaled, raising my arms in front of me, elbows straight, to the count of 10. On the exhale, I lowered them just as slowly. And again. Again.

I cycled through a series of stretches, counting to 10, repeating each three times; bending forward and back, circling my hips, squatting, arching, folding at the waist and touching the deck with flattened palms. I lunged and pointed, my arm like a spear, first one direction, then another.

And finished in the same standing position, feet apart, arms relaxed at my sides.

I walked inside, my body loose, my mind both settled and expanded. My meditation cushion was calling to me.

But it was my landline that rang.

The woman on the other end was sobbing so hard I couldn't make out her words. Then the baron's dreaded combination of clipped consonants and drawn-out vowels was back.

"Mr. Norrr-gaaay?"

"It's Nor-Bu. Norgay was the sherpa."

"I do apologize. Mr. Norbu, my wife and I are a bit worried."

"Go on."

"Collie is gone, you see. He appears to have left Cambridge. I'm so sorry, I don't mean *left,* he hasn't graduated, he's gone away. Isn't answering his phone, most unlike him. He seems to have missed his last two sessions with his tutor and the porter can't remember when he last saw or spoke to him."

Lord Purdham-Coote had clearly been busy rousing people all over campus.

"Couldn't Colin have skipped class?"

"That's just it, you see. No one has seen hide nor hair for several days. I had the porter check with the students on his hall. Everyone assumed we'd called Collie home for one of Winnie's events. She does like to wave the family flag."

His voice grew slightly petulant—the verbal equivalent of Collie's fretful Facebook posts. "It is simply unacceptable. I can't imagine why nobody thought to call us."

"Maybe your son decided last minute to come here to Los Angeles. On a whim."

"Well, but why on earth would he? I just, I'm simply stymied."

And clearly not used to the feeling.

"Have you filed a missing-persons report?" I was assuming their protocol was similar to ours.

"I plan on doing so next."

"Up in Cambridge?"

"Good lord, no. My solicitor and I are going to the Belgravia station. It's just down the street, off Buckingham Palace Road. They know me there. I shall be keeping a very close eye."

"I'm sure you will." I didn't envy whoever was manning the front desk.

"How do you know Collie, anyway?"

"I don't."

I explained what I did know, which wasn't much.

"Well," Purdham-Coote said. "*Someone* knows where Collie has got to, and that someone appears to want you to know as well." He sighed. "Winnie's fit to be tied. I thought we were through with all this nonsense."

"What do you mean?"

"Never mind," he said. "I suppose we shall have to hire you now, as well."

"Are you saying Colin has run away in the past?"

"No, no. Nothing like that. He's just been . . . difficult. Went through a bit of a stage. But he's been sorted for months. Still, this is all very worrying." His voice grew resigned. "How much do you charge for your services?"

I glanced at the stack of envelopes I had not yet mailed. Pictured a gleaming white four-story, seven-bedroom house in the most expensive part of London, complete with peerage.

A lot.

I gave my greed a time-out. Desperation did not lead to good decision making.

There was something very suspicious about the situation. I wasn't going to commit fully to this employment opportunity until I figured out what was going on. That is to say, sure, there was such a thing as intuitive ease when solving a case. And once in a great while, there was even such a thing as ridiculous luck.

Getting the driver's license of a misper with filthy-rich parents hand-delivered to your home? There wasn't even a category for that.

For whatever reason, I was being played. I needed to know by whom.

"Let's make sure your son is missing first, Lord Purdham-Coote, shall we?"

CHAPTER 16

"Pancakes and bacon? Are you serious?"

I meant the question to be light, but Julie's tone was defensive.

"That's what Geshe Sonam requested. He kept repeating the same thing: 'I would like round pieces of warm bread, and meat. Not thick meat. Very thin.' I guess he had pancakes once in New York. Some UN conference on world religions. I was convinced he meant pepperoni pizza, but we got there eventually."

"Sonam's full of surprises," I said.

I cracked the last egg and dumped it onto a mound of powdery ingredients. Julie was brisk as she flew around the kitchen in her purple apron, wielding tongs like a weapon. She flipped two spitting pieces of bacon in the hot frying pan and transferred two more onto a folded paper towel.

The Tibetan contingent had been whooshed outside to the deck to watch the sunset. I looked at their still forms, columns against the darkening sky, with longing.

"Do you want me to mix this stuff?"

"I'll do it," Julie said. "And by the way, about the bacon? I thought you were a vegetarian because you were a Buddhist, not because you were, you know, a vegetarian. You never told me monks ate meat."

"You never asked. Anyway, not all monks eat meat."

"All of these do. As far as I can tell, the only thing they won't eat is seafood, which is the only thing you will. And even then, I have to beg."

I kept quiet. When it came to food, Julie's passions ran high. No need to remind her tonight about my hippy mother

in Paris, whose diets ranged from macrobiotic to foie gras festivals, depending on her current lover. Or my brief foray into meat eating during the Heather years. Julie would go ballistic if she found out I'd consumed my first Langer's pastrami sandwich without her.

Sometimes wisdom meant waiting for the right time.

She measured and poured buttermilk and whisked the batter into submission. Grabbing a teaspoon, she dribbled water onto the hot greased griddle. The drops of water hissed and leaped.

"Homer can have these first ones," she muttered, ladling circles of batter onto the griddle. The batter bubbled up.

"Nothing I love more than round pieces of warm bread," I said.

"Ha ha." She mopped her forehead with her forearm.

I moved next to her. She stiffened slightly.

"I'm sorry about this morning," I said. "I don't want to be like this right now."

She softened slightly. "I'm not exactly at my best either," she said.

"I called Eric for an appointment."

She shot me a look. "You did?"

"I did."

From inside my back pocket, the brides, to my mind sounding a little more desperate every time, started singing. I glanced at the screen.

"It's Bill . . . I probably should . . ."

"Take it, love. Take it. To be continued."

I moved into the living room.

"Hey," I said.

"You got a job yet?"

"Maybe. Ask me tomorrow."

"Sorry about Martha. She confessed to her unprovoked attack of meddling."

"Not to worry," I said.

"So, I got back the crime lab analysis on the Griffith Park mystery ink."

"Already?"

"Yeah, well, there's gotta be some perks to my job."

"And?"

"Get this. It's blood all right, human blood I mean, AB negative."

"Interesting. That should help narrow things down." AB negative is one of the rarer blood types.

"But what's really interesting is, there's more than one."

"More than one blood type?"

"Not blood type. Type of blood. There's regular blood, and that-time-of-the-month blood."

"Oh."

"Exactly. Plus off-the-chart levels of sulphur."

"Sulphur?"

"Yeah. Sulphur. Plus semen, plus heavy traces of mercury."

"Thanks for killing my appetite, Bill."

"So, what do you think? Any ideas?"

"Julie!" I called. "What foods contain sulphur?"

"Tons!" she called back. "Broccoli. Artichokes. Bacon. You name it!"

"Nothing specific comes to mind," I said. "Too bad we don't have the stomach contents."

"Not to mention the stomach."

"So what's next?"

"We're treating it as a crime scene, just in case," Bill said. "The investigators collected what they could. Unfortunately the site was already somewhat contaminated by nosy tourists and such, but Sully and Mack did a pretty good job of securing it until we figure out what the hell's going on." Sully and Mack, known to most as S&M, were old-timers, like Bill, but neither had moved up the ladder.

"Any hikers reported as missing?"

"We're checking."

"How about the tag? Any luck identifying the gang?"

"Tags. There were two. Not so far. The initials *JMM* mean anything to you?"

"No. Sorry."

"Yeah, well, I may shoot over the crime scene photos if we keep hitting walls. S & M aren't the sharpest tools in the box." Bill sighed. "Something about this thing's giving me the heebie-jeebies."

"Why Bill, how unscientific of you. You almost sound like me."

"Asshole," he said.

"I meant it as a compliment. And yes, send me whatever, whenever. I'm happy to help. Anything else? I have monks here for pancakes."

"I don't even want to know. Okay. Later, gator."

"Not that much later."

"Right. Tomorrow night, gator. Ommmmm," and he hung up.

I'd forgotten how much lamas eat, given the chance. Julie and I were kept busy replenishing plates.

For the record, I stuck to pancakes. Homer, on the other hand, planted himself underfoot and kept vigilant watch for dropped pork. Yeshe slipped him an entire strip of bacon, which wouldn't bode well for his digestive system later. Maybe Homer could sleep on the deck tonight. Serenade the owls.

I broke out the Sapporo, which goes better with breakfast than you'd think. Lobsang had two full glasses, and finished off the meal with a loud *BRRRAPPP*, the highest of compliments to the chef.

Yeshe cleared and Lobsang and I stacked the plates by the sink. Sonam directed TJ and Wangdue to wash the dishes. He stretched out on the sofa.

Finally I was able to hustle Yeshe and Lobsang onto the deck. Enough with the communal living, I needed them to myself.

We stood in a row, shoulder to shoulder, looking out at the canyon. As we settled into our bodies, our breathing slowed, becoming gentle, almost synchronized. This was what I missed most of all, this silent communing. Sometimes

we'd managed to link in meditation, but such an experience was rare.

"Can you see Saka from here?" Yeshe asked.

"I don't know," I said. "Maybe that one?" I pointed across the canyon to the first star of the evening, a dot of light.

"Yes, I think that Saka," Yeshe said happily.

"Hanh," Lobsang said, unpersuaded.

The distant call of a coyote set off a chorus of echoing yips and chuckles. Their feral song faded into silence. More stars twinkled to life. The moon, Dawa, was midway through her cycle. She would add thin crescents of light until she reached fullness again.

"Your house is just like picture I paint in my mind." Yeshe said. "I like very much."

"I'm glad. And Los Angeles?"

"I like too! Big roads. So many fancy cars!"

"Too much cars," Lobsang said.

"At least they follow rules," Yeshe said. "Not like India."

"Hanh, in India, too much cars *and* too much fools," Lobsang said.

The conversation soothed me. Yeshe could look at any situation, no matter how bleak the weave, and find the thread of gold. Lobsang's grumpy pragmatism served as yang to Yeshe's yin.

"I'm glad you like it here," I repeated. "This is home now." Saying it almost made me believe it.

Another animal cry echoed through the canyon, the call of the hunted, or the haunted. Just below me on the shadowy slope, a cactus was reaching up with prickly paddles, as if asking for a hug. But who would choose to embrace a cactus?

I crossed my arms.

"Everything is okay, Tenzing? You are okay?" Yeshe asked the question, but Lobsang turned his head to watch me answer.

"I don't know," I said. And then, "No. I'm worried about work. I'm worried about money. I'm worried about . . . everything."

It all spilled out in a flood: the panic attacks, the paranoia, the sudden appearance of Colin's license and the disappearance of the young man himself. After I finished, neither friend spoke for some time. Nor did I. This was our way.

"You need find this boy." Lobsang's voice, when it came, was firm. He was always the practical one. "Father pay you well. He already say so."

"But I can't right now. You're here. I'm going to be driving you around."

"Driving not your dharma," Lobsang said. "Finding boy? That your dharma."

Yeshe touched my arm.

"I am sad for your troubles," he said. His voice grew urgent. "Is Saka Dawa. You need chant. Make merit. I chant, too, for you feel better."

"Hanh," Lobsang said. "Chant for him find missing boy with rich father."

Their friendship wrapped me in its folds, a moment of pure protection.

"Lama Tenzing?" TJ was standing in the doorway like a red-robed ghost, Wangdue just behind him. Their heads gleamed, reflecting the light from inside.

"You can give us code for Wi-Fi please?" TJ held up his iPad.

"Of course," I said.

Like all things, the moment had passed.

Chapter 17

It was late by the time Julie got home from ferrying the monks back to Los Feliz. I was in bed, reading a long and rambling Swedish mystery, one of my preferred sleep aids.

"Save me," I said. "I'm lost in a swamp of Scandinavian Burgs, Borgs, and Stads."

"You have only yourself to blame." She stripped off her clothes and pulled on a tank top and a pair of my boxers before ducking into the bathroom. I heard the hum of an electric toothbrush.

I set my Kindle on the floor.

Julie climbed into bed. She smelled of jasmine and a hint of lemon. She leaned against the headboard, hugging her knees, and met my eyes.

"So," she said. "Eric."

I could lie by omission, or at least dilution, or I could recognize the tightening of my stomach muscles as a warning delivered in body code. Danger: Opportunity to Lose or Gain Intimacy Straight Ahead. Barricades between partners don't manifest in an instant. They grow over time and start with a single, seemingly innocent pebble.

"I've been experiencing these flashes of . . . fear, I guess," I said. "It happened again this morning. I couldn't breathe. I don't think it's physical, but it feels that way. Plus, you know, that nightmare about the tower. I keep having it."

"Okay."

"So I called Eric today, or rather left him a message. I think I need to meet with him. Talk to him."

"Talk? Or, like, *talk*."

"The second kind, I think." I shrugged. "Just a consultation, you know?"

"About the nightmare."

"Yes. Among other things. None of this is about you, or us, don't worry."

"Uh huh." When Julie starts to smile, a faint dimple appears. Only on the left cheek. It comes and goes quickly, like a wink of well-being. Easy to miss.

"What?"

"Ten, I've been in therapy, remember? It's never about what you think it's about." Her smile faded as her eyes darkened with a fresh worry.

"What is it?" I asked.

"I just . . . we're okay, right? You and me, I mean?"

"Of course we're okay."

"Because, we don't have to go through with this."

"Jules," I said. I tugged at her wrist. "Come here. You feel too far away."

She lay down, her body inches from mine. Her breath was warm.

"I'm all in," I said. "Got it?" I traced the constellation of freckles sprinkled across her collarbone.

"Got it." Julie leaned in and touched her lips to mine. Such a light kiss. A brush of butterfly wings, there, then gone.

"I'm glad you are going to see Eric," she said. "Really. But be prepared. Deep-sea diving ain't for sissies."

"I know that. I'm with you, aren't I?"

My turn to kiss her. Her lips parted. I tasted peppermint. I let my hands wander. My body responded.

Then hers did.

Then ours did.

But afterward, I lay awake for a long time.

Chapter 18

The eighth day of Saka Dawa dawned clear and mild. Mere weeks ago, Los Angeles had been close to paralyzed by a relentless parade of 100-degree temperatures. Power outages turned apartments into ovens. County officials scrambled to set up cooling centers and splash pads throughout the city. The air was so hot and dry that the act of breathing scorched the throat. Finally the triple-digit surge had broken, mercifully receding like a rogue wave.

I padded barefoot to the kitchen. The hardwood floor was cool instead of radiating sun-blasted heat from too many scalding days and nights. I poured a mug of coffee. Julie and Homer had already left in the Ford van. Early start for all of us today. I would be following the instructions of both my friends, Yeshe's first.

I took the coffee onto the deck. A light breeze ran cool fingers over my face and arms. Maybe Green Tara got word that the monks of Dorje Yidam were on their way to L.A. and decided to intervene with the local weather gods. The fruits of karma can ripen for good as well as for ill, and the month of Saka Dawa was a notably auspicious time for *puñña*—merit-making. The benefits of any right action increased many times over. And on the actual day of Saka Dawa Duchen—the full moon that landed midmonth—a monk could multiply his meritorious blowback by 100,000. As Bill would put it, Saka Dawa Duchen gave you much more bang for your buck.

At Dorje Yidam, our monastery teachers implored us to use this propitious month wisely. To consciously and specifically deepen our commitment to the three grounds of "right" action: mental purity, generosity, and morality.

Some of the other novices even listened.

The dawn sky was pale blue, the ocean a barely perceptible rub of green in the distance. Dorje Yidam was on the other side of the world.

"You need make merit," Yeshe had urged me.

Mental purity. Generosity. Morality. Those were the stated goals of Saka Dawa. I resolved to do more meditating, giving, and right-acting. Beginning now.

I stepped behind the screen, sat on a cushion, and alternated chants and meditation for a full hour. Maybe it was psychosomatic, but time felt especially fluid and nonlinear, and the hour was over in an instant.

Before allowing myself a second mug of coffee, I logged online to make a contribution to the Dorje Yidam Kickstarter fund.

My eyes widened. Unless the number across the top was wrong, the campaign had raised $15,000 electronically since the first of May. Times had changed since monks went door to door for lentils and rice.

There were three ways to make a donation to the fund: PayPal; something called Dana-puñña; and that modern equivalent of a bottomless begging bowl, the credit card.

I charged $100 to a piece of plastic, an act of faith. I would donate the same amount on Saka Dawa Duchen, the full moon power spot next week, $200 in total. Who knows? If Green Tara was feeling beneficent, maybe I'd land a $20 million job before the end of June.

No nightmare last night either. I was feeling dangerously close to smug. It wasn't even ten o'clock, and I had already meditated and performed an act of generosity. I could check two out of three meritorious feats off my list. All that was left was a good deed.

My cell phone sang. Did changing ringtones so I didn't kill myself qualify?

"Hi, Jules."

"Hello, my one. How are you? I miss you."

"I'm pretty good." And I was. "I miss you, too." And I did.

"So listen, I've got a huge favor to ask. Today is Martha and Bill's day to see their marriage counselor, and usually I watch the girls, but I can't, it's too crazy over here. I know you have to work, but Martha's desperate. It would only be for a few hours."

"Done," I said. Twins. Maybe that counted as double.

"You're a saint. She'll bring them to you. Then you can drive the girls here for the ceremony. Take the Subaru—I've got car seats. Thanks, love."

"See you tonight."

Tank was sleeping by his empty food bowl. He lifted his head.

"See how easy that was?"

He was unimpressed. For Tank, the only good deeds worth mentioning involve tuna juice or raw liver.

Across the living room, my work phone was flashing. I hadn't heard it ring while I was meditating. Maybe what I called excellent concentration was in fact acute sleepiness.

I had three messages.

"Detective Norbu? Lord Purdham-Coote. This is urgent." No drawls, and not one iota of condescension—more like desperation. "Call me as soon as you get this message. It's about Collie." He recited two numbers, including one I already had. I opened a file folder and added the other to the contact list I'd started yesterday, just in case these odd events should evolve into a job.

I listened to the second message.

"Yeah, Tenzing Norbu? Yeah, so gimme a jingle. Purdham-Coote told me to call. Been his watchdog over here. For the kid, I mean." The voice was blunt and scruffy. "I'm up early, and I'm up late. I fuckin' never sleep, you wanna know the truth of it. Oh, I'm Bertie. Bertie Andrews."

Definitely not upper crust. More like working man's white bread.

On to three.

"This is a message for a Detective Tenzing Norbu. This is Detective Chief Inspector Nigel Garfield of the City of

London Metropolitan Police. That's Garfield. Gee, ay, arr, eff, eye, ee, el, dee." He rattled off a phone number, thoughtfully including all necessary city and country codes.

I took a moment to enjoy the moment. A message from the London Metropolitan Police, aka New Scotland Yard. How many nights had I spent at Dorje Yidam seemingly huddled under a scratchy blanket with a flashlight, but in fact striding the foggy cobbled streets of London with my hero, pipes clenched in our mouths, connecting clues? Now the Yard was calling me. Life was growing more propitious by the minute.

I dialed Lord P-C's number first.

"Yes! Yes! Hello! I'm here!" he said. The man sounded truly frantic.

"Lord Purdham-Coote. Tenzing Norbu here, calling you back."

"Did Bertie call you, Detective Norbu?"

"Bertie called and left a message, as did . . ." I found the name, "Detective Chief Inspector Nigel Garfield. And please, call me Ten."

"But you haven't spoken to them?"

"No."

"So you don't know."

"Know what?"

"Cambridgeshire sent a couple of constables to search Collie's room. He's gone. They say the circumstances are suspicious. They're assessing the risk now, but they're not ruling out anything. I fear our son may be, oh God . . ." His voice broke.

The image of Lord Purdham-Coote and his wife stared at me from the opened file, a portrait of invincibility. Nothing in their world could go wrong, because they held the reins. They were in charge. They knew how life worked. No one warned them, and they had yet to learn, that invincibility is an illusion born of fear and mocked by reality.

The Buddha, too, had been born to wealth and anointed with power. But for him, prestige brought only pain. He'd

sought different truths, and found the solution to suffering the hard way.

Purdham-Coote's suffering was no less valid because it was wrapped in cashmere.

I directed unspoken words of compassion his way. *May the suffering of the present lead you to a path of wisdom. May you have ease.*

"Please, will you help us?"

"If I can," I said. "I need to speak with the lead detective. Would that be Garfield?"

"DCI Garfield. Yes. Collie's temporary residence is at Queens' College, and it looked like they might take the reins, but I persuaded everyone that the Metropolitan Police should retain supervision. This is his home. Our home. They know us here."

"I understand," I said. "I'll call you back once I've connected with DCI Garfield."

"I pay well. Ask Bertie. I'm a man of my word."

"I'm sure you are."

It was 7:30 A.M.—4:30 P.M. over there. Worth a try.

"Detective Chief Inspector Nigel Garfield here." His voice was firm, but not unpleasant.

"This is Tenzing Norbu, calling from Los Angeles. I just hung up with Lord Purdham-Coote."

"Oh, hello. Yes. His lordship mentioned that he'd like me to coordinate things with you. In what official capacity, may I ask, are you connected to the Colin Purdham-Coote investigation?"

"Official capacity?"

"Sorry, yes, I just want to be sure we are following protocol."

"Protocol?"

Nigel's voice grew just the tiniest bit sharper.

"Protocol. As regards your police department and ours, Detective."

Ah. "I'm afraid you may have been misled," I said. "I'm not LAPD. I'm a private investigator. I work on my own."

The dead silence with which this information was greeted spoke volumes.

"Well," DCI Garfield huffed. "In that case, I'm not sure how I can help you, *or* his lordship. We are in the very early stages of this investigation. Time is of the essence, and we must spend that time wisely. I don't see how talking to you is helpful. Do I make myself clear?"

I took a deep breath in, and then exhaled slowly, allowing another long-held idealization to disperse with the out-breath. There were blowhards in New Scotland Yard, just like everywhere else.

"Look," I said. "I may have precipitated this situation, but I didn't seek it out, it found me. Lord Purdham-Coote and his wife are extremely worried about their son. And I don't blame them. Maybe *his lordship* was afraid if he told you the truth you wouldn't talk to me. And it sounds like he had a point."

Garfield said nothing. I ploughed on.

"I happen to specialize in mispers. I was also a member of the police force over here for over a decade. But whether or not I coordinate with my colleagues at the LAPD, including my ex-partner Detective Bill Bohannon, Rank Three, Burglary-Homicide, depends upon what I find in the course of my own investigation. Meanwhile, I would very much appreciate it if you could include me in yours. Who knows? We might actually help each other find Colin."

Garfield sighed, his version of taking a nice, deep breath. "I apologize," he said. "I've spent the better part of the past fifteen hours talking, or rather listening, to Lord Purdham-Coote."

"Understood," I said. We left it at that.

"Shall we start fresh, Detective Norbu?"

"I'd like nothing better."

"I understand you have evidence pertaining to the case?"

"Potential evidence," I said. I gave him the shorthand version of the envelope and its mysterious contents.

"Actually, this is quite helpful," he said. "When the university constables searched the boy's premises, they weren't able to locate his passport. His Oyster card's gone as well but we're already onto that."

"I'm sorry. Oyster card?"

"Travel card. Prepaid, for public transportation. Bus, tramlink, light rail, national rail, and the Metro, of course. People mostly use them for the Tube."

"Ah. We don't have Oyster cards in Los Angeles. We barely have oysters."

"Ha! Good one. In any case, he topped up his Oyster card last month. We've asked London Transport to take a look at his account and report back to us once they've determined where and when he used public transportation over the past few weeks. Unfortunately, he seems to have left his ATM and credit cards behind. We have also learned, with a little help from his father, that Colin cleaned out his Bank of England account last week. Quite a healthy balance, in fact. All in all, we're closing in on a fairly accurate set of time parameters regarding travel. Your information helps with the geography."

"May I ask you something?"

"Of course."

"Isn't it possible that Colin has just run away? His father seemed to suggest that his son's past might have been somewhat troubled."

Garfield cleared his throat. "Ah, yes. Is he missing, or merely absent? And if he is missing, what is the level of risk? All good questions. We do seem to have conflicting issues at play. On the one hand, we're not dealing with a child, but rather a young man over the age of consent who seems to have left his current premises suddenly, but with no clear evidence of foul play. And yes, he does have a few minor blots on his record, although they have more to do with recreational drug use than anything more suspicious."

He delivered the information in a confident British accent. If I closed my eyes, he could be Holmes.

"On the other, we have the son of a high-profile citizen and a potential target of blackmail, or worse. And it's not been his pattern to go away without leaving word." Garfield paused, as if weighing his next words. "We have a saying over here, Detective. 'If in doubt, think murder.' Far too often an unexplained absence is the first indicator of a much more serious event."

"It's the same here," I said, thinking back to all the times when "missing," turned out to be "murdered."

"I haven't shared that with Lord Purdham-Coote, I'm sure you understand why. But there's more than one good reason for us to err on the side of caution. Preliminarily."

"So you're treating him as missing."

"Yes. With a high level of risk, for the time being."

"Why high?"

"How current are you with the phenomenon of online targeting, Detective Norbu?"

"As regards victims of human trafficking? I know a bit." The tangled snare of Indra's Net moved across my vision. I knew more than a bit, after last year. I knew too much.

"Well, yes, that, but I'm talking about something else. I'm talking about radical elements using social media to profile and then draw in vulnerable young men and women for their own political purposes. It's becoming a real issue over here."

"Terrorists? Colin doesn't strike me as the type."

"No, but then again most of our homegrown radicals don't. We're not ruling anything out, not yet. We consider every missing-persons investigation to be fluid, rather than fixed. Our approach tends to be cyclical and collaborative, as opposed to linear."

"That's commendable," I said. *If it's true*, I thought.

"Yes, well, that's the hope, anyway," he said, as if reading my mind. "Doesn't always turn out that way in practice. But we try to adjust our strategies on a daily, if not hourly basis, and deploy resources accordingly."

"Hmm," I said.

"To summarize, as of now, Colin Purdham-Coote's whereabouts have not been established, the circumstances of his absence are out of character, and he may be at risk. Until we locate him and hear what he has to say, we must remain flexible and open-minded as to the cause. Meanwhile, we've notified the UK MPB, as in Missing Persons Bureau, and the NCA, as in National Crime Agency. Sorry. Everything's an acronym these days, have you noticed?"

"I have."

"There you have the long and short of it."

I was impressed. They hadn't even reached the 24-hour mark. Over here, we'd probably still be debating whether or not to fill out a preliminary missing-person's report.

"What's next?" I asked. "Passenger manifests?"

"Precisely. We've already placed him on the PIW, sorry, police information watchlist, and put in a request for information on his movements, in or out of the country. Anything shows up, we'll access relevant CCTV for visual confirmation." Garfield's phone beeped. "I have another call coming in. I need to take it."

"I appreciate you being so forthright. Is there anything I can do to help?"

"Not at the moment. If we're looking at a cross-border or transatlantic situation, someone here will get in touch. And if Colin should happen to show up on your doorstep looking for his driving license, persuade him to give his parents a call. You'll be saving her majesty a lot of money."

I could see why Lord Purdham-Coote didn't want to let go of DCI Garfield. If I were Colin's father, I'd feel the same.

But if I were Colin's father, I'd also want to leave no stone unturned.

I called Purdham-Coote again. He answered on the first ring, as if his hand had been hovering.

"Yes! Yes! Hello!"

"This is Ten. I'll take the case," I said. "DCI Garfield is terrific, but if it turns out your son is over here, I'd like to get a head start on things."

"Excellent, Detective Norbu. Excellent. Shall we start with an advance of, say, two thousand? Pounds? I believe that's over three thousand dollars. I can wire it today."

It was a start. Maybe not a 100,000-fold, but 15-fold, give or take. Which was a whole lot better than nil.

I'd make my second donation the minute we hung up.

"I'll fax you a contract," I said. "I have a small commitment to take care of this afternoon, and then I will focus all my efforts on finding your son Colin." Twin-sitting might not be a priority to any other private investigator, but I knew better. Karma can turn on a dime.

"I am so appreciative," he said. "Naturally, I had Bertie look into you. He assures me you have had a good bit of success in this area. And Detective Norbu, so far we've kept the vultures at bay. I'm sure this goes without saying . . ."

"I will be completely discreet."

"Thank you. Use this line. It's unlisted. We are hoping against hope to keep our situation out of the tabloids. Those people are shameless. And now the Yard is considering bringing someone on from counterterrorism. In case . . . well . . . it's all so worrisome. Lady Purdham-Coote is shattered. Completely shattered."

"I'll do my absolute best."

"Please." His voice faltered. "Please do that." He hung up.

I would spend the next few hours entering the relevant information into the databases of both NamUs and the FBI's National Crime Information Center. I would check the local hospitals, as well as the morgue, for possible matches. I would put together and prioritize a list of tasks for myself and catalog any further questions for the Purdham-Cootes; Bertie, my London doppelganger; and DCI Garfield, my new best friend. I wanted to be ready, should Collie turn out to be here, as the presence of his driver's license suggested.

DCI Garfield was clearly an extremely competent detective, and my ego was eager to take on the challenge. But the adrenaline now fizzing through my body was not about winning a competition. I had opened myself to passion again, to doing what I did best and loved most.

CHAPTER 19

Maude stood just inside the kitchen, red hair tamed into braids, fingers in her mouth. Behind her, Lola pressed her face against the screen door, eyes pinned on her mother's van in the driveway. Martha made an awkward three-point turn in the narrow space and drove slowly away, wheels crunching on the gravel.

Maude unplugged her mouth.

"Where's Homer?" she said.

"He's with Aunt Julie. You'll see him later."

She replugged for a quick charge of self-soothing, her eyes scanning the kitchen. Out came the fingers. "Where's Tank?"

I pointed. Maude shifted her head to find Tank sprawled at the base of the kitchen window, the tip of his tail flicking.

Lola finally turned from the door. Her eyes were suspiciously bright, but she mustered a small smile.

"Uncle Ten?"

"Yes?"

"I need to tell you sumping."

"Okay."

"I need to tell you that Momma needs you to babysit us because she and Daddy have to go talk to a special lady."

"I see. Is that what your mother told you?"

"Yes. Because Momma and Daddy have . . . they have . . ." Lola frowned. "What do they have again, Maude?"

Maude freed up her mouth. "Tissues," she said.

"Because Momma and Daddy have tissues," Lola repeated. Her lower lip pushed outward. "Uncle Ten, is that a bad thing? To have tissues?"

Oh, boy. We weren't even 10 minutes in.

"I can't say if it's bad or good, Lola. But I'm pretty sure everybody has them at some point or other. I know I do."

That seemed to satisfy both girls.

I set today's ground rules. Rule one: only two cat treats each for Tank. Rule two: no burying the Buddha statue outside, although rearranging the contents of my altar table was okay. Rule three: only 15 minutes of playing trampoline on the bed. (That one might have to stay between them and me.)

They decided on jumping first, which was fine by me. It gave me a chance to revise, print out, sign, scan, and attach a PDF of my adjusted standard contract to Lord Purdham-Coote.

I could hear the twins' squeals of laughter over a series of loud thumps.

"Ten more minutes," I called out.

I checked messages, but the circuit between here and the UK had gone silent. Neither Bertie the Sleepless nor Scotland Yard's best had picked up earlier when I called, and they had not answered my voice messages since. Maybe they'd found their own leads and were loathe to share. Maybe they resented having a Tibetan American half-breed added to the team.

Maybe I should stop being so paranoid.

It had gotten ominously quiet. I half rose from my chair.

"Uncle Ten?" Maude was standing in front of the sofa, staring at me. "I'm hungry."

"Uncle Ten! I need to show you sumping!" Lola called from the bedroom.

"Just a minute, Lola!"

"I'm hungry," Maude said again. "Aunt Julie always makes us a-vo-ca-do on toast." She pronounced the word proudly, as if it were recently learned.

"Uncle Ten, it's really, really important!"

"I'll be right there, Lola!"

"Uncle Ten?" Maude's eyes darkened with doubt. "Do you know how to make a-vo-ca-do on toast?"

I opened my mouth to answer.

"Bang," I heard. "You're dead."

Adrenaline karate-kicked my heart into my throat.

The body is always the first to know.

Lola was in the living room, her chubby 4-year-old hand wrapped around 11 ounces of deadly weapon. She was pointing the Smith & Wesson at her sister, maybe two feet away.

An AirLite works best at close range, like a fist. It can kill three men in five seconds.

My lungs shut down.

I was so exhausted the other night. I must not have spun the combination lock on the safe.

I couldn't remember removing the bullets.

"Lola," I said, my voice forced into false calm. "Listen to Uncle Ten. I want you to stop walking. Stop. Walking. Right. Now."

Lola froze, her eyes uncertain.

"Good. Now put the gun on the floor, okay? Just lay it right on the floor, just like this."

I illustrated.

"Am I in trouble?" Her lower lip trembled.

"No, sweetheart. You're not in any trouble. Just put the gun down, okay?"

She did as I said. I was at her side in three strides. I picked up the revolver, wheeling away from both children. I thumbed the release and snapped the cylinder open. The fact that it was empty of bullets did little to slow my heartbeat or stem the hot rise of shame.

"It wasn't a rule! You didn't say no looking in the closet!" Lola threw both arms in the air before collapsing onto the floor.

"Lola, I'm not mad at you. I promise."

She was spread-eagled and wailing, like a widow on a funeral pyre. I jammed the revolver deep in my back pocket and knelt next to Lola. I laid my hand on her back.

"Lola, it's okay. I'm not mad at you."

She lifted up her head, her nose and eyes streaming.

"I just need to be sad for a little while, Uncle Ten," she sobbed. "I need Lola time, right Maude?"

Maude nodded, stolid and unperturbed. She had her own agenda.

"Uncle Ten," Maude said. "I'm still . . ."

"You're hungry. Got it," I said. "Just . . . just hang on, girls, okay? I'll be right back."

I ran into the bedroom. The black plastic AirLite case lay on the closet floor, its lid raised. The open door of the gun safe was an invitation to disaster. I pressed the Smith & Wesson back in its foam cutout nest, snapped it shut, stored the case inside the safe, and double-spun the dial on the lock. I checked the safe door. Checked it again.

My palms were slick with sweat. Make that my whole body. My heart was chattering like a machine gun. I was up to my neck in tissues.

I placed my hands on my bent knees and forced myself to count off 10 deep breaths.

In the living room Lola had stopped crying. It was risky, but I had to make sure they both understood.

"Girls, I need you to make me a promise, okay? A really really important one."

They nodded, their faces solemn.

"Promise me if you ever find a gun, here, or anywhere else, you won't touch it. Not even if you think it's a toy. Can you promise me that?"

"We promise, Uncle Ten," Lola said.

"We promise," Maude chimed in. "Can we have lunch now?"

"Okay, good. Two treats each for Tank, and two avocados on toast for my two favorite girls."

I am always amazed at the emotional resilience of children, especially children who haven't been taught to repress their feelings. It seems so counterintuitive, to just sit quietly by and allow them to experience their pain. But pain allowed is pain that passes. Just as unacknowledged or forbidden suffering has no place to go but underground. There,

like a buried spore, it can only intensify and grow. I ought to know.

I fished out a bag of cat bribes from the cupboard under the sink and let Maude and Lola pluck out their treats. Tank magically manifested from whatever realm he'd been inhabiting. The girls held out their palms.

What if the gun had been loaded? What if Lola had pulled . . . ?

Bill chose that moment to call.

"Bill?" My voice was high and tight. I needed to change gears, and quickly. *Fake it 'til you make it*, Jean likes to say. *Works with jobs. Works with feelings.* She may be a waitress at Langer's, but for me she's the downtown deli version of a Tibetan oracle. I cleared my throat and tried again, forcing heartiness.

"Bill! Hello!"

"What the fuck's wrong with you?"

The trouble is, I've never been very good at the "faking it" part.

"I'll tell you when I see you," I said. "I almost messed up. Really messed up."

"Almost only counts in horseshoes."

"Not this time."

"Whatever. So listen, Martha and I just got out of our session with the shrink. The lab called while I was in there. More news on the body snatching. Nothing earth shattering, but news is news. Whoever was donating his or her precious bodily fluids liked to smoke hash and weed, big-time. All the blood had a THC reading that was off the charts. You know, Cheech-and-Chong level."

"Who?"

"Cheech and Chong. Jesus." He sighed. "Never mind. Also, according to S&M, no matches from NamUs, NMPDD, or that missing-kids clearinghouse, though it's early days." The LAPD had instant access to numerous web directories, the biggest guns being the National Missing and Unidentified Persons System, aka NamUs, a detailed data site compiled by the Department of Justice, and the FBI's National

Missing Person DNA Database, NMPDD. We lowly private investigators had the same access—it just took longer.

"The blood type helped eliminate most contenders," Bill added.

"So what's next?"

"Nothing, that's what. Zilch. You're off the hook. We're kicking this over to Gangs and Narcotics. Like you said, it's probably just vandalism. Some wannabe gangbanger with a sick sense of humor."

Gangs and Narcotics would probably shelve this as well, as long as it stayed this side of a homicide. I twinged with resistance. I hate unsolved mysteries.

"What about your heebie-jeebies?"

"Yeah, well, we still don't even know if there's been a crime. GND promised to take another look. The tag's the key. Four hundred and fifty gangs out there. Who's to say this isn't number four hundred and fifty-one? Not to worry. Either way, your tax dollars will be put to work. Not that you pay taxes. Gotta earn money to pay taxes, last I heard."

I could barely keep up. The therapy session must have been pretty stimulating—Bill was acting like he'd been mainlining pure caffeine.

"How about the girls," he added. "They behaving?"

I glanced into the kitchen.

Maude must have reopened the bag of cat treats. Her thumb and forefinger held a small brown nugget of mystery meat. Her hand rose slowly to her mouth.

Technically, she wasn't breaking any rules.

"You have no idea," I said.

CHAPTER 20

I merged onto the 134 East. The heavy clot of traffic immediately thinned. I had allowed plenty of time, as the 101 almost never flowed openly anymore. No major freeway in Los Angeles did. The public thoroughfares had been designed for thousands of commuters, not millions.

To quote Lobsang, too much cars *and* too much fools.

The girls were buckled into their car seats behind me. They sipped from straws jutting from little waxy containers of apple juice. They'd had to instruct me on how to use the pointed end of the straw to pierce the tiny foil circle on the top of the box. That was after they showed me where to find the actual straws, bivouacked against one waxed wall. Baby-sitting the twins was always instructive as well as humbling.

Behind me, a throaty roar announced a motorcycle, coming up fast on my right. I'd noticed a crazy-looking bike splitting traffic earlier, and I half hoped this was the same one. I really wanted a closer look. I was in the fast lane, and I moved left a little more, in case he wanted to pass.

The growl grew louder, and a low-slung bike pulled alongside us. Lightweight but powerful, it was a beautiful thing. Orange and black, built like a modern work of art. Gold-anodized track rods operated a hub-centered steering apparatus. The handlebars were set wide apart on a swing-arm instead of the usual fork.

The rider gripped them lightly. He stayed parallel to us, reining the bike in, and it seemed to almost buck. A black leather glove saluted, as if the rider were doffing his cap. But in this case the cap was a gleaming black helmet, its lowered visor tinted smoky gray.

"Look, girls. See that motorcycle? That's called a Vyrus. You don't see one of those every day." I was intrigued. I'd researched the Vyrus after noticing a pure black one fly past me in Malibu. Only two people in Los Angeles owned them, both famous, neither of them this guy. I could tell by the color.

"Pretty," Lola said.

The Vyrus hovered an instant longer and then zoomed away like a supercharged hummingbird. A long black rope of hair spilled from the rider's helmet in a tarry rivulet. Another moment, and he was gone.

The thrill subsided. I was still in a Subaru with two four-year-olds in car seats, sipping from boxes of apple juice.

Ganden Gyatso, my former temple, was just off Figueroa Street in the area east of Eagle Rock known as Highland Park. I noted the exits: Pass Avenue, Forest Lawn, San Fernando Road. The sharp familiarity of the route cracked the casing of my subconscious.

I was on my way to Ganden Gyatso again. After 15 years.

The temple was only a few years old when I first arrived, built at the behest of a wealthy Pasadena developer, Roderick Paul. He'd finally abandoned his rusted chassis at the age of 94 and slipped into the sacred mindstream with the hope of flowing into a newer, sleeker model of mortal coil. To that end, he'd willed three contiguous lots of undeveloped land—prime Highland Park real estate overlooking the San Rafael Hills—to the Dorje Yidam Monastery of Dharamshala, India, as well as earmarking 1.8 million tax-free dollars to construct a Buddhist temple in Los Angeles.

His kids went ballistic.

Mr. Paul had heard the 14th Dalai Lama speak during His Holiness's first visit to Los Angeles. The young lama with a shaved pate and wearing a red robe talked about a middle way, about a path to freedom from suffering and the inevitability of disease and death. And Roderick Paul had listened and learned, following up with several visits to Dharamshala, where he was a guest at Dorje Yidam.

As his final will and testament showed, Paul especially took the notion of neutralizing karma to heart. Apparently he felt guilty about some of his actions, though shrinking the estate for his progeny was not one of them.

The courts ruled that his bequest to Dorje Yidam, while unusual, was fully legal. My father, as abbot, sent his trusted friend Serje Rinpoche Neysrung to oversee the design and construction of Ganden Gyatso, or "Joyful Stream," in 1992. Two years later Rinpoche consecrated the gleaming new temple. We held our own blessings ritual in our prayer hall in Dharamshala.

Rinpoche returned to India, but he stayed connected to Ganden Gyatso. And it was at his urging that a novice lama by the name of Tenzing Norbu, 18 years old and full of a restless rebellion, was sent to Los Angeles five years later to be a part of the center's youth-outreach program.

"Uncle Ten?"

"Yes, Maude."

"I'm ready to see Momma now."

"Almost there, Maude. Look for a sign that starts with the letter *F*."

Like a foster child, I was placed with Dr. Leonard and his wife Adina, early Gelugpa converts. I helped conduct weekly discussions on lamrim, the stages of the path, and taught meditation classes in both Tibetan and English.

Let's just say that for me, it was not a good match. I never fully embraced the monastic life in Dharamshala, and I certainly didn't embrace it in Los Angeles.

Having a youth program at all was an overly optimistic plan. Highland Park was gang central back then, and we weren't exactly swarming with eager young seekers. They were much too busy waging turf wars and killing one another in nearby Glassell Park. This stronghold of the deadly Avenues gang made youth outreach risky, if not lethal.

I did manage to befriend a few members of the patrolling police force. I found their approach to improving the

lives of others much more to my taste. Plus, they got to carry guns. Legally, I mean.

The moment I completed my GRE, I applied and was accepted into the Los Angeles Police Academy. I swapped my robe and Buddhist vows for a cadet uniform and the promise to protect and serve.

"I think I . . ." Maude started.

"*F*! I see it!" Lola said.

"No fair, I saw it first!" Maude said.

"Well, I saw it last, so you both win," I said.

I almost missed the ramp. Highland Park exits could be treacherous. The Subaru took the turn a little hot, and the girls squealed with delight.

I steered past Mexican bodegas, Vietnamese diners, and organic cafés. One final, steep left dead-ended onto Arroyo Ridge, a long curve that eventually looped back down to Figueroa.

Fifteen years was a long time.

I consciously loosened my grip on the steering wheel, finger by finger.

"Uncle Ten?" Lola was looking out the window, but her mind, like mine, was already inside the temple.

"Yes, Lola?"

"Is Homer friends with them?"

"Friends with . . . ?"

"The goats. Is Homer friends with them?"

"I'm sorry. What goats are we talking about?"

"The goats! The ones that are having the party!"

I was mystified. "Maybe you can ask your father about the goats," I said.

The lot was almost full, one or two luxury sedans furtively stashed amid the horde of guilt-free hybrids and electrical cars. The eight-seat Ford passenger van loomed over all like a white whale, also a guzzler, but a necessary one.

I parked next to Martha and Bill's Mazda.

The temple shimmered in the setting sun, luminous and vibrant. Faded but still-colorful flags hung overhead. The

multicolored wooden awning was as brightly striped as a beach towel, and California poppies crowded the planters, the paper-thin petals of scarlet and orange incandescent, like tiny flames.

"It's so fancy," Lola said. "Like a Fancy Nancy house."

A pair of scowling stone lions guarded the front walkway. Behind them, red wooden frames housed barrel-shaped prayer wheels, 10 to a side.

Maude liberated her fingers.

"Anyway, Lola, they're not goats." Her voice was matter-of-fact. "They're llamas. In red pajamas. Right, Uncle Ten?"

Chapter 21

The polished oak double doors cracked open and Martha's head poked through.

"Martha! Over here!" I called.

She stepped outside, smiling. The girls took off.

I stayed put. I desperately needed a few moments to myself. I followed the footpath to an enclosed patio and cactus garden at the back of the temple. Lotus-shaped succulents, their pointed petals tipped with purple, hunkered between spiky yuccas on either side of the dirt path.

Out back, more prayer flags hung in the still evening air, limp cloth necklaces strung between posts. I set my palm against a rough boulder. The surface was jagged, like my nerves. Three more randomly studded the landscape, as if dropped by mistake.

Just past the paving stones that marked the sitting area, the small marble fountain was bone dry. Its bottom was black with baked sludge, residue from the heat wave. A pair of carved doves, gray with marbled veins, perched on their arid centerpiece of stone flowers. They seemed as mournful as my memory had painted them, one gazing across the yard, the other tucking her head beneath her wing. Their throats must be parched. The ground beneath my feet was desiccated and hard as brick.

I did not want to be here.

I retraced my steps. I hadn't seen a soul since the girls ran to their mother.

I passed between the stone lions. My skin shrank: the prayer wheels were spinning on either side of me, as if brushed by invisible hands.

I entered the temple swiftly.

An oblong table was pushed against one corridor wall, covered with offerings in parallel lines. Flickering candles floating in metal bowls of ghee. Paired sticks of incense emerging like antennae from dried yellow rice. Single pieces of fruit, an apple, a peach, or a nectarine. Floating blooms, gardenias and pink spiky chrysanthemums.

A familiar framed sign hung on the wall by the door. I could have recited the listed items with my eyes closed.

Temple Etiquette:

- Please remove shoes before entering the temple.

- Please do not place prayer books or Dharma images on the floor.

- Please do not step over Dharma books or images.

- Please do not point the bottom of your feet toward the teachers or altar.

But then, a new one:

- Please turn off all cell phones.

At Dorje Yidam, the rules of Buddhist etiquette had numbered in the hundreds and were far less rational, but I bristled nonetheless.

I slipped out of my canvas slip-ons—they were called boat shoes, but I'd purchased them for the ease factor. Neither they, nor I, had ever been near a boat.

My black socks were scattered with tiny skulls, a conscious, if puny rebellion.

I added the shoes to a pile of footwear, between 50 and 60 pairs in total.

I muted my cell phone instead of turning it off, a second act of resistance, and moved to the doorway at the back of

the prayer hall. The man in me appreciated the opportunity to revisit the past. The boy in me wanted to grab my boat shoes and sail away forever.

The prayer hall was crowded with people. Some sat cross-legged, some knelt on their haunches, feet carefully aimed backward.

No sign of Julie, but about five rows in, I spotted Bill's gray-blond head floating above the sea of strangers. To his left, Lola, then Maude and Martha. Eric and Adina were on Bill's right.

Eric had never called back. Maybe that was a good thing.

Up front, the massive Shakyamuni statue had been wrapped in a robe of marigold-yellow silk. His hair was a domed knot of black and his ears hung low, as if someone had pulled hard on the lobes before they'd had time to set properly.

Five foam cushions with navy canvas-backed supports were lined up in front of the Buddha. Bright wings peeked from either side, as if giant canaries were back there, preening.

My favorite goddess, Green Tara, was also on the dais, a bronze statue sitting in a jeweled lake of lotus flowers, left leg tucked under, right foot outstretched. She looked ready to leap to her escape. I could relate.

I was no longer a captive of these commitments and vows. I could even appreciate the powerful spiritual energy—it permeated the hall like ozone. But I not only felt resistance, I tasted dread. My skull-covered feet refused to cross the threshold.

Adina appeared at the door, a twin in each hand.

"Potty break," she whispered. "They're starting the ceremony in a few minutes. We saved you a seat." She cocked her head. "Everything okay?"

"Everything's great," I said.

I made my reluctant way up the aisle, Bill's head serving as a beacon.

I slid sideways past a Tibetan couple in traditional peaked felt caps, wide-sleeved white cotton shirts, and brilliantly

embroidered aprons and tunics. Their clothes smelled faintly of mothballs.

Bill pushed to his feet to face me. Usually we clapped shoulders and executed awkward man hugs but the heat in his eyes held me back.

"You're late," Bill said. "Too chicken shit to face me?" Anger rolled off him like thunder.

The AirLite.

"Lola told you?"

"She told me enough." His fists clenched. "Do you have any idea how many kids die that way? What were you thinking?"

I held Bill's gaze. "I am so sorry. I have absolutely no excuse. It was a rookie mistake."

"You got that right!"

"If you guys never want me to watch the girls again, I totally understand."

Bill scrubbed at his scalp with one hand. I waited for the verdict.

"Ah, hell," he said, "I left my Beretta in the holster once last year. Hanging on the back of the bedroom chair, full of bullets. Still gives me nightmares, just thinking about it. Only difference was, I got away with it. Now my phone's set for daily alerts, reminding me to check."

"Good idea," I said. "I'm thinking about putting a separate lock on the closet."

"Better put two," he said. "Lola's worse than Houdini."

He made room for me to pass. I was excused, although not yet absolved.

Laughter rippled through the crowd. Julie was up front, scanning the room. Homer lolled happily in her arms, his mournful clownish face, as usual, causing a reaction.

Julie caught sight of me, and her face cleared. She walked off the dais, Homer glued to her chest. I guess they were waiting until I got there to start.

As I took a seat next to Eric, his face brightened. "I got your message. A slot just opened up tomorrow. It's yours if you still want to see me."

My brain gave off a high-pitched whine, like the stripping of gears.

"Not sure about wanting to," I said. "But I definitely need to."

"Eleven o'clock okay?"

That meant getting up before dawn to start my new transatlantic job, but given the time difference, I'd be doing that anyway.

"Yes. Where?"

"Los Feliz. I work out of home now."

We scrambled to our feet as the five visiting monks processed through the side door. Ceremonial saffron silk was draped over their red robes. Their expressions were stern.

Then Yeshe seemed to register where he was, and a huge smile illuminated his face. I honestly think he had no idea such a prayer hall might exist outside of India and Tibet. He and Lobsang would be hounding me to attend temple functions after this.

Adina hurried in with the twins as we took our seats.

"What did I miss?" In one graceful motion, Adina sank into a lotus posture. Her spine, like Eric's, was straight and firm. Experienced chanters, they'd brought their own foam-and-canvas back supports.

Sonam remained standing. "Welcome, welcome. As you know, this time of year, Saka Dawa, is very auspicious, as we honor Shakyamuni's birth, enlightenment, and death. Special thanks to this beautiful temple for bringing us here to celebrate."

People started clapping, but Sonam waved everyone quiet.

"So. We begin."

He sat, and picked up a stack of narrow rectangular pages resting on a pillow at his feet, our chants for the evening. Each page was covered with rows of Tibetan characters, boxy and crimped.

The monks hooked their right hands behind their stools and returned with curved yellow hats hedged with saffron bristles, which they pressed onto their heads. They looked gloriously crowned, like roosters.

Yeshe, Lobsang, TJ, and Wangdue reached behind again, this time with both hands. I half expected them to pull out 10-foot Tibetan horns, like some sort of magic trick, but these ritual instruments were easier to manage.

Their right hands clasped *damarus*—monkey drums, we called them. Wooden double-sided hand drums shaped like hourglasses and trailing feathered tails of silk and beads. In their left they grasped *drilbus*, burnished handbells embossed with tiny masks, petals, and Tibetan mantras. Now I knew what was in all those boxes.

Lama Jamyang's creaky voice reached across time, once again leading our beginner's class on the ritual use of tantric implements.

"Right hand, children. Right hand for the monkey drum," he would croak. With his hooded eyes and curved spine he resembled a vulture, but no one was better at banging a drum, ringing a bell, or sculpting butter. "Always the male hand to proclaim the sound of great bliss!" He would illustrate, his wrist a blur as he set loose the dangling strikers. I couldn't work out what that nervous metallic chatter had to do with bliss.

Meanwhile, across Lama Jamyang's lap, his left hand—the female hand—rang his drilbu, supposedly generating wisdom by producing another oxymoron, a clanging sound of emptiness.

Our awkward wrist flicks had rattled pellets against goatskin and sent bronze clappers back and forth in jingling collision until we thought our hands would fall off.

I shook off the memory as this row of monks sat silently, instruments in their laps.

I leaned left to find Maude and Lola. I needed to see what they thought of these fantastic drums and bells, and the crazy crayon-yellow rooster hats.

They stared ahead, captivated. Lola sat closest to me.

"Lola," I whispered. "What do you think of my fancy friends?"

Lola turned and beamed at me, her copper curls glowing.

She had a bright red bindi in the middle of her forehead. Perfectly round, like a scarlet target.

No.

My blood tingled. Something was very off.

Bindis were part of the Hindu tradition. They had no place in a Tibetan Buddhist ritual.

Lola clambered over Bill and squeezed next to me.

"Uncle Ten, I have to tell you sumping!" Her bright voice trilled in the silent hall. Someone laughed. Martha's head whipped sideways, her mother alarm activated.

I sent her what I hoped was a reassuring smile.

"Soft voice, Lola. Like this," I said, using my best whisper. I touched her arm. "How did you get that mark on your forehead?" Maybe the hush in my voice would hide the panic.

"The lady gave it to me." Lola's voice was breathy as she strained to speak quietly.

A man sitting in front of us turned and put a finger to his lips. I ignored him.

"What lady?"

"The pretty lady. When I went to go potty. The one wearing the nightgown."

My pulse crashed against my eardrums. *Whoosh. Whoosh. Whoosh.*

"Lola," I whispered, "is the lady still here?"

Lola glanced around, but she wasn't really looking.

"No. But she told me to tell you sumping." Lola's girlish voice kept sneaking in. "She said to tell you, um . . . she said to tell you, it's time."

Her words set off a chain reaction: cold to hot, chills to sweat.

The man turned again. "Shhh!" he said. My right fist clenched.

Breathe, Ten.

"Are you sure that's what she said? Lola, are you sure?"

A small line formed, a vertical dash of worry. Her eyes were blue marbles of light.

I would kill anyone who harmed her.

"Yes. That's what she wanted me to tell you. It's time. She called you Uncle Ten." Lola's lower lip trembled.

"I believe you," I said. I placed my palm against her back.

She calmed under my hand. "She was nice, Uncle Ten." Lola's breath smelled faintly of apple. "She had a polka dot on her forehead. Like Fancy Nancy. When I told her I liked it, she made one on me."

With a chattering, clanging eruption, the ritual began and Bill hooked Lola and reeled her onto his lap.

I climbed past Eric to Adina. I gripped her wrist, my fingers like talons.

"Who gave Lola that bindi?"

"What are you talking about? Ouch, that hurts."

I loosened my grasp. "The bindi. The red mark on Lola's forehead. Where did it come from?"

The thumping and ringing increased, an urgent summons, but I was feeling neither bliss nor wisdom.

"I have no idea," Adina said, freeing her wrist. "The girls asked me to wait in the hallway while they peed. The bindi was on Lola's face when they came back out. I figured the girls found some lipstick or something."

After the cacophony, the abrupt hush was as shocking as an icy bath. The monks had set down their instruments and sat with eyes closed, palms in prayer position. For the first time, I understood the power of emptiness. How it could ring with expectation, or in my case, dread.

Sonam pursed his mouth. An impossibly low sound emerged, dark and guttural, like a rumbled rush of black. *Sang gyay chodang tsog kyi chog nam la.* The monks wove their own threads into the chant, some low in pitch, some medium, some high. *Jang chub bar du dag ni kyab su chi.* Their tonal range blended, creating a harmonious path of sound.

*Sang gyay chodang tsog kyi chog nam la, Jang chub bar du
dag ni kyab su chi . . .*

How many thousands of times had I chanted these
words? *I take refuge until I am enlightened, in the Buddhas, the
dharma, and the sangha. Through the merit I create by practicing
giving and the other perfections, may I attain Buddhahood for the
sake of all sentient beings . . . I take refuge . . .*

I turned back to Adina. She'd closed her eyes and started
to sway, her lips moving. I touched her shoulder, gently this
time.

"Did you see anyone else leave the bathroom? A woman,
maybe, wearing a caftan or a robe?" Adina opened her
eyes reluctantly.

Eric leaned across, his voice concerned. "Everything
okay, Ten?"

"Adina," I pleaded. "Think."

"There was no one," she said. "I would have noticed."

Sonam moved on to the 10-syllable prayer to Green Tara:
I prostrate to the Liberator, mother of all victorious ones.

Closing her eyes again, Adina mirrored Chonam's fluid
hand ballet as she laced her fingers into an intricate con-
figuration—the spirit-subduing mudra; little fingers linked,
index fingers pointed sideways, ready to scold and threaten
any hovering malignant entities. Her palms fanned outward,
like a raptor mantling its prey.

The frenzied hand drum in my chest would not be
consoled.

I scoured the room, front to back. No one but the monks
was wearing a robe. No one else was marked with a daub of
red.

I returned to the girls.

Maude stared at the front stage, her smooth forehead
fragile and pale as the shell of an egg. Lola was in constant
motion, watching the chanting lamas, watching everyone
else watching the chanting lamas. She reached up to scratch
at the bindi. Her finger came away smeared, as if with blood.

If it were a bullet hole, she'd be dead.

Black dots swarmed my vision, executing a crazed and dizzying dance. My throat constricted. The container protecting my sense of self collapsed.

I moved in a clumsy crouch until I reached the side aisle and could make my way to the outside corridor. I ran past the flickering butter candles and smoking sticks of incense, past the list of temple rules, past the piled shoes, stopping only to grab my own. I shoved open the double doors and staggered into the night.

The chanting followed, the haunted medley of a choir of ghosts.

CHAPTER 22

The streetlamps emitted weak beams, as if exhausted from the effort of caring. Their watery light cast a hazy sheen across the sidewalk.

I turned right, and then left.

The road was empty.

I jogged to the temple parking lot and wove between the rows. Every parking space was full, every car vacant.

Running now, I traversed the paved ridge of road that lay like a narrow bandage between brushy cliff-side and the terrain sloping toward civilization. The farthest point north was a cul-de-sac. It was deserted. No barking dog, no blue-lit blare of a flat screen. Only a ramshackle house, its windows dark.

I sprinted the other way, running harder, my shoes slipping at the heels. Except for a faint ringing and banging from inside the temple, the entire length of the street was stone quiet, as if under curfew. Completely absent of moving cars or mysterious women.

Something snagged my vision, and I bent to look, lungs bellowing.

Skid marks, where the south end of the road veered left before making a somewhat sudden descent back to Figueroa.

I pulled out my phone and found the flashlight app. I aimed the bright beam onto the asphalt.

Diagonal smears of rubber. Two thick tires, one fatter than the other. The marks indicated a motorcycle caught in a dangerous fishtail. For a split second I thought the bike must have skated right over the cliff. But no. The marks straightened.

Whoever pulled out of that slide was very skilled. Or very lucky.

I switched to the camera function and snapped a few images of the skid marks. The smears were generic, and probably impossible to trace, but I was willing to bet these tires were custom and belonged to an Italian motorcycle that cost more than most people earned in a year. I'd seen it up close on the 134. A Vyrus.

How appropriate. A virus can be hard to identify, and harder to contain.

Dangerous. Deadly even.

Why was that biker following me?

I shook my head. I was creating stories to justify my fears. Next thing, I'd be walking around with my hands permanently fixed in the spirit-subduing mudra, fending off foes. When I was rattled like this my anxiety groped for any explanation, logical or not, like a hat looking for a hook.

I returned to the temple garden and leaned against the edge of the fountain. Nothing made sense.

Someone's coming. My hand snapped to my waist for a gun that wasn't there.

"Ten?" Julie stepped out of the shadows, leash in hand. I tucked my hand into my pocket.

Homer snuffled at my feet. He peered at me between folds of skin, tongue flap dangling, before carrying on.

"Too much for you in there, hunh." Julie moved to my side.

Homer lifted his back leg and anointed one of the boulders. Mission completed. He sat on his haunches and sniffed the air.

Julie reached into her pocket and pulled something out. I assumed it was a treat for Homer, but in fact the treat was for me.

"Khapsay?" She held out the puffy triangle. I opened my mouth and she popped the pastry in.

I was seven years old. Banished to Dorje Yidam for another summer, aching with loneliness. Lama Sonam had just

discovered me hiding in the dormitory. He brought me into his living quarters. We drank sweet tea and shared a platter of warm sugared khapsay. Every bite had tasted like loving-kindness . . .

It still did. I let the dough soften on my tongue, once again taking refuge in its sweetness.

"Let's sit for a minute," Julie said.

We moved to a stone bench next to the empty fountain.

"They've been at it for almost an hour," Julie said. "Do they always chant for this long?"

"This? This is nothing." My voice grew bitter. "Try five hours straight with your father glaring at you from the shadows. Watching your every move."

Julie made a soft sound.

"You poor thing," she said. "No wonder you need therapy."

"Ouch," I said. "Low blow."

"It wasn't meant to be."

Julie turned her head to look at me.

"What is going on, Ten?"

I opened my mouth. Closed it again.

What could I say? That I was sure someone was after me, but I didn't know who or why? Or even scarier . . . if? That I wasn't sure if Julie and I were, in fact, okay? That I felt less and less worthy of love?

I settled for the only truth I felt comfortable sharing.

"I'm seeing Eric on Wednesday." I shrugged. "I guess it's official. I'm a hot mess."

Over by the trees, Homer inched forward, head lowered to the ground. He was using his nose to sniff and push at the soft dirt. With his blocky body and small, wide-set ears, he resembled a rooting pig.

Julie's voice was fierce in the darkness. "I don't care if you're a mess. Who isn't? It's the people who don't know they're a mess that scare me."

I reached for her hand and gave it a light squeeze. It wasn't much but it was the best I could do.

I would sleep on things. No need to upset Julie tonight, or anyone else for that matter. Who knew if my demons were real or simply leftover fragments of old and broken fears?

"Are you coming back inside?" Julie's voice was neutral, neither warm nor cool. It was the best she could do, too.

"In a minute."

"Homer, come." Homer trundled behind his mistress, just a few steps behind.

In the morning, I would jot down the sore spots in my awareness, the ones that seemed to trigger unease. They were lodged deep, like buried splinters. Eric would help me bring them to the surface. He would help me pull them out.

I crossed the garden to where Homer had been digging but nothing was there but clods of earth.

CHAPTER 23

A different set of bells rang me awake—my landline in the living room. The digital numbers on the bedside table glowed red: It was one o'clock in the morning.

Julie groaned and buried her head in the pillows.

I ran to the phone before voice mail kicked in.

"H'lo?" I cleared my throat and tried again. "Hello, this is Tenzing."

"Detective Norbu? DCI Garfield. Sorry for the ungodly hour, but I thought I should let you know. We found him."

"You found Colin? That's wonderful news." It was. Not for my bank account, maybe, but a found misper was always cause for celebration. "Is he okay? Is he back with his parents?"

"Sorry, what I meant to say is, we've zeroed in on his whereabouts. The Oyster card usage turned up a British Rail ticket from Cambridge to King's Cross, at which point he took the Circle Line to Paddington. From there, he caught the express to Heathrow."

"Alone?"

"I'll get to that. We can now confirm he was at Heathrow based on two further pieces of evidence. NBTC, sorry, National Border Targeting Centre was able to check our information against outgoing passenger lists for the day of travel. Thanks to you, we prioritized flights to the States, with a possible final destination of Los Angeles. A passenger by the name of Colin Purdham-Coote II, or at least a passenger using his passport, departed London Heathrow on Virgin Atlantic Flight Seven on the day in question."

"Quick work."

"This kind of situation, we have to be quick."

"And you're sure it was him."

"Yes. Because of the travel card, we were also able to pinpoint his arrival at Heathrow, and access CCTV for the times and terminals involved. We now have visual confirmation of Colin from numerous sources."

"Wow." I was wide awake now. I had also woken up my computer, and I pulled up the desktop calendar. "When was this, exactly?"

"Monday past."

My chest reacted initially, lungs compressing from a feeling of heavy pressure beneath the clavicle. My pulse fluttered like a trapped bird.

The body is always the first to know.

"Are you saying Colin flew into Los Angeles on Monday, June second?"

"Precisely."

"What time did his flight land?" My voice was calm, but my heart was doing handstands.

"Let's see. Fight Seven departed eleven twenty-five A.M., due to arrive Pacific Daylight Time two thirty P.M., but it was slightly delayed, and landed closer to three o'clock. Something else, and this is slightly worrying. When Colin entered London Heathrow, he was dressed casually. Blue jeans. T-shirt. Hooded jacket. But at some point after checking in and passing through security, he changed clothes. An airport security camera inside the gate shows him wearing a disguise. I'm not exactly sure how to describe it, but he was dressed like a . . . in, well, in some kind of . . ."

"Robe. Like a caftan. With a shawl over his head."

DCI Garfield's voice grew cold. "How on earth could you possibly know that, Detective Norbu? If you've been withholding information . . ."

"I was there," I broke in. "I was at the international terminal in Los Angeles when Colin landed. Waiting at customs." I realized how crazy this must sound. "DCI Garfield, I think I may have actually seen him. Not on purpose, of

course. I was there to meet friends arriving on a flight from India."

"That's . . . that's quite a coincidence, wouldn't you say, Detective?"

"Yes, I would."

And suddenly I remembered why the long tunics on that group of shiny-eyed young people looked familiar. The sleeves were configured like Tibetan Buddhist robes—one long, the other exposing most of the arm. But the robe itself was a simple cut of cloth that required no wrapping or tucking. I had encountered caftans exactly like these last year, on Sasha's grandmother, from Bosnia. Which made no sense.

"I'm not a big believer in coincidence, are you, Detective?"

I wasn't sure how to answer that. In my experience, the more in tune I was with my inner compass, the more my actions seemed to attract synchronicity. But this . . . ?

"No," I said. "I don't believe this is a coincidence."

The memory sharpened. Irena Radovic had been dressed in the gray tunic-like robe the first time I met her, at Bill's house on the Fourth of July. She hid inside her fog-colored robe and head scarf and spoke barely a word, but her grim satisfaction was palpable as she witnessed her daughter Mila shattering Bill and Martha's world. And a month later, in a long blue tunic the color of ice, Irena had taken her own life. Her eyes, too, had gleamed with devotion but the shine of absolute surrender couldn't conceal an underlying madness.

"Do you have any explanation offhand?" Garfield's voice was still guarded.

"I think Colin arrived as part of a group, if that helps. There were several young men and women wearing the same kind of robes."

I gave Garfield a shortened version of why I was at the international terminal and what I saw. He was still not satisfied, understandably.

"To recap: you just happened to be there when Colin landed, and his driving license just happened to be delivered

to you in an envelope the following morning? I'm sorry, but it's most peculiar."

"I have to agree."

He thought. I waited.

"I would be more suspicious but for the fact that you set everything in motion by calling Lord Purdham-Coote in the first place. And as far as I know, you haven't mentioned the word *ransom*. But this strains credulity."

"I am as mystified as you are." I changed directions. "How about his fellow travelers? Any red flags? I have someone at Homeland Security I could call."

"Let me worry about that. Meanwhile, Detective Norbu, I suggest you think long and hard about your part in all of this. You may not be directly involved, but you are involved nonetheless. We'll talk again later."

I sat in the semidarkness for several minutes, my mind racing from one end of this new trail of information to the other. But I was faced with too many fragments of fact, and not enough mental clarity to piece together anything coherent. I tiptoed back into the bedroom, set the alarm on my phone, and crawled under the covers carefully, so I wouldn't disturb Julie or Tank. I fell into a troubled sleep.

Chapter 24

The cell phone vibrated like a trapped bee.

No.

I swatted it silent.

3:30 A.M.

I can't.

C'mon, Ten, you used to do this all the time when you were a novice lama on kitchen duty.

Tank's round mask of silvered fur rose from the foot of the bed, green eyes unblinking, a feline moon. I sent him a silent message: not time for breakfast yet. Message received. He lowered his head to his paws and closed his eyes.

I resisted the temptation to do the same, to draw Julie close and sink back into sleep.

Coffee. The only thing that would make this better was coffee.

I pulled on sweatpants and yesterday's T-shirt and added a hoodie from the closet. The season of early-morning fog was upon us, and the canyon would cling to its cool air until well past dawn.

In the kitchen, I filled the kettle with filtered water and set it on the burner to boil. A small mason jar awaited on the counter. I unscrewed the lid and inhaled the rich, earthy scent of Ethiopian beans, roasted to smoky perfection—the last of my personal stash of politically incorrect coffee. The coarsely ground beans were the color of tobacco and the consistency of steel-cut oats.

I'd rescued my abandoned French press from the back of a kitchen shelf—an expensive gift to myself after closing the deal on the Topanga Canyon house. My mother had owned

one just like it in Paris. I'd make myself very small on my kitchen stool as she swore at her *cafetière*, trying to force the mesh plunger. Desperate to treat her hangover with scalding-hot caffeine.

Making a great cup of coffee might not be rocket science, but it was science nonetheless. Basically, there were three phases, however you chose to brew: immersion, dissolution, and diffusion. Just like the three phases of the lama's journey from ignorance to wisdom: slow brewing as a devotional path.

When your mind is trained to seek, everything is practice.

The first step, immersion, was crucial. Saturating the grounds released the carbon dioxide trapped in their cells. Total concentration provided the ideal environment in which to bloom.

Next, dissolution: the solids confined in the cells needed to dissolve into the hot water solvent, like pure thought dispersing into consciousness.

Finally, diffusion: all that concentrated flavor spread throughout the surrounding liquid, creating the beverage some called coffee that I called the absolute made manifest. Bliss. The bhakti path to joy. I no longer practiced it personally, but I believed in its worth.

I filled the bottom of the press with about two inches of the coarse grind.

I snatched the kettle off the burner before its faint whistle became a scream. I found the stopwatch function on my phone and pressed "Start." I let a full 30 seconds pass before pouring. With a lighter roast I would have added the water right off the boil.

Why was I there when Colin landed?

I filled the beaker carefully, stopping a few inches below the rim.

Glanced at the stopwatch. Total saturation, commencing now.

Where was he going?

Breathe in to the count of 10, breathe out to the count of 10. In to 10, out to 10.

The stopwatch read 01:15:33. Perfect.

Why did I have his license? Who brought it to me?

I gave the mixture a thorough stir. Dissolution. The grounds swirled and circled before gradually settling to the bottom of the glass cylinder. The process calmed my own whirling thoughts.

I placed the lid on the press, plunger rising out of it like a flagpole.

And what about the blocked call, the whispered message, *We're here*?

Two minutes had passed. I moved on to phase three, diffusion.

I set the timer for eight minutes and again pressed "Start." The countdown began.

I set my questions aside. Time for my own act of diffusion.

I moved the phone to the kitchen table, where I'd set out a legal pad and my favorite Space Pen. It was silvery and sleek, like an elongated bullet. It worked underwater, in extreme heat or cold, upside down, and even in zero gravity, should the opportunity arise.

Stop procrastinating, Ten.

07:00. Seven minutes left. And, GO.

I rolled the pen between my thumb and forefinger.

Just start. Start anywhere.

I wrote down *space pen*. Then, *I love my space pen*. Idly, I crossed out the word *pen*. Replaced *love* with *need*. I read the new sentence.

I need my space.

My hand flew across the page: *I need my space. Never alone. Always lonely. Wedding invitations. Orphan. No family. Pressure. For ever and ever. Failure. Chasing failure? No. Being chased. Following. Being followed. Being followed by my failure. Why?*

I checked the timer.

Four minutes left.

The dream. Don't forget the dream.

Tower dream. Every few days now. Why do I keep having it? Why can I never reach the top floor?

Tank jumped onto my lap and kneaded my thighs.

"Hey, buddy."

Bindi, I wrote. Then, *Who is she?*

My pen hovered.

It's time. Time for what?

The writing gave me a sense of control. I had a list. Questions to place at Eric's feet like offerings.

A jangling sound startled me. I checked my phone. **Timer done.** I reset, giving myself another minute.

Julie.

My chest tightened. I didn't want to write anymore. But I did.

What if I can't?

This time the alarm was my liberator.

I jumped upright, dumping Tank. He yowled.

"Sorry. Don't want to overbrew."

I hurried from the unsettled thoughts once again clouding my brain.

I depressed the plunger, trying to maintain a steady pressure that was both gentle and deliberate. As the dark brown liquid rose, the grounds descended.

The plunger tightened under my palm. I backed up an inch. Let more grounds settle before resuming.

Good coffee could not be forced or rushed.

Good coffee required absolute commitment.

CHAPTER 25

Lord Purdham-Coote had faxed the completed contract overnight. I scanned the print. No changes to the terms of employment, and he had signed and dated the last page, as of today. I filed the form in my legal documents folder.

It was 11:30 A.M. over there. Not too early, not too late. I had two overseas calls to make. First I'd reach out to the hand that was feeding me.

I used my business line.

The double ring went immediately to voice mail.

"Lord Purdham-Coote, this is Ten. Please call me when you get this. If I don't answer here, try my cell." I recited both numbers and hung up. It rang immediately.

"Lord Purdham-Coote?"

"Naw. This is Bertie. Bertie Andrews. Lord Purdham-Coote's on another call. Saw it was you, told me to give you a jingle. Sorry I di'n't call earlier. I just got back from Cambridge. I was under orders to wait. Until you were part of the team, like. Wotcha got? Good news, I hope." His voice was graveled from nicotine and the words tumbled into a disorganized heap. I sorted through the pile before choosing an answer.

"No news yet." I rubbed my eyes. "It's three thirty in the morning. I've only been on the job for a few hours."

"No need to get yer knickers twisted," Bertie rasped. "I wasn't implying anything. Gave you the thumbs-up, di'n't I?" He paused, as if reassessing. "Yer a bit touchy, aren't you? For a monk, I mean. Thought you'd be more like that bald bugger. Whatshisname. Gandhi." A phlegmy laugh morphed into a fit of coughing. "Sorry. Fuckin' cigs. Harder to quit

than my ex, and almost as bad for me, though give 'er a few pints and she'll be more than happy to tell you exactly how it was the other way 'round."

I needed to redirect this conversation before it took us both to places better left unvisited.

"I have several questions, Mr. Andrews. And I'm sure you have more than a few for me."

"Bertie. Call me Bertie. Mr. Andrews would be my dad, God rest his coal-black soul."

"Anything further on your end? DCI Garfield and I talked earlier."

"Hizzoner's talking to Garfield right now. Fighting with him, more like."

I waited. Bertie clearly loved to talk. I'd learn more by keeping my mouth shut.

"They want to drop it, don't they? What with the postcard 'n' all."

"What postcard?'

"Came today. Kid sent his old man a fuckin' postcard of palm trees and that tourist sign, like he was on holiday."

"The Hollywood sign?"

"That's the one. Only Collie didn't say 'wish you were here,' did he?"

"Let me guess. Collie told his father not to worry. That he's found a new family, he's never been happier, and his parents shouldn't try to contact him."

"Mate! Almost word for word!"

"Don't be too impressed," I said. "I live in Los Angeles, remember? It's a mecca for megalomaniacs, religious and otherwise. I mean, Scientology owns half the city."

"Yeah, I read about them. Bunch of bollocks. We wouldn't let that wanker's ship dock over here, way back when. Otherwise, who knows? Maybe they'd have their headquarters in the Tower of London."

"I worked the Missing Persons Unit before I moved up to Burglary/Homicide," I said. "I can't tell you how many calls I took from frantic parents on the receiving end of messages

like Collie's. Calling off the family is a pretty standard first move for cults. Sounds like maybe he's joined one."

"Yeah, makes sense, given the robe and all. Trouble is now the Yard wants to bow out. Says Collie doesn't need a deputy chief inspector, he needs a deprogrammer."

"What does Lord Purdham-Coote say?"

"Well, he's shittin' bricks, i'n't he?"

My eyes strayed to the yellow legal pad and my cursory notes for the session with Eric. I flipped to a blank page.

"Can I ask you a few questions?"

"Ask away, mate. Looks like he's gonna be on with DCI Garfield awhile longer. Purdham-Coote's used to getting his way. Won't take no, will he?"

"Were you present when the constables entered Collie's room?"

"Yeah. Lord P-C wanted me there—second set of eyes."

"I understood from DCI Garfield that Colin didn't take his cell phone with him."

"iPhone. And no. They found it in his room. Sim card next to it, or what was left of it. Smashed it silly, di'n't he?"

"Computer?"

"MacBook Pro. Under his bed, wiped clean as a baby's arse. iPad's missing, but in case you're wondering, they're saying he erased all his data remotely, and now no one can access shite. He had that find-your-phone thingy, but turns out, when you dump the data, you disable the other thingy that helps identify your devices. No data means no tracking. No tracking, no trace of Collie." A note of admiration crept into Bernie's gruff voice. "Kid did a wallop on us all, di'n't he? Smarter than he let on."

"Something for everyone to keep in mind."

"Wasn't all he left behind. Clothes. Books. LPs. Moped. Little bugger left his *life* behind. Well, you would, wouldn't you? Clean slate an' all. His friends don't know shite. Or his tutor. The university's washing its hands. Cocked things up royal this time, Collie did." Bertie sounded almost pleased.

"So based on what you're saying, DCI Garfield's point is valid. Collie not only abandoned his old life deliberately, he's now trying very hard to make sure no one finds or follows him into his new one."

"Looks that way."

I stared at the lined yellow page before me. Still blank, except for a big question mark I must have drawn unconsciously. I circled it, over and over, pressing so hard that my Space Pen tore right through the paper.

"Then why the hell did someone put his license in my mailbox?"

"Yeah, well, that's the big question, innit?"

He let the moment hang, the perfect move for an interrogator, fishing for a confession. His suspicion was misplaced, but understandable. I'd have done the same if our positions were reversed.

I was innocent, but for the second time this morning I felt guilty. My respect grew for the interview techniques of British detectives, on the Scotland Yard payroll and off.

Muted mumbles, as if he'd covered the phone.

"Hizzoner wants a word," Bertie said.

"Wait. Bertie?"

"Yeah?"

"Can you scan a current photograph of Collie, and also the postcard, front and back, and e-mail them to me?"

Maybe the handwriting on my envelope would turn out to be a match with Colin's, although I doubted it. Number one, it made no sense. Number two, block print is notoriously hard to compare, not to mention analyze.

"Yeah, sure. Anything else?"

There was, but for a moment I couldn't bring it to the forefront of my sleep-deprived mind. *Photo . . . postcard . . .* My eye fell on the driver's license.

"Does he have any tattoos or identifying scars? Anything specific for the missing-person's sites?"

"Besides the scar on his left wrist? Cry for help, that. More of a scratch than a gouge. Don't know about anything else. I'll ask around."

We said cordial enough good-byes, and he passed me over.

Scar on his left wrist, I wrote.

"Ten? I understand you're up to speed." Lord Purdham-Coote's voice cracked with exhaustion. "DCI Garfield says he'll call you again soon."

"That's good."

"They're quite certain Collie's in Los Angeles. That he arrived safely, and he did not leave under duress. I've persuaded the Metropolitan Police to keep DCI Garfield assigned to the case for a few more days, but that's as far as they'll go. They've changed the priority grade from high to low, simply extraordinary, but there it is, which means almost no further allocation of resources. I was hoping for more, but . . ."

"I understand."

"I don't, but so be it. So you see, it's down to you, Ten. I've wired the money. You should have it in your account by tomorrow."

"I appreciate that."

"Winnie and I are prepared to fly over there, if you think that might help. We can bring Bertie as well. Many hands, and so forth."

"That's not necessary." That was all I needed—a trio of Brits to keep tabs on in addition to my Tibetan tribe.

But there was more. I chose my next words with care. "Sir, I must warn you, if and when I do locate Colin, the end result might not be to your liking. You do understand that, don't you?"

"What are you saying?"

"I'm saying Colin's not a child anymore. There's a big difference between 'missing' and 'not wanting to be found.' If he's committed himself to a cause, there's a good chance he won't want to leave his new situation right away. And maybe not for a long time. Are you prepared for that?"

Lord Purdham-Coote's breath was ragged.

"Just find my son," he said, and hung up.

CHAPTER 26

I roused my computer and checked my e-mail. I hadn't fully decided where Bertie fell along the spectrum between "highly competent" and "grossly incompetent." His response to my request would serve as a simple but invaluable test.

As with so many things, I owed this insight to Lama Sonam. Years ago, I'd poured out my struggle to understand the behavior of my fellow human beings. So much of the time I felt like they were from Planet Earth and I was from Planet Ten. Their motives baffled me and their choices confused me. Who were they, really? Could I trust them? How could I know for sure? "Don't overcomplicate things, Tenzing," Lama Sonam used to say. "Look at their actions. What people do is who they are. And who they are is who you're with."

Ping. The e-mail subject was "Collie photo and postcard." Bertie had come through.

My landline rang.

So had DCI Garfield.

"Hello?"

"Detective Norbu?"

"Yes, this is Ten."

"You heard about the postcard."

"Yes."

DCI Garfield sighed. "We're in a bit of a quandary over here. Now that the subject of our investigation has been in touch, technically this no longer qualifies as a high-risk case."

"They're sure the card is from Colin?"

"Yes. Mother and father both confirmed the handwriting. He wrote it, all right."

"Maybe under duress?"

"Maybe, but highly unlikely. In conjunction with everything else, we're taking it at face value."

"How about the rest of his group—did you . . ."

"There were four others, just as you said. All from the UK, all young adults, mostly early twenties, like him, although Colin was the only son of a peer. Two females, two males. No red flags, none is on any of our watch lists. In fact, no one on the plane or in the cockpit set off any alarms, officially or otherwise."

"Did you find out why they were coming here?"

"Not exactly. We looked into his companions' backgrounds and made contact with a couple of baffled parents, an indifferent older brother, and one jilted sweetheart, but that's it."

"Not much to go on."

"We did discover all five purchased one-way tickets. I don't think they're planning on coming back any time soon."

Lost souls, I thought. Leaving mystified friends and heartbroken parents in their wake, wondering where they'd gone wrong.

DCI Garfield's thoughts had followed a similar path.

"It's sad, that. But not the end of the world. Chasing after some ersatz guru may be misguided, but it isn't dangerous. It's not ISIL we're talking about here."

I remembered the shiver of threat at the airport, and I wondered. But I kept that to myself. An attack of goose bumps doesn't qualify as proof of anything more extreme than an active imagination.

I scanned my mental files to see if there was anything else I needed to ask. And found the obvious.

"Did you happen to find out anything about their leader?"

"Hang on, I've got it in a file here somewhere," Garfield said. As I waited, my chest fluttered. Anxiety? Excitement? The outcome was up to me, and what I did with my breath. After two deep inhales and exhales, tingling anticipation enlivened my entire body.

I used the rest of the wait to open Bertie's e-mail and click on the attachments.

The first scan was a photo of a smiling, fresh-faced Collie—much like the picture of him and his friend on Facebook. In fact, looking more closely, I was almost certain it was the same picture, only cropped. The extra hand dangling over Colin's right shoulder sported a gold ring on the middle finger. If you looked closely, you could see the amber cat's eye.

I opened the second attachment—three scans making up one PDF. I glanced at the first: a postcard—a color photograph of the Hollywood sign. This version included matching palm trees and, for some reason, a fluttering American flag. They used to sell a hundred different varieties of this iconic image in postcard stands all over Los Angeles. I had sent one to Yeshe and Lobsang soon after I landed here, just about 15 years ago. But postcards were dated, soon to be obsolete. Nowadays people snapped selfies with the lettered sign arched over their shoulders and posted the results online.

"I found the file," DCI Garfield said. "Let's see what we've got . . . okay. The leader's a female. Mid- to late thirties, give or take. Darkish complexion, maybe Indian, or even a Paki? Can't tell from the CCTV photo. We caught her leaving some kind of musical gathering in Cambridge, along with our boy Colin."

Female guru. Indian-ish, I wrote down.

The last page of the PDF was a scan of the back of the postcard. Colin had handwritten the message in his almost illegible scrawl. As I feared, there was no way to compare the handwriting to my envelope's blocky anonymous print. I could barely decipher the actual words. Luckily I already knew the gist. I picked out *fine, happiest I've ever been,* and

please don't as I scanned the slanted cursive, mostly listening to DCI Garfield.

"Where in Cambridge?" I asked.

"Central Cambridge. Lovers Walk, just back of Humberstone Road. Some kind of warehouse that rents out space."

"Did you . . ."

"Yes. Paid in cash, and the contact information was a fake address and a burner phone."

"Too bad."

"What else, let's see, we did a little digging and discovered she just started touring recently. Still small potatoes in terms of followers, though to be fair they all start out that way, don't they? She's only been active a year or so. Here's her name, though I'm sure it's not her given name. Ready? Em, Ay, Aitch, Ay, Em, You, Dee, Arrr, Ay."

As I jotted down the letters, my eyes landed on three words, just above Collie's dashed signature . . .

Maha Mudra, I wrote.

"Maha Mudra," Garfield said. "Ever heard of her?"

Jai Maha Mudra, I read.

I stared at the words.

"Yes. I have." My head felt hollowed, from the inside out.

"Not much else to go on here," Garfield continued. His voice grew faint, as if the handset was suddenly stuffed full of felt. But the felt was inside my brain. "Black hair. Got one of those red dealies on her forehead. She's a looker, I'll give her that."

Looker, I wrote. *Bindi.*

Events of the past few days clustered around the stem of my brain like metal filings, though I still didn't know who or what constituted the magnet. But the pieces were there: the flier outside Kim's father's apartment in San Diego—beautiful woman with long black hair, a red bindi, and the words *Jai Maha Mudra*. A beautiful woman with long black hair and a red bindi inside Ganden Gyatso, cornering Lola, using the child to send me a message. A Vyrus motorcycle, following, then passing me on the freeway, its rider of medium build

and physically compact, with a long black braid streaming down his back.

Her back.

And there was something else, I was sure of it, but once again, I couldn't access the source.

"You still there, Ten?"

"Sorry," I said. "Just trying to put a few things together. You don't happen to have a current location for this Maha Mudra, do you?"

"No. Not over here, anyway. We can't figure out when or even if she's spent much time in London, but she definitely wasn't born and/or raised in the UK. She seems to be no-madic. And she's careful with her digital footprint—doesn't even have a website. Well, that's about it from our side. I'll send you the CCTV image, if you like."

"Yes, that would be helpful."

"As I'm sure Lord Purdham-Coote told you, we're filing this under *harmless* for the time being. We did manage to keep the press off Purdham-Coote's back, so there's that." DCI Garfield sighed. "The boy's just following his bliss—isn't that what they call it? He's not the first to drop out of uni-versity, and he won't be the last. So his Lordship's out nine thousand quid—it's a bloody shame, but it isn't a crime."

"No, I guess not," I said.

"Anything changes, we'll let you know. I'll ask you to please do the same, if you would. All things considered, you're a much better bet for establishing contact with Colin, as I told Lord Purdham-Coote. And Detective? You figure out the connection between you and that young man, I'd love to know what it is."

"Of course."

"Right then. I'll be off."

The connection was already there, although hard to ex-plain. It originated in my near past, and continued to haunt me. Irena, Sasha's grandmother, had worn a robe identical to Colin's when she'd arrived at Bill's doorstep with Mila. Weeks later she'd put a bullet through her brain, but not

before pointing the gun at me and conveying a message, her eyes deranged with fanaticism.

He says to tell you. He's coming.

A robe and a fanatic, they were my links to Colin Purdham-Coote the Third. If he was following the same spiritual leader as Irena had, he was on a treacherous path indeed, and I feared we were both pawns in the unfinished game of an unknown adversary. I didn't know how yet, but I could feel the truth of it, deep in the marrow of my soul. Collie and I weren't just linked, we were shackled.

He says to tell you. He's coming.

And now, a second message, from another messenger: *It's time.*

Dawn was close by, layers of darkness peeling off the night sky almost imperceptibly. I sat for some time, staring at the downloaded image of Colin's face. He beamed back at me from the computer monitor, his eyes fervent with promise. "I have the answer! Come join me," he seemed to say.

Where? Join you where? But stare as I did, nothing stirred, much less floated to the surface. My brain, like his smile, remained fixed and frozen.

CHAPTER 27

I parked the Mustang in the Leonards' driveway, walked around to the back. Sure enough, a steep set of flagstone steps led to a small stucco outbuilding. Eric's office must have been part of the remodel. Trellises thick with jasmine vines lined both sides, their leafy stems bursting with tiny star-shaped flowers. I headed up. A hummingbird darted off, its throat a patch of scarlet. I pinched off a white bloom and held it to my nose. The sweetness barely registered.

I reached a small deck at the top of the stone risers. I was short of breath and dizzy, but not from the climb.

The office door consisted of vertical slats of worn timber in faded shades of blue, green, red, and yellow, repurposed from someone else's place of refuge. Across the way, a concrete statue of the Buddha sat cross-legged on a wrought-iron stand. Both hands rested on his knees, palms up. Someone had placed a plump, homegrown rose in his right hand. The splayed pink petals were loose and starting to yellow at the edges. I added my tiny offering of jasmine.

The landing offered the same view of Griffith Park as the deck off their living room. I found the spot where the owls might be nesting. What had Eric said?

Bronson Caves.

A distant bird circled there, maybe a hawk, maybe a crow.

I had dressed up for my appointment. My dark blue Levis were clean and almost new, my white cotton shirt had all its buttons, and my brown lace-up shoes were polished. I sat on the bench, unlaced them, and lined them up with a pair of suede Hush Puppies.

A small bell hung from a twisted red rope to the right of the door. I gave the rope a slight shake. The bell jangled with a bright enthusiasm I did not share.

Eric opened the door smiling. His aquamarine shirt matched his eyes.

"You made it. Adina and I had a little bet going."

"And?"

"Let's just say I don't have to do the dishes for a while."

I stepped inside.

The office was a roomy, well-lit square. An oval rug of twisted yarns covered the floor. A striped armchair faced its twin across a glass coffee table, as well as an overstuffed sofa covered with navy burlap. I eyed the sofa suspiciously.

An open laptop was asleep in the corner. Maybe a dozen wire-bound notebooks in different colors stood upright next to the laptop, propped side-by-side in a mesh metal basket. The far wall was all built-in shelving. I moved closer to take a look.

The recessed shelves were wall-to-wall books, interspersed with icons from every religious tradition. A carved Ganesh; a porcelain Saint Francis; a miniature oil painting of a mosque; a watercolor of Krishna. Even his carved wooden Buddha rubbed shoulders with a crucifix.

My eyes landed on a strange-looking tool with a tapered wooden handle, a silk ribbon tied in a bow midshaft. The dark blue head was shaped like the casings on our ritual handbells. Our name for it was *tho-ba*.

What was Eric doing with a vajra hammer?

"Is this what I think it is?" I said.

"An antique tho-ba," Eric confirmed. "Adina gave it to me for our thirtieth, maybe my favorite present ever. Isn't it something? And so apt. The vajra hammer's purpose, as I'm sure you know, is to smash the evil dispositions that block liberation." He smiled. "Don't worry, I've yet to use it on a client."

"Good to know."

The books told a similarly eclectic tale: Bible; Koran; Bhagavad Gita; Torah; *Mahāyāna*; *I am Thou*; *Be Here Now*; Book of Mormon; *Dao De Jing*; Freud; Maslow; Erikson; *Diagnostic and Statistical Manual of Mental Disorders* . . .

My head was starting to swim. I turned away.

"To quote Ram Dass," Eric said, "'I'm a generalist.'"

"A generalist," I said. "I like that."

"Adina would disagree. She believes it's better to have both feet firmly planted in one boat. Although as I love to remind her, the boat itself has changed more than once over the years."

I couldn't put it off any longer.

"What happens now?"

"Take a seat," Eric said. "Or not. Whatever you like."

I lowered myself into the armchair.

"Water?"

"Please."

He opened the bathroom door. A ceramic water dispenser sat just inside, on a stand. He filled two glasses and set them on the coffee table. He claimed the chair across from mine.

My throat was gritty. I took a sip of water.

"Relax, Ten," Eric said. "I promise I don't bite."

I inhaled deeply. On the slow exhale my shoulders lowered.

"That's good," Eric said. "Most of my clients forget to breathe."

I studied the twisted yarns of the rug, trying to decipher a recognizable pattern.

"Ten?'

"Yes," I said to the floor.

"When you look at me, what do you see?"

I raised my eyes. The air swirled thick with something resembling dust motes, but the particles were transparent, as if made up of bits of air.

"I . . . I can't really see you," I said. My heartbeat started to race. "I can barely see you at all." I gulped down half the water in my glass.

"That's fine," Eric said. "And understandable. You don't trust me right now. I don't blame you. Why should you?"

I pulled the list from my pocket. My hands were damp, my fingers clumsy as they unfolded the lined yellow paper with its bumpy chronicle of deterioration.

I latched onto the dream first. Therapists loved dreams, right?

"I have this recurring dream," I said. "About a tower. When it first started, maybe five or six years ago, I felt like it was there to help me. And it did at first. I asked it for guidance, and it led me to solutions for a couple of cases I took on."

"You interacted with it. So, a lucid dream?"

"I suppose so, yes."

"About a tower."

"A tower. And my father's usually in it, or lately my mother. And there's this voice that talks to me, it's really, really close, like someone's mouth is pressed to my ear. Sometimes the voice even wakes me up. I used to have the tower dream maybe once every six months. Now it's every few days." I swallowed. "I'm sorry, can you open the window? It's kind of stuffy in here."

Eric moved to the wall and cranked a handle on one of the sills. The framed window swung outward, leaving a screen in place. The smell of jasmine invaded the room, sickly sweet. I felt ill.

"Also," I said, "I've been having these, these attacks. Where I feel completely trapped, and I can't seem to breathe. I wrote down a list of triggers. I mean, it's pretty random, but . . ."

I cleared my throat and went to read my list, but the words looked like gibberish.

The space behind my eyes pulsed, and I was hit with a fist of dizziness.

"Ten." Eric's voice came from far away. "It might help you to look at me."

His face floated behind the visual barrier of swirling matter. His features were in pieces, like a Picasso painting.

"Look into my eyes," he said.

"Can't breathe," I gasped.

"Yes," he said. "You can."

I focused on his eyes. His pupils were steady pinpoints of safety.

Slowly, my breath returned to normal.

"I don't know what's wrong with me but it has to stop. I'm becoming incapacitated. This is affecting my work. Julie and me. Everything." I stood up.

"Can you think back to when it all started?"

I started to pace. "The panic attacks? Maybe eight months ago, maybe a little longer. At first, they barely affected me. Just a little dizziness now and then. I chalked it up to hypoglycemia."

"Anything else change in your life around then?"

I stopped in my tracks. "Only everything," I said.

"Ahh." Eric said.

I sat back down in the chair.

"Julie?" Eric's voice was so kind.

"Julie. Among other things."

"I'm going to take notes. Do you mind?"

I shook my head. Eric flipped a wirebound notebook to the first page and plucked a ballpoint pen from his shirt pocket.

"Old school," he said. "I think better when I write things down."

"I'm the same." I was feeling better, suddenly.

He jotted notes as I described the sequence of events over the past year—the harrowing trip to Bosnia-Herzegovina triggered by the shocking discovery that Bill had an illegitimate son. How affected I was by the fallout, the near-demise of Bill and Martha's marriage. And yes, the arrival of Julie during that same time, reengaging with her, merging households, asking her to marry me.

The dread I woke up with now, almost every morning.

"Dread? Can you be more precise?"

"I feel as if I'm underwater. Every move is like dragging a heavy load of stones behind me."

"What's happening to your breath right now, Ten?"

I took a moment to check. "What breath?"

"Exactly."

I reintroduced my lungs to the magic of oxygen.

"Any idea when you might have felt dread like this before?"

Dorje Yidam. It took all my strength not to jump up again. I gripped the arms of the chair.

"Let's leave that for now," Eric said, his voice soothing.

I took another sip of water.

"I'm working you pretty hard. Do you want to take a break?"

"No!" My vehemence surprised me. "No," I repeated. "There's more. I feel like I'm being watched. Followed, Eric. All the time. At the airport the other day. Driving to the temple yesterday, and afterward, inside Ganden Gyatso. I can't shake the feeling that someone or something is after me."

"After you?"

"Yes. Someone who wishes me harm. And I can't completely discount the feeling, because in the past when I've had it, I've been right more times than I've been wrong."

Eric wrote down a few more things. He glanced at a round wall clock hanging above his desk. I did the same, and was shocked to see how much time had passed. My entire body clenched.

"My next client canceled, right before you got here," he said. "I don't always recommend this, Ten, but I'm thinking we should consider having a double session."

My chest muscles released their clutch. "My breath seems to agree," I said. "Which is weird. A few minutes ago every cell in my body wanted to get up and leave."

Eric clapped his hands. "What a pleasure this is!"

I must have looked as confused as I felt.

"To work with someone like you," he said. "Someone who's not only willing to change, but open to the idea that mind and body are equal partners when it comes to healing. Well done, Ten!"

I basked in his approval and felt the first small stirrings of hope.

"So you can help me with this stuff? The panic attacks? The paranoia?"

"I will do my very best," he said.

I had to smile at that.

Eric raised his eyebrows. "What?"

"I say that to my clients, too. To reassure them, when I can't promise anything."

"Caught. But only because it's not just up to me." Eric leaned forward, his voice serious. "Therapy isn't a quick fix, Ten. These issues of yours didn't start eight months ago, or even eight years. The seeds were planted long ago, and the roots reach deep. They won't be resolved in a day, or even a month."

"I know that." I swallowed back a flutter of panic. "But what if I can't . . . ?"

Eric raised his hand. "That said, I think I can help you, at least with some of the overt symptoms you've been experiencing."

"Really?" A thought invaded. "I'm not interested in taking drugs."

Eric nodded. "Even if you were, I'm not that kind of doctor."

"But you still think you can help me?"

"I believe so. I'm a generalist, remember? I like to mix and match modalities, depending on the client. So yes, I can address the symptoms short-term. Long-term solutions will require a deeper commitment on both our parts. But we don't have to make that decision right away."

I focused on the words *short* and *term*. I clarified. "You're saying there's something you can do quickly. To help with the panic, and the nightmares."

"Yes."

"Like, today?"

"Yes. If you're willing."

"How?"

"It's a form of hypnotherapy. I've had great success with it in the past. We'll use your own subconscious to guide us there."

"Guide us where?"

"Back into the tower."

Chapter 28

We took a short break. Eric left the office to go into the house, and I stepped into the bathroom. I met my eyes in the mirror as I washed my hands.

"You are getting sleeeepierrr . . ." I said, but the joke fell flat.

I walked outside. Sunbaked paving stones warmed the soles of my feet through my thin cotton socks. The sprig of jasmine had turned brown and curled in the Buddha's palm, but the scent was still heady. I powered up my phone and checked for messages—there was a text from Julie, asking me to call her when I was done, but that was it.

I walked back inside and took a seat. Eric joined me almost immediately. He pushed the coffee table to one side and moved his armchair a foot or two closer to me. He sat, hands clasped in his lap. He seemed utterly at ease.

"So how does this work?"

"Pretty simple, really," Eric said. "I will guide you into a relaxed state of awareness, and from there you and I will explore the troubling aspects of your dream. Let's see if we can restore some balance."

I shifted in my seat. "I should tell you, I'm not great at giving up control."

Eric shrugged. "If you're not susceptible to hypnotic suggestion, you're not. But the fact that you've expressed a willingness to try, coupled with your long-term practice of a concentration technique and your self-reported sensitivity to your environment makes me think you have nothing to worry about."

I was at least as worried the hypnosis would succeed as I was that it would fail, but some things were better left unsaid.

"Ready?"

"Ready."

Eric leaned back in his chair. I did the same.

"We all dream," he began. His voice was soothing. "Every night, even if we don't remember our dreams the next morning. Most dreams are composed of flotsam and jetsam, bits and pieces of our days carried over into our sleep. People, places, things: everything that has left an imprint. But sometimes the events and experiences that make up our life carry a little more weight—actions left undone, expectations unfulfilled. An emotional need that is aroused but left unsatisfied. Then, our dreams step in to complete the circuit."

Eric's quiet voice seemed to invite my muscles to relax, one by one.

"Maybe something is confusing to us. Puzzling, or perhaps even frightening. Or something threatens us, whether or not it is real. Then our unconscious mind longs to complete the pattern, and creates a 'bad' dream to do so. It thinks it's helping, but the solution only adds another layer of problem. Do you follow me?"

"Yes." Eric's voice was like balm, adding layers of delicious weight to my body. I sank deeper into the chair.

"Good," he said. "So the more we take conscious steps to ease our anxiety during the day, and the more we actively problem-solve any challenges, the less likely we are to have nightmares. Yes?"

"Yes." My eyelids drooped. I forced them open. The air grew dense, but this time the experience was pleasant. Like being blanketed in calm.

"That's it . . . And you can focus your attention inside and just, yes, just close those eyes right now . . ."

I closed my eyes with a soft groan of relief.

"That's it . . . And sometimes a certain dream comes anyway, and then we can assume it may have an even deeper purpose. We don't want to dismiss such a dream, do we? We want to bring it closer. It wants so much to help us, you see. Yes?"

"Yes." My breath was deep and slow.

"Good . . . Now, as you prepare to become very relaxed . . ."

If I get any more relaxed, I'm going to fall off the chair. A bubble of hilarity formed in my throat, and it was all I could do not to burst out laughing.

"That's it," Eric's voice said. "Feel the joy . . . the pleasure . . . And this dream of yours, it wants to support you. To help you. It is an expression of your imaginative mind, such a wonderful mind, the same mind you can now draw upon to notice a bright green square, vivid green, right in front of you, like a beautiful screen, yes?"

A glowing square of neon green floated in front of my mind's eye, wafer thin. Close enough to pluck from the air. *I'll bet it tastes like fresh lime.* A tart flavor of citrus spread across my tongue.

"That's it . . . and just beginning to relax with this inward focus . . ."

Eric's voice swam in and out of my consciousness, like a glowing eel. The tang faded.

". . . and sometimes you will see the green square clearly and sometimes you'll just know it's there . . . that's it . . . and what if that bright green screen could change and become a fiery red triangle?"

The triangle was crisp and red, vibrant where it hung. And then it shifted into a circle, deep sapphire, shimmering, radiating healing blue light . . . and I was in the middle of somewhere but no, I was nowhere except the reality of knowing and inside the knowledge of my intuition and deeply relaxed but also deeply aware and far, far away in the distance, I saw the tower again—I loved that tower so much and I started to walk toward it and a great feeling of euphoria came over me the answer was in the tower and I was going to walk inside the tower and climb up the steps and finally reach the top and find it.

"That's it," from miles away. "That's it . . ."

I flew up the steps, light as a feather. And at the top there was a figure. I couldn't see who it was yet. A hood was pulled low over its face. I wasn't sure I liked this person. And I frowned.

"And you can stop climbing whenever you want to, you can move that old dream of the tower as far away as you want, you can put it onto that screen over there . . ."

The figure in the tower was reduced to an image on the thin screen, a distance away. It started to dance, a monkey dance, arms and legs lifting. *Silly monkey! It doesn't want to hurt me, it's my friend! It wants to play!* My laugh was light, like a child's.

"That's it . . . How wonderful to feel the joy that waits for you in the tower."

I was back inside the room at the top. The figure reached up and removed the hood.

Everything went black.

"Ten? Tenzing?"

I opened my eyes.

Eric was smiling at me.

"Not susceptible at all, are you?"

"What happened?" I blinked a few times. "I feel a bit strange."

"You did it, my friend. You embraced your fear. Literally."

"What are you talking about?"

"First of all, how do you feel?"

I felt into my body. "Light," I said. "Spacious. But also grounded somehow. I feel okay." I elaborated. "I feel like myself. Which is strange. I mean, who was I before?"

Eric nodded. "I have this client. She loves to meditate more than anything. Her life isn't that great, mind you, but her meditations are spectacular. The other day she couldn't wait to tell me about an out-of-body experience she'd had that morning." Eric smiled. "I told her my job was to bring her fully *into* her body. She wasn't too happy with me, but it's the truth. Everything I do is about returning you to you. To

my mind, there's nothing more spiritual than understanding and accepting your own in-the-body experiences."

"The Buddha would agree."

Eric cocked his head. "Can you recall what happened?"

"Not exactly."

"How about now?" Eric reached over and touched my shoulder.

And I was back in the room, and the figure turned to face me.

He reached up and removed the hood. His head was shaved. A blackish shadow marked the hairline on his scalp. He smiled. He was 19 and strikingly handsome. His eyes were dark and flecked with gold. Muscular, lean, a sleek greyhound of a young man. His smile celebrated me as if I were a treasure. "Brother," he said. "I've missed you."

Nawang?

"Nawang," I said out loud. "Oh."

"Yes." Eric looked down at his notes. "That's the name you used. Who is he?"

My eyes filled. Part pain, part relief. "I'm . . . he's . . . Nawang is my brother. Half brother, technically," I said, "at least, he seemed to think so."

"I see," Eric said. "How interesting. Am I right in remembering that when you moved here, you said you were an only child?"

"I thought I was." Vague images shuttled by: a flash of a three-sided dagger. Yeshe and Lobsang and I fleeing the prayer hall. The city of Dharamshala in flames. Nothing coherent, just a jumble of faint impressions.

"I don't believe this. I must have pushed Nawang completely out of my mind." Another memory arose, this one clearer. "He left the monastery the same summer I was expelled. I was only twelve at the time. Something . . . something pretty bad happened, a kid died in the village. An Indian boy, from one of the local tribes and I think . . . I think they blamed me. There were riots. I had to leave Dorje

Yidam right away. A few months later my mother died." My voice became matter-of-fact. "So I came back."

"I'm sorry. That sounds like a very painful time."

I shrugged. "Not really. Like I said, I can barely remember what happened."

"The mind does what it must to help us survive."

"I'm still not sure Nawang even existed. No one at Dorje Yidam ever mentioned him again, or anything else about my expulsion. My father's orders. And I sure wasn't going to bring it up." I tried for a lighter tone. "So what do you think, doc? Do I have a brother, or is he just a figment of my imagination?"

"It's not what I think that matters. It's how you feel. As I'm sure you know, significant characters in our dreams, imagined or not, also represent aspects of our own psyche. That said, I'm guessing he's real. And happily for both of us, there are others you can ask, some of them currently staying right downstairs."

"Good point."

"I don't think it's coincidental this has come up now for you. Hopefully our friends can shed some light. The unconscious hates unfinished business, even from decades past."

"And if all else fails, there's always Google." I was only half joking.

"Whatever works, my friend. Whatever works." Eric flipped his notepad closed.

I stood up and stretched.

"Wow. I really feel terrific."

"Don't forget what I said, Ten. This relief is real, but it's not necessarily permanent." He stood as well. "Think of your life as two silos, one full of consciousness, the other full of crap. Something tells me you've been avoiding going anywhere near the crap silo for a very long time. And guess what? It's starting to overflow. These panic attacks? They're just your unconscious waving a red flag—letting you know it's time to pick up the shovel and get to work."

He slid the notepad in between the others in the mesh basket. I was dying to count them. How many of us were there?

"What do I owe you?" I reached for my wallet.

Eric waved his hand. "I never charge for the first session. Again, not what the powers that be recommend, but I like my clients to understand what they're committing to. I think it went pretty well, though, don't you?"

I gave him a look that said *are you kidding me?* and he laughed. "Yes," I said. "I want to continue."

"Good. I'd like you to come in again soon, maybe in a few days. Monday okay?"

"Monday's fine."

"In the meantime, take it easy. You did some powerful work today. And please, call me if you need to. Like I said, I'm here." He moved to his desk. Our session was over.

My shoes were tied, but I stayed put on the bench, relishing the spaciousness inside and out. Across from me, the Buddha seemed to smile. The jasmine was intoxicating. Everything looked sharply etched and saturated with color—the trees, the hanging baskets of flowers, the gleaming saffron flanks of my Shelby Mustang, parked below.

Maybe I'd take a walk before getting back in my car and battling my way through traffic. Yeshe and Lobsang would understand. This heightened sense of awareness was precious. Who knew how long it would last?

Nawang. I mentally unearthed the Tibetan translation: the possessive one.

You belong to me. And I belong to you.

I pulled out my phone and called Julie.

"Hey," she whispered. I heard the deep familiar throb of Tibetan throat singing.

"It's happening?"

"Thank God. They forgot to unlock early for us, so it was a mad scramble, but we started on time. Adina's ecstatic. Huge turnout. Hang on, let me move outside."

My gaze shifted to the park. Now there were maybe 10 or 12 birds circling Bronson Canyon. That meant crows. Hawks flew in pairs.

"How are you?" Julie's voice was concerned. "How'd it go?"

"Actually, I feel pretty great. Eric was amazing. Just . . . amazing."

"I'm almost jealous. I used to fantasize as a kid about having Yoda as my special friend."

"I got hypnotized."

"Seriously? Okay, now I am jealous." Julie laughed. "Jeez. I let you out of my sight for two days . . ."

"I think we discovered something. Don't freak out, but I think I have a brother out there somewhere."

Julie was silent.

"It's a lot to process," I said. "Sorry. Don't be upset."

"I'm not upset." She took a moment. "Well, maybe a little."

"Just to be clear, I wasn't keeping it from you. More like keeping it from myself."

"I get it," Julie said. "Listen, I really want to talk more about this, but they need me inside. How soon can you get here?"

"Soon."

"Good. They're about to sketch the design. They'll start pouring sand right after lunch."

Now there were over 20 crows, some circling, some darting out of sight. Their caws were faint, but insistent.

"That's so weird," I said.

"Really? I figured you'd know all about sand mandala ceremonies."

"No, I mean I'm watching something weird. I'm still at Eric's, and I'm looking across at Griffith Park. There's a flock of crows flying around, more every minute."

"A murder."

"What?"

"That's what you call a group of them. *A murder of crows*. You know, *pride of lions*. *Gaggle of geese*. Kind of like a metaphor."

"Oh. Right." But my body wasn't buying the circling birds as metaphor. My body wanted to close the distance between the black birds and me in three strides, so I could find out what was underneath them.

A murder of crows.

"Can't wait to see you," Julie said. "And babe?"

"Yes?"

"I hope it's true. The brother thing."

Chapter 29

My phone pinged. A text had just made its way across the ocean from Bertie's thumbs to my eyes. My feeling of spacious ease was dissipating rapidly.

RE: IDENTIFYING MARKS. NO TATTOOS. TWO SCARS. ONE ON LEFT WRIST. ONE FROM APPENDIX REMOVAL 2001. ACCORDING TO MEDICAL RECS. COLLIE BLOOD TYPE RARE: AB NEG.

I hurtled down the stairs. The second I reached the driveway, I scrolled for and pressed Bill's number.

"Hola," Bill said. "How's the head-shrinking going? Any nasty secrets I need to know about?"

I'd mentioned my appointment with Eric to Bill last night. He'd refrained from immediate ridicule. He knew that I knew he currently had two therapists, one for him, one for them.

"I'll tell you mine if you tell me yours," I said, crossing the driveway. "But that's not why I'm calling. Did you guys think about bringing Fran and Shirley in on the Griffith Park deal?" Bill and I had worked with the human-remains detection dog and her handler, Fran Hoagland, with great success in the past.

"Shirley Bones? No. No reason to. Like I said before, no missing hikers, no missing anyone that matched the time and place, and nothing else turned up in the surrounding area. As for a broader search, we're talking four thousand acres of land, much of it inaccessible. Why?"

"Well, Eric's office is in Los Feliz. Adjacent to Griffith Park. I'm looking across at an area known as Bronson Canyon."

"Yeah, I know it. A head showed up in a garbage bag there a couple years back, hands and feet soon to follow. So?"

"So there's a lot of crows right now, circling and diving in the vicinity of Bronson Caves."

"And?"

"And I'm thinking murder."

"What did that shrink do—give you acid?"

"Bill, listen. That job I was telling you about yesterday? The young man from the UK?"

"With the rich parents. What about him?"

"According to the police over there, he definitely flew into L.A. this past Monday, before he dropped out of sight. He was listed as a passenger, plus there's visual CCTV confirmation from Heathrow, plus written confirmation from the kid himself."

"Okay."

"Plus something else. His blood type's AB negative. I just found out."

"What the hell?"

"I know," I said.

"You're telling me he's missing, he's AB negative, and he's in Los Angeles?"

"Affirmative."

I waited. Bill's gears were grinding. Best to let him reach his own verdict.

"Stay put," Bill said. "I'll get back to you in a few."

I reread the text. I knew I was right about this. Collie had been on that Griffith Park trail, or at least his blood had. And the crows weren't circling a discarded bag of take-out.

My phone buzzed.

"We're in luck," Bill said. "Shirley and Fran are free. They can be there in an hour or two. You'd better be fucking right about this."

"If I'm not, feel free to lay the blame at my feet."

"Yeah, but you're not on the LAPD payroll anymore, are you?" Bill's voice was sharp. He hated having to answer to people as much as I did.

"Sorry. I shouldn't joke. What do you want me to do?"

"I'm coming over right now. Meet me at the gated entrance at the top of Deronda Drive. You said you were in Los Feliz?"

"Yes."

"Right. Take Los Feliz to Franklin to Beachwood then left on Ledgewood until it meets up with Deronda. I'll notify the rangers. We'll need an escort from that entrance point. Do not, I repeat, DO NOT go anywhere near the site without me. I've sent word to S&M to get their butts over there. Usually Fran likes to take a look-see first, but I'm pretty sure she's familiar with the overall terrain of Griffith Park. Shirley, too. It's a popular dumping ground, unfortunately."

"I know." During one 15-day-period a few years ago, six bodies had turned up, scattered throughout the park like so much debris. The combination of paved roads cutting through inaccessibly mountainous terrain proved irresistible to murderers looking for good hiding places.

"If I know Fran, she'll want to give Shirley a good sniff around the original scene before she lets her loose," Bill mused. "Remember what I said. Wait for me." He hung up before I had a chance to argue.

I brought up the location. I was 15 minutes from Deronda Drive. Knowing Bill and traffic, it would take him at least an hour.

I leaned against my car. The bright yellow metal warmed the seat of my jeans.

I had a decision to make. I could call Lord and Lady Purdham-Coote, or I could wait until I had more information.

Just find my son.

If this turned out to be a false alarm, I would regret the impulse to share information prematurely. Hearts were at stake.

And if I told Bertie Andrews, he would be obligated to tell them.

There was one person over there I could call. I checked the time, added eight hours. Still only 9:00 P.M. in London. I found Garfield's number.

"DCI Garfield."

"It's Ten. Sorry to call your cell so late, but I have news." I brought him up to speed.

"This is most concerning. So you'll know more later today?"

"Hopefully, yes. DCI Garfield?" My voice had tightened. I took a page from my session with Eric. Inhaled deeply and let the outward flow of breath carry my dread along with it. I tried again. "DCI Garfield, what's the protocol if we find a body? I mean, if we find a body, and it turns out to be Collie?"

Garfield's answer was prompt. "Where the body lies," he said.

"I'm not sure I understand."

"Pertaining to incidents where a victim of homicide has crossed borders, jurisdiction is determined by where the body lies. Your country, your case."

"I see."

"Not that we wouldn't do everything we could to help from over here, if it comes to that. Let's hope it doesn't. Thank you for calling. I'll await word, either way."

Where the body lies.

I sent Julie a text message: SOMETHING'S COME UP. I MAY BE DELAYED. SORRY.

Then I closed my eyes and sent a different kind of message to whatever or whoever lay out there near the caves, a powerful series of mantras that can transform any physical or mental impurities into the pure body, speech, and mind of a Buddha: *Om mane padma hum.*

CHAPTER 30

No reply from Julie, which meant she was busy, or irritated. Either way, I was starving.

I checked the time. I had 45 minutes, plenty of time.

Franklin Boulevard had several food options, discounting the Scientology Celebrity Centre. I wasn't going to eat or drink anything they served. Kool-Aid—that's all I have to say about that. Victor's Deli seemed like the fastest choice, so I turned right on Bronson Avenue, just past Gelson's.

The deli I remembered had morphed into a hipster café, complete with outdoor tables on a narrow sidewalk patio. They provided the perfect urban Instagram setting for men in porkpie hats and sunglasses and women who looked like they ate maybe once a month.

The café had its own small lot, but the car directly in front of me—a low-slung black Maserati—veered left and snagged the last empty space. I pulled into the larger adjacent lot and squeezed into a narrow vacancy in the far corner, directly in front of a pet-grooming store. A few faint barks followed me across the tarmac.

Inside, the café was both frenetic and somewhat dysfunctional. A long line of customers to my left waited to give their coffee and pastry commands at a glass counter; a shorter line had formed in front of a harried cashier who was taking food orders.

I scooped up a premade baguette of Brie and mango chutney located in a refrigerated glass case filled with artisanal cheeses and unpronounceable dried meats. The sandwich honored the French-Indian cuisines of my youth. The cup of black coffee-to-go was American cop, all the way.

The total cost? Ridiculous.

I moved outside. A narrow counter bordered the café's picture window. I perched on a fixed metal-and-wood bar stool. The baguette was wrapped in brown paper. As I pulled off the wrapping, a pigeon landed on the pavement next to me, which reminded me that I was on Bronson, and that there was a murder of crows right at the end of the street.

Bill had warned me off the original crime site. He hadn't said a word about the caves.

In minutes I was driving north up Bronson while gnawing at the baguette. I gave up after three bites, peeled the remaining Brie off the gluey chutney-smeared bread, and ate the cheese straight up, rind and all. Prorated, it came to about $3 a mouthful. The gourmet coffee was also just okay, nothing special. I guess you paid extra for the hipness factor.

The road veered east toward the hills. Bigger trees, nicer cars. Speed bumps materialized as the houses got grander and better protected. I had driven these parts a few years ago, riding shotgun on a Brangelina prowl with my paparazzo friend Clancy, before he repurposed his skill set into freelance private investigating.

Every side street warned off nonlocals: "Preferred Parking," "No Access to the Hollywood Sign," "Not a Through Street," "No Outlet," go away, go away, go away.

Residential development seceded to nature as I passed beneath an arched canopy of leafy branches and entered the beginnings of Bronson Canyon. The grass was green here. I guess the city could still afford to water. There were two small, kid-friendly pocket parks at the entrance. Farther along, a bleached sycamore trunk angled low over a grassy expanse, begging kids to shimmy along its thick stem.

The large public parking lot was surprisingly empty considering the direct access into Griffith Park. I counted six cars, only one of them a rental.

Twenty-five minutes. I'd be cutting it close. I couldn't see the crows from here, but I could hear them. They traded caws like insults, somewhere ahead and above.

I kept a spare set of clothes and a pair of old running shoes in the in-case-of-emergency duffel bag stashed on the floor behind the driver's seat. I changed shoes and swapped my button-down for a black T-shirt and a binocular necklace.

The packed dirt road was ideal for running. I started with an easy jog, passing a 10-foot-tall spear of an agave plant beginning its centennial process of blooming. The dirt crunched under my feet, a satisfying sound. The road made a sharp turn, cutting back on itself as it climbed. In the distance rocky outcroppings and steep cliffs warned of a much rougher terrain.

The variety of vegetation was almost shocking. Trees with paint-by-number trunks, trees with leaves the size of dinner plates, trees with ferns for arms. Giant needled conifers with green-scaled pinecones, and spiky seedpods that pocked the edges of the wide dirt path.

I accelerated to a sprint, clutching the bouncing binoculars to my chest with one hand. My feet pounded up the steady incline, lungs working hard, thigh muscles burning.

You should be there by now.

I leaned over, panting. Where was my head? The caves were a five-minute stroll from the entrance. I'd been running flat out for 10.

A California jay scolded: *Pay attention to your life.*

I waved down a speed-walking woman, ponytail bobbing, buds plugged in. She made one ear available.

"Caves?" I said.

"Fire road," she said, thumbing the way I'd come, without breaking stride. "Smokey the Bear!" she called over her shoulder.

I reversed course, jumping the high red curb at the switchback to save time. It was downhill all the way, and I reached the fire road in a couple of minutes. The large Smokey the Bear sign marking the side road was hard to miss, unless you were me.

I skirted the metal vehicle barricade and kept running.

The push and pull between nature and man was clearly delineated in this direction. Houses marched up terraced hills to one side and uninhabitable ridges witnessed the urban madness from across the way. One brave soul had placed a gazebo on a quartet of skinny stilts at the top of the hillside overlooking the park. This was earthquake country—might as well put your trust in toothpicks.

The fire road snaked left and so did I.

The cave was gouged straight through the thick face of rock. A square black mouth, permanently open. Two smaller caves flanked it, semicircles of blackness hanging close to the mother cave like cubs. Not a crow in sight, but I could hear them cawing, not that far away.

The tunneled darkness gave off an impression of coldness and damp, but an arch of bright sunlight beckoned from the other end. The other two caves were more cramped and unwelcoming. I decided to explore from left to right, weaving back and forth.

I ducked inside the first cave. Using my phone as a flashlight, I scoured the narrow, craggy walls and low ceiling. Nothing troublesome marred their surface. The cave dumped me into sunshine, a wide sandy area. Someone had formed a spiral maze out of stones, worth investigation, but I was in a hurry, so I dove into the middle cavern, again finding nothing but rough rock.

One more to go. The opening was narrow and forbidding. I crouched low and ducked inside. Dank air closed clammy fingers around my neck. It smelled of hostility in here. I fumbled with the flashlight.

Nothing.

Except . . . I moved closer to the rough rock face about halfway in. Someone had made a faint marking with chalk. It looked like a dash, followed by the letter *M*, and then an *N* maybe? The lettering was blurred. I took a photo, using the flash function, and got out of there.

I emerged next to the spiral of stones. They culminated in a strange formation of pebbles, a half-moon on its side,

cupping a round ball, and something else on top. I snapped another photo. If I hurried, I'd still get to Deronda before Bill.

My phone pinged.

Or not.

Bill's text was condensed, but I got the point: GET UR BUTT OVER HERE.

It took my butt five minutes to reach the car and another eight before I was turning north onto Beachwood. A large solar-powered digital display cautioned tourists against stopping, smoking, parking, or trying to reach the sign—against existing, basically. I was willing to bet the digital messages were paid for by the wealthier residents who lived up the hill—NIMBYs, Bill called them. Not In My Back Yarders.

Driving up Beachwood itself was an adventure of braking and swerving to avoid impervious pedestrians. They darted in and out of the middle of the street, blind to any hurtling sheet metal, their phones and cameras held aloft.

My sympathy for the locals grew a little.

After a mile and several stop signs, a pair of stone gates marked the entrance into upper Beachwood. The gates were also from the '20s, and composed of rough blocks of gray stone. The one on the right was tall and turret shaped, and its base formed a pedestrian arch over the sidewalk. It reminded me a little of the tower in my dream.

I tested my response to it. No chilly fog of fear descended, not even a wisp.

CHAPTER 31

Bill pointedly looked at his watch.

I squeezed into a spot behind his car. The Hollywood sign loomed across the canyon treetops. On either side, homes crouched behind walls and fences, their windows shuttered, their inhabitants vainly attempting to block out the fact that they lived in the shadow of the world's cheesiest icon.

Bill was waiting next to a white Suburban stenciled with the words *Park Ranger*. A green gate was wrapped in a thick chain bracelet dangling with padlock charms. A stocky park ranger in a gray uniform and a jaunty straw hat was unlocking the last of the padlocks.

"Sorry I'm late," I said. "I had to eat something. Hypoglycemia."

"My ass."

The ranger looked up from the padlocks.

"This is Ten," Bill said. "Ten, meet Ezekial Foss. Big Dodger fan."

"Zeke," the ranger said. He swung open the gate. "Let's go."

We climbed into the Suburban. Zeke drove at a snail's pace. The rutted road was paved, but barely, and we stopped more than once to make way for joggers, hikers, and tourists. They were the safari animals and this was their habitat.

"It's just up there," Bill said.

The road widened slightly. Zeke parked the Suburban parallel to the shoulder, hugging the inner part of the trail. He turned the radio on—some kind of sports station. Two men were yelling about how bad the Dodgers were right now.

"Rockies tonight," Bill said. "Coors Field. Balls'll be flying."

"Yep." Zeke settled in his seat. A man of few words.

Bill and I walked to the scene of the noncrime. Yellow tape fluttered, attached to a pair of stakes driven into the soft dirt shoulder. The road beyond twisted and turned, forking through miles of parkland.

I faced the view, trying to get my bearings. The copper domes of the Griffith Observatory sprung from a hillside to my left. Straight ahead, the downtown skyline jutted like a city of toy blocks. A sprawl of flat urbanization culminated in a thin strip of ocean, where distant haze mounded into vague humps, the islands of Catalina. And finally, to the right, the dual towers of Century City.

"So what do you think?" Bill said.

I redirected my attention to the asphalt art at my feet.

The body tracing was much as Bill had described: a life-size silhouette of a prone human being. The colored lines were now more brown than red, but that was the nature of exposed blood.

I circled the form. And knew immediately. My heart started to hammer.

This message is for me.

Dots of black started their swirling dance, and a second voice kicked in— soothing, rational.

You don't know that, not for sure. Take a deep breath.

I took a deep breath.

That's it.

"Interesting," I said.

"What?"

"The positioning of the arms and legs."

"What about them?"

I walked around the pictograph a second time, using my forefinger like a pointer.

"See how the right elbow is bent with the fingers pointing upward, and the left arm is straight, with the hand aimed toward the feet?"

"Okay . . ."

"And how the legs are almost parallel?"

Bill tipped his head. "Hmmm. It is a little unusual."

"It's more than unusual, it's impossible. No one would fall this way. But what if it's posed? What if you were trying to depict a specific posture? Say, this one?" I illustrated, standing with my legs hip-distance apart, right elbow bent, palm forward and left arm down, fingertips stretching toward the ground.

"I got nothing," Bill said. "Enlighten me, oh wise one."

"The Buddha wasn't born the Buddha. He was born a prince, Prince Siddhartha."

"Ten, even I know that. What's that got to do with anything?"

"But there were signs that he'd be special, starting with this dream his mother had about a huge white elephant." I saw Bill's face. "Okay, scratch that. The elephant's not important. So, he was born in a grove of trees, and the story goes, his birth was marked by a shower of flower petals and streams of colored light pouring from the sky."

Bill opened his mouth. I held up my hand.

"I'm setting the scene, okay? So here's this baby, maybe a few minutes old. And what does he do? He stands up and walks. And how does he do it? With one palm reaching upward, and the other pointing down toward the earth." I took the pose again. *"Comme ça."* I had Bill's full attention now. I let my arm drop. "It's a classic symbol of godlike power, known to Buddhists everywhere." Another thought crossed my mind. "One more thing. He didn't just walk, he talked."

"I'm guessing he didn't say *mama*?"

I closed my eyes, retrieving Shakyamuni's first words. "I alone am the world-honored one," I recited. "Heaven above and earth below revere me."

Was it my imagination, or had the world gone briefly silent? I opened my eyes.

Bill was watching me, his expression unreadable. "So you're thinking this is some sort of religious statement?"

But my attention had shifted to the three-lettered tag a few feet to the right of the traced figure. *JMM*, written with the same bodily fluids.

I pulled out my phone. Compared the letters to the chalked lettering inside the cave. With a little imagination, the monograms were the same.

And another insight clicked into alignment.

"What," Bill said. "What are you seeing?"

"This." I motioned. "*JMM*. It's not a gang tag, Bill. The letter *J* stands for *jai*."

"Jay, like the bird?"

"No. *Jai*, like the devotional greeting. From the Hindu tradition. It doesn't translate easily. *All victory to*, maybe. Or, *blessings upon*, or even *long live*, as in *long live the Queen*."

"Okay, this is actually interesting. Keep going."

"If I'm right, the two *M*'s stand for the Sanskrit names Maha and Mudra. So *Jai Maha Mudra* translates as *all victory to Maha Mudra*."

"And?"

"And my misper, Colin Purdham-Coote, came over here to join a cult, led by a female guru called Maha Mudra. He signed off with those same three words on a card to his parents. Postmarked four days ago, from Hollywood." I met Bill's eyes. "Which ties this scene directly to my missing person's case."

"Jesus, Ten." Bill walked a few more yards up the path and waved me over. "You're batting a thousand so far. What about this one?"

The second marking, painted in the same darkened red-brown, was about six inches high and four inches across, an odd stacked series of shapes crowned with a small crescent, like a quarter moon lying on its back. The crescent cupped a round ball topped with a tiny flame. The design was unusual, more like a hieroglyph. Or . . .

"It's got nothing to do with gangs either," I said, "unless there's a gang of Gelugpa monks we don't know about.

Because this is definitely some kind of Tibetan Buddhist symbol."

And I had found something similar constructed out of pebbles by the caves.

Bill returned to the body tracing. "I don't suppose you can tell me what any of this means."

"I can't. But I know people who can."

A wave of dizziness sent me to the aluminum safety fence. I grabbed it with both hands and leaned over, eyes closed.

Not cured.

Never okay again.

Always alone.

After a moment, the panic passed.

I straightened up, ignoring Bill's look of concern.

Eric was right. I needed to know more, to verify the truth. Everything was connected. Everything traced back to my childhood.

It usually does.

A joyous string of yelps behind us announced the carefree presence of a dog.

"Shirley! *Wees stil, wees stil!*"

A muscular German shepherd bounded in our direction, towing her handler behind her. Black markings crisscrossed the thick brown coat, and a soft shield of white spilled across her chest like foam. She skidded to a stop a few yards away and sat. Her tail swept the ground in wide, fringed arcs.

Her dark-haired handler was out of breath. Her name was Fran Hoagland, and I was pleased to see her again.

"Hey, Bill." Fran caught sight of me and brightened. "Hey there, stranger. Haven't laid eyes on you in a while. Good Lord, you don't age. Still drinking that Trappist swill?"

"Absolutely."

Fran was a double-Scotch-no-rocks girl. She didn't see the point of wine or beer.

She, too, appeared unchanged. Her hair was so black it was almost blue. The blunt cut was all sharpness and angles, sides curved inward like pointed scimitars. She was dressed

for work: bright blue shirt with a yellow and blue coroner's shield sewn onto the left front pocket; black cargo pants; black cop shoes. I'd never seen her wear anything else.

Shirley was also in uniform. The tan harness yoked beneath her collar sported a bright yellow Los Angeles Coroner's Office medallion, stitched onto the front.

"So, Fran," I said, "you break a hundred yet?"

"One thirty-nine, suckah!" Her grin was wickedly pleased.

When I left the force five years ago, the K-9 team of Fran Hoagland and Shirley Bones had only been at the County Coroner's Office for two years, but they'd already recovered remains on more than four dozen homicide cases. They were close to the best— if not *the* best—in the country.

One hundred and thirty-nine meant they had almost tripled that count. "So where's that put you?"

"Third. I've been stuck there forever, feels like. But June is always a pretty good month, statistically."

"Still checking your stats every day?"

"I can't help it. I'm obsessed."

"There's a term for that, you know. *Comparing mind.* According to the Buddha, nothing puts you on a faster track to suffering."

Fran shrugged. "Fuck that. We all do it."

Bill was on his phone, listening and frowning. Fran pulled out hers and started to thumb through e-mails.

I checked on Zeke. He had pulled the straw brim low over his face. He appeared to be taking a nap.

A couple with a border terrier off the leash jogged into view. Shirley's low warning grumble culminated in a sharp bark. She pushed to her feet.

"*Zitten!*" Fran commanded in Dutch, and Shirley complied, but her eyes followed the trio until they were a safe distance past.

Shirley was born in the Netherlands. She'd arrived here with formal papers, some training, and an unpronounceable surname. Meanwhile Fran, like me, had grown up on a steady diet of Sherlock Holmes. When she joined the K-9

training unit she'd already picked out a name for her future search dog.

But he was a she, so Sherlock became Shirley.

The Bones part came later; something to do with an actress who starred in a television series about pigeons, or partridges, or something.

"How's working for yourself, Ten? You miss the fast lane?"

"Sometimes."

"I'd go nuts."

I didn't envy Fran her job. Cadaver searches were difficult and often fruitless. By definition those that ended successfully ended badly.

For most people, the work would be too grisly and morbid to bear. For Fran, the job was a mission of mercy. She saw herself as a vital piece of the homicide process, maybe the last piece standing. Be the voice of the victims, and bring answers to their families.

This was the second thing we shared. The unsolved dead and unrecovered missing haunted us.

Shirley yawned, her tongue curling. She bumped her head against her handler's thigh. Fran stroked the thick ruff of fur while keeping a tight hold on the leash.

Bill ended his call.

"What are we waiting for?" Fran said to Bill.

"Sully and Mack," Bill said. "But you know what? They're running late, as usual. So screw 'em, let's get started."

Chapter 32

Fran led Shirley to the outlined body. The dog seemed to extract information out of thin air, nose quivering. Then she lay down, resting her head against her forepaws.

"What did you say this fluid was composed of?" Fran asked Bill.

"Blood, menstrual blood, and semen. Plus a couple of organic chemicals, namely sulphur and mercury."

"Charming," Fran said. "But not extracted from a carcass, right Shirley?"

Shirley's tail wagged.

"Shirley's been proofed off of live scents. She'd be on high alert if it wasn't, uh, fresh, so to speak. This particular combo's a new one, though."

Fran gazed across the expanse of park, dotted with paddled cacti and scattered brush. "So you're thinking there might be a body . . . where?"

I pointed right. "Over there. Brush Canyon." A few black specks circled. "See those crows?"

Fran squinted. "Ravens," she said. "Common ravens, if they're in Griffith Park."

So much for my murder of crows.

"Ravens, then. Anyway, whatever they're circling isn't in the caves, but close by, over the next couple of steep ridges."

"And you just happen to know that, how?" Bill had trained his legendary glower on me.

"I might have checked out the caves before meeting you here."

Bill turned to Fran. "You see what I have to put up with?"

We woke Zeke from his afternoon snooze and he drove us out. Moments later, Bill and Fran were following me, caravan-style, back to the Bronson Canyon lot. We parked in a row next to a porta-potty and a Dumpster.

Shirley was already on alert in the open bed of the coroner's truck, tail wagging, nose testing the air.

Sully and Mack tore up the road and pulled in beside us.

"Okay," Bill said, opening his trunk. "Who besides me remembered crime-scene kits? Norbu, you get a pass." Fran raised her hand. Sully and Mack looked at the ground. "As it happens, I have two." Bill loaded up a backpack with two kits and a digital camera and slung it over his shoulders. "We find anything, that should be enough to hold us over until the troops arrive."

Bill hadn't been out in the field for months. He looked 10 years younger.

Fran kept Shirley reined in tight as we took off at a half-run. I led the way, Bill, Fran, and Shirley right behind.

We reached the caves in five minutes, at least four of us did. Sully was an oversize person. Mack was thinner, but he smoked. By the time they turned the corner, Sully's bright red face was beaded with sweat and Mack wasn't doing much better.

"How's this work again?" Sully swiped at his forehead with a wrinkled bandana he'd pulled from his pocket. Maybe he didn't remember the drill, or maybe he just wanted to catch his breath, but I was glad for the chance to review procedure. It had been quite a few years since I'd participated in a K-9 operation.

Fran rested her hand on Shirley's head. "Shirley will conduct the search following a scent cone pattern. She'll be moving in a kind of serpentine configuration, gradually reducing the area she's covering. I'll be shadowing her closely. You guys follow my lead. And don't worry, if she finds anything indicating a cadaver, she knows not to taint the evidence."

Bill and I exchanged a look—Sully and Mack could take a page out of the dog's book.

Fran unhooked the leash and belted the length of chain around her waist. She hunkered face-to-face with the dog. They locked gazes, bright brown eyes meeting bright brown eyes. The connection between hunter and handler was palpable.

"All right," Fran said. "*Sook. Shirley, sook!*" Shirley took off, and the *sook* was on.

The dog zigzagged over dirt and brush, tail up, nose close to the dry packed soil. Fran was right on her heels. We held back, maintaining a gap measured in yards. But fallen rock and scrubby undergrowth made the steep route up the first jagged incline a challenge, and our progress was painfully slow.

"Should have brought my hiking boots," I said to Bill.

"Tell me about it."

By the time we reached the apex, Fran and Shirley had already made the sharp descent and were crossing a dried gully that bordered a second, even steeper ridge. Dog and handler continued shifting both laterally and vertically as they descended like snakes.

"Jesus Christ," Sully gasped behind us. Mack added a painful moan.

"You two stay put," Bill barked. "We'll let you know if they find anything."

Bill and I skidded into the gully. We leaped across the dry streambed and scrambled up the second incline. We'd gone maybe a mile, but it felt like 10. My right shoe slipped, sending a cascade of tiny pebbles behind me.

"Over here!" Fran's call was urgent, and my heart rate picked up speed. I dug in, Bill huffing and puffing behind me.

We crested the second rise. The jagged ravine below was choked with brush and a few stunted trees. A hot haze lay over everything, as if the earth was exhaling exhaust. Fran's back was to us. She was looking past her dog at whatever the shepherd had found.

Shirley sat rooted in place, a statue. She stared fixedly at a tight trio of blooming creosote bushes.

Fran looked up at us. The pain in her face required no translation.

Without a word, Bill pulled out the two crime-scene kits, and we pulled on paper gowns, gloves, and booties. A sickly-sweet smell wafted our way, and we added face shields. As we picked our way down, the smell grew stronger. I swallowed back bile.

Whatever was down there was past fresh, and in an early state of decomp.

When we reached Fran, Shirley was curled at her feet, munching happily on a rawhide cruller. Their work was done. Ours was just beginning.

We moved to the body, stepping with care in our paper booties. Later, the crime scene investigators would take the same path.

Tiny yellow blooms decorated the creosote bushes, bold if bittersweet reminders of new growth, given what lay beneath them. Bill indicated the location with a stack of small stones. I guess his kits didn't include evidence markers.

I crouched carefully, noting what I could, careful not to touch or disturb anything. This close, the smell was rank, an attack to the soul and like no other scent on the planet. I pressed the mask tighter against my nose and mouth.

The body was almost naked, though a strip of cotton had been twisted around the groin area, like a loincloth. The legs were shoulder-width apart. Right elbow bent, fingers reaching upward. Left arm aimed down.

Ragged holes where there should have been eyes.

Bill had pulled out his camera and was shooting from different angles: *Click, whirr. Click, whirr. Click, whirr.*

Focus, Ten.

Adult male. Partially decomposed from heat, and the avid pecking of beaks.

Darkish skin, could be a side effect of death, or from overexposure. Black hair.

Black hair.

Not Collie.

The relief was short-lived. For I recognized him now, even without eyes. Or rather, I recognized his ring. The wide gold band cut into the swollen middle finger, but the amber cat's-eye glowed. Not Collie, but rather the remains of Collie's elated companion, his beaming cohort in the image posted on his Facebook page.

"It's not him, Bill. Not my missing person," I said. "But I know him. Not by name, but he and Colin hung out together in England. I recognize the ring."

"Poor kid," Bill said. He scanned the narrow gorge and cliffs, natural barriers to access. "What a nightmare. Getting forensics down here is going to be hell. We'll need a chopper to airlift the remains."

"I figured."

"Oh, well. At least it won't be hard to secure. This isn't exactly a destination point." Banter at times like this tended to blunt the horror.

Bill held up his cell phone, waving it left to right. "No signal, of course." He walked a few yards up the slope, testing the air for a digital source.

Fran had put Shirley back on the leash and was keeping her distance. Her face was grim.

"You okay?"

"I'm used to bones," she said. "Our finds aren't usually this fresh. And that smell. I never get used to it. Brutal."

I stayed put. I wasn't being paid to look away, and a thorough investigation included taking precise inventory of the damage.

Maybe this time the act of objectifying mortal wounds would lessen their nightmarish impact.

Bill returned. We scanned the body in silence.

"There's something almost ritualistic about this," I said.

Bill grunted, which meant maybe, maybe not.

Click, whir. Click, whir.

Both arms had been sliced open. The incisions were clean, vertical, and quite deep. No hesitation marks that I could see. The dusty ground beneath the body had hardened

into a dark bed of spilled, desiccated blood. Blood spatter clotted the dirt in and around the branches of creosote.

The thighs and shins had been both stabbed and sliced and in some places stripped of skin.

In addition, here and there the flesh looked puckered, as if beaks were involved.

The face was bloated and the neck arched, mouth open, lips pulled back in a grimace. A trickle of something like dried foam crusted the corners. Traces of the same fluid left small dark stains under each nostril. The stomach area, too, was distended.

These were all common events in untended corpses—we may die, but the millions of microorganisms and enzymes in our internal organs don't. They start to self-digest, creating fluids and gases that have to go somewhere. It's a form of life after death, a transformation of matter, but one that we have succeeded in sanitizing and embalming right out of our culture and consciousness.

So he'd been here at least a few days. No visible maggots, though. Which meant less than a week.

His eyes—I hoped that was the work of ravens or some other raptor, after his spirit-self abandoned ship.

So much for objectivity. My chest ached. Every inhalation was a struggle. I swallowed hard, but all I could taste was this young man's pain.

I offered the only antidote I could: *May your passage through the bardo be protected. May your journey be filled with ease. May you find peace. May you be free.*

"Ten. Over here," Bill said. He had moved several yards away.

He was photographing a plant with gray-green velvety leaves. A limp trumpet of a flower, creamy white streaked with violet, wilted in the afternoon sun. A handful of walnut-size, spiny capsules lay at the base of the plant. Most had split open, revealing crowded colonies of flat seeds the size of peppercorns.

"What is this?"

"Datura," Bill said. "Angel's trumpet."

"Or Devil's snare. Take your pick," Fran said, coming up behind us. "The seeds are loaded with tropane alkaloids. Plus a little scopolamine. They'll make you high as fuck, if they don't kill you first."

"Exactly. Which is why I find this interesting." Bill's gloved finger pointed to an empty husk, both sides scooped of seeds. He again marked the area with a stack of three small stones. They dotted the crime scene now like forensic stupas.

"You're not going to bag it?" I asked.

"I'll leave the packaging to the pros. Clearer chain of evidence. The courts like it better that way."

"You're thinking he might have been poisoned," Fran said.

"Maybe."

"Here's another possibility," I said. "We have a version of this plant in India. Also called datura. It's been around forever, it's even mentioned in ayurveda, a Hindu system of healing over five thousand years old."

"Here we go," Bill said.

"No. I want to hear this," Fran said.

"Thank you. Some ayurvedic healers say it's a poison, others, an aphrodisiac. But I can almost guarantee you there are Indian gurus who still use datura as a way to honor Shiva and achieve higher states of enlightenment."

"So the fuck what?" Dehydration was making Bill grumpy.

"So maybe he swallowed the seeds on purpose."

"Or maybe there's a hallucinating coyote out there who thinks he's a camel," Bill said. "I'm not ruling anything out at this point. I'll have the lab test for it. They'll need to do a full tox screening anyway."

"Better mark this area, too. There may have been a struggle." I pointed to a spot near the body where blood loss and multiple footprints had churned and stained the earth.

Bill photographed the chaos.

"I'm seeing lots of prints," he said from behind the camera.

"Bare feet," Fran added. "And bleeding like a mofo."

"Like a death dance," I said.

I turned back to the body. Whatever the cause, or purpose, his passing had not been gentle.

A raven landed next to the corpse.

"Get! Get away!" I shouted. Careful to avoid the bloody carpet of soil, I stepped toward the bird, waving my arms. Something metallic glinted from deep within the creosote's gnarled roots.

"Bill."

I could just make out a knife of some sort. I crouched.

The knife had an ornate eight-sided handle and a curved iron blade that finished in a hook, like a deadly curl. The flat part of the blade was encrusted with blood. The knife lay on a folded garment of gray cotton.

A robe.

A pair of hiking boots was neatly placed to one side.

"Bill!"

My ex-partner knows me very well. He ran.

I moved aside. Bill studied the weapon and robe for some time before turning back to me. His expression was unreadable.

"So, the knife's a sacred weapon, sacred to the Tibetan Buddhist tradition." I swallowed. "My tradition, as it turns out."

Bill nodded as he stacked three more stones.

"Ceremonial," I said again. "For use in rituals, to . . . to root out ignorance, greed, and aggression. Symbolic use."

"What rituals?"

"I'm not sure. Yet."

Bill's mouth tightened, but he gave a short nod.

Shirley barked, her canine nose far more attuned than ours to any alteration in the status quo. Where we smelled a single note, she smelled a symphony. Now Sully and Mack staggered into view, gleaming gods of sweat. A

THE FIFTH RULE OF TEN

black-and-white helicopter chopped its way across the sun-streaked sky.

Shirley and her handler had tracked down their fallen, lifeless prey. Bill and I had established enough grounds for suspicion concerning the cause. Now the experts in deciphering acts of mortal violence would converge, pulled as one to this particular place at this particular time by the negative forces of an unlawful death.

CHAPTER 33

Julie wouldn't even meet my eyes. I slipped into the empty chair next to her. A waiter scurried up.

"*Pho Tai?* Noodle with beef?" Julie and Lobsang raised their hands, and two steaming bowls landed. The fragrance hit like a punch.

"Noodle with beef and meatball?" Yeshe and Sonam made room.

"*Pho ga?* Noodle with chicken, very good!" TJ took the bowl. Everyone but Wangdue and me had food.

"Don't worry," Julie said, her voice curt. "I ordered for you." *Uh-oh.*

A second waiter arrived.

"*Pho chay.* No meat. Only veggie. No meat."

"Here." Once again, I was the lone outlier.

Well, not quite. Wangdue's place setting was still empty. "What about you, Lama Wangdue?"

"Saka Dawa," he said. "I fasting."

Right. Rigorously observant lamas spent the entire month eating only one meal a day, in the midmorning.

Platters of crunchy bean sprouts, sprigs of fresh Thai basil and cilantro, and slices of lime followed.

Julie's anger lay like a wall between us. I busied myself with condiments, adding this and that. Every table sported a round white tray with plastic squeeze bottles of soy, hot, and hoisin sauces. I reached for the plastic bottle of thick, sweet-and-sour hoisin.

"Don't," Julie said.

I froze, bottle poised.

"Hoisin ruins a good Pho broth. It's like putting ketchup on steak tartare."

I put the bottle back.

I couldn't get a signal at the site, and getting sprung from the crime scene had taken much longer than I'd expected. But honestly, getting to a sand mandala ceremony was the last thing on my mind once I'd caught sight of the ravens circling the caves.

By the time I'd checked in with Julie it was dusk.

"I wanted to come," I said to Julie. "One thing just led to another."

"It's not that you didn't come. It's that you didn't call. For hours. It's not like you. The new you, I should say." She gestured, her eyes hurt. "Ten, I thought we made an agreement about this."

An ancient resistance welled up, the notion that anyone who claims to love me really just wants to control me. Thankfully, I recognized it for what it was, an old idea. My issue, not Julie's, and based on a stifled, powerless past. But this was the present, and I did have a choice.

I chose to allow the resistance to rise, and then dissolve.

"You're right. I wasn't thinking. I'm sorry. I'll be more mindful next time."

It was Julie's turn. She could either ratchet the argument up or down. As I waited, the tension drained from her body.

"Thanks," was all she said, but it was enough. She picked up a flat ceramic spoon and scooped hot broth into her mouth. "Oh. My. God." She waved her spoon at Lobsang. "Did you taste this, Lobsang? This can't be legal."

Pho Café was tucked in the corner of a strip mall off Sunset in Silver Lake; impossible to find, but extremely popular with Vietnamese locals and foodies like Julie with discerning taste buds.

The décor was minimalist, featuring plain white walls, laminated pine tables for two, and an exposed kitchen where the magic happened. A big-bellied Buddha beamed from the far corner of the counter, seemingly delighted by the vases

of fresh sunflowers surrounding him. No sign out front, no reservations, yet it overflowed with diners most of the time.

Our four small tables had been pushed together to make one and we sat elbow to elbow on curved chairs of bright orange vinyl. The other diners shot sideways glances at us, and a few took furtive pictures with their phones, as if the monks were rock stars.

"How did you manage to get us in so quickly?" I asked. We'd skirted a group of restless hipsters milling outside in the dark.

"I played the Buddhist monk card," Julie said. She maneuvered a twisted knot of rice noodles into her mouth with the house chopsticks. "Turns out the owner's a follower of Thich Nhat Hanh."

"Convenient."

"I had a feeling."

She nudged me. "Eat, love, before it gets cold."

I spooned up some broth and tasted both smoke and tang, a blend of mushrooms, herbs, and diced hot peppers. Julie was right. Hoisin would have wrecked the delicate balance between earth and fire. I plucked out a few cubes of tofu with my chopsticks. They were dense and firm, exactly the way I liked them, and the white rice flour noodles had been perfectly simmered, not too hard and not too soft.

Julie had plucked three strips of steak from her bowl. She folded them in a paper napkin. A certain bulldog waiting in the van was going to be ecstatic.

For a moment, I was miles away from the broken body in the park.

But only for a moment.

I set my chopsticks aside, my appetite gone.

"You finished?" Lobsang asked.

"Yes."

"I can try?"

I passed over my bowl.

"What's wrong?" Julie said. "You barely ate."

I hadn't wanted to burden her, but withheld truth creates its own unhealthy weight.

"We found a body in Griffith Park. Not my client's son, but someone Colin knew." I paused. "It was bad, Jules."

Julie reached for my hand. "I can't imagine how hard that must have been." Her response was perfect, like perfect pho. She didn't try to change how I was feeling, or make things better. She didn't start a sentence with *oh well, at least* . . . She just held my hand. And the darkness lifted.

Now I was sorry I'd given Lobsang my noodles.

Wangdue touched my shoulder.

"Tenzing. I hear you say you find body. I must ask. Dead?"

"Yes," I said. "Dead."

"In park?"

"Yes."

Wangdue removed a string of carved sandalwood prayer beads coiled around his right wrist. He cupped the beads in both hands, as if weighing their worth.

"I chant for him," Wangdue said. He closed his eyes. His lips moved as he fed the beads from hand to hand. I knew what he was doing. He was keeping count of his mantras. The more you recited, the closer you were to achieving Buddha mind. He was probably as obsessed with his stats as Fran.

I shifted in my seat.

Self-righteous jerk.

I caught myself and had to smile. Judgmental mind is right up there with comparing mind when it comes to obstructing one's path to ease.

Yeshe was directly across from me. He sent me his own smile, one of deep affection, as if he'd both observed and understood this entire sequence of responses.

We had spent over a decade side by side in the prayer hall at Dorje Yidam, wrestling with the maddening parade of hindrances to tranquility.

I rolled my eyes and his smile widened.

"Show him your hat, Yeshe," Julie said. Yeshe rummaged inside his cloth bag and pulled out a blue Dodger cap.

"Martha brought them to Yeshe and Lobsang today," Julie said. "Courtesy of your ex-partner."

"Leave it to Bill." Bill was more enthusiastic than ever for the team, now that new ownership was firmly in place.

Yeshe pulled the cap on. He flashed me a hand sign, middle fingers bent, pinkie, forefinger, and thumb up. He looked so pleased—I hated to burst his bubble, but common sense prevailed.

"Yeshe, where did you learn that?"

"Man on street today. He wearing blue cap like mine, and shirt with Dodger name on front. I smile at him. He make sign like this. Is for Dodgers, yes? Dodger mudra!"

"Not exactly."

My early beat had included East Los Angeles, and I was well versed in the hand tags flashed by local gangs. Weirdly, Yeshe was right. They did resemble mudras. Unfortunately their purpose was to wreak havoc, not protect against it.

"Do me a favor, Yeshe. Don't try that when you're driving around Pasadena, okay?" That was all we needed—Yeshe getting mistaken for a member of the Pasadena Latin Kings.

"Ten," TJ called from the front corner of the table. "Why you not tell me I have my own store? Trader Joe. TJ. Get it? TJ! Like me!"

I could barely muster a smile. I was suddenly exhausted—the hindrance of torpor, lowering its elephantine trunk. I'd been up since three in the morning. Tomorrow would be more of the same, with several transatlantic calls to make.

I caught Sonam's eye.

"Geshe, I need to talk to you about some things," I said. "Soon."

"Of course. Tonight?"

"Not tonight. I'll come by the gallery tomorrow."

Julie gave me a look.

"That's a promise," I told both of them.

Wangdue's fingers danced through the sandalwood beads. His eyes never opened and his lips never stopped moving. But I felt him listening just the same.

Chapter 34

I ascend the tower stairs, my steps feather light.

The round room at the top is spacious and filled with a luminous glow. A man in a golden robe stands directly across from me, looking out a circular window. A portal.

I step inside.

The man turns. His face is thin and drawn, but full of peace.

"Apa?"

My father points to something resting against a wall.

A sky blue suitcase.

CHAPTER 35

My throat throbbed, pulses of blood coursing through the carotids. Julie lay still, her breath steady.

I bolted from bed. A container, I needed a container.

Laundry hamper.

I dumped rumpled T-shirts, boxers, and jeans on the floor and carried the empty wicker cube into the living room, using my elbow to flick on the light switch. I stepped behind the paneled divider and set the hamper by the altar.

In went the Buddha and the Green Tara. The picture of my mother as a young woman, in love with my father and high on nothing stronger than pheromones. The red-tailed hawk feather, the dried lavender and sage, the whorled shell, the mangled bullet. The program from John D's memorial service. The faded photograph of Kim and her brother, his young arm protective around her small shoulders.

The altar was empty. Now for the maroon cloth. Faint lines of dust marked where the robe hung over the planked corners. I tugged it off and shook the dark red rectangle. Powdery particles danced.

I held the zhen to my nose. It smelled faintly musty, but that was it. I'd expected more. This robe had wrapped itself around years of joy and resistance, friendship and dread. My young lungs had learned how to breathe inside this robe. My heart had learned how to break.

I pleated and folded until the zhen formed a plump burgundy square. I set it on top of the spiritual bits and pieces. It reminded me of yesterday's robe, a cushion for the bloody dagger.

I hope I'm ready for this.

The redwood top to my makeshift altar was still a source of pride—two wide planks, sanded smooth, planed, and glued together using tongue-and-groove joinery. I had constructed the covering my first fall living in Topanga, reincarnating scraps from the deck I'd also built, off the kitchen.

I ran my hand across the planks. Still no cracks or buckles. My work had held together well.

I lifted the top from the frame and leaned it against the wall. The suitcase was underneath. Waiting.

Hard-sided, light blue, no wheels. A hard vinyl handle and two brass clasps for locks. Maybe 20 inches wide, a little over a foot high, and 6 or 7 inches deep. I rubbed my thumb across the word *Starlite*, affixed below the right-hand latch.

This suitcase had traveled with me between Dharamshala and Paris year after year, holding my belongings, and sometimes a secret or two. The clasps locked and a pair of inner side pockets zipped closed. To my young mind, this made invasion harder for prying eyes and fingers.

Why had I continued to keep it, I now wondered? The key was long since lost. Unlike my duffel, it was a remnant of my past that no longer held any purpose. But it had been my mother's, long ago. And something in me hadn't wanted to part with her Starlite suitcase, even when I was leaving everything else behind.

I snapped open the brass fasteners. The satin lining had once been dark blue, but time had perverted the color to a liverish purple. I sniffed. The nylon material smelled faintly of lemon-lime. The hint of citrus teased out a memory.

She sits at her bedroom vanity. She is staring into the oval mirror, but I can tell she's not seeing see her own face. My mother's dress is pretty, all the colors swirled together like finger-paints, orange and green and blue. She opens a side drawer and sticks her hand inside. I hear clinking. She pulls out a bright yellow bottle. She stands up to face me. She waves her arm in a circle spraying a misty cloud into the air. She scrunches her eyes closed and walks straight through the mist. My eyes sting. A sharp smell hits my

nose. Like lemons, only sweeter. My mother's smell—I never knew where it came from.

"What is that?" I ask.

"Eau de Cologne," Valerie says. "Jean Naté. It reminds me of my grandmother." *Her voice sounds different, not mad, but something else.*

"You have a grandmother?"

"Had," she says. "No more questions, Tenzing, okay?"

I winced at the memory. I should have taken my cue from the tone in her voice.

How could you know? You were only seven years old.

Still . . .

She'd gone straight from the bedroom to the cabinet where she stored her wine . . .

I unzipped the pocket on the right-hand side. Reaching inside, my fingers grasped something soft. I fished out a crumpled Kleenex, so old it dissolved into shreds at my touch. I set the wisps of tissue aside. I felt again. Nothing else in there.

The pocket on the left bulged in a more promising way.

Breathe, Tenzing. Breathe.

The white handkerchief was bandaged around something hard and odd shaped, all curves and angles with a neck, like a swan. The hankie was stained here and there with yellowish marks, as if invisible patches of impurity had darkened over time. I unwrapped the cotton with care. My fingers felt clumsy and leaden.

The small metal pot had a narrow protruding spout and an ornate feathered topper. All the surfaces were inscribed with elaborate symbols—at least it seemed that way. The beaten silver had oxidized over time and the rounded bowl and arched neck were almost black. I rubbed my thumb against the smoky tarnish, but the surface remained stubbornly opaque. I moved on to the topper. A thin strip of

brocade bound three miniature peacock feathers together. They jutted from the narrow cone that served as a plug for the pot.

Bumpa. That was the word for this ceremonial vase. Bumpa.

I removed the feathered sprinkler and tipped the vase to the light. The pot was empty. I sniffed. Closed my eyes, and inhaled again, more deeply. The heady bouquet separated into specific strands of smell. Saffron and juniper, the warm kiss of sandalwood and sharp bite of camphor. Stale ghee, and a flicker of molasses.

For the second time this morning, a potent scent from the past acted as a catapult. For the second time, I was flung backwards in time to my habitual role of spectator, bearing witness to a ritualistic deed.

I am with Nawang in his private quarters—he is special so he gets to sleep in his own room. I like watching him get ready for his acts of puja. He walks in a circle, sprinkling the scented water here and there. He says he is ridding his world of impurities. The peacock feathers and special nectar turn ignorance and craving and hatred into wisdom. Now he puts the bumpa back on his altar. He stands before the thangka and takes refuge in the Buddha, the dharma, and the sangha. He starts his 100 prostrations. My job is to count. Legs behind, trunk down, forehead to the floor, arch up, back to his feet. One. Legs, trunk, forehead, arch, feet. Two. Three. Four. His body moves like he doesn't have any bones. Like a snake.

The hammered silver vase had grown warm in my hands. More moments with Nawang pressed forward, clamoring for attention. As if this tarnished bumpa were some kind of key, unlocking a hidden compartment that had imprisoned vital events for decades. Only yesterday, Eric had suggested such a compartment existed. Today, the door was thrown wide open.

I closed my eyes.
Allow.

The memories surged:

Nawang, rescuing me from confusion, my 11-year-old body changing and growing faster than my understanding of sexual things.

Nawang, urging me to talk to the beautiful village girl Pema, my attraction to her so powerful it tied my tongue.

Nawang, talking about the powerful goddess Viswamata.

Nawang, debating with me in the courtyard, tapping my forehead, *tok*! Propelling me into a wild dance with infinity.

Nawang, wearing my shoes and hoodie, his arm raised, stabbing . . .

My mind slammed shut. Dense confusion swirled in its place.

A sudden craving for a cold beer sliced through the fog, almost painful. It was either far too late or far too early to drink, but my brain didn't care. The need was absolute.

A telephone rang, a clanging summons. *Wake up!* it said, and I did. A deep breath was all I needed, all it took to wedge the smallest of gaps between thought and action, reminding me alcohol was not the cure.

My poor mother had never understood that creating the gap was everything.

I placed the blackened silver *bumpa* on top of the folded robe and hurried to my desk to answer what I saw was a call from the London Metropolitan Police.

"DCI Garfield, hello. You got my text."

"Yes."

"Sorry I wasn't more specific. This felt like something we should discuss voice to voice."

He said nothing.

"A body turned up in Griffith Park yesterday. Not Colin's, but I believe the death may be related to your case."

"Griffith Park. I've heard of that. It's quite sizeable, is it not?"

"Yes, over four thousand acres, some of them fairly inaccessible. We found the body in a somewhat remote canyon."

"I see."

"We're waiting for the autopsy report, but the circumstances were unusual and very suspicious." I pictured the stabs and incisions, the stripped skin and missing eyes. "The death, whatever caused it, was violent in nature."

"You said it might be related to Lord Purdham-Coote's son?"

"Yes. I wanted to talk to you right away, because I believe I recognized the young man. I saw two photographs of him on Colin's Facebook page, the last two before he stopped posting. They may have even traveled here together. The victim is dark complexioned, black hair, perhaps of Indian descent, approximately the same age . . ."

"Paresh Kapoor," Garfield said. "Pee, Ay, Arr . . ."

"I've got it, thanks." I wrote down the names, both fairly common in India.

"Right. Well, your suspicion is well founded. If it is Paresh Kapoor, he was on the same flight from Heathrow."

"You're sure?"

"Yes. He was on the passenger manifest, and we received confirmation from your end that he entered the country as a tourist. During the course of our follow-up inquiries, we also made the social media connection with Purdham-Coote via Facebook. Kapoor wasn't at Cambridge. He attended a regional college nearby, in Peterborough. We believe they met shortly after the new term began."

"Family?"

"Both parents dead, killed in a car accident on the A1 two years ago. They were en route to visiting him, poor sod. One older sibling, a brother, Mihir Kapoor. He moved to Mumbai five years back to join a digital start-up company." Garfield's voice hardened. "Made sure to tell me at least three times that he went to Oxford. They don't seem to be close. In fact, when we finally made contact with the brother, he admitted he hadn't spoken to Paresh since the parents' funeral."

No parents, and an older brother who was both arrogant and uncommunicative. Paresh Kapoor must have felt so lost. A lonely, vulnerable boy, hungering for validation of his own

worth, for simple answers to life's hardest questions. An easy target for a beautiful guru promising both.

I gave DCI Garfield Bill's name and number. He promised to get in touch with the older brother to facilitate confirmation of the identity. I painted the broad strokes of what led us to finding Kapoor. Assuming it was Kapoor.

"So you were responsible for tracking down the body?"

"In a way."

"Good work, Detective."

His praise was sweet, flowing, as it did, from New Scotland Yard.

I made two more calls, first to Lord Purdham-Coote and then to Bertie Andrews. The Purdham-Cootes had heard nothing more from Colin, and as I suspected, my report caused both relief and dread.

Bertie did have something interesting to add.

"I went back to Cambridge yesterday, poked around a bit more," he said. "One of his classmates recalled seeing Collie and an Indian bloke walking out've a round church on Bridge Street, a few days before he went missing."

"A round church?"

"Not a, the. That's what it's called. The Round Church."

"But it's an actual place of worship?"

"Yeah, well, not anymore. Visitor center now. Built ages ago, maybe a thousand years give or take, but the fellow in charge said it was considered holy ground even before then. We're talking bleedin' druids, you know, like Stonehenge. And something else. According to him, the place is crawling with ley lines. You heard of them?"

"Yes."

"I figured. Load of rubbish. Anyway, he remembered Collie and the Kapoor kid. Said they spent over an hour just walking around. Hard to do. Place is no bigger than a snail shell."

"Anything else?"

"No. Except they asked to go into the tower."

The tower.

"I see. And did you?"

"Climb the bell tower? Nah. Fuckin' druid bollocks."

I waited.

"What?"

"Nothing. Just, I wish you'd checked out the tower. Call it a hunch."

A metal lighter snapped, followed by a deep suck of breath. Bertie's exhale must have let loose a billowing cloud of nicotine. "Ah hell. Sometimes a hunch is all we got, innit? I'll take another look-see."

After the call, I sat thinking for some time. But wherever I aimed my attention, it kept looping back to my dream tower and the man inside it.

I started a fresh page on the legal pad.

1. *Nawang*

What was his last name?

Gephel, that was it. *Nawang Gephel. The possessive one* and *builder of merit.*

A chill ran up my spine.

The possessive one.

CHAPTER 36

Julie stumbled into the living room, her eyelids at half-mast, and moved behind the standing screen. She reappeared, a small furrow between her eyebrows. She spotted me and the frown line smoothed.

"Oh," she said.

"Morning, Jules."

"What happened to your meditation room? Are you moving somewhere?"

"Long story."

Julie blinked a few times, one foot still firmly planted in sleep consciousness.

"Maybe you should go back to bed, love."

"Can't. Too much to do."

"In that case, the coffee pot's primed and ready to go."

"Bless you." She shuffled off. Julie was not a morning person, good for a chef, not so good for other things. She crawled into consciousness every morning like the first amphibian emerging from the primordial ooze.

I returned to the list.

1. *Nawang Gephel*

I was now fairly certain Nawang existed, but frustrating pockets of memory remained sewn shut. This made me think at least some trauma was involved. Still, my work with Eric had led to last night's dream, which in turn had finally unearthed something concrete.

I elaborated:

2. *What did N. do?*

3. *Where did N. go?*

4. *Maha Mudra*

I added a short list of questions for Geshe Sonam and another list for Yeshe and Lobsang.

I returned to Maha Mudra and underlined the name. More than anything, I needed to locate this woman. Finding her meant finding Colin and Nawang, I was more and more convinced.

So I had at least two more people to trace, besides Colin. Either or both had information I needed. Either or both were of primary interest.

They were sure to be elusive, and running them to ground should have felt daunting. Not for me. I felt energized. My adrenal glands might be thumb-size, but once they start pumping out cortisol, beware.

Fran had Shirley Bones. But I had Mike Koenigs, and I'd put his cyber-tracking skills up against any nose, canine or otherwise. I checked the time. Five A.M. equaled dinnertime for Mike, which meant interrupting a meal of pepperoni pizza and several cans of Red Bull.

The house filled with the rich aroma of brewing coffee. My insides whimpered. Before I could move a muscle, Julie set a steaming mug on my desk.

"I could kiss you. In fact . . ."

But Julie had already moved onto the sofa with her own mug. Her hair was a tousled mess. She was wearing an old T-shirt of mine, and the threadbare hem barely covered her thighs. Her breasts pressed against the thin cotton. My groin tingled to life.

She blew across the steam, took a tentative sip, and raised her head.

The rims of her eyes were swollen and red.

"What is it? What's wrong?"

"Everything!" She set down the coffee and covered her face with her hands. Her shoulders shook. Homer waddled out of the bedroom. He tried to climb the sofa, but his barreled body wasn't up to the job. He pawed uselessly.

Tank arrived next. He assessed the situation. Three feet up? No problem. He leapt lightly and stuck a perfect landing next to Julie.

I tugged some Kleenex from the box on my desk. "Here."

Julie accepted the Kleenex, but she kept crying. I stood by the sofa, feeling helpless. Finally, I lifted Homer onto the end of the sofa. Tank abandoned ship as a matter of principle, so I took his spot. I put my arm around Julie.

"What's going on?" I said.

"Nothing. I just, I hate my life!"

Oh. I wanted to contradict her, but I knew better. She had just presented me with an unarguable truth.

"Every dress I've tried on makes me look like a fat meringue, and I'm tired of not making any money, and, and, my fucking lawyer finally called but I can't even talk with you about it because suddenly you can't stand to be around me, and it all just sucks!"

She honked into a tissue.

"Jules."

She held up her hand. "Not yet. I need to talk to you about something else. It has to do with us."

"Okay," I said. But I didn't feel okay. I felt trapped in a brutal tug of war between Mr. Fight and Mr. Flee.

"You know how you get out of bed early in the morning and leave? Like this morning?"

"Julie, I'm really sorry, it's just that I can't . . ."

"Ten, I need to tell you this before I lose my nerve. Please, just listen. Do that breathing thing if you need to, but let me finish."

Good advice. I took a deep breath in. Let it out slowly. My lungs reminded my brain that whatever was coming, they, at least, remained committed to keeping me alive.

"It's just, sometimes I feel relieved. I like sleeping with you, I mean, I love it, most of the time. But sometimes I feel like everything's just gotten too . . . crowded—with you, and me, and Tank, and even Homer. Like there's not enough room for me to just . . . be." She shook her head. "Crap! Just saying this makes my stomach hurt. I'm scared to death you'll, you know . . ."

I finished the sentence for her. "Freak out? Want to leave you? Call off the wedding?"

"Yes. Yes!"

"Not gonna happen," I said.

"It's not? Are you sure?" She looked down. "It's happened before."

I pulled her closer. "Hey, it's okay to need space," I said. "It doesn't mean we don't love each other."

Homer chose that moment to crawl onto Julie. His considerable weight spilled over both sides of her lap. He groaned with pleasure.

She shook her head. "What are we going to do with us?"

"Figure it out," I said. "Or not."

She gave me a watery smile. "The good news is I feel ten pounds lighter inside."

"The confession diet. Those suckers called secrets weigh a lot."

I felt closer to her than I had in weeks.

"So, not to bring up a sore subject," I said, "but what did your lawyer say?"

"Same ol' same ol'. There are suddenly a bunch more forms to fill out. More permits needed. More regulations, this time from the county."

"So that's okay then. That means it's just a matter of time."

"I guess."

Julie set Homer on the floor. She circled her knees with her arms. I reached underneath the flimsy cotton to stroke the arched bow of her spine, running my thumb down the bumps of her vertebrae, top to bottom, until I reached the

base, where the Kundalini snake sleeps. I pressed firmly on the curved tip of bone.

"Mmm. That feels amazing."

I rested my palm there, cupping the nest of energy.

"Spending this time with the monks has been . . ." Julie turned her head to me. "They're like kids, you know? Everything they do is a form of play. Well, maybe not Wangdue, he's Mr. Serious, but Yeshe and TJ, for sure." She smiled. "Even Lobsang. He likes to pretend otherwise, but his heart is as open as they come. They find such joy in their work. I'd almost forgotten what that felt like."

I nodded. I knew the feeling.

"I watched them building a work of art out of nothing but tiny grains of sand and I felt this peace, this contentment. Then my lawyer called, and bam, the anxiety hit. Worse than anxiety, actually. Dread. Because it's not going to stop with the permits, you know?"

"What do you mean?"

"I've worked in restaurants my entire adult life. Who am I fooling? Say I do get the permits, and the financing. Say we do find a site. Say I do open next year. Then what? There'll be the same insanity happening on a daily basis that always happens in restaurants. The only difference is, it'll be my insanity to deal with, even when it isn't mine. That's what being a chef-owner means. Crisis management all day, every day. Forget having a life or a family. Forget cooking, even. I'll be lucky if I get to boil an egg."

I could see her point. Julie had more kitchen stories of aberrant behaviors and dangerous loonies than I did, and I'd worked in Burglary/Homicide for over eight years.

"Whatever," Julie said. "I've already spent thousands of dollars to get to this point. It's a little late to have doubts."

I searched for the right thing to say.

What would I want to hear? Then I recalled a time when I was just as stuck, and the words that helped me make a shift.

"What does your heart truly long for, Julie?"

"It's not that simple, Yoda."

"Maybe it is. Come on. It's worth a try."

She nodded. She closed her eyes. "Ask me again?"

"What does your heart truly long for?"

She rotated her shoulders back and forth, and her neck side to side. Finally, she was still.

I waited.

"I want to cook food I love for people I love, or at least don't hate," she said. "To have fun with it again. The freedom to make spontaneous, mind-blowing art with my cooking."

She opened her eyes.

"Sounds like part of you isn't confused at all."

"Great. So what am I supposed to do now?"

I kissed her cheek.

"Do that," I said.

CHAPTER 37

"Hey, Mike. Can you talk?"

"Dude, we were just about to crash," he grumbled.

"It shouldn't take long."

"Whenever you say that, I worry."

"Ten minutes maximum, I promise."

It took 25, but most of that was Mike's fault. He wanted to hear details about the hypnotherapy, and exactly how the recurring nightmare was in fact my unconscious mind waving a desperate flag.

"That's so dope," he said.

I added *dope* to my list of Koenigs terminology, although I wasn't sure whether it meant good, bad, or insane. Most of the adjectives he used were open to multiple interpretations.

"So this long-lost brother of yours. Nawang. His last name Norbu?"

"No. It's Gephel, I'm pretty sure. Can I get back to you on that?"

"No problem. And Maha Mudra? Just a wild guess—that's not her real name."

"Probably not."

He waited, but I had nothing else to add.

"You don't have a clue in the world who she is, do you?" he asked.

"No. I wish I did."

"Okay, well, I'll start with her. Especially if she's still here in Los Angeles. Someone's bound to know something."

"I'll text you whatever else I can find out about Nawang. I'm sure to have more after meeting with Sonam."

Mike covered his mouthpiece to have a muffled conversation.

"You're in luck, boss. Tricia's heard of the Mudra chick. Says our friend's been to one of Maha Mudra's concerts."

"Satsang," I heard.

"Satsang. Whatever the fuck that is."

"It's a Sanskrit term," I explained. "A satsang is like a social gathering, only spiritual. A devotional coming together."

"Whatever. We'll see if we can track her down. Our friend, I mean. Her name's Lia Pootah. You'll like her, she's cray. *Ciao.*"

Cray, meaning good? Bad? Insane?

I was betting on insane.

Before signing off, I encouraged Mike to grab a few hours of sleep before setting his digital hounds loose. Fatigue leads to stupid mistakes, and I didn't want either of us to make any.

Julie and Homer were on their way to Los Feliz. Again. As for me, I was tired, but also wired, a state that meant the adrenaline surge was alive and well and sleep would be impossible.

That said, I dreaded the digging process ahead of me. These shadowy events from the past had occupied the crap silo, as Eric so graphically put it, for a very long time. Their grip was sure to be tenacious and the act of uprooting them would be painful.

The whole thing was making me very grumpy.

I wandered into the kitchen. Three days' worth of mugs and dishes filled the sink and the garbage can was overflowing. What a mess, and Julie was MIA. Once again it was up to me to restore order.

I caught myself. Resentment was like any other mood-altering drug; indulging in it felt good—until it didn't.

I decided to make cleaning the house today's spiritual practice.

May I cultivate gratitude with my heart.

I dry- and wet-mopped all the floors, feeling the solid surface beneath my feet, counting breaths with every swipe

across the wood. I cleaned and emptied Tank's cat box, inviting appreciation for his healthy digestive system as I refilled the box with fresh litter. I pulled my damp clothing from the washing machine.

I am grateful for hot water. I am grateful for cleanliness.

I hung the clean laundry on the clothesline we'd strung between two poles outside, a householder's display of domestic prayer flags.

I am grateful for the sun.

I sorted through mail, putting bills to one side, shredding everything else. This had become part of Kim's job, but she wasn't due home for another week or two.

I am grateful for Kim.

I wasn't sure what to do about the deconstructed altar, so I left everything as it was in my meditation nook after mopping and dusting the exposed surfaces.

I am grateful for my path.

By 10:00 A.M. the house was returned to harmony and so was I—or I would be once I'd showered. I had stripped and was heading for the bathroom when the County Coroner's Office number showed up on my cell phone screen.

"Hello?"

"Ten? It's me."

My stomach tightened. I hadn't talked to Heather in more than a year, but I'd know her voice anywhere. The last I'd heard, she'd been on a leave of absence to deal with some health issues. A relapse of some sort, or so the rumor mill claimed. She'd confessed to a long battle with bulimia when we were together, and the thought that she might have lost another skirmish made me sad at the time.

"Hey, Heather. How are you?"

"Better, thanks. Day at a time, like everything else. You?"

"I'm doing well." I wasn't sure if she knew about my engagement to Julie, but now wasn't the time. "So, you're working weekends these days?"

"And weekdays. You know me."

Heather was a brilliant forensic pathologist, both driven and meticulous. She was also tall, blonde, and strikingly beautiful, genetically blessed with the kind of flawless looks

that turned heads, both male and female. We hadn't made a great match as lovers or as mates, but our hearts were always in the right place.

I am grateful for past loves, and for letting go.

I am grateful for Julie.

"I'm phoning you about the Griffith Park body, Ten. Bill was just here. He gave me the go-ahead to contact you. He thought you might want to know the initial autopsy results."

"I do. It's connected to a case I'm working on."

"Right, that's what he said."

"So you can tell me what killed him?"

"I can tell you more than 'what.' I can tell you 'who.'"

"How is that possible? Oh." I answered my own question. "He took his own life."

"Affirmative. It's a suicide. Probably one of the stranger suicides that's crossed my path, but I'm ninety-nine-point-nine-percent positive the wounds were self-inflicted. They're comparing his prints with those on the weapon as we speak, but there's no doubt in my mind."

"Can you hang on a second?"

I pulled on a cotton kimono and moved to my desk. I put the phone on speaker so I could take notes.

"Okay. I'm ready for specifics."

"You sure about that?"

"I already saw the body, Heather."

"Right. I knew that. Okay, so, I've ruled the official cause of death as exsanguination due to multiple sharp-force injuries sustained from self-inflicted puncture and incised wounds, consistent with a curved knife."

My pen flew across the pad. "Exsanguination. Loss of blood, in other words."

"Massive loss of blood. There were . . ." She paused. "There were ten knife wounds in all, including a vertical incised wound along the underside of each forearm from elbow to wrist, longitudinal axis blah, blah you-don't-need-to-know-that . . . Two horizontal slashes across the left upper thigh, two puncture or chop wounds to the calf and the same on the right, a pair of longitudinal cuts across the thigh, and two stabs to the calf. The circular carvings on his chest and

stomach area were more like scratches—insignificant in terms of actual damage. And finally, there was the additional removal of several strips of epidermis."

"Can you tell which knife wounds came first?'

"Either the chest and stomach or the thighs and lower legs. They were shallow enough to cause great pain, but not fatal."

"But the arm wounds were. Fatal."

"Eventually, but here's where it gets interesting. He managed to implement two fairly deep arm wounds while avoiding any major veins or arteries. Not easy to do, especially when using his weaker hand to cut the right arm."

"He was right-handed?"

"Best guess. I don't like to speculate, but the wounds were self-inflicted, and the directionality is clear."

"So . . ." I tried to picture what had happened. "So, he took off his robe, folded it, put it under the bush, took off his hiking boots and laid them next to the robe, scratched a circle on his chest and stomach, cut his thighs, stabbed and skinned his calves, made a deep slice down his right arm with his left hand, and then another down his left arm with his right, placed the knife on the robe, danced around barefoot on the dirt, lay down, positioned himself in a symbolic pose of power, and bled to death."

"Can't confirm the dancing or the pose. He was past rigor when they brought him in. I can confirm that he was lying on his back when he died, and nobody moved him to or from there, before or after. Livor mortis was fixed, though not pronounced. The rest of your description sounds about right."

"And the time of death?"

"Everybody's favorite question. I can give you an approximation. It's always trickier when there's exposure to heat and other elements. But the cold core temperature, combined with the lack of stiffness and early stages of decomp, indicates he's been dead approximately thirty-six hours."

"A day and a half?"

"Give or take. But not much longer than that. I'd say forty hours, max."

"Any particular reason?"

"Coyotes. Hawks. I'm betting the next round of carrion eaters were closing in from all directions when you found him. Once they arrive, its circle-of-life time. Bye-bye soft tissue, hello, skeletal remains."

"Jhator," I said, realizing.

"What?"

"Jhator. Sky burial. It's a traditional Tibetan Buddhist burial method. Once the individual's consciousness enters the bardo state, the physical body is readied for excarnation and left out in the open. It's a final act of generosity—providing sustenance to other sentient beings."

"Wow. Like becoming at one with nature?"

"That's a little lofty. More like becoming a snack."

"How common is the procedure?"

"Well, it's still around, but barely. As a burial technique, jhator has become largely replaced by cremation. The Chinese positively hate the practice."

"For sanitary reasons?"

"Political. Historically, invading nations merge with those they overtake. China prefers obliteration. So sky burials have gone underground, excuse the pun."

I mentally compared what I knew about jhator with the crime scene.

"Not everything jibes," I said. "Most sky burials in Tibet take place on a flat rock, called a mandala, which has been transported, along with the body, to as high a point as possible. A mountaintop, for example, or a cliff. Whatever terrain overlooks the surrounding areas.

"So by snack, you mean Clif Bar?"

"Good one."

We shared an amused moment. Heather's wit was alive and well.

"I've missed you," Heather said. "This."

In the awkward silence that followed, I did a gut check and found, to my relief, that I didn't. Now was the moment to mention Julie.

I let it pass.

Heather's voice was light. "Moving on, you were saying? Most sky burials are up high?"

"Yes. But this corpse was in a gulley, partially under a bush. Still, the number and placement of the wounds fit the sky-burial pattern. *Approximately* fit, to use your favorite word. Thankfully."

"Why?"

"Well, the completed procedure results in a major disassembling of the flesh. To make things easier for the vultures."

"Charming."

"Yup. The *rogyapas* pretty much strip the body of all its parts, like a stolen car in a chop shop."

"Rogyapas," Heather said, as if tasting the word.

"Body breakers. They're very adept at dismemberment. Actually, you would make a good rogyapa, Heather."

"No comment."

"Anyway, thirty-six to forty hours puts time of death at . . ." I counted back, "Wednesday night? Approximately?"

"Correct."

Pancake night at our house. Paresh Kapoor had only been in Los Angeles for two days.

"Can you send me the final report?"

"Sure, in a few weeks. Toxicology is backed up, as usual."

"Right. The datura plant."

"The alkaloids weren't what killed him, but they might have made the ride more interesting. Anything else I can help you with?"

"No." The thought rose again—*I should mention Julie.* I let it float away. "Thanks so much, Heather. This was really helpful."

"No worries. Anything for an ex-boyfriend. An ex, engaged-to-be-married, spineless-when-it-comes-to-talking-about-certain-things boyfriend."

"Heather . . ."

"Body breaker, my ass." And she hung up, laughing.

Chapter 38

I walked outside to the deck. Heather and I had smoked a joint here. Shared our first kiss here. Exchanged a few truths and a few more lies here. Talked. Talked some more. Talked endlessly, struggling to make things work. The fact that endless communication never led to actual connection should have been a clue.

A motorcycle downshifted, shifted again—the back-stitched hum of a fine-tuned machine; someone nearby was riding into the day, rubber side down.

Someone on a high-end luxury machine.

Sharp gravel bit into the soles of my feet as I pounded down the driveway to the mailbox, kimono flapping.

The steep ribbon of Topanga Canyon Boulevard was empty in both directions.

I listened, my ribs heaving. A distant, mosquito-like whine was all that remained of the motorcycle's presence. Dropping to my knees, I scoured the ground, where asphalt and gravel met the soft, grassy shoulder.

Were those tracks? I couldn't really tell.

I opened the mailbox as if it held a scorpion.

A white envelope awaited, my name on the front in block letters. Flap unsealed. Plump with something, but nothing good.

I opened the envelope. A small vial of dark red fluid was capped with a black screw-top lid. I closed the envelope. Maybe I'd get lucky. Maybe the glass surface had retained prints.

Can't breathe! Can't . . .

Another voice broke in. *Yes. You can.*

The iron clamp around my lungs loosened.

That's it . . . That's it . . .

I gulped hot air. The sun had burned off any remaining fog. But as I walked up the drive, I was shivering.

A scanned photo attachment from DSI Garfield awaited me on the computer.

I printed it out. The blurred forms of the female guru and her band of followers were almost impossible to decode. But the image gave me an idea.

This time, Dave Smith answered my call.

"Smith here."

"Corporal? Ten Norbu."

"I know. Says on the phone."

"How are you doing, sir?"

"Fuckin' balls out, thanks." He sighed. "How the hell do you think I'm doin'? Lungs don't work, my leg that I don't got anymore aches, and I can't see for shit."

"I'm sorry."

"Yeah, well, it is what it is."

"I have a favor to ask you."

He said nothing.

"When I drove down last week, there was a flier on the bulletin board in the front lobby of your building. I'm wondering if you could check if it's still there."

"Oh," he said. "I thought maybe . . ."

"What?"

"I thought maybe you was calling about the kids. You know . . ." His voice hardened. "Why should I lift a finger for you? All you did was open me up to a world of hurt."

I considered his words. "If you hurt, that means you still care. Corporal Smith, I promise the next time I get a chance, I'll put in a word to Kim and Bobby." I didn't extend it to a "good" word, but maybe just a word would be enough.

He cleared his throat. "What you want me to do now?"

"If the flier's still there, I could use your help telling me what's on it."

"What kind of flier?"

"It's got a picture of an Indian woman on it, and a website on the bottom, I think. What I need is any contact information."

"Call me back in ten," he said. "I gotta strap on my leg."

I gave him 15, using the time to study the smudged form of Maha Mudra for clues, as if staring might sharpen her edges.

Even so, he was gasping for breath when he answered.

"Corporal Smith? Do you need more time?"

"Nah. I got it right here. Hang on." Something crashed. A distant *"Shit!"*

"Okay, I'm back."

"Everything all right?"

"Had to get my headlamp out of the closet. My eyes aren't what they used to be." He was still breathing hard. "She some kind of Muslim or something?"

"I don't think so. I don't really know, actually."

"Reason I ask, there's no phone number, but there's one of those website links on the bottom. And a picture of something purple, looks like a mosque."

"A purple mosque?" My heart rate sped up. "Could it be an onion?"

He wheezed through a few breaths. "Yeah. Maybe."

No wonder Maha Mudra was hard to trace. She hid out in the dark web. On Tor, otherwise known as The Onion Router. Where people with secrets liked to live. "Can you give me the website?"

"Lemme . . . hang on, I've got a magnifying glass somewhere." More silence. "Okay. It says 'info at W W W dot R J R P R T R T dot com. That's all. Plus the onion."

I wrote it down. The letters meant nothing to me. I sent Mike a quick text with the link. Use tor, I typed.

"Corporal Smith, I can't tell you how much this helps."

"Any time," he said. "Feels good to be useful, you wanna know the truth. What's all this about?"

"There's a young man missing, and a father out there hoping to get him back."

Silence.

"Corporal?"

"We took this gook prisoner one time. Just a kid. Hell, we were all just kids. Anyway, he spoke a little English. Enough to tell us all about something called karma. Ever heard of it?"

"Yes."

"I did some awful things over there. Picked up a lot of bad karma. Weighs on a man, you know?" His voice trailed off.

"But not today," I said. "Today, you let some of that weight go."

CHAPTER 39

The sound reached me first. Metallic scraping, like copper cricket wings.

Yeshe, TJ, and Lobsang huddled on the floor around the mandala blueprint. They had tied white scarves around their faces, makeshift masks to protect their lungs from any loose particles of sand. They looked like holy bandits.

Scrape scrape scrape.

Each monk held a silver funnel-shaped cone, called a chak-pur. They'd positioned the narrow ends over a curved quadrant of the mandala blueprint, which was sketched directly onto a framed board. Grasping thin metal rods in their right hands, they grazed the length of the serrated cones as if they were grating cheese. Particles of colored sand flowed from the tips like liquid sapphires, filling in the rimmed circumference with a steady stream of cobalt blue.

About 30 onlookers observed in the gallery auditorium, some watching with their eyes, others through their phones. Julie and Homer were nowhere to be seen, but she'd texted me that she might take him for a waddle around the Rose Bowl.

Scrape scrape scrape.

I'd missed my favorite element of the ceremony, yesterday's drafting of the design. Using rulers, compasses, white-leaded pencils, and an elastic chalk line, they laid down the intricate measurements by memory. Each *pop* of the stretched string not only left behind a guiding line of chalk, but also acted as a mindful alert to stay conscious of the profound nature of their activity. The process could take hours or days, depending on the size of the mandala.

Once the blueprint satisfied the senior monk in charge—in this case, Lobsang—the chalk was brushed away, leaving behind a detailed penciled outline. All that remained was to fill in the lines with brilliant hues, as in a child's coloring book. But in this case, rather than a unicorn or a butterfly, the final representation depicted an aspect of Buddhist cosmography powerful enough to tip the world on its axis.

Scrape scrape.

Yeshe pushed to his feet and arched and straightened his stiff spine. I waggled my fingers, and his eyes crinkled above his white mask. I smiled back. He moved to an oblong table set in the corner, where bowls of colored sand glittered. He tapped out a few loose blue grains, dipped the funnel into a bowl of brilliant orange, and returned to the mandala to kneel and abrade once again.

The process was painstaking and had been for thousands of years—ancient designs taking meticulous shape, accompanied by the steady rasp of rods against funnels. The result was a flawless depiction of compassion, or healing, or some other universal truth. Then, in an act of mindful sabotage, the offering was swept away, a reminder that perfection, like everything else in this world, was impermanent.

No wonder people found them spellbinding.

I moved closer to study the central image of this mandala. Nested within a square formed by orange, yellow, maroon, and white triangles was a central chamber, a perfect circle made up of all four colors. Inside were two shapes: a cobalt blue vajra, or scepter, and to the left of it, a round red dot.

I let my mind drift back to an earlier time. Scepter and orb, scepter and orb.

Of course, they represented archetypal Buddhas, the masculine and the feminine. I looked closer, and saw that yes, the chamber rested on a bed of eight lotus petals holding eight more dots of color—the eight Shakti goddesses, generators of the compassionate and enlightened heart.

Building outward, delicate white lines awaiting their filler of color marked an intricate path. Eight, twelve, twenty-eight petaled lotuses, upon which deities danced, but always around the central couple. At the circumference, there was a repeated pattern of seed syllables—mantras associated with the planets, the solar and lunar mansions, and infinite space and time. This outermost rim of perfection was critical—it protected the divine community within, 722 entities in total, all emanating from the central image of male and female, scepter and orb.

I was looking at the building blocks of a Kalachakra Mandala: concentric circles moving outward, depicting earth, water, fire, air, and space. The shapes and symbols created a visionary map of the subtlest states of enlightenment. Kalachakra, and his consort Vishvamata, together embodied the highest form of Buddhahood; omniscient, omnipresent, all-powerful. And any bodhisattva who followed the Kalachakra path could expect nothing less than total transformation, inside and out. Or so I had been taught.

The Kalachakra Mandala: my friends were constructing a visual ode to universal tantric power.

Wangdue was manning another table, a movable store loaded with Tibetan treats—prayer beads, altar cloths, CDs, even packets of prayer flags the size of playing cards. He was busy making change for a woman with a substantial mound of purchases. In the clash between nonattachment and attachment, the latter had won hands down.

She moved away, happily clutching her treasures.

"Lama Wangdue, do you know where I can find Geshe Sonam?"

"Chanting." Wangdue gestured to a curtained area. I could just make out the hem of a red robe.

"Thanks."

Sonam sat in a folding chair in front of a small tray table. On it rested the chant master's three basic tools: scepter, handbell, and chants. His dorje was maybe three inches in length and shaped like an hourglass. Small, given that it

represented the indestructible state of absolute reality. His drilbu, or handbell, was twice as big.

But the real power lay in the stack of Tibetan termas, the sacred texts that imbued every ceremony with import. Without these teachings, an event like today's was just monks playing with sand.

Sonam moved his lips in silent concentration, eyes lowered to the rectangular, yellowed manuscript covered in rows of delicately hand-pressed characters.

He raised his eyes, sensing my presence.

"Lama Tenzing. Come, come! Sit with me!"

"I'm not disturbing you?"

"Our enlightened teachers have been listening to these mantras since the beginning of time. I'm sure they welcome any break from the endless entreaties." Sonam leaned close, a glint in his eye. "As do I."

I moved a second chair across from him and sat. Anxiety collected at the back of my tongue like rust. I cleared my throat.

"You are worried about something?" Sonam's voice was gentle.

"Yes."

"Many things?"

"Yes. I can't make sense out of certain events. Certain memories. I need to know what happened, if I'm right about them."

"Just so. You are suffering, because you are looking for labels." A statement, not a question.

"What do you mean?"

"All negative emotion is the result of labeling. Of looking for a single definition, a final answer. We love to find meaning, to put importance on each moment. But everything is interdependent." He wagged his finger. "Nothing is singular, or permanent, Tenzing. Except for impermanence."

"But my fears seem so real."

"They are. Because you make them so." Sonam spread his hands. "But also not-real. The component that determines

whether you have a pleasant or unpleasant experience is the same now as when the Buddha first taught. Come, Lama Tenzing. You remember this, surely? The root of all suffering?"

"Grasping?"

"Just so. Grasping. But grasping only makes sense if you believe in permanence, yes? Otherwise, what is the point? Either you let go of the idea of permanence, or you leave this world with your fists clenched tight, clinging to illusion."

My mind skidded sideways, as it had when I was a novice monk grappling with this same idea.

Sonam pressed harder. "The minute we attach permanence to anything, suffering grows. The poisoned blooms are many—greed, jealousy, fear, anger. On and on, so many ways to feel unease. But pull up any one of them? You will find the same root."

"I don't . . ."

He held up his left hand. The tremor was quite visible. "This is my hand, yes?"

"Of course."

"Ten years ago, it was also my hand, and yet a different hand, a hand that did not shake like a leaf in the wind. If I desire today's hand to be my 10-years-ago hand, I suffer. I am resentful. I am afraid. Why is this hand not working the way it used to? What are these spots on the skin? Will my hand work at all in 10 years' time? But if I accept that yesterday's hand is gone, today's hand is like this, and tomorrow's, well, who knows? If the only permanent thing about the state of my hand is that it will never stay the same, I can relax. Enjoy my hand, just as it is."

A shift in perception tugged at the sleeve of my mind, tantalizingly close.

"Just like the self. Essential nature is permanent, but actual existence is divisible."

"So our sense of who we are stays the same over time," I said. "And yet in reality we are composed of nothing more than a series of present moments." The profound truth of

this resonated, bone-deep and beyond, triggering a flash of freedom.

I grasped at the insight, and in the grasping, it was gone. I groaned in frustration.

Lama Sonam touched my arm. "You have bad traffic here, yes?"

"Yes."

"And when you sit in the long line of cars, nobody moving, the logical mind knows that you will not be sitting like this always, for the rest of time. The logical mind understands that traffic not moving is a temporary state. But the mind attaches eternity to the situation anyway. And the moment the mind does that . . . ?"

"We start to suffer."

"Just so. We yell at other cars. We bang the steering wheel. We try to force the cars forward with our agitation." Sonam's eyes gleamed. "It's the same with all suffering. Completely illogical!" He clapped his knees, delighted by the absurdity of human nature.

For a second brief moment I was bathed in expansiveness. And also, insight: liberation arises from fully accepting reality's absolute impermanence—if fear doesn't get there first.

"Okay, lesson on intrinsic nature of reality over," Sonam said. "You have questions for me, yes?"

It was easier to broach the subject, in light of my impermanent state. "I need to talk to you about Nawang."

Sonam flinched, as if recoiling from an unexpected assailant.

"Geshe Sonam, please. I know my father forbade us to talk about that summer, but Apa has moved on. And memories . . . bad memories are arising in me."

"Maybe it's better not to fiddle so much," Sonam said. "Maybe it's better to leave them there, Tenzing."

"I can't," I said.

"Why not?"

"Because I believe Nawang is coming after me. And I don't know why."

CHAPTER 40

Yeshe rounded the curtain on the stage. "Ahh. Here you are," he said. "We go for lunch. You come?'

Sonam spoke rapidly in Tibetan. Yeshe shot me a troubled look before hurrying out.

"He will bring us food, and also Lobsang," Sonam said. "They should be part of this conversation, yes?"

"Sure. Yes."

"Good." Sonam folded his hands in his lap and closed his eyes. For the time being, the conversation was on hold.

I probably should have done the same, but the lure of the smartphone was too great. There was an e-mail from Mike, flagged as urgent, and a missed call and message from "unknown." The number was local, a (310) exchange.

I slipped out of the auditorium and found my way to the outside courtyard. A few plump koi traced circles in an overgrown fishpond, streaks of orange hinting of the joy to be found, even in murk.

Mike's e-mail was brief. "Hey boss, gave Lia Pootah your cell number. Contact info attached. Following another possible lead on M. M."

I added the contact to my address book. The last name, Chang, raised an eyebrow.

I played her message: "Tenzing Norbu? Lia Pootah Chang here. And yeah, I'm Chinese. Get over it, I grew up in Monterey Park, okay? Call me back."

Her message was spring-loaded with hostility. No way was I calling her back. She would do me no good. She was my sworn enemy.

Or was she?

I was labeling again. I heard *Chinese* and assumed *foe*. A toxic reaction, without investigation.

I pressed her number.

"Lia Pootah here. Who's calling?" Her voice was light and musical, but edged with anger.

"Tenzing Norbu."

"No way. I'm shocked."

"What do you mean?"

"Let's just say a couple of Buddhist do-gooders in my Comparative Religions class at SMCC blamed me personally for the entire Tibetan diaspora. They weren't even Tibetan. Nice little white girls from Beverly Hills."

I relaxed. Anyone who used the word *diaspora* correctly couldn't be that bad.

"So, do I call you Tenzing, or Norbu, or what?"

"Ten is fine. You?"

"Lia Pootah, please. *Lia* by itself screams Jewish-American Princess, *Pootah* sounds exactly like the word for slut in Spanish, so . . . My mother's an anthropologist, okay? She came across this tribe, the Lia Pootah, in Tazmania. Half-breed by-products of conquering white men raping and pillaging defenseless Aborigine women. Classic case of masculine privilege."

"Did she study the tribe?"

"What? Fuck, no. She just liked the name."

I hadn't misread the hostility earlier. I just hadn't realized it was all encompassing and impersonal.

"You're calling about Maha Mudra, right?"

"I am."

"What do you want to know?"

"Everything you do."

"Okay, well, it's not much. So, I'm an audio-visual conceptual artist, did Mike tell you?"

"No. He just said you were, um, cray."

"He did?" She sounded pleased. "So, I'm currently working on a multimedia piece that will counterpoint iconic religious images and thought with the spiritual viewpoints of

powerful women. Specifically, using feminist interpretations to challenge classically male-dominated belief systems."

"Okay . . ."

Silence. She appeared to want more, though of what, I didn't know.

"So you, ah, you're interested in challenging belief systems," I said.

"*Male-dominated* belief systems. Like Christian fundamentalism, Orthodox Judaism, extremist Islam. Even polytheistic systems such as Hinduism. I mean, once the Laws of Manu came into existence, boom! Women were regulated to the same compliant binary roles as always, seductive temptress or submissive wife. You're either a whore or good mother material."

"Uh huh." I moved to the other side of the pond. The koi were nowhere to be seen. They were probably lost in the weeds, like I was.

"By the way, I also put Buddhism in this category, big time. I don't care what the Dalai Lama says, they are not female friendly. Though if the next one's a woman, believe me, I'll be the first to eat my words."

Yeshe and Lobsang crossed the courtyard and hurried into the tunnel entrance carrying white paper to-go bags.

"I'm not saying it's popular. Good thing I don't give a shit about what other people think." Lia Pootah's laugh was sharp.

"Uh huh." I kept my voice neutral.

"So anyway, I heard through the grapevine about this woman guru who was talking about the same kind of things."

"Maha Mudra?"

"Maha Mudra."

Yeshe stepped out of the arched entryway and into the sunshine and caught my eye. He mimicked eating, his expression a question mark.

"She was a total trip."

I pointed to the phone and held up five fingers. Yeshe nodded and left. "You saw her?"

"Well, sort of. I taped an interview with her, but she disguised her voice. Wouldn't show her face either. Too dangerous, she said."

"And you believed her?"

"Of course. Ask Malala Yousafzai. What's riskier than challenging the fundamentalist masculine status quo? Maha Mudra has some strange ideas, though. I mean, she's out there. I may not even use her."

"Can I see the interview?"

"Sure. I guess. It's rough."

"I can handle it."

"I mean, unedited. I'm still in the process of gathering raw footage before I create the actual piece, you know?"

"When? Where? Can you meet me this afternoon?" I gripped the phone so hard my knuckles whitened.

Grasping.

I inhaled and exhaled. Just like that, things shifted, a slightly looser Ten replacing the wound-up version. Another quick lesson in the divisible nature of self.

"I don't mean to push, Lia Pootah. It's just, there's a young man missing. We think he's with Maha Mudra. At the moment, you are my only link to finding him."

"Mike said."

"I can come to you."

"Where are you?"

"Pasadena."

She thought for a moment.

"Meet me in Mike's loft in a couple of hours."

"I'll be there. And thanks. I mean it. Thank you." But she had already ended the call.

Chapter 41

Lobsang's scowl was epic. Nobody else said a word.

"Really? Nothing to add? Not one of you?"

We'd finished up our Peruvian takeout from Cholo Mama. Lomo saltado burritos for them—burrito-wrapped, stir-fried tenderloin with rice, Peruvian beans, shredded cheese, and creole salsa. Tofu soltado for me, which consisted of French fries, tofu, and an extra scoop of rice on the side, in case I didn't have enough white things on my plate.

"It have *mama* in name," Yeshe had announced, handing out the food. "Mama always mean good!"

"Maybe for you," I'd replied.

All was well, until I brought up the subject of Nawang.

"Guys, come on," I continued. "I have his bumpa. I remember watching Nawang use it. I know he was at Dorje Yidam when we were, and I know he left the monastery the summer I was sent home early to Paris. I know my father worshipped him and hated me. But I don't know why."

Yeshe and Lobsang exchanged a long look.

"Will someone please fill me in here?"

Sonam spoke first. "You must understand, Tenzing. We all held your father in the highest esteem."

"Really?"

I had to laugh at their blank expressions.

"I'm joking. Of course you did. I know that. And I respect your respect, I really do." I thought Sonam would move on, but I was wrong.

"When your father left this plane and entered the bardo realm, he also left behind certain . . . causes and conditions. Beyond the five aggregates."

"But not karma. Karma still follow." Yeshe's voice was solemn.

Lobsang was getting more irritated by the minute. "Not our job to put attention on unskilled actions, now that he is gone, hanh?"

"What unskilled actions?" I countered.

"How does breathing air into a lifeless body help anything?" Sonam begged. "Your father's karmic destiny is set. His intentions were always pure. Let him be."

"What. Unskilled. Actions?"

Sonam reached for his dorje and ran his fingers across the closed prongs on either side, studying the motion. He glanced up at me. "I saw him again, you know. After he left."

"Saw who? Apa?" I envisioned Sonam squinting into the distance as my father's shadowy apparition floated past.

"No. Lama Nawang."

The shock of confirmation caused my spine to straighten. "When?"

"Maybe ten or eleven years ago. His Holiness was conducting Kalachakra initiations in Bodh Gaya."

There it was again—Kalachakra.

Yeshe interjected. "Where Shakyamuni reach enlightenment." His nod was firm. "Some day I go."

"At first I did not know Lama Nawang," Sonam continued. "He had abandoned the zhen for a loincloth. He looked . . ." Sonam fussed with his own robe, tugging an end off his shoulder, flipping it back into place. "He looked more like a beast than a man."

"What do you mean?"

"Like a sadhu, you know? A Hindu ascetic. His hair hung in twisted knots. His dhoti was torn and stained. And he was thin. Very thin. I could count every rib. As if, like Shakyamuni, he ate nothing, only a grain of rice a day." Sonam shrugged. "But the eyes. The eyes were the same."

Yes. His eyes.

Black pools, ringed with gold. Like luminous mirrors: in themselves, nothing, but reflecting everything.

"Then what happened?" I said.

"Nawang pushed to the front of the crowd as His Holiness walked up to the Mahabodhi Stupa. I noticed him because he did not bow or prostrate. He just stood there. Staring."

"Did you talk to him?"

"I tried. But he shook his head, pointing to his closed mouth. I think maybe he took a vow of silence."

I tried to absorb this information.

"Lama Nawang at Bodh Gaya?" Lobsang broke in. "He do Kalachakra initiations? Even higher ones?" Lobsang sounded offended.

"I don't know," Sonam replied. "There were over two hundred thousand people in Bodh Gaya receiving wisdom from His Holiness."

"I'm sure he wanted to," I told Lobsang, and another memory materialized out of the smoky past: the painted silk hanging of the male deity Kalachakra and his consort that decorated an entire wall in Nawang's private quarters. It was the first thing Nawang had showed me, right after we met.

I said, "He was completely obsessed with Kalachakra and Vishvamata, even back then."

Especially Vishvamata—bare breasted, with multiple arms wrapped around her partner; the blue-limbed god. Yab yum, Nawang had called their coupling. Outer and inner. The sword and the vessel.

"He tell you this?" Yeshe asked.

"Yes, he told me. Anyway, it was obvious. A Kalachakra thangka depicting their sacred union hung over his altar." I shrugged. "Nawang wanted to obtain Buddhahood through the supreme integration of emptiness and bliss. More than anything. His commitment was absolute."

Sonam nodded. "I remember now. He revered the Kalachakra path."

"Nawang didn't just want to follow Kalachakra," I said. "A part of him wanted to *be* Kalachakra."

A strange feeling came over me. "Geshe Sonam, can you talk to me about the role of mudras during these secret practices?"

"Mudras? Why do you ask?" His voice was sharp.

"I wouldn't, if it weren't important."

"You are like a boa constrictor, Tenzing. Once you latch onto an idea, you squeeze and squeeze."

I let my silence do the squeezing.

Sonam sighed. "What aspect of mudras?"

"What aspect? I'm not sure I understand."

"Mudra can mean a ritual gesture. But also, mudra can mean a woman." He shook his head slightly. "No, not a woman exactly. Female essence, in the form of a woman."

My pulse quickened. "Tell me," I said.

Sonam's eyes narrowed. He looked into mine as if plumbing their depths for any sign of weakness. I kept my gaze steady.

"More than one," he replied quietly. "Three. Three mudras. Three female principles. Real, imaginary, and inner. Karma, inana, and maha."

I was closing in on something, I just didn't know what yet.

Beyond the curtain, voices murmured, followed by a belly laugh I recognized and loved.

Yeshe stood up abruptly. "Lobsang, we go now. Continue with mandala." Lobsang rose as well, but reluctantly.

"Tell Julie I'm with Geshe Sonam, but I'll see her soon," I told Lobsang. His nod was followed by a pointed look as if to say *don't forget a word*. He trailed Yeshe into the auditorium.

"Please, go on, Geshe Sonam," I said. "Three mudras."

Sonam leaned back and closed his eyes. "*Mudra* comes from Sanskrit, yes? It's the same in both languages. It means seal, or stamp. Spiritual masters need mudras to seal energies, to stamp together, or merge, the male and female essence to achieve the highest realm of Buddhahood."

"But are they actual women? Are they real?"

Sonam opened his eyes. "There you go again, Tenzing. How you love your labels. The essence of energy is neither real, nor not real. Neither male, nor female. Karma Mudra represents the feminine essence as it exists in the material plane of existence." His mouth thinned. "Do some unskilled monks take that to mean—how did you put it?—a real woman? Yes. Are they right to think so? No. But delusion cloaks itself in many forms, including the human body." He spread his hands. "The Buddha himself was tempted. As he sat under the Bodhi tree on the brink of enlightenment, Maya attacked wearing the disguise of an army of beautiful, naked women."

Every novice was told this tale over and over, but this time I heard it differently. Lia Pootah had a point. Whatever the belief system, it was always women tempting men, wasn't it? And why were they always naked and beautiful?

"But Tenzing, karma mudra is symbolic, yes? No more manifest than inana mudra, or even maha mudra."

"What did you just say?"

"No more . . ."

"No," I interrupted. "After that. You said *maha mudra*."

"Yes. Inana mudra is the imagined feminine essence, summoned in meditation, but still existing in the realm of forms. But maha mudra is formless, called upon to embody reality and illusion both. Maha mudra is the most powerful of mudras, the most essential to the success of the practice."

"The most essential," I repeated, my heart pounding.

"Both are necessary, yes? Without the feminine principle, the masculine cannot survive." Sonam clasped his eight-pronged scepter in his right hand and the handbell in his left. "Like so," he illustrated. "Dorje and drilbu. Method and wisdom. Lotus and thunderbolt."

"Kalachakra and Vishvamata," I said. "Deity and consort." I jumped to my feet. Finally, a connection between Nawang and Maha Mudra that made sense. She was his lotus, the embodiment of the feminine. He needed her to complete his mission.

Sonam cocked his head. "I have helped you?"

"You have." I started for the edge of the stage. "Thank you," I called over my shoulder. Sonam picked up his sheet of mantras. Good thing, because otherwise I would have forgotten my other question.

"I'm sorry. One more thing." I pulled out my phone and scrolled through my photos until I found the clearest image. I enlarged the stacked characters so they filled the screen.

"Can you tell me what this is?"

Sonam held the screen close to his eyes. Recognition washed over his face. Then something else.

Alarm.

"Where did you find this?"

"It's part of the missing-person's case I'm working on. Why?"

He handed the phone back. I glanced at the design, though I didn't need to. I could picture it in my sleep. "I know it's not a mantra, Sonam, but it's some kind of Tibetan symbol, right?"

"*Namchuwangdan*," Sonam said, his voice low. "In Sanskrit, the *dasakaro vasi*. From the Kalachakra tantra practice." He swallowed. "Sometimes the bird, Garuda, flies overhead as well, swallowing a snake."

"But what is it? A mantra?"

"Not exactly." He pointed with a shaky forefinger. "See the interwoven letters? The five elements? The lotus? And here, the sun and moon? See the flame on top, the demon Rahu?"

"Yes . . ."

"This is an anatomical map. The microcosmic body of the most powerful of all the Buddhas. So no, Lama Tenzing. Not just any mantra." I had never heard Sonam so serious. "This symbol is the global mantra, controlling all the energies that constitute creation."

"Namchu . . .?"

"Namchuwangdan. The symbol of the Adi Buddha." Sonam lowered his voice. "The Buddha of all Buddhas."

I remembered hearing about the Adi Buddha a lifetime ago. *The highest one. He who knows not the circle of time.*

Sonam stared at the image, mesmerized.

"Some of the older boys at the monastery whispered that His Holiness was the Adi Buddha," I said.

This broke the spell. "Ha! His Holiness would laugh to hear such silly talk. No, Tenzing, our spiritual leader's power lies in his humanity. And his humility. Do you know how he started last year's address in Bodh Gaya, on the steps of the Mahabodhi Temple?"

I shook my head.

"He said, 'There are seven billion human beings on this earth. And I am only one of them.'" Sonam's eyes shone. "Can you imagine? The whole world, awaiting his wisdom. And before anything else, he invites his own insignificance to stand by his side." Sonam seemed struck by the moment all over again. "The moment he mentioned seven billion lives, he reminded us of the seven billion deaths to come. Including his own. Adi Buddha?" Sonam brushed the thought away. "He would be the last person to claim the title of Adi Buddha."

"I understand."

"Do you? I hope so. Claims of personal power have no business in our hearts, or minds. We commit to the well-being of others, not personal advancement."

"Always good to be reminded of that."

Sonam's eyes grew troubled. "This symbol has a second meaning, as well." He paused, as if reluctant to continue.

I touched his arm. "I think you'd better tell me."

"It means . . ." Sonam firmed his voice. "It means, the Power of Ten." He met my eyes.

"You must take care, Ten. Someone is luring you into playing a dangerous game."

CHAPTER 42

"You look like you've just seen a ghost." Julie was sitting on a bench by the fishpond, Homer in a heap at her feet.

"In a way, I guess I have." I rested my hand on Homer's solid back. His flat stump of a tail wagged.

"So? Any news? On the brother front, I mean?"

"He exists. He's alive, Julie, at least as of ten years ago."

"Ten, that's great!" She saw my face. "Isn't it?"

"I don't know. Honestly, I have a pretty bad feeling about all of this." My crossed arms formed a tight shield across my chest. I lowered them, but the exposed feeling lingered.

I sat, searching for the right words. "Nawang was . . . different, even back then."

"In what way?"

"He was so confident. Fearless, even. And he made me feel the same way, as if I could do anything. Would do anything, at least for him."

"You admired him."

"More than that. I worshipped him. I was in awe." I smiled. "Not just me. Everyone he came into contact with felt the same way. He was only seventeen, but already there was talk that he was destined for greatness."

"So what happened?"

My face flamed—shame does that. "I happened. Or maybe I should say, *we* happened. He asked me to steal something, and I did. An ancient terma."

"Terma?"

"A secret teaching. In this case, a forbidden one."

"And you stole it?"

"Yes. Then I got cold feet, but it was too late. It led us both down a dark path."

"In what way?"

I met Julie's eyes. "That's just it. I can't remember. All I know is, a local Indian kid died, I was sent home, and Nawang disappeared. But the actual event is just out of reach, you know?" I shrugged. "I do think I'm getting closer. Eric is helping."

"But Nawang is definitely your brother?"

"Half brother. Same father."

"But a different mother."

"Yes."

"Wasn't that unusual? I mean, for a Buddhist monk?"

"That's one word for it."

I'd been so distracted by Sonam's sighting of Nawang that the subject of my father's "unskilled actions" had died on the vine. Maybe that was Sonam's intention.

I groaned. Every time I grew close to trapping a truth, it wriggled out of reach.

Julie took my hand. Her grip was both firm and pliant. The middle way. "Maybe it's time for you to see Eric again."

I kissed her cheek. "I'm going Monday, first thing."

Homer yawned and stretched, rump raised.

"So, the boys want me to take them to Rodeo Drive," Julie said.

"They do?"

"They like to 'eye shop,' apparently. That's what Yeshe calls it."

"Has anybody warned the Beverly Hills police? I'm not sure they're ready for five Buddhist monks and a bulldog."

Julie gave me a sidelong glance. "I thought I'd check out the wedding bands at Harry Winston."

"Sounds good. Buy me a Bugatti while you're at it."

Julie was wearing thin cotton leggings. I touched the top of her thigh. Julie shifted closer and a current of longing passed back and forth between us. I was glad to feel the pulse of desire again.

"I wish . . ." she said.

"I know. Me, too."

TJ appeared across the courtyard talking into a phone, his face animated.

"TJ has his own cell phone now?" I asked.

"Refurbished. He bought it for his brother. I guess his family lives in some Tibetan village out in the middle of nowhere."

TJ ended the call and hurried back inside.

"I'd better go back," Julie said.

I checked the time. "Same here." I stood. "I'm meeting someone at Mike's loft. A conceptual artist by the name of Lia Pootah Chang."

Julie raised an eyebrow.

"Don't worry. She's Chinese."

"Tenzing Norbu. She's a sentient being, isn't she? Where's your loving-kindness?"

"Sorry, Jules. Not happening with a Chinese girl. Not in this lifetime."

She was laughing softly as my mouth found hers.

"Even so," she murmured.

I reached around her waist and pulled our bodies closer, pressing my length against hers. Our beating hearts were inches apart.

In this moment, the pulse of our love was strong and steady.

Chapter 43

"Enter." Mike's mop of hair stuck out every which way, as if he'd just rolled out of bed. No doubt he had—late afternoon was early morning to Mike.

He was dressed for work: a tie-dyed shirt and lightweight drawstring pants that hung low on his bony frame. The hems were frayed from dragging on the floor.

These were also his sleep clothes.

"You're up early," I said.

"Don't start." He stepped aside. The lack of furniture and proliferation of electronics gave his spacious loft an industrial feel.

"That's new." I pointed to a sectional sofa.

"Tricia," Mike said. "She's desperate to domesticate me."

A petite stranger stood by the large picture window. Behind her, the angled metallic wings of the Disney Concert Hall glinted in the sunlight.

Mike pulled me forward. "Lia Pootah, Ten. Ten, Lia Pootah. Okay, you two. Be nice." He scuffed to his ergonomic perch in front of three computer screens, a mouse, and a two-tiered keyboard.

Lia Pootah Chang was tiny, but she radiated intensity. Coal-black eyes, black hair, black fingernails, black toenails. A black-cat tattoo curled around her right bicep, and a short black skirt and sleeveless top completed the monochrome look. Only her lips were a daring slash of bright red.

She looked like she could body-press twice her weight. Then again she probably tipped the scale at 90 pounds.

"Thanks for meeting me," I said.

"No worries." She bit at a thumb cuticle then caught herself. "Sorry. Bad habit." She moved to the far wall and made

minuscule adjustments to a row of framed black-and-white photographs—homeless people doing a dance, it looked like.

"Burning Man," she said. "I took these."

"She's fierce with a camera," Mike announced from the corner.

I wanted to sit but felt awkward about it, since Lia Pootah wouldn't stop moving. I settled for leaning against the back of the sofa. "I'm curious to see this interview," I said.

"Yeah, well, about that . . ."

"It's bullshit!" Mike called.

"Tell that to my lawyer!" Lia Pootah shot back. She shrugged at me. "No can do. I forgot I signed an agreement. I can't let anyone see the interview until Maha Mudra gives the go-ahead. And I can't seem to reach her."

A bitter taste filled my mouth. "That's disappointing."

"And ludicrous," Mike chimed in.

Lia Pootah's eyes gleamed. "Relax. She didn't say anything about letting someone *hear* it."

Mike marched over. He had about 14 inches on Lia Pootah. Add on his wild crown of hair and he towered over her. He held out his hand. "Give."

She handed Mike her phone. He laughed. "You're kidding, right?" he teased.

"What? This is my backup audio! You're the one always talking about backups, asshole!"

Their fiery friendship was fueled by a particular kind of heat. If I were Tricia, I'd take note.

I stored the thought in the bulging "Not My Business" file, where it would stay. Nothing good came from nosing around in there.

Mike found a USB connection and hooked her phone to a deck that looked like a trash can full of wires. He fingered through cables, following two that led to a pair of tall speakers. Just watching him made my head hurt.

He nodded to himself and pressed something on her screen.

"Testing, testing." Lia Pootah's voice. Sort of. If she was a robot on a strict diet of rusty nails.

"What the fuck?!" Mike fiddled with the speaker connections.

Lia Pootah buzzed to his side and slapped his hand away. "Hey! It's on purpose! I used a voice-changing app."

Mike's look was admiring. "Shut the front door!"

"I know. Sick, right?"

If this Gen-X foreplay went on much longer, I was going to need my own brain-changing app. "Can I hear the interview, please?'

"You be the kahuna," Mike said. Lia Pootah giggled. Mike started the recording again.

"Testing, testing. Interview with Maha Mudra, Monday, May twenty-ninth, two thousand and fourteen."

The first day of Saka Dawa. Interesting.

I'd brought along my notepad and pen. I flipped to a blank page and wrote down the date and its significance.

Lia Pootah's voice continued; robotic, almost disembodied, but my ears quickly adjusted.

"So, Maha Mudra. I like your name, by the way. What does it mean?"

"Nothing," an equally toneless voice answered, though a little lower in pitch. "Names are meaningless. What matters is Atma."

Atma, I wrote down. *Hindu term? Same meaning as Buddhist Atman?* The first referred to the individual soul, the second to a kind of collective world spirit. I appreciated Lia Pootah's next question.

"Atma? Can you be more specific?"

"At ma. I am that. That which cannot be destroyed. Uncuttable, like the atom. Decide to be that first. Otherwise, you revisit old wounds again and again. Like chewing old gum. You want to chew old gum? Go for it. Or don't."

Chewing gum, I wrote. Added *old*. Then crossed the whole thing out. It looked ridiculous.

"So you're saying . . ."

"That is the role of guru. *Gu* means sticky stuff. *Ru* means the one who removes. Guru is the one who removes the stickiness of life. Guru is heavy inside, from swallowing all the ignorance."

Guru = removing sticky stuff.

I set the notebook aside. Sticky or not, none of this was adhering. Maybe Lia Pootah would send me a link to the interview.

Lia Pootah sounded pretty befuddled herself, or her robot version did. "Can we just . . . can we talk about your attitude toward the feminine in your spiritual practice?"

"Always the male and the female," answered the flat mechanical voice. "Without both present, how can we have ultimate beauty?"

"So you see them as equal?"

Mike repeated the question with a mocking robotic delivery. "So. You. See. Them. As. Equal." Lia Pootah threw a punch at his arm, but he hopped out of the way.

"Atma," the monotoned voice continued. "Nothing else matters. That intense feeling you think only exists between two people? That one special love? Temporary madness. A tiny drop of what is possible. You must want Atma more than anything else. You must be mad for beauty. Mad for love. Are you listening?"

"Yes, but as regards the male dominance of certain . . ."

"What looks like madness is the soul, searching for commitment. For devotion. For bhakti. This is not madness, this is sanity."

"I'm sorry. Bock tea? Can you spell that?"

"You are here for a reason."

"Yes. I'm interviewing a lot of . . ."

"You are here for a reason. You came to me. Something in you craves bliss. Do not waste this opportunity. This is what the guru is for."

"Okay, well . . ."

"Nothing is permanent. Nothing else matters but this. The day you move to another womb, you leave all your toys behind. I have enough. Say it."

"I'm sorry? Another room?"

"Womb. Mother's womb. Say it. 'I have enough.'"

"I have enough."

"I have enough."

"I have enough."

"This is embodied Atma. Buddha-nature. Bhakti."

"But you still haven't answered my . . ." A pause. "Where are you . . . ? You're leaving already?" Lia Pootah's robot voice could not disguise the stress.

"You waste my time. Just as you waste your life. Nam-chuwangdan. He's coming. It's time. But you will be asleep."

The sound of a door opening, then closing.

Dead air. Then Lia Pootah's unaltered voice returned, taking charge: "Shit. Wow. Okay. So, umm, that was pretty weird. Interview concluded with Maha Mudra. I guess." And a final, brittle laugh.

"Yeah, so, that's it," Lia Pootah said.

I looked up from my notebook to see Mike twirling a finger around his right temple. "Seriously," he said. "That bitch is nutso."

"I know. Right?" Lia Pootah bit at another cuticle. "No way am I using her for my show, now that I listened to that again. Can you imagine the troll comments? Talk about flame bait."

"What do you think, boss?" Mike turned to me. "This stuff should be right up your alley."

I reread the phrases I'd just written down. *He's coming. It's time.* "Lia Pootah, where did this interview take place?"

"Some empty warehouse waaayyy downtown. The whole thing was pretty random. I didn't even find out the location until a half hour before we met. By anonymous text. Talk about paranoid."

"Can you get me the address?"

"Sure, I can look it up, but like I said, the building was empty. She said something about curtains, though."

"Curtains."

"Yeah. That people went there for curtains."

This jiggled something loose, but it floated off before I could grab hold.

"Use the bathroom, Mike?" Lia Pootah didn't wait for an answer. She ducked inside a door to one side of Mike and Tricia's raised king-size bed.

Mike had returned to his cove of computers.

"So boss, that website you sent me? I moused it up, but no dice. Shut down already." His fingers flew across the keyboard as he stared at one of the monitors. "Come see." He motioned me over.

The screen displayed a "This website is no longer active" message. "Been finding a buttload of these, by the by. Fundraising events. Spiritual gatherings. They show up for a few days, and then they're gone, straight into the black hole. All of them routed by Tor and connected to your favorite server."

"Indra's Net?'

Mike pointed to me. "Bang."

"But why? What does that mean?"

"Means they want to be seen, but they don't want to be found."

My head was spinning. *Like Collie.*

A key turned in the front door and Tricia shouldered her way inside. A heavy canvas bag swung from the crease of her right elbow. She set the bag down with a thud and it tipped, spilling textbooks. Her left arm balanced an extra-large pizza container.

I gave Tricia a little wave.

"Hey, Ten!" She stepped over the spilled books. Her voice cooled several degrees as Lia Pootah emerged from the bathroom. "Oh. Lia Pootah."

Mike looked like a spooked giraffe galumphing across the floor to Tricia. "I got that." He grabbed for the pizza.

"I can do it." Tricia spun away and stalked into the kitchen area.

Uh-oh. Tricia and Mike were on the brink of slipping into the three-step waltz of bad relationship roles: victim, rescuer, persecutor; victim, rescuer, persecutor; *one-two-three, one-two-three.*

By the counter, Tricia was a ramrod ready to force its charge. She didn't say another word. She didn't have to.

"Okay, well, thanks Mike." I edged for the door. "You coming, Lia Pootah?"

Spots of scarlet marked her cheekbones. "What? Oh. Yeah." She disconnected her phone from the tangle of wires and followed me out the front door.

We rode the elevator down in silence. With any luck, a sweaty conversation was taking place above us. If not, there was sure to be more trouble ahead.

We stood at the crosswalk, waiting for the light to change. I'd somehow snagged a metered spot directly across from Mike's building. Multistory apartment complexes lined both sides of this avenue, and available parking was rare.

"Need a ride?"

Lia Pootah was staring at the ground.

"It's not like anything happened." She knuckled her cheeks. For a split second, her tough veneer cracked. "I just think he's cool, you know?"

Maha Mudra's robotic voice seemed to echo through the urban canyon.

That intense feeling you think can only be between two people? That one special love . . . ? Temporary madness.

I passed Lia Pootah my handkerchief.

"Thanks." She wiped her eyes, leaving black smears. "Oh, great. Now I look like a fucking raccoon." Her smile was watery as she handed the hankie back. "Horrible animals."

"Hey," I said. "Raccoons are sentient beings, too, you know. Where's your loving-kindness?"

She laughed, and I realized I no longer disliked her.

The human heart isn't Chinese, or Tibetan. It just is. And sometimes, it just wants what it wants. Until, being human, it gets distracted by something else.

Lia Pootah's eyes widened. "Is that your Mustang?"

"Yes."

"Sixty-five Shelby?"

I nodded, impressed.

"Oh, snap!" Her good humor restored, Lia Pootah opened her iPhone, scrolled through some images, and flashed me a photo of a beautifully restored gold El Torino. "Meet Baby," she said. "I did the work myself."

I tried to enlarge the image, but swiped to the next picture by mistake. A selfie. The right half of Lia Pootah's face grinned in an empty parking lot. Behind her was a squat cement building with a row of narrow openings lining the top like bunker windows.

"Weird."

"What."

"I feel like I know that building," I said.

She took the phone. "Oh. That's where I did the interview. I have the address somewhere." Her fingers danced. "Here it is. Eleventh and Main."

Adrenaline sent my energy spiking. "I knew it. I've been there. They hold underground concerts in that place. Electronic music. I went there a few years ago, to meet Mike."

The experience came back in a rush. The secret codes and texts from the organizers. The switched locations and times, keeping the event off the radar of any authorities. The warehouse room packed with young people, high on X, arms waving.

The woman at the door with the red bindi.

"Whatever." Lia Pootah shrugged. "Like I said, they use it for curtains now."

"Lia Pootah, you're a genius! Not curtains. *Kirtans.*"

"That's what I . . ."

"With a *K*. A kirtan is a special form of devotional chanting. Part of the bhakti tradition. They have huge kirtan concerts in India. All over the world now, actually."

I pulled out my phone.

"Who are you calling?"

"Mike." *Oh.* I paused before I pressed his number. "Sorry, I . . ."

But Lia Pootah was halfway down the sidewalk. "Knock yourself out," she called over her shoulder.

CHAPTER 44

The 101 North was at a standstill. Across the median strip, the traffic heading south was no better. Impatience tightened around my temples.

Okay. Standing still was good—standing still offered the perfect opportunity to reflect and review.

I'd settled for a call-me-when-you-can text to Mike, and he hadn't responded. He and Tricia were probably still fighting, eating, or making up after fighting and before eating. None of these options warranted further interruption.

But even without Mike, I knew I was nearer to discovering what lay behind Maha Mudra's success at eluding everyone. And a step closer to finding Collie.

Fragments of information marched across my mind, a parade of partial clues.

- Maha Mudra was a nomad—she had no "headquarters," no website, no tangible (or intangible) home.

- Maha Mudra was attracting followers, both here and abroad.

- You could only reach Maha Mudra via sites located on Tor.

- Even then, the contact sites were temporary.

- She was part of a bhakti, or devotional tradition that was somehow connected to a preexisting network of underground techno events.

I edged left to allow for a Harley splitting traffic. He roared past with no acknowledgment. Typical HOG behavior.

- And, she rode a Vyrus. Time to track down that lead.

- Maha Mudra was linked to Nawang.

But how?
Acolyte, probably.
I frowned. She didn't sound like anyone's acolyte.
Partner then. Partner, lover, coconspirator.
Maybe.

Or maybe my first instinct was right. Maybe Nawang *was* this guru's guru. Her personal sage. Her Adi Buddha. Maybe Maha Mudra's job was to spread Nawang's teachings, and she was here in Southern California, a nexus of spirituality, to prepare the way for him. The Buddha had his first cadre of monks, Jesus his disciples. Mohammed his early converts.

All men.

My mouth formed a grim smile; it would be just like Nawang to enlist a beautiful woman as his principal devotee.

The traffic tourniquet loosened and cars began to flow.

DCI Garfield had mentioned "grooming" as the latest online technique for attracting converts to radical belief systems. Was that what we had here? Was she bait? A seductive lure to hook new followers?

And was Nawang directing her every move—the actual power, the mantra in the center of the mandala?

It's time.

My pocket vibrated. I fumbled for the phone and somehow managed to put the call on speaker.

"Boss."

"Hi, Mike." I asked without asking. "Everything okay?"

"Yeah, s'cool. Tricia and I just had to backspace a little. Clear up a few things. We're good."

"Good."

"I got your text. What's up?"

I explained my new theory.

"Whoa. Okay, so normally I'd say you were on crack, but you may be onto something."

A car flashed its brights at me. I switched on my headlights. Somehow dusk had fallen. I couldn't wait to be out of this car.

"Explain, please," I said.

"Well, there's this new thing happening. Raja rap, they call it. Weird shit—like . . . who's that famous Hindu goddess? The one with all the arms?"

"Lakshmi?"

"That's the one. So, raja rap's like if Lakshmi and Fatboy Slim had a baby."

"English, Mike. Speak English."

"I'm trying! Look, you're the one suggesting this Maha Mudra chick might be a part of the underground electronica circuit. I'm saying, there's a new kind of gig happening. I went to one, which was plenty by the way. I mean seriously. Bletch."

"In what way?"

"In every way. Picture a woman chanting Hare Krishnas and pumping a harmonium, and right next to her a pimply kid throwing down house beats. Meanwhile a dude in dreadlocks is spouting some kind of quasi-spiritual rap. Not to mention the guy in the corner blowing a hella horn. Had to be eight or nine feet long. A didgeridoo maybe."

Or a Tibetan long horn.

"How did you find out about the concert to begin with?"

"Oh, you know," Mike said. "Once it gets around you're interested in this kind of thing, they find you."

He fell silent, as the import landed. I shivered, remembering the haunted eyes of a young Bosnian girl, just a child, but the victim of terrible things. Mike must have been nosing down the same trail. The dark web provided the ultimate venue for communicating things best kept secret.

"Raja rap retreat," I said, realizing. "R. J. R. P. R. T. R. T."

"Shit," he replied. "Maybe this *is* connected to the old Indra's Net."

"Mike, what if they're letting their followers know about events the same way your electronica raves do? You know, with last-minute texts to a private list? Remember that downtown deal you deejayed last year? The one I came to?"

"Of course."

"Well guess what? Maha Mudra used the same warehouse to meet with Lia Pootah."

"No shit."

"It's the same communication model. I'm sure of it."

"Makes total sense."

My Mustang crested the ridge and slalomed down Topanga Canyon Boulevard. Almost home.

"Mike, I need to get on that invitation list. If it exists. But they can't know it's me, okay? Is that something you can do?"

"Sure. But boss, I'm starting to think you've got a serious banana problem."

"What does that even mean?"

"You're like that kid, the one who said, 'I know how to spell banana. I just don't know when to stop.'"

I rolled into my gravel driveway. The house was dark. Julie must still be eye-shopping, or else she was stuck in her own sheet metal nightmare, aka rush hour.

The headlights landed on my living room window, illuminating a pair of green spheres; emeralds in a Persian feline setting. So he wasn't hiding this time.

The eyes vanished. Tank preferred to greet me at the kitchen door—closer to his favorite cupboard, the one filled with cans of cat food.

"Mike? You still there?"

"I'm just giving you one last chance to change your mind."

"I can't. I have to find these people."

I turned off the ignition. The silence was interrupted by the *tick-ticking* of cooling exhaust-pipe metal.

"Give me a couple of days," Mike said.

CHAPTER 45

Making love when half-awake has a quality of timelessness. Our boundaries were indistinct, our rhythm gentle and unhurried in the pale shadows of almost dawn. First Julie reached her peak of pleasure, looking down at me as she rocked, her eyes widening in that way I loved. I grasped her hips and we rolled over in one smooth motion. She hooked her legs tight around my back. Her smile was an invitation.

I let myself go and dissolved into piercing sensation.

We stayed physically connected for as long as we could.

"That's better," Julie murmured.

"So much better," I echoed. Our skin cooled. I touched her cheek. "Can you go back to sleep?"

"Already there," she said, turning onto her side.

Tank had commandeered the rumpled bedclothes for a nest. I straightened the top sheet, pulling it high enough to cover Julie's shoulders.

Wrapping my cotton kimono tight, I walked to work.

The office phone weighed heavy in my hand. There was nothing concrete to report. If I were Lord Purdham-Coote, I'd demand a refund.

I flipped open the file for Purdham-Coote's number.

A *ping* announced an incoming text on my iPhone. Mike's message was succinct: CALL ME. IT'S ABOUT NAWANG.

Saved by a techie who kept vampire hours.

Mike answered immediately. "Seriously? Now who's up early?"

"Forget that. What have you found out?"

"Before you get too excited, the scent on Nawang went cold a few years ago. But I've managed to piece together quite a few things."

"I need whatever you've got."

"Okay. So. I pulled most of this early stuff off an old bio I tracked down—from your monastery in India, actually. Nawang Gephel was born in a small village in the foothills of northern Tibet, although *village* is pushing it—more like four huts on a rocky slope. Farming, yaks, stuff like that. His mother raised him as best she could. Tough, lonely life for a kid, reading between the lines. Then . . ."

"Hang on."

"What?"

"What about the father?"

"No mention of a father."

Anger flared. I tamed it with a deep, cooling breath.

"Go on."

"So—this is according to an official temple bio, meaning it follows a certain predictable path—but Nawang showed an early propensity for the monastic way of life. Like, almost before he could talk. Always running off to meditate under trees. Wouldn't wear regular clothes, only robes. Insisted on shaving his head. Like that. He begged his mother to let him take vows, and finally she agreed. He entered the . . . hang on . . . the Dhankar monastery at the age of eight. By that time, the mother had married a herdsman and had another son, so I guess that made the decision easier."

This was news.

"He transferred to your monastery, Dorje Yidam, when he was sixteen, 'to advance in his studies,' it says here. Then there's more stuff about empowerments and further teachings. A bit of a prodigy, sounds like."

That part I knew.

"Anyway, all that stopped the following year, I guess when he turned seventeen. They pulled the biography, and he pulled a disappearing act."

I was almost 12. "Nineteen ninety-three?"

"That's right."

"Then what?"

"Well, as far as I can tell, he started guru-hopping all over India. We're talking years. I found evidence of him joining ranks with a guy called Sri Sri Baba Sai, another dude called Karoli Maharaj, etcetera etcetera."

Siddhartha Gautama had traversed India in the same way, sampling different paths, seeking a solution to human suffering.

"I can send you names if you like."

"Yes, please."

How on earth had Mike found all this out?

He answered the question before I could ask it. "They've all gone digital now, so if you know what you're doing, you can search through their membership lists. It's all about branding and fund-raising, my man. Gurus included. Nawang still stayed connected to Buddhism, though. He did something called kala . . . kala sha . . ."

"Kalachakra inititiations. Ten years ago, in Bodh Gaya, right?"

"Eleven. And that was the second time. First time was in '96, in West Benghal."

Only 20 years old. Nawang had not lost any of his passion for spiritual transformation. If I weren't so threatened, I'd be intrigued.

"So the final hit I got was from three years back. He briefly joined some Buddhist offshoot in the UK. Another tongue twister. Bear with me: Doll-gee-al Shug . . ."

"Dolgyal Shugpa." I cleared the knot of fear forming in my throat. "His Holiness issued a warning about their practices."

"Yeah. Well you'd know more about that than me. After that, nothing."

"It's a pretty dark road to go down."

"Speaking of dark roads, maybe six or seven months later, Indra's Net first came into being. Coincidence?"

"I'm guessing not."

"I'm sorry to say I agree."

"Thanks, Mike. This helps a lot."

"One last thing," he said.

"Go ahead."

"It has to do with his family in Tibet. This was a while ago."

My chest tightened. Something about Mike's voice.

"The circumstances were gruesome enough to make the news."

"What happened?"

"So, no one had seen them for a while. I guess a neighbor went to check. The smell was the first clue. He found Nawang's family inside their hut. They'd been dead for several days. All three of them."

My mouth was dry. "How?"

"Stabbed. And skinned in some places. Some sort of ritualistic murder-suicide. They believe the mother was responsible."

I carried the phone out onto the deck. I needed air.

"You still there?"

"I'm here," I said. The sky was marbled pink and gray.

"Anyway, about that other thing? About getting you onto the concert list?"

"Yes."

"It's done."

A pair of mourning doves traded their five-note refrain, a sorrowful call and response.

"That's good, Mike." I turned away from the canyon. "So, what's next?"

"What's next is, I keep digging, and you wait for the next event. And Ten?"

"Yes?"

"While you're waiting, do me a favor. Pay a visit to the target range. I don't like where any of this is heading."

I left messages for Lord Purdham-Coote and Bertie, letting them know I was zeroing in on Maha Mudra.

A hard, sweaty run helped clear my head, a six-mile loop through Topanga Canyon Park via Trippet Ranch. By the time I got home, Julie was up and gone. The deconstruction ceremony started at noon, and there was a lot for her to do before then.

For me, as well.

A cold shower and two mugs of hot coffee kept fatigue at bay. I added a squeeze of tuna juice to Tank's can of mixed grill—I'd been neglecting him lately—and fueled up with a quick fried egg sandwich.

I transferred my .38 Wilson Supergrade and S & W snub nose AirLite into a hard nylon pistol case. I double-locked the zipper—I'd learned my lesson. I'd buy bullets there. No hollow points were allowed, and I was out of full metal jackets.

I headed downtown to the Los Angeles Gun Club to rent a booth and do exactly what Mike suggested. Practice pointing and shooting. The doors opened at 11:00 A.M. on Sunday, and I planned on being first in line. My goal was to achieve consistent 1.5-inch groups at 21 feet with both weapons, but it had been a while, so I might have to settle for 2-inch groupings.

Target practice followed by sacred sand mandala deconstruction.

My story, in a nutshell.

Chapter 46

The clanging reverberation of the drilbus faded into silence. Five mouths pursed into *O* shapes, and Geshe Sonam led the others into another round of throat singing.

Sonam stepped forward and the crowd pressed even closer. It was standing room only, and the misguided few who'd arrived a little late, such as me, were forced to squeeze inside the doorways. The combination of heat and bodies was stifling. Here and there, wilting observers fanned themselves with shiny brochures describing ancient Tibetan arts. Baking alive was not one of them.

Sweat trickled down my spine and pooled at the small of my back. Someone needed to turn on the air-conditioning.

The completed mandala glowed on its black frame, a perfect circle in jeweled tones. Breathtaking. Impossible. The chamber at the center, with its scepter and orb, seemed to pulse with life.

Maude and Lola hunkered in the front row, held tight by Martha and Bill. Bill's son Sasha was there, too, looking fit; apparently the police academy training was agreeing with him.

I experienced a surge of appreciation for what my Tibetan friends had created: at their commitment, and sheer skill. The Buddha called this feeling *mudita:* sympathetic joy, and it was the polar opposite of resentment.

Sonam's face was calm yet focused as he began to circle the mandala in a clockwise direction. Moments earlier, Lobsang had dropped a magnolia blossom onto the right-hand quadrant.

Sonam scooped up the bloom and now placed it in the center. He circled a second time.

My gaze followed, tracing the multicolored rim, alternating parallelograms of color etched with scrolled black lines.

One of the patterned sections didn't match.

Impossible. It had to match. Equanimity demanded absolute balance. I craned my head to better see what had snagged my vision.

And recognized the tiny stack of symbols. Namchuwangdan. My knees buckled.

"Easy, buddy," the man next to me whispered. "You okay?"

I straightened, steadying myself. "Sorry," I murmured. "The heat."

Was Nawang here?

The sense of déjà vu almost overwhelmed me as I again scanned a crowd for a malignant presence and again found only friendly faces. Bill and his family; Eric and Adina; Julie, with Homer leashed and panting between her feet. Others I recognized from the Highland Park temple, along with a slew of smiling strangers. All benign. All absorbed in the dismantlement ceremony proceeding before them.

Sonam pressed together two fingers and a thumb to form a point with his right hand. He knelt close. He placed the makeshift plow at the center of the mandala and carved a furrow, passing through the first of the four gates to the outer circumference. Returning to the midpoint, he repeated the action three more times until he had divided the mandala into equal quadrants.

The Power of Ten symbol remained where it was, a flaw on the far edge of the cosmos, promising chaos.

Why had no one removed it?

Whoever put it there knew what he was doing, for the image was expertly applied. While the need to correct mistakes was rare, if errors occurred the chak-pur could also be used to suck up errant grains, using the breath. Someone had

carefully vacuumed up the initial design before replacing it with this new symbol.

The chanting increased in volume.

Lobsang and Sonam switched places. Lobsang was holding a paintbrush. Hand steady, he brushed from the midpoint outward. Each swipe transformed vivid blocks of color into a blended mixture. Strip by curved strip, Lobsang eradicated the exquisite design with crescent-shaped strokes of the brush.

Even though this was expected, the crowd seemed stunned by the methodical act of benevolent destruction.

All that beauty, all that effort, reduced in a moment to a blurred pile, like so much dust. Nothing is permanent. Nothing.

Julie's gaze was fixed on Lobsang's hand as he completed his task. A tear rolled down her cheek. She must have felt me looking at her, for she raised her eyes to meet mine.

We shared an intimate moment, a bittersweet recognition of mortality. I don't know when I've loved her more.

The mandala was no more. The Power of Ten symbol proved as temporary as anything else.

Sonam pinched up a few grains from one of the mounds, removed his yellow hat, and placed the sand on his scalp. The sand was an offering, the gesture a tradition that honored the passing of the recent dead. Sonam met my eyes as he replaced his curved hat. I knew what he was doing. He was inviting me to join him in sending ease and compassion to my father's restless spirit.

I couldn't do it.

The chants faded into silence.

The scattered clapping was tentative. Nobody knew the protocol for this kind of thing.

"Tank you," Lobsang said, and the applause grew. TJ and Wangdue started sweeping the four mounds into a central pile. I lost sight of them in the jostling crowd.

"Can I have your attention, please?"

Adina stood in front, skin glowing. I'd missed her opening remarks today, but was sure she'd held everyone spellbound as she voiced her thanks and promoted the Dorje Yidam cause.

"Please, form a line," she now called out. "There's plenty of sand, enough for everybody!"

An assembly line of monks divided the pile into individual portions. I was desperate to reach Sonam, but there was only one pathway and it started at the end of the long queue.

I inched forward. Finally, I stood before him. His smile faded at my grim expression.

"Geshe, didn't you see? The namchuwangdan . . ."

He leaned close, touching my forehead to his. "Not now," he said, his voice low. "Later."

He pulled away. Yeshe passed him something, which he handed over to me. My fingers closed around a small cylinder of glass.

I opened my palm. The black-capped vial was half-filled with multicolored mandala sand. But it was otherwise identical to the one I'd put in my pocket this morning, sealed in an evidence bag. The one filled with blood.

I pushed through the crowd to Bill. He stood with one arm slung across Sasha's shoulder.

"Ten! Guess who came first in marksmanship?" Bill said. "Chip off the old block."

"I need to speak with you." I caught myself. "Sorry. That's great news, Sasha."

Sasha peered at me. "Talk to him, Dad," he said to Bill. "I'll catch you guys later."

He'd read the situation perfectly, and this—more than his capacity to hit a paper target—told me Sasha would make a great detective someday.

Bill followed me into the crowded courtyard. I pulled him to the far side of the fishpond and handed him a sealed bag holding the glass vial of blood. This morning I'd filled out the chain-of-evidence form as best I could, considering the case was closed and I was no longer a cop.

"What the hell is this?"

"It was in my mailbox yesterday. Anything about it look familiar?"

I held up the other, sand-filled vial.

"Right," he said, comparing the two. "Just like the party favors."

"Think you can get forensics to check it out?"

Bill sighed. "Ten, I don't know what to say, except someone has a sick sense of humor."

"What are you talking about? It's more evidence."

"Evidence of what? Look. The dead kid is a suicide. The missing kid is missing on purpose. No one, including you, my friend, can find anyone who knows jack shit. And I've got a triple homicide and two gang-related drive-bys that just landed on my desk. Which means I get to work on Sunday again. Woo-fucking-hoo."

"So you're saying no."

"I'm saying, stand in line. But it's basement priority, kiddo, so you know what that means."

"Fine." I grabbed the pouch back.

"Sorry."

"No. I get it. It's like everything else. Nothing happens, until something really bad happens."

Bill glared at me. "Give me the damn bag," he said.

CHAPTER 47

The courtyard had emptied. I ran to the parking lot just in time to see Eric drive off with Sonam in the Leonards' Lexus. Homer's snout was pressed against the rear window. I walked up to Julie.

"Sonam's not overseeing the disbursement?" I was surprised. The final step of mandala deconstruction was critical. It required pouring a portion of the sand into a body of water, to further spread the benevolence.

"Change of plan," Julie said. "The Arroyo Seco is too seco. We're going a little farther away, to some waterfall Adina knows about. Sonam took a pass. He needs to rest."

I would have to rely on Yeshe and Lobsang for answers.

With Lobsang supervising, TJ and Wangdue stacked the last box of mandala supplies in the back of the van.

Adina was loading a backpack with bottles of water. "It's going to be hot there."

"Where?" I said.

Nobody bothered to answer me.

"Okay," Adina continued. "Cooler? Check. Water? Check." Adina's eyes were vibrating with energy. She seemed even more intense than usual, almost frantic. Maybe it was spillover from the success of the event. The glass donation jar had been stuffed with bills.

"Adventure pass?" Adina fished a big salmon-pink ticket out of her purse and handed it to Julie. "Check!"

Adina hefted the backpack and slipped it over my shoulders. It must have weighed 20 pounds.

"Not too heavy?"

"Depends on where we're going," I said.

"It's a piece of cake," Adina said. She stuck out her palm. I slapped her five. She gave me a look.

"Nice try. Keys."

"What?"

"You're going in the van. The pass is only good for one vehicle. TJ and I are taking your car back to our place. Keys, please."

There went my plan to drive Yeshe and Lobsang separately.

"We go fast in Mustang!" TJ was wearing new aviator sunglasses. "Like James Bond!"

"Uh."

"Relax, Ten," Adina said. "I was raised on a stick shift. Ask anyone. I'm hell on wheels."

Was that supposed to reassure me?

Adina patted the backpack. "Precious cargo, don't forget."

"The water?"

"The sand, sweetheart. Pure sattva."

Of course. The sand. That explained the weight.

"Okay, guys." Adina's eyes glittered. "Stay hydrated. And remember, the planetarium show starts at eight forty-five. If you're late, they lock you out."

I'd totally forgotten about our field trip to the Griffith Observatory. Yeshe and Lobsang were going to go nuts.

I shrugged off the pack and stuck it in the back of the van with the boxes. Julie was waiting for me up front.

"Looks like I'm going with you," I told Julie.

"Do you want to drive?" she asked.

I moved close, careful to keep my voice low.

"Jules, I need to sit in the back with Yeshe and Lobsang, okay? *Just* Yeshe and Lobsang."

She didn't miss a beat. "Wangdue!" she called. "You're up front with me today!"

I slid open the side door. Yeshe was already buckled in, smiling under the brim of his Dodgers cap. I climbed next to him and Lobsang followed.

Julie steered the van up Los Robles onto Corson and merged onto the 210, heading east. Up front, Wangdue gazed out the window, silent as usual. His hands fingered through his prayer beads. The kid never stopped.

"How long is the drive?" I asked Julie.

"Half an hour, max." She turned on the radio and punched a few buttons. Classical music, something with a lot of violins, filled the van.

Half an hour. I'd better get started. Where to begin?

Lobsang beat me to it. "You see mistake?" he said. "You see namchuwangdan?"

"I did."

He twisted to face me. "I notice first thing when we come in this morning. Too late to fix. Who does this thing?"

Yeshe leaned across me. "Why it matter? Is finished now."

"No, Lobsang's right. It does matter," I said. "It matters a lot."

My voice quiet, I gave them a truncated account of my talk with Sonam. I pulled up the namchuwangdan images on my phone.

"This is part of a pattern. And it's aimed at me, although I don't know why." I turned to Lobsang. "Who had access to the sand mandala? Besides the museum officials, I mean."

"We have key," Lobsang said. "Just to gallery. After they come so late the first morning, they give to us. We keep in our place." He corrected himself. "Eric and Adina's place."

"Was it there last night?"

Lobsang nodded. "And this morning. Always on small table next to door. We give it back already."

"Okay."

Yeshe looked concerned.

Up ahead, a solid bank of brake lights announced a major slowdown. Julie made an immediate exit off the freeway. She continued east on Sierra Madre Boulevard, and we entered what must have been a supermagnetic zone for Christians. I counted at least five churches in a four-block range.

Yeshe glanced at Wangdue. He turned back to me, his voice troubled. "Tenzing, last night, I wake up for some reason. And I notice something." His distress was evident. "TJ and Wangdue, they sleep at other end of room, yes?"

"Yes."

"Last night I see two mattress. But only one body under blanket. I smile, because it remind me of you, when we are boys. How you like to go outside."

Lobsang made an impatient sound.

"What? I am thinking only someone still have jet leg. Probably out taking a walk!"

"Lag." Lobsang said. "Not leg."

I steered the conversation back. I was grateful for the swelling strings on the radio. "Could you tell who was missing? Or how long he was gone?"

Yeshe shook his head. "No. I just go back to sleep."

So either TJ or Wangdue had the means and opportunity to deface the mandala, although that made no sense either. What did they do, hitchhike to Pasadena and back?

Up ahead, Wangdue remained a silent witness to the world streaming past.

We'd turned toward Angeles National Forest and were winding up a steep series of switchbacks leading into the Angeles Crest. A hawk spiraled up into the blue void.

Lobsang spoke, his voice grim. "Nawang," he said. "Nawang do this."

For a moment, the air darkened. I closed my eyes. This was not the time to succumb to another panic attack. When my lungs finally cooperated, I opened my eyes again.

"What happened that summer?" I said. "The summer Nawang disappeared?" I turned to Lobsang. "Please."

Lobsang offered a short nod, as if making a decision. "A local Indian boy, he die in Dharamshala, hanh? A shepherd boy. A Gaddi."

"His name Bhim," Yeshe added.

"Bhim," I repeated, nodding.

Yes. I remember.

"Someone kill him," Lobsang said. "Another boy. A Tibetan, they say."

"Bhim was murdered?" The clamp on my recollections loosened.

"Stabbed," Lobsang said. He glanced at me, then away. "With phurba."

Nawang lurches close. A blade flashes. One! Two! Three! The boy falls.

Can't breathe.

I reached across Yeshe to open the window, but it wasn't that kind of window. I was sealed in tight.

"They say you are there. They think maybe you do this!" Yeshe broke in. "But Tenzing, we know it cannot be true. We know you cannot kill boy."

Can't breathe.

I choked out the words. "But Nawang could," I said. "And Nawang did."

The van pulled into a parking area.

"We're here," Julie said, an echo of my first clue that something was wrong.

CHAPTER 48

A carved wooden sign listed several destination points. The mid-afternoon sun beat down on us, baking hot.

"Sturtevant Falls, two point eight miles," I read. Not exactly a piece of cake, at least not in this heat.

Julie frowned. "Adina said it was super short. I should have double-checked." She eyed her phone. "Okay, well, it's almost two o'clock. What do you guys think?"

Like me, Julie was wearing running shoes. Wangdue's Tevas would probably work. I studied Lobsang and Yeshe's worn leather sandals dubiously.

"How difficult is the hike?" I asked Julie, who was reading the Yelp description on her phone.

"It says here kids can do it. Dogs, too."

Lobsang took charge. "We eat. And then we walk to falling water."

We wolfed down Julie's ciabatta creations—fresh mozzarella and pesto for me, prosciutto and swiss for everyone else. Only Wangdue abstained. He was still keeping to his Saka Dawa, one-meal-a-day fast.

And I was still resenting him for it.

Julie had put some beer in the cooler, but Wangdue's willpower was chastening. We stuck with bottled water.

The public restroom was a simple wooden structure, dull brown and buzzing with flies. As I waited my turn, I scanned the adjacent bulletin board. A bright orange sign carried a stark warning, printed over the image of charred tree trunks: ONE CARELESS MOMENT.

There were several cars in the lot. I checked them out, a cop's reflex. And was glad I did. One black Toyota Highlander

with tinted windows was suspiciously tricked out. My limbic lobe—the primitive lizard part that's prewired to sense danger—lit up like a neon sign.

And my guns were in the Mustang, heading for Los Feliz.

"Oh no," I muttered, but Julie heard.

"What?"

"My guns. They're in my car."

"With TJ?" Her eyes widened with alarm.

"Don't worry. I locked the case," I said. But I shared her unease, if for a different reason. That SUV sure looked like the kind of wild bull gangbangers loved to ride.

The hike began in reverse, with a steep descent down a narrow asphalt fire road. Tiny gnats dive-bombed our faces. The air remained hot and still, though overhanging foliage provided occasional shade.

The sound of leather slapping against concrete followed me down the hill. I slowed my pace until Yeshe and Lobsang drew parallel.

"Sonam said some troubling things about Apa, yesterday. Didn't he, Yeshe?"

"Look!" Yeshe pointed to another wooden sign. "Wisdom everywhere!"

I read the carved yellow lettering: *Take care of the land . . . Someday you'll be part of it.* "Yes. Very wise." And hopefully not prophetic—at least not today.

I aimed my next question at Lobsang. "You referred to my father's unskilled actions. What did you mean?"

"Tenzing, your father . . ." Lobsang waved at the air to disperse a sudden swarm of gnats. "The Buddha says, intention of the doer is important when examining certain choices, hanh?"

Yeshe nodded eagerly. "Yes! Karma not always so clear."

I came to an abrupt stop. "Okay. There's a term for what you're both doing. It's called 'beating around the bush.' Just stop, okay?"

Julie and Wangdue were several yards ahead. Wangdue's robe flashed red in the dappled light as they rounded a curve.

"Before your father die, he ask to meet with us," Lobsang said. "In private."

"Also Geshe Sonam, he is there," Yeshe added.

"Your father says he want to . . ." Lobsang muttered a word at Yeshe.

"Admit," Yeshe said.

"Hanh. Admit something. He says he feels bad about certain things, and he wants to explain. So we will understand."

"He feel sorry about how he is with you," Yeshe said.

"Hard to imagine, but okay," I said. "Go on."

The road flattened out. We crossed a slatted wooden bridge with metal railings. Beneath it was a bed of sticky mud. In wetter times the bridge might be necessary, but not today.

Asphalt gave way to cracked soil. Yellow honeysuckle vines crowded both sides of the trail.

"Yesterday, we talk about Kalachakra. Wheel of Time initiations, hanh?" Lobsang's sandals scuffed, hemming his robe with dust.

"Yes," I said.

"Some say, Kalachakra tantra the root and crown of the teaching."

We passed a land-lease cabin balanced on a rocky pile of river stone and surrounded by dying pine trees, their needles red-brown. A limp American flag hung from a pole out front, its borders barely riffling.

"With Kalachakra initiations, many stages," Lobsang continued. "First ones are for everyone, for public, but after that, initiations more secret, for higher levels."

"Okay."

"To reach final stage of perfection, some think it necessary for woman to be present."

"Special woman," Yeshe said. "Like empty vessel. Willing to surrender. Karma mudra."

"Right," I said. "Sonam and I talked about this."

More cabins appeared alongside a trickle of stream. Here and there, stagnant water collected in shallow pools, oily

black and alive with insects. An uneven row of cement steps branched upward to the left, ending at a lone, lopsided shack.

A slash of red caught my eye. I looked closer. A gang tag marred the final riser. The jagged letters were incongruous in the middle of this forest glen. Not *JMM*, thankfully. A co-incidence of that magnitude might have sent me out of the forest screaming.

PLK. Pasadena Latin Kings.

Lobsang picked up the thread of our conversation. "Tradition says karma mudra should be woman with pale skin, white like moon and without blemish. Beautiful. And young. No more than twenty years." He wouldn't meet my eyes.

My mother, Valerie, was 19 when she and my father met.

Now Lobsang was almost pleading. "Tenzing, your father, he wanting very much to progress. To achieve final stage of perfection, so he can remove karmic stains of others. He wish to master his body. He make commitment to this."

Yeshe said, "He is thinking, if attainment of goal is meant to be, right woman will appear."

I realized what they were saying and also not saying. "Valerie showed up at the monastery. My mother was the answer to his petitions."

Yeshe touched my arm. "Yes. So when they practice Kalachakra tantra, intention is for liberation. Right action, for bringing more *sattva*, more goodness into world. Not for . . ." Yeshe looked pained. "Not to . . ."

"Not to make a baby," I said.

It made a certain sense. After all, what did my father know about birth control? And as for my mother, she was gullible to the point of delusion. One was completely ignorant, the other, blindly trusting. But both burned with a fierce desire to taste enlightenment.

They'd felt sexual attraction and assumed a sacred imperative. Mistook temporary madness for that one true love. *The minute I met your father, I knew we were soulmates*, my mother used to say when wine had rendered her maudlin.

So they'd entered into a crazy pact and made a sexual commitment to a higher cause, with one disastrous result.

Me.

The possibility of pregnancy hadn't occurred to them. Not when their intentions were so pure. So when I arrived, squalling and discontent, I didn't just signal naivete. I served as living proof of my father's utter failure to advance. He not only didn't achieve the stage of perfection, he broke his vows in the process.

No wonder he was so hard on me.

The rage started as a kernel of heat in my solar plexus.

"No," I said. "He wasn't that naive. Apa knew this could happen. He knew."

"What you mean?" Yeshe said.

The heat spread. I was seething. "Nawang."

Their expressions were blank. They still didn't know.

"My father didn't tell you about Nawang, did he, during this big confession? How convenient for him."

Lobsang waved a hand, as if to ward off what my words implied.

"I do not understand. Did not tell us what?" Yeshe said.

"My mother wasn't Apa's first vessel," I said. "And I wasn't his first mistake."

CHAPTER 49

Lobsang scowled, but said nothing. Yeshe seemed to shrink inside his robe at my words.

The air darkened. Shadows reached from either side of a rocky gully, brambled and thick with growth. Our path had narrowed and now sliced between a pair of cliffs like a wound.

Lots of cover here; perfect place to stage an ambush.

We had lost sight of Julie and Wangdue, but just ahead another weathered wooden sign pointed us right, to Fiddler's Crossing and the falls beyond.

Male voices shouted. Raucous laughter. And then, ominous silence.

We hurried over fallen boulders, zigging left and right toward the sound of tumbling water.

And then we were there. Leafy limbs arched green across a natural stone grotto, carved slowly over time. A narrow stream skipped down multiple levels of mossy granite and fed into an oval pool at the base—not exactly thunderous, but a waterfall nonetheless.

Julie and Wangdue had stopped at a grove of trees a short distance from the water. Julie shot me a look of warning and gestured slightly in the direction of the waterfall.

I focused on the four young men thigh-deep and shirt-less in the shallow swimming hole. They glared at us, arms crossed. Discolored ink marked their necks, trunks, and fore-arms. Their skin tone was in that same indeterminate range as mine—the tea-colored no-man's-land between black and white. Everything else pegged them as Hispanic gangbangers.

One of them, the alpha of the pack, met my eyes, all lean muscle and meanness. He raked back a dark slick of hair. His flat stare hinted at violence and a close acquaintance with untimely death.

He stepped forward, a clear challenge.

I moved in front of Yeshe and Lobsang.

His hostile eyes skimmed past me and took note of Lobsang's shaved head and red robe. He lingered over Yeshe's Dodgers cap and cocked his head, as if puzzled.

Alpha looked back at his three friends. *"¿Qué son?"* he asked, his voice mocking.

"Payasos," a second man answered.

The leader turned back, his smile a sneer. "My compadre, he thinks you are clowns. But me? I see your colors, and I think maybe you are bad boys." He directed his next question at Yeshe. "Are you a bad boy, *chava*? Where are you from?" His crew moved beside him, hands reaching for the pockets of their baggy, low-riding shorts.

The situation was escalating quickly, but why?

"You from Sacramento, bitch?"

Sacramento? And then I understood. Unbelievable. This idiot saw burgundy robes and high cheekbones and actually thought we were part of the Sacramento Bad Boys, a nasty Asian-American gang making inroads in Los Angeles. If it weren't so potentially deadly, the situation would be laughable.

"We from Dorje Yidam," Yeshe answered brightly. "In Dharamshala."

Alpha chewed this over, scowling. I needed to diffuse the tension before we found out what was in those pockets.

I quickly read Alpha's tats for clues, registering the ribbon-banner inked across his flat belly, displaying the Latin words *Veni, Vidi, Vici*; the naked woman on his upper torso; the iron cross at his throat; the handguns on both biceps.

There.

Directly over his heart was a crude, five-pointed crown. Above it, the initials *PLK*. Pasadena Latin Kings.

Of course. They'd left their calling card on the trail.

I knew what to do.

"We come in peace," I said. "These men are Buddhist monks. They're from Tibet, and they live in India." I gestured. "But Yeshe here already met another friend of yours in Pasadena." I willed Yeshe to understand. "Remember? He taught you their special mudra, didn't he, Yeshe?"

"Oh, yes!" Yeshe said. Beaming, he held up his palm: middle fingers bent; pinkie, thumb, and forefinger up. The Pasadena Latin Kings' hand sign.

After a moment of stunned silence, the leader burst out laughing. His soldiers relaxed. "No shit," he said, and flashed the same sign back. "Welcome to L.A., homes."

CHAPTER 50

In the end, it was Wangdue who did the honors, his river-walking Tevas sealing the deal. As rituals go, this was turning out to be pretty makeshift. Just the way I liked it.

I fished two handbells out of the backpack, followed by a heavy globe-shaped container bundled in embroidered cloth. I unwrapped the cloth and found a large sand-filled urn. Adina had wisely sealed the rim with plastic wrap and tape. I peeled off the temporary lid and handed the urn to Wangdue.

He waded into the swimming hole and crossed to the far end, where glinting drops of water tumbled in a narrow sheet.

Yeshe and Lobsang began the chant, invoking Green Tara's blessings. They asked that the healing powers of loving-kindness merge with the water, that the intentions dissolve, evaporate, form into clouds, reincarnate as rain, and fall like healing tears of compassion onto a suffering earth.

The bangers were long gone. Too bad, they might have gained something by hanging around.

Or were they? A movement caught my eye, high and to the left, by a forked trunk at the edge of the tree line. I shaded my eyes, squinting into the direct sunlight. Nothing stirred.

There you go again, looking for trouble.

Wangdue tipped the urn, releasing a steady flow of sand. Colored particles clouded the water before sinking out of sight. Julie and I rang the drilbus, and the clanging echoed in the steep canyon before fading into silence.

This time, it was the snap of a branch that set my nerves jangling. I spun toward the noise but found only a clump of straggly bushes clinging to a steep path.

"Good," Yeshe said. "Is finished."

Wangdue waded out, his robe dripping. He handed me the empty urn and bowed. And finally, something in me shifted.

Wangdue was exactly like me, before I rejected my vows and any part of me that believed in them. His one-pointed focus was disconcerting. That didn't mean it was bad. As my sober friend Joan loved to remind me, "You spot it, you got it." Worse, Wangdue's stern nature also reminded me of my father. My dislike had been automatic and without investigation—the polar opposite of mindful.

"You did well," I now told Wangdue, and bowed back. His eyes widened in surprise.

A rabbit shot across the rocky slope to my left, flushed out of its hole by something. Or someone. My pulse accelerated.

"I'm going to check out that trail," I said to Julie.

Her expression was dubious. "It looks pretty steep. Are you sure?"

I was already moving.

"We should leave in twenty minutes, Ten." Julie pulled out her phone. "I'll let Adina know." She frowned at the screen. "Nope. No signal."

I reached the base of the slope and started climbing.

"Be careful."

There was no time to be careful. I traversed slippery shale, urging my body to move quickly. Real or not, I could smell danger.

The hillside started out steep and quickly grew steeper. The angled rock face was pimpled with boulders and bearded with scrubby brush. A pair of chipmunks skittered past, as the narrow path quickly became a perpendicular twist of dirt. I pushed between tangled branches and granite, using crevasses as footholds and roots as pulleys.

At the top of the cliff I found the forked trunk where I'd first seen movement. The dying tree marked a split in the path. A narrow stone lip wound to the right. Beyond it lay

the falls. I edged toward a flat ledge of rock overlooking the tumble of water. It would provide the clearest view of the area.

The sound of rushing water grew louder.

I reached the ledge. The 100-foot drop was almost vertical. For a moment, my legs turned to jelly.

Crack!

The sound was deafening. A rock to my left splintered.

Crack!

To my right, stone shattered, spitting up shards.

"Julie! Get down!" I yelled into the void, my voice muffled by the ringing in my ears. "Everyone down! Someone's shooting!"

Crack!

This one didn't land, not that I could see. Where was the shooter?

A faint shout—Lobsang, maybe—followed by Julie's panicked cry.

"I'm coming!" I shouted.

I shimmied across the narrow rim, my hands splayed against rough stone. If I lost my footing, I'd fall to certain death—that's if a bullet didn't kill me first. I hit the path and broke into a crouched sprint, zigzagging in tight angles until I could take cover behind the forked tree trunk.

There was no easy way down, especially not at top speed. I plunged anyway, scrambling, sliding, grasping at roots, colliding with stones. I grabbed something thorny and pain stabbed my left palm.

Crack!

Too close. My eardrums shrieked.

Was I hit?

I assessed. No blood. Still breathing. So, no.

The bullet had entered a tree six feet to my left. A thick branch hung at an odd angle, partially snapped off.

The dirt. Check the dirt.

The earth beyond was untouched. No tunneling, no telltale mound.

It didn't go through.

I tucked and rolled sideways until I was by the trunk, its damaged limb bent and dangling. I stood and yanked hard, praying this brief, exposed pause wouldn't prove deadly. A second wrench, and the branch splintered off. Hunkering again, I half scuttled, half sprinted until I reached the steepest part of the descent, somehow keeping hold of my broken prize.

The path below was riddled with twisted roots. A straight drop.

I flipped onto my stomach and climbed down backward, rung by rooted rung, the wooden tree limb awkwardly pinned across my chest. At times I had to point the branch straight up like a spear so it wouldn't catch. Finally the trail spilled back onto the bouldered hillside overlooking the swimming hole. I turned and sat on my haunches, balancing the branch across my lap, and slid down the steep slope. Pebbles cascaded in front of me. Below me, the grotto was silent.

This is taking too long!

I stood upright and slung the thick limb. It arched through the air and landed on the ground below. I would complete the final yards at a dead run.

I took a giant stride, but the ground gave like loose grain. There was nothing to break my momentum and I pitched headlong. My brain said *curl and roll* but my body said *break the fall.*

The crash came hard. My right wrist took the brunt of the impact. My forehead landed second, striking hard ground and snapping back. A sudden, brutal hit.

I tasted blood.

"Ten!" Julie's panicked voice came from behind a group of boulders.

Sheer adrenaline compelled me to my feet. I cradled my arm and ran. I found them all huddled in a group.

"Are you okay? Is anyone shot?"

Julie's face was white. "No! We heard gunfire, so we hid."

"Good. Good. Did you call for help?" Julie's helpless expression reminded me: no service up here.

"Baby," Julie said. "God, are you okay?"

I inventoried my body. "I think so," I said. "I'm not shot, anyway." My right arm looked strange, the wrist thickening before my eyes. But there was no pain, only a numb weightiness. I flexed the fingers. Made a fist. "I may have sprained my wrist," I said.

"You're bleeding." Julie touched my lip.

"Bit my tongue. It's nothing." My forehead throbbed. I located a tender bump the size of a golf ball. My tongue was sore. A sharp, needling pain in my palm was a reminder where the thorn had pierced. I didn't even want to think about what other bruises might be forming.

All because I just had to sprint those final few yards.

One careless moment.

Lobsang touched my shoulder. "Tenzing, you see who is shooting gun?"

"No."

Wangdue squinted up at the cliffs, his expression thoughtful.

Yeshe's voice was distressed. "Those boys from before? Is them?"

"Maybe. But probably not," I said. "Drive-by is more their style."

"Then who? Who want to harm us?"

"I'm not sure," I said. "But they were mostly shooting at me."

"Why?" Julie said. "I don't understand why."

"I don't either, Jules."

Yeshe mustered a smile. "You very lucky man. Good karma for you today. Bullets not hit you."

"That's me. Mr. Lucky." I didn't tell Yeshe how close I had come to becoming part of the earth again.

Someone wanted me dead. But who?

The bullet might tell me.

The broken tree limb lay where I'd tossed it. I dashed over, snatched it off the ground, and raced back.

The forest was silent. Watchful. Not even the chipmunks stirred. My sense was the shooter or shooters were gone.

My right wrist definitely felt strange.

"Lobsang, hold this?"

He took the branch, maybe five feet in length.

"Rotate it?" He looked at me. "Turn it slowly."

He rotated it like a spit.

"Stop."

A narrow bullet had lodged in a knot in the thickest part of the branch, just about eight inches from the end.

Maybe I was lucky after all. I had Wangdue break off that portion and zip it in the backpack.

We waited as long as we dared, before finally heading back up the path. I jumped at every random noise, and scoured the cliffsides at every turn, but the sniper was gone, or was hidden. We finally reached the lot. A handful of hikers lingered by their cars.

By then, my head hurt so much that a bullet to the brain didn't sound that bad.

CHAPTER 51

"It's not broken." My functioning hand patted a temporary sling fashioned from a strip of Yeshe's robe. "And anyway, you fixed me up."

Julie's expression was stony as she steered the van back to civilization. The three monks were silent in the back. We were all exhausted. Lobsang had even managed to fall asleep. I was much too wired to even try.

"It's irresponsible, and you know it," Julie said. "You took a bad fall."

"The Advil is really helping. If it's worse tomorrow, I promise I'll go straight to the doctor, okay?"

"No. None of this is okay." Julie's voice broke.

"Jules?"

"Someone tried to kill you, Ten. I'm scared, okay?"

"Understood." An earlier version of me would have tried to talk her out of feeling scared, but I skipped that part. "Look. Bill's meeting me at the observatory. I've got the bullet to give him—that should tell us something. And he's sending a team to Sturtevant Falls in the morning to take a closer look."

"Do you think they'll find him?"

"Probably not," I admitted. "My gut tells me whoever's behind all this stuff is long gone."

Julie shot me a look.

"All this stuff?" Her fingers tightened on the steering wheel. "What do you mean, all this stuff? There's more?" Julie's voice rose. "Babe, you have to talk to me."

So I did. I ran through the series of baffling events—young Colin's license, the person on the Vyrus, Lola's bindi,

the vial of blood. And the Power of Ten symbol, following me like a malevolent shadow.

"Someone's trying to gaslight you," Julie said.

"Gaslight me?"

"Manipulate your reality. Make you think you're going crazy."

"Well, it's working."

Yeshe's voice floated from the seat behind me.

"Tenzing, when you first notice these things?"

So he'd been listening. Which meant Wangdue had, as well.

"Good question." I mentally rewound the troubling events of the past week or so.

"I guess when I opened that first envelope," I said. "No, wait. Before that, even. At the airport. The day you landed. I felt like someone was watching me. And then I got that call."

Hram hram hram hram.

"I feel something there at airport also." Wangdue's voice. "Something dark. Like demon."

Lobsang chose that moment to let out a loud snore. I jumped. I think we all did. A moment later, he cleared his throat. "When dinner?" he asked.

It felt good to laugh.

"So listen," I said, when the laughter settled. "Bill is already on it. I don't want to worry the others. Let's keep the sniper to ourselves, okay?"

Los Feliz Boulevard was jammed, as usual, but it was late enough in the day that Observatory Drive had opened up. Eric was waiting for us at the upper lot. He directed the van to a reserved spot. We trudged toward the gleaming white walls of the Griffith Observatory as if on a pilgrimage to Mecca.

The elegant art deco structure was fashioned out of concrete and dreams; part Parthenon, part Taj Mahal. Three copper-topped domes glowed like opals in the flame-colored sunset.

Fellow travelers were scattered across the grounds. More were visible in the galleries above, human beads strung around every dome.

Two manicured rectangles of emerald lawn were fenced off from pedestrians. Adina had spread a blanket on a third lawn, this one an open patch of dead and dying grass. Sonam sat in a folding lawn chair, a cane resting between his legs. TJ had stretched out alongside him.

Wangdue or TJ? Wangdue or TJ? I still hadn't decided on the culprit, but I was leaning toward TJ now.

I lowered myself next to him. He smiled, but I noticed how quickly he flipped the magnetic cover over his iPad screen. He was wearing a dark blue hoodie over his robe. I hadn't seen it before.

"Nice hoodie."

"Yes. I buy for my brother," he said. His eyes shifted away. Maybe he thought I was judging him. He sat up. His boots were also new—Dr. Martens. I refrained from comment.

Wangdue set the backpack next to me and wandered off to explore a monument in front of the entrance. The carved sides were of seven white-robed sages—saints of astronomy holding their sacred instruments of science. From here, I could see Newton, Kepler, and Copernicus.

TJ pointed out a carved bust on a pedestal. "James Dean! Very famous actor!"

"I guess that counts as a star," I replied.

Adina was doling out burritos, plump tubes wrapped in foil that smelled of rice and beans. When she got to me she paused.

"Whoa," she said. "You weren't kidding. That's some bump on your noggin."

I'd called Eric from the van to warn everyone about my spill.

Julie unwrapped my burrito for me. It felt strange eating with my left hand. I took a tentative bite.

"Jesus, Ten. Since when is strolling in the woods a contact sport?" Bill kept his voice casual, but his forehead

dripped and his shirtsleeves were marked with half-moons of sweat. He'd wasted no time getting up the hill.

"You should see the other tree," I said, a twist on an old joke between us. I handed Julie my barely touched burrito.

"That's it?" she said.

"My stomach feels a little funny." I struggled upright— everything was more work with only one arm. I nudged the backpack toward Bill with my toe. He took the hint and picked it up.

We moved several yards away. Bill unzipped the pack. "This it?" He pulled out the 18-inch section of tree limb.

"That's it."

He squinted at the narrow burrow tunneling straight into the knot. "Well, you're right about one thing. This probably wasn't a PLK gang hit. That's a twenty-two hole."

"A twenty-two? Are you sure? It sounded like a howitzer."

"A two twenty-two military, then?"

"Louder."

"O-kay." He activated his phone flashlight and aimed the bright glow at the hole. "That's pretty deep, a lot of energy. So maybe a twenty-two two-fifty. Wildcat cartridge."

"Meaning?"

"Meaning someone was shooting a varmint rifle." He thumbed off the light and pocketed his phone. "Meaning you were the varmint."

"A hunting rifle?" Another fact that made no sense.

"Yeah. Seven hundred Savage. Maybe a Browning. Bolt-action, certainly." He bagged the branch. "The lab will dig this out first thing. I'll put a rush on it." He shot me a look. "Hell, I'll put a rush on the vial of blood, too."

I resisted commenting. Nobody wants to hear *I told you so*.

"May I?" Bill gently tugged apart my amateur sling for a closer look.

"It doesn't hurt." Technically, this was no longer true. A deep ache had taken permanent hold in my forearm. Plus, my fingers resembled five fat sausages.

"You need to see a doctor."

"I need to do a lot of things," I said. "But right now I need to be with my fiancée and friends, gaze at a few planets, and hope to survive the annihilation of humanity."

The planetarium show supposedly highlighted an ancient Mayan prediction of a current global apocalypse. The date of which had already passed. But still.

Bill didn't even blink. He was used to me saying things like this.

"Whatever," he said. "Try to stay out of any more trouble."

Adina walked up.

"May I? This should help." She rubbed something brown and oily into the bulge on my forehead. "Arnica." She stepped back and locked eyes with me. "Honey, what happened out there?"

"Nothing," I said. "I tripped. I fell."

We rejoined the others and headed up the central walkway to the entrance. The doors were bronze and glass medleys of planetary symbols, glossy and polished. We pushed inside. Like the outside shell, the pristine interior reflected a lot of recent care and renovation.

"Okay, everyone, we only have an hour," Adina announced.

"Bit skimpy," I joked. "Considering how long it took to create the universe."

"Somebody's feeling better," Julie said.

"That's because somebody else gave him Advil," I answered.

Inside the central rotunda a crowd surrounded a massive Foucault pendulum, suspended by a wire from the ceiling. Its steady, mysterious sway was subtle proof that the planet we occupied was also in constant motion.

The movement was making me dizzy.

Adina pointed to the ceiling, and I looked up instead. It was covered with murals, some illustrating celestial mythology, others illustrating scientific methodology, but all

paying homage to human nature's compulsive need to explain creation.

"Who build this place?" TJ asked, his voice hushed.

"That would be Griffith J. Griffith," answered a guide. She was young, with cropped, purple-tipped hair and a T-shirt that announced *Back in my day, we had NINE planets.* According to the museum ID card pinned to her chest, her name was Trixie.

"Mr. Griffith was awesome. A visionary," Trixie-the-guide continued. "Like, literally. He got to look through the first sixty-inch telescope up on Mount Wilson right after it was built and was, like, totally transformed. He decided everyone had to see the sky that way so he gave enough money to build this place. He wanted to change the world."

TJ's eyes shone. "Yes. Change world," he breathed.

"Amazing story," Julie said.

"Check out the downstairs," Trixie added. "If you ask at the desk, they'll let you hold an actual meteorite."

Adina tapped her wristwatch. "Keep moving," she said. We hurried after her into a smaller rotunda and buzzed past a camera obscura, a Tesla coil, and a series of timekeeping instruments, magnifying lenses, and telescopes.

So many ways to quantify and observe the cosmos, I thought, and not one of them able to pinpoint the source of mankind's suffering.

TJ was glued to a glass-encased model of the observatory. Underneath it was an interactive row of buttons and descriptions. He kept pushing the same button over and over, lighting a segment to the right.

He caught me watching. He strolled off, self-consciously casual.

"Be right back," I told Julie.

I pushed the same button. The right-hand corner of the structure lit up. I checked the description. "Transit corridor," I read.

Why was he so interested?

The transit corridor ran alongside something called Sunset Terrace on the lower level, next to a café. Also next to the Stellar Emporium gift shop.

Mystery solved. TJ had located another store where he could eye-shop, or better yet, shop-shop. He'd been bitten by the highly contagious bug called *wanting-stuff-you-don't-need*. Once infected by craving, it's very hard to recover. Ask the Buddha.

The monks had crossed the main rotunda and were wandering through a fresh series of exhibits. TJ again was stalled. Julie and I joined him at a demonstration of the phases of day and night across global time zones.

"This is desert?" he asked Julie, pointing to a flickering image of cactus trees. Washes of light and dark time-lapsed across the spiked and knobby cactus limbs.

"Yes. Those are Joshua trees," Julie said. TJ stared, captivated by the accelerated time loop.

"Let's go downstairs," Julie said to me.

We descended two flights of stairs and followed a curved hallway downward. The outer wall traced the formation of the universe, starting with the big bang. Markers noted highlights of evolution over the billions of years it took to form life out of carbon and chance, eventually leading to the tiny speck of time called the present.

This whole place was one long lesson in insignificance.

The corridor dumped us into a cavernous space. Giant planets hung from the ceiling like luminous baubles. Julie made a beeline for the information desk. A pale, angular man in horn-rimmed glasses was tapping at a keyboard.

"Excuse me? Sir? Trixie upstairs said we might be able to hold a meteorite." Julie offered the man her best smile.

His expression unreadable, he wheeled his chair sideways, opened a drawer, and pulled out a wooden box. He opened it, laid a small mat of felt on the counter, and lifted out a craggy blob of blue-black iron. He set it on the mat.

"How old?" I asked.

"Four, four and a half," he answered. "Billion."

I stroked the crust, the edges shiny where fingers like mine had rubbed.

"May I hold it?" Julie asked. He nodded, and she picked it up. "Whoa. It's heavy."

"How can you tell it's not just terrestrial rock?" I asked.

"Other than cutting it in half? One, it was found next to a huge meteor crater. And two, it's pure iron."

"Deduction," I said.

"Yes, logical reasoning, therefore deductive. Or inductive, I suppose, depending on where you start. As in, I have good reason to believe given the circumstances that this is a meteor, although the truth is not guaranteed. Unlike Sherlock Holmes, by the way. He used abduction, despite what he claimed. Out of many possible explanations, he abduced the single most correct one. Nobody seems to understand the difference."

Nor did I. My head was swimming.

"Don't get me wrong, I love Sherlock," he added. "I've read every book."

Apparently, we Arthur Conan Doyle fans were everywhere, even in the bowels of the Griffith Observatory.

"Ten, look."

Julie pointed to a massive wall showing multiple galaxies, millions of celestial objects normally naked to the human eye.

But all of my attention had moved to my wrist. The anesthetizing shock had fully worn off and the slightest move unleashed searing pain. I reached behind with my left hand to adjust the sling.

"Let me." Julie tightened the knot. "Better?"

I nodded, biting back nausea. Julie's body was haloed, as if eclipsed by her own private sun. Great. Add concussion to my list of ailments.

"I don't feel right about leaving for Ojai tomorrow," she said. "Maybe I should bail."

"No. You made a commitment. They need you."

My forearm throbbed. How was I going to get undressed? Take a shower? Open a can of cat food?

I wavered. "Unless maybe Adina . . . ?"

"I already asked. She's got other plans." Julie chewed at her lower lip.

"Go," I said. "I'll be fine." For the first time all week I regretted giving Kim time off. Just when you're sure you don't need other people, life lets you know you do.

"Please make your way to the west terrace if you have tickets to the eight forty-five show," a voice blared over the PA system.

Both our phones beeped with the same text: SOUTH GALLERY ON FIRST FLOOR. NOW. A.

Eric, Adina, and the five monks were already occupying a pair of benches just outside the planetarium entrance, next to a handicap sign. Apparently Sonam's cane meant we got to go inside first. A young male guide guarded the closed double doors.

Why is he holding a Taser?

Trixie joined Taser-guide. They pulled open the doors.

"Tickets," Taser-guide said and raised his arm, and I realized my addled brain had misinterpreted his bar code reader for a weapon. He leaned close to me. His face rippled like water. "Time's up," he said.

"What? What did you say?"

Adina stepped past me. "I've got all the tickets to *Time's Up*," she said.

I had to get a grip. It was the name of the show, not a personal warning.

We followed behind Adina like obedient schoolchildren. The floor felt spongy under my weight. I worried it was another symptom until I looked down and saw the cork flooring. The seats were plush, like little thrones. Adina led us to reserved seating, the last row on the left. We settled into eight seats. TJ was left standing by himself.

"Take mine, TJ." Eric pushed to his feet.

"No," TJ answered quickly. "I sit over here. Is good." He claimed an empty chair by the side exit. I envied him. I was feeling distinctly queasy and the show hadn't even started.

The room filled quickly. I multiplied rows and seats and came up with 300. Counted again and got 200, so I quit counting.

"Please turn off your cell phones," Trixie announced from the doorway.

My left hand fumbled with my iPhone.

Julie held out her hand. "Let me, babe."

I passed the phone over.

A large projector was positioned front and center, its bulbous satellite nose pointing skyward like a catapult.

Lobsang leaned across Yeshe. "Fiber-optic," he told me in an excited whisper. "State of art!"

Julie was right. They were like little kids. A wave of affection for them was followed by a sharp surge of nausea.

I bit back the wooziness as the show began, and a familiar beach scene filled the domed screen overhead. The Santa Monica Pier bustled under a deep blue sky. It was all very carefree, but for the ominous drumbeats and discordant horns that warned of trouble brewing.

Meteors materialized overhead, distant at first, milling aimlessly like wasps.

Bile pooled at the back of my throat.

The iron projectiles plummeted. Exploded. The crust of the earth cracked wide in response. Landmasses sheared away. Buildings collapsed and flattened.

The kettledrums had somehow invaded my brain and were pounding the inside of my skull as a loose planet spun out of orbit and sideswiped the moon. Dawa disintegrated, setting loose a sea of tumbling blue monkeys, sprouting wings.

Tiny pinpoints of pain danced behind my eyes.

"Hold on, hold on!" This from a live female narrator, standing at a podium. "Just stop, already. Humans are always

predicting the end of the world, but let's go back to the beginning, shall we?"

With the sound of a scratching needle, both images and music reversed, a handy rewind of an epic disaster.

My stomach heaved. I wasn't going to make it.

"I'll be right back," I whispered to Julie.

I burst into the outer hallway. The men's room was just around the corner. I stumbled straight into a stall and leaned over the toilet.

There wasn't much to lose, but I emptied my stomach.

Back at the row of sinks, I rinsed the sour taste from my mouth and splashed tepid water on my face, one-handed. My contusion looked like a bruised Saturn, rings of purple and green surrounding a raised lump, stained with brownish oil. My right eye was completely bloodshot.

"Hello, handsome," I said.

I headed back to the closed entrance. Just as the thought occurred that I might be locked out, a maroon-red streak crossed the corridor in front of me like the tail of a comet.

I ran to look. And saw TJ sprinting down the double flight of stairs, dodging startled bodies.

I hurried after, clinging to the rail, and ran past the calendar of time until I'd reentered the lower level, the depths of space. Planets dangled, massive eyes watching me as I combed the room. TJ had vanished like vapor.

Think. Think. Where could he have gone?

I pictured TJ pushing the button, lighting up the lower right-hand corner.

Transit corridor.

I bolted past the shuttered café and gift emporium and pushed through a pair of glass doors to an outdoor terrace.

The patio tables were empty, their umbrellas still open. The terrace was bordered by a metal railing over meshed wire.

I ran to the rail and leaned across it. Nothing to my right.

I looked left.

Just short of the corner, a red-robed figure hugged the wall.

"TJ!"

He turned. Alarm spread across his features like wildfire. Then he was gone.

I vaulted over the waist-high fence, ignoring the slash of pain in my forearm. At the corner of the structure the ground fell away. A cement support propped up the foundation, creating a three-foot gap. I scurried underneath like some kind of rodent.

"TJ!" My voice bounced uselessly between sturdy concrete struts.

I ducked and scrambled, emerging onto a dirt footpath littered with empty beer bottles and rattraps, the boxy kind that are supposedly humane. I was cradling my arm close. Every step was painful and clumsy.

To the left rose a dark expanse of parkland. To the right and far below spread a carpet of city lights. No sign of TJ.

I had no idea which way to turn, up into wilderness or down toward the city. Then the one-eyed growl of a motorcycle below and to my right made the decision for me.

I almost missed the turn—a strip of trail pointing like a spear at the headlamp of a custom Vyrus.

I followed the steep path downward.

"TJ!"

Below me, a flashlight flicked on and then off.

I kept running. The dirt path broadened into an oval of land surrounded by scrub and trees. Live oak. Toyon. A fallen log. And something else, right where the light had winked.

It looked like a gravestone, but there was no time to investigate.

Earth became pavement and I picked up speed and hope. Then I hit a roadblock—a looming chain-link barricade, too wide and steep to go around, too high to climb over. On the far side lay houses and a road that by my calculations connected to Los Feliz Boulevard.

The motorcycle rumble faded away.

How . . . ?

At the lowest point of the fencing a flap of woven steel wire bent upward. TJ must have scuttled downhill sideways like a crab to reach it, fingers gripping mesh.

There was no way I could follow, not with one hand.

I grabbed for my phone and came up empty. It was still with Julie.

Julie.

She'd be frantic.

I hustled back the way I'd come, uphill all the way. But the memory of that blink of light stopped me at the oval clearing. Near the fallen log, I found a hollow metal structure, the size and shape of a headstone and covered with graffiti.

Maybe some kind of abandoned junction box?

I touched the front panel and felt a seam. I tugged it open. Inside was a rusted metal shelf. And on the shelf, a crumpled maroon zhen and dhonka, and a white silk khata, personally blessed by His Holiness.

TJ had left his past behind.

Every inch of my body hurt as I stumbled back up the footpath to the observatory. I couldn't see vaulting the mesh fence a second time, so I circled the grounds until I hit the pedestrian walkway leading to the front entrance. It was just past 10:00 P.M. Officially, the observatory was closed.

The front entrance was locked. I pounded on the bronze door with my working fist. After a moment, Trixie-the-guide opened it, her features pinched.

A sea of worried faces greeted me in the main rotunda, including more guides. A cluster of official employees in matching blue shirts froze at the sight of me, walkie-talkies glued to their ears.

"Lama Tenzing!" Yeshe's voice was joyful

Julie hurried to my side. "We were so worried. Where did you guys go?" Her smile faded as she looked past me. "Isn't TJ with you?"

"No. I tried, Julie, but I couldn't stop him." I held up the wrinkled evidence. "TJ's gone." Scalding pain migrated from my arm to a charred point midway between my temples.

The giant Foucault pendulum swung back and forth, back and forth. The floor undulated and the triangles of tile churned.

A park ranger pushed his way inside. Heavyset. Familiar. His body swelled like a balloon, then shrank to the size of a molecule.

"Understand you got a missing monk," Zeke said.

"Catch him," a disembodied voice called as I plunged into milky darkness.

CHAPTER 52

"You still blazed, boss?" Mike was luminescent in my bedroom doorway. A black aura surrounded his face like tangled electricity.

Or maybe that was his hair.

"You are a beautiful sight," I said. "You know that, right?"

"Reason I'm asking, you have visitors. Julie brought your monk friends by."

"I figured out why Percocet works, Mike. The pain's still there. You just stop caring about it."

"They're on their way up to Ojai."

"What day is it again?" I'd probably asked that question 20 times in as many hours.

"Monday. And it's night. Eight o'clock."

So I'd been here 18 hours, flat on my back, my semipermanent splint raised in a semipermanent greeting. Tank had established an early paw hold along my left side, and he lay there now like a furry plank of warmth.

Moderate traumatic brain injury and fracture of the ulna. The emergency doctor at Hollywood Presbyterian had delivered the news casually, like it was no big deal. "You're lucky," he'd added. "No bleeding in the brain. And usually with this kind of break, the radius is fractured as well."

Lucky—there was that word again.

His midnight diagnosis had followed a series of unpleasant procedures like a CT scan, palpation of the forearm, and realignment of my cracked bone. I'd downed Percocet like it was candy.

"You don't understand," I'd told the doctor's bald spot as he molded fiberglass and wound elastic bandaging up and

down my forearm. "It can't be broken. I'm right-handed. It's life or death."

"You screenwriters," the doctor had muttered, shaking his head.

But I wasn't talking about the ability to write. I was talking about the ability to shoot.

He sent me home with a multilayered sugar-tong splint that immobilized my arm from elbow to palm crease. A black sling pinned the splint diagonally across my chest, hand just above the heart.

And now I was under concussion watch, which meant every two to three hours someone had to monitor my state of awareness. It was that, or get checked into the hospital. Julie had only agreed to leave my side this afternoon, when Mike volunteered to take over.

The pain pills definitely helped.

"Let me check your pupils." Mike's face loomed close.

"I see nose hairs," I teased.

"Well, you're definitely still loaded, but I don't think you're concussed anymore."

"Hey, you." Julie leaned around Mike. She'd tied her hair into some kind of knot, but several rebellious curls had managed to escape. Even on no sleep, her skin was a celebration.

"I want to lick every inch of your body," I said dreamily.

"Hold that thought, big guy." Julie turned and gestured. "Okay, you can come in. Drugstore Cowboy's awake."

Yeshe, Lobsang, Sonam, and Wangdue filed inside. They crowded around the bed, their solemn expressions dampening my high.

"No word from TJ?" I asked.

They shook their heads.

"What about the police? Have you filed a missing-person's report?"

"They say to wait," Lobsang said. Yeshe nodded.

"Typical. Okay, well, has anyone gotten in touch with TJ's family? His brother?"

No one spoke.

"What?" I looked around, growing more concerned by the second. "What?!"

"Tell him, Lama Wangdue," Sonam said.

"TJ have no brother," Wangdue said. "No family. He is orphan."

"But . . . I thought . . ."

"TJ not always good at saying what is true."

Sonam clasped his hands. "Thoknay Jampa came to us as a very troubled child, and grew up to be an even more troubled young man. But lately, he seemed much more at ease, especially after His Holiness blessed him with a silk khata. When the tour invitation came, we thought the trip would be good for him."

I pushed into a sitting position. "You're saying this change of personality was recent?"

"Maybe since six months," Lobsang said. Yeshe nodded.

"Because the Dalai Lama noticed him?"

"Also, he get iPad," Wangdue said.

His iPad. An invaluable source of clues. I straightened up at this.

"He take with him," Wangdue continued, and I slumped.

"Phone, too," Yeshe put in. "Your friend in kitchen ask already."

"Mike asked me for TJ's cell number," Julie added.

"Good."

Julie opened her hands, a helpless gesture. "He says the phone's dead, and the data on both devices has been wiped out."

I shifted my weight. The mild slice of forearm pain made me wince.

"Time for another pill?" Julie reached toward the bedside table.

"No. No more pills." I was missing something, but my furry brain couldn't pinpoint what.

Julie cocked her head, but she didn't push. "Okay, well, we'd better get going. Bill's coming by soon." She brushed her lips lightly against my forehead, avoiding the bruise.

"You do look a little better. We'll be home before you know it. Mike's taking the night shift, and Martha will be here to check on you first thing tomorrow."

I said nothing as they trooped out. I don't do helpless well.

Sonam lingered, dark worry ringing his eyes. The fingers of his left hand fluttered like the wings of a moth.

"Lama Tenzing, I have to ask. Do you think TJ is with this Maha Mudra?"

"Yes."

"And Nawang?"

"I think they'll meet up with Nawang soon, unless it's already happened. So, yes."

"You believe Nawang is . . . capable of wrong action?"

It's time.

"Yes, Geshe, I do. I think he's planning something, something big, and something bad." I swallowed. "He's not right in his mind."

Sonam fumbled inside his cloth bag. He pulled out a thin sheaf of papers. He placed them on the bed in front of me.

I picked up the top page. Sonam's cramped scrawl covered the paper in tight lines. The words were in English, slanted, and barely legible, as if written in haste. I read the heading out loud: "Ganachakra tantra." I met Sonam's eyes. "What is this?"

"Something I never gave you," he answered, and left the bedroom.

CHAPTER 53

"Special delivery." Bill set the hard nylon case on the closet floor, in front of the safe. "You gonna make a habit of this? Leaving your guns lying around?"

"The bag's locked, Bill. Give me a break."

"Yeah, yeah, yeah." He put the Mustang keys on the bedside table, next to my new, prepaid burner phone. I'd just checked it again, but no text messages, not yet.

"Thanks for getting the car," I said.

"Hey, if breaking your arm is what it takes to finally let me drive the Shelby, so be it." Bill plopped onto the foot of the bed. The sudden motion disturbed Tank's nap. "Sorry, cat." Tank leaped to the floor and sauntered out of the room.

"So?" I said.

"So, I was right. The bullet's a twenty-two two-fifty, from some dandy little hunting rifle. Browning, most likely."

"What about the blood in the vial?"

"O-positive this time, but the same gnarly mix of male and female bodily fluids. They also found elevated levels of synthetic progesterone. So, maybe a woman on hormone replacement therapy?"

"Will you run the DNA?"

"Not unless we have to—no immediate connection to a crime, budget constraints, blah blah blah."

"Let's hope we don't have to, then."

I surreptitiously checked the screen of the burner phone. Still nothing.

My arm throbbed incessantly, but my head was finally clear. I'd slept for 10 hours straight, and spent most of

today alternating between dozing and poring over Sonam's cramped handwriting.

I was reeling from the contents.

"Oh, and I thought you should know, they went ahead and cremated that Kapoor kid." Bill shrugged. "No one wanted to claim him."

"You spoke to his brother in Mumbai?"

"Yeah. What an asshole."

If nothing changed, Paresh Kapoor's ashes would end up in the county cemetery in Boyle Heights, along with hundreds of other unclaimed dead. Hopefully his consciousness, at least, had entered a better mindstream. Still, I felt sad.

"Here." Bill fished out an evidence bag. "I brought you his ring."

The amber cat's-eye glared, accusing me of failure.

I tried to put the ring on, but I couldn't manage it.

"I got it." Bill slipped it on my left middle finger. He clasped his hands to his heart. "At last! It's official!"

I had to laugh.

"Speaking of which," Bill said, "Martha's not happy with the lack of progress on the wedding front. Not happy at all."

Yesterday, Martha had brought by homemade blueberry muffins and several samples of engraved invitations. I'd thanked her for the muffins.

"Don't worry," I said. "I have an idea. It's inspired, if I do say so myself."

"Yeah, but is that you or the drugs talking?"

"Ha ha." My smile faded. "I can't take much more of this, Bill." My awkward gesture included the splinted arm, the bed, and the tray with its untouched bowl of congealed soup. "It's like being tied to a tree, knowing a tornado's about to hit."

"Tough," Bill answered. "This tornado, as you call it, is officially out of your hands. Once you hear back from these nut jobs, you are passing that information along pronto, so the LAPD can move in. Are we clear?"

"I guess." I wasn't convinced an armed response was wise. History wasn't on our side; true believers throughout time had made a practice of choosing mass death over the dishonor of captivity. Masada . . . Rajasthan . . . Jonestown . . . Waco . . .

"Hey, you're the one always saying things happen for a reason," Bill interrupted my grim inventory. "That broken wing of yours? That's your get-out-of-jail-free card. Let us do our job. Yours is to heal, so you can walk down the aisle, or whatever cockamamie plan you've cooked up." He picked up the tray and left.

Tank slipped inside the door and hopped on the bed, reclaiming his turf. I stroked his back, eliciting a deep, low purr.

I could hear Mike and Bill talking in the kitchen.

I checked the disposable phone again. No calls. No texts. Nothing to indicate there was a Maha Mudra event happening any time soon. Mike had delivered the burner phone to me this afternoon.

"Are you sure they won't know it's me?" I'd asked.

"Yup. You're armor plated. As far as Maha Mudra's people know, you're just another kirtan groupie. I gave you the perfect new-age handle. Harry."

"Harry?"

"Yeah. Harry Harry, like the George Harrison song."

Since then I'd checked for texts dozens of times, but Hare Hare was getting no love.

I pulled out the ganachakra tantra, rereading the portions I had highlighted. This detailed account of the ultimate stages of Kalachakra initiation described highly secret rites, both powerful and dark. The mandala held 723 entities, but the ritual required only 64. Under the watchful eye of the master, or guru, the initiates participated in a series of orgiastic, if not violent, rituals involving ceremonial objects, tantric transmutation, and even moments of self-inflicted harm. All of this, of course, was meant to be symbolic—internal acts of surrender and self-sacrifice purely spiritual in nature. But

in the mind of a madman, the document in front of me was an invitation to a bloodbath.

The kitchen was quiet again. I kicked off the covers and hobbled to the window, just as the Subaru headlights came on. Bill drove away, his silhouetted curls visible. Tricia's Mini was parked by the Neon. Soon Martha's Mazda would replace it.

As Lobsang would say, "Too much cars *and* too much babysitters."

I peed and got right back in bed. I hadn't attempted a shower yet, and the thought of another sponge bath overwhelmed.

No texts.

I was seeing Eric tomorrow afternoon. I'd booked a double session. I'd be paying him this time, but whether for therapy or as a business expense remained to be seen. I might have a lot of tissues, but I also had questions. Oh, yes, I had questions.

I set my iPhone alarm for 6:00 A.M.—I owed my employer an overseas call first thing. As I went to return it to my bedside table, the phone warbled in my hand—weren't those women married yet?

It was Julie.

"Homer misses you. He says to tell you Ojai's beautiful."

"How funny. Tank was just mentioning how empty the house feels without you."

"Clever pets." Her breath was soft across the ether. "Are you taking it easy?"

"Any easier and I'd be in a coma."

She laughed. "How's the arm?"

"Itchy, thanks."

We lapsed into silence. After a moment, we dropped into an even deeper connection—that linked intimacy I still wasn't completely comfortable allowing.

"How are you doing?" Julie's voice was warm. "Really."

"I'm not sure," I replied. "I'm worried about TJ, and I'm pretty sick of lying in bed. But it's so good to hear your

voice." I thought about what I'd been reading. "And I'm glad you're safe and sound in Ojai. How about you?"

"I'm worried about TJ, too. The others are handling it much better than I am. Plus, I haven't heard boo from my lawyer. I think he's avoiding my calls." She sighed. "Are you sure I shouldn't just come home?"

"I'm sure," I said. "Have they decided where Saka Dawa Duchen is going to be held up there?"

"Nope. I guess Adina's still working on it. The sand mandala is taking place at someone's house, but it's not big enough for the full moon ceremony. Any chance you'll make it for that?"

I glanced at the burner phone, stubbornly silent. "I don't know," I said. "I hope so."

We ended the call soon after, and the bittersweet missing-Julie heart cramp joined the other aches and pains still claiming space in my body.

But there was also relief. If I was right about Nawang and Maha Mudra, Julie and the others would be secure in Ojai, protected from potential harm. And if I was wrong, well, so much the better. Either way, by next week things would be back to normal.

They had to be, right?

I tried Martha and got her voice mail. "Martha? I have a big favor to ask you."

At least I could set one plan in motion before sleep.

CHAPTER 54

Lord Purdham-Coote finally spoke. "So you're saying this cult Collie has joined is planning some sort of mass ritual?"

"That's right. And soon. If I had to guess, no later than Thursday." I spared him the details—how Thursday featured the most auspicious full moon of the year, landing as it did in the middle of the most potent month. How Saka Dawa Duchen was a day when merits multiplied 100,000-fold and destinies could be created. Or destroyed.

"Will it be dangerous?"

"Possibly, yes."

"And you still don't know where this is taking place?"

"No. But I will."

"You're certain?"

I pulled back slightly. "Almost certain."

Purdham-Coote sighed. "Yes, well, nothing's one hundred percent, is it? I appreciate your honesty." Suffering a total loss of control had softened his ironclad persona. Pain is never welcome, but I liked him the better for it.

"How are you for funds?" he said.

I felt positively weepy at his concern, from which I deduced, induced, and abduced that Percocet still lingered in my system. "I'm fine, sir," I said.

"Just say the word, understand?"

"I appreciate that. Try not to worry. I'll let you know the moment I hear anything."

"Please do. And if you will, call Bertie. He has been most distressed over something, but he won't tell me what."

I retrieved Bertie's number from the file on my desk. Using my left thumb, I awkwardly tapped on the keys on the face of my work phone. It felt good to be up and about again.

Bertie answered immediately.

"Whaddya know, ladies and gents? He's alive."

"I have a good excuse." I explained about the accident and my mysterious sniper.

"Goes to show. Everyone over there has a bleedin' gun." His lighter snapped, and he inhaled.

"Lord Purdham-Coote said you had news for me?"

"Yeah. Didn't want to worry him, but I went back to the Round Church, like you asked. Found some scribbles in the tower, on the wall. Same initials, *JMM*, and some kind of whatchmacallit. Hi-ro-glyph."

"Written in blood?"

"Yeah. Or something that looked just like it."

I waited. There had to be more.

"So I started to sniff around." He paused for a hit of nicotine. "I discovered three more suicides. Same pattern. Troubled kid runs away. Turns up a little later dead. Robes. Self-inflicted stab wounds. Skinned in places like a rabbit."

"And nobody connected the deaths?"

"Nah, they were all over the map. St. Ives. Trowbridge. Yarmouth. Different boroughs. Months apart. Nothing to link 'em, unless you knew where to look."

"But you did."

"Yeah. On account of them being on the same watchamacallit, ley line, as the Round Church."

"You figured that out?"

"Yeah."

"Bertie, that's brilliant." I'd forgotten about the ley line connection. I mentally added it to what I'd recently learned. One more puzzle piece.

"No biggie," he said, but he sounded pleased. "I let Garfield know, in case there are more." Bertie's voice darkened. "Some guru. Fuckin' nightmare. I could wring her Paki neck."

"She's not . . ." I stopped. Now was not the time to address racial miscasting.

"You want me in L.A.? Sounds like you could use the help. Lord P-C's prepared to ship me over anytime."

"Thanks," I said. "But no. Not yet, anyway."

He rang off. I took physical stock. My arm still hurt like hell, but otherwise I felt much better this morning. Mike had persuaded me to eat a small bowl of oatmeal with half a sliced banana. I also managed the first cup of coffee in two days. Maybe some of the cerebral ache had been due to caffeine withdrawal, because my head was pain-free for the first time since I'd landed on it.

Mike let out a long, low whistle from his temporary kitchen-table office. "Ho-ly shit."

"What is it?"

He loped into the living room. He'd been here since last night, and his hair was a turbine experiment gone very wrong. "So I've been tracking various cryptocurrency money trails. You know, looking for overlap between your boy TJ, Indra's Net, and Nawang. Impossible task, by the by." His fingers raked through his mane. "But I think I just found a link, to that Buddhist temple. Your alma mater."

"Dorje Yidam? Makes sense. Nawang was there for a while, remember?"

"No, boss. The temple here. In Highland Park."

"Ganden Gyatso?" A vein at my throat pulsed.

"Bang." Mike started to pace. "So, you remember how Indra's Net—I'm talking about last year's version—exclusively used the cyber currency DNAcoins?"

"Yes." When Mike first stumbled on it, NDRSNT was a flourishing peer-to-peer marketplace for the worst kind of consumers. As Silk Road was to drugs, NDRSNT was to human traffickers, at least until Bill and I ran their Bosnian branch to ground. Then the server, and everything else, went dead—switched off like a light.

Decoding the acronym NDRSNT came a little later, when my mind finally connected the dots. I realized the

letters stood for *Indra's Net*—a pre-Buddhist concept of the interconnectedness of time. A notion that had morphed for Buddhists into . . .

My blood chilled. How had I missed this connection?

. . . had morphed into our very own Kalachakra tantra. The Wheel of Time. The Power of Ten.

It's time.

Holy shit, indeed.

". . . crytpocurrency exchange site," Mike was saying, as he marched past me.

"Sorry, Mike. Can you repeat that? And can you please stop pacing around?"

Mike put on the brakes. "Boss, you gotta listen. This is crucial. I *said*, I managed to track down a cryptocurrency exchange site, where you can switch up your cyber dough. Bitcoins, BlackCoins, Auroracoins, like that. But strangely, no DNAcoins anymore." He pointed at me. "But here's the thing. I did find something called Dana-puñña. And I remembered you thought DNAcoins stood for Dana-coins, so I put two and two together."

"Wait, Dana-puñña? I saw that term recently." I racked my brain. "On some website, maybe?"

"Uh, yeah, try the Ganden Gyatso website. Better yet, try the Ganden Gyatso fund-raising link to your monk-friends' tour."

Dana-puñña. There it was again, Sanskrit roots, connecting to Tibetan tradition. *Dana* was the Vedic word for purification, until it also became the Buddhist term for generosity. *Puñña* meant merit. And the cultivation of generosity and merit were cornerstones of our spiritual path.

"It's fucking brilliant, actually," Mike said. "All that virtual money, automagically changing names but not hands. Millions, maybe billions in untraceable cash, disappearing onto benign sites for nonprofits. You could payroll a lot of things that way."

Yes, you certainly could. And if Nawang was using spiritual websites as a front, that meant he was once again manipulating Indra's Net for his own dark uses. No wonder Maha Mudra's mission seemed to spring from nowhere yet was spreading as quickly as a virus.

The Vyrus. Another thread I had dropped.

"Really good work, Mike."

"No worries. I actually really dig this dark web spy stuff." He stifled a yawn. "That said, I might not last much longer. These last two days taking care of you have been killer. Now I know what life must be like with a newborn. No offense."

"Go home," I said. "Get some sleep. I feel fine."

"Roger that." Moments later, he and the Mini had vacated the premises.

The Vyrus motorcycle website listed 10 dealerships worldwide. I eliminated all but three, using my own favored method of deduction: hunch.

That left Mexico, the UK, and Vyrus North America, which was in Raleigh, North Carolina, of all places.

I called the UK dealership first, located in Surrey, but no one answered the long string of double rings. Vyrus Mexico was no longer in service. Only North Carolina remained. I dialed the number—it, too, rang and rang.

So much for hunches. I jammed the phone into its charger. Hadn't these people ever heard of voice mail?

I typed out an e-mail on my computer, lowercase, one key at a time. I included both phone numbers and a fairly detailed query, as well as the bike's orange-and-black color scheme. There were so few Vyruses, color was up there with DNA when it came to identification.

I copied and pasted the e-mail addresses of all 10 dealerships worldwide, a painstaking process. If there was a language issue, let them deal with it.

By the time I pushed "send" it was almost time for Eric.

The act of getting dressed was as uncomfortable as it was humiliating. My clothes were loose, but not in a good way. I'd lost muscle mass, already.

Tank's expression was dubious as he watched me wrestle with the buttons on my fly.

"What?" I asked. "You try doing this one-handed."

The Neon was the only possible choice of wheels. No stick shift for me, not for a while.

I threw the burner phone onto the front seat, but I had little patience, and even less hope.

CHAPTER 55

How quickly Eric's office had become a place of refuge. I scanned the bookcase from my chair, enjoying the assorted amulets and tomes of wisdom. My eyes fell on the vajra hammer. The head was made of rugged blue-black iron, vaguely familiar.

"Eric?" I called. "Is the head of your vajra hammer from a meteorite?"

He emerged from the bathroom with two tumblers of water. "Very perceptive," he said. "It is indeed."

"How old does that make it?"

"As old as you need it to be. Pick a number." Eric put the water on the table and settled across from me. "Well. You've had quite a week."

I reached for my glass. The shift in position caused me to flinch.

"You're still in pain. I'm sorry."

"On the plus side, I've been so busy beating myself up, I haven't had a panic attack in days."

"I can help you with that."

"My sense of failure?"

"Your pain."

"Well, you are a psychologist."

"I mean literally, Ten."

"Really?"

"Look. You're extremely depleted. In fact, I'm surprised you even made it here. Don't misread me, your coming sends the right message to the part of your psyche that wants to be well. But you're physically hurting and mentally shaken— not the ideal platform for deep therapy."

I wasn't sure how to respond.

"We can, however, work with your innate ability to reach a trance state. There's a phenomenon called arm catalepsy. You might find it useful as a pain suppressant."

My arm was suddenly on fire, as if triggered by the mere suggestion of relief.

"I'm game," I said, "but first, can I ask you about something else? It has to do with Ganden Gyatso's finances."

Eric steepled his fingers, but didn't answer.

"I can ask Adina, if you think that would be better."

"It would, actually. But Adina's at a weeklong retreat."

"I thought she was in Ojai."

"Nope."

I must have misunderstood Julie. Inside the splint, pain snaked up and down the ulna nerve.

"Okay, here's what I'll do," Eric said. "I'll answer what I can. And if I feel I'm breaching confidentiality, I won't."

"How did this tour come about?" I asked.

Eric took his time answering.

"The temple received a rather large donation," he finally said. "Very generous, and very specific."

"Who from?" I asked, without a lot of hope.

"It was anonymous." Eric's answer validated my pessimism. "At first we assumed the benefactor was the family trust of Roderick Paul, our founder. But I put in a call to the trust manager, to thank him, and he denied making the donation. We still don't know where it came from."

"What do you mean by *specific*?"

"Again, this is Adina's area of expertise, but I believe the terms and conditions regarding the contribution were quite explicit. Tour dates, types of events, right down to the choice of sand mandala. Even the monks were handpicked."

This startled me. "All of them? Including TJ?"

"Yes."

I followed that trail. "Plus my two best friends growing up. Plus my mentor."

"I think I see where you're going."

"So whoever orchestrated this knew me. Knew my past. Knew exactly what it would take to draw me back in. Had the financial means and created the opportunity."

"You're thinking Nawang."

"Who else could it be?" Fear balled in my chest. "Eric, I need to know what I'm dealing with here."

"What do you mean?"

I lifted my sling an inch, ignoring the pain. "Look at me. You already said it. I'm weak. Mentally and physically. I have none of my normal skills to fall back on." My voice rose. "You never met Nawang. I did. He was like some kind of twisted god, even back then. I would have followed him anywhere! And now he's using this Maha Mudra ruse to pull in Colin and TJ, and who knows how many others? And no one can find any of them. They're like ghosts!"

"More like pied pipers," Eric said.

"What?"

"Malignant pied pipers, these cult leaders. Malevolent gurus. Jim Jones. Charlie Manson. Some even put Osama bin Laden in that category."

"Oh, great."

"Ten, they're monsters. But they're also human. And if anyone can meet Nawang at the level of his humanity, it's you."

"Why?"

"Because whatever he has planned, he clearly needs you to ensure its success. He's obsessed with you. And that obsession is the chink in his armor."

The knot loosened a little. "I'm listening," I said.

"Personality types like Nawang, or . . ." Eric paused. "I'll focus on Nawang. He and Maha Mudra are clearly fused in some way, but she's submissive to him in this partnership."

"I agree. Can I tape this?"

"Please."

With a bow to Lia Pootah, I found the recording function on my iPhone and thumbed it on.

"Okay, it's recording."

"I was saying, messianic personalities share certain traits. They're good at reading people, not to mention manipulating them, often by using a combination of inspiring rhetoric and personal magnetism."

"Showmen."

"Yup. They can raise any roof with their testifying. They're aloof at times, but can also be incredibly warm. They seem to be available, but in fact are completely detached, and that detachment, too, feeds the impression of spiritual superiority."

"Sounds like Nawang."

Also a little like me.

"What else . . . They're usually highly empathic. Unconventional. Rebellious. And completely convinced that they are messengers for a higher truth. That's part of their appeal. They're narcissists, but they genuinely believe in their prophecies."

I thought about this. "The Buddha talked a lot about dependant origination. You know, causes and conditions. What conditions give rise to a Nawang?"

"Funny you should ask."

"Why?"

"Because many of those same conditions have also given rise to genuine prophets. Including the Buddha. None of this is ever black-and-white."

I took another sip of water. Eric glanced at the clock.

"Please," I said. "This is helping me so much."

"Okay. Well, the journey to personal prophecy tends to follow distinct stages. Usually there's early evidence of at least one excessively doting parent. Doting, yet also conflicted. And that unhealthy bond is often followed by a traumatic loss of some kind."

My mother, Valerie.

"The child incubates with a sense that there is something *different* about him or her, of not belonging anywhere, or to any group."

Yes.

"He becomes almost radically autonomous. In constant conflict with authority, yet also very good at acquiring practical skills."

Like building a deck. Or shooting a gun.

"But the key shift comes in the form of a spiritual awakening. A moment of total transformation. The burning bush, if you like. But this personality type is not content with experiencing such a shift just for himself. He wants the world to follow. This becomes his mission. A dark mission, in the case of Nawang and others like him."

So here was where Nawang and I parted ways.

"But why?"

"Good question. Nobody knows exactly, but I have a theory. When the self one has constructed is false, external props are required to keep it upright. The weaker the false structure, the more support required. Survival is at stake. At any cost."

"Which means lots of followers."

"Exactly. So they use their considerable talents to recruit and retain others. Devise rituals to give their followers a taste of transcendence. Regulate their reality wherever possible. But it all goes back to a false self, and the overwhelming terror of facing that inner vacuum."

I thought back to Dorje Yidam. To the young confused boy I was, desperate for attention and value. "They prey on the weak, don't they?"

"You bet. It's part of their genius, an almost primal ability to identify and seduce people who are at especially vulnerable points in their lives. People on the cusp of change."

Like I was then.

Like I am now.

But was Nawang's intention to lure me back as acolyte or destroy me once and for all?

What if the answer was both?

Chapter 56

Delicious weightiness. Utter surrender.

"That's it . . . and your awareness can start to fade into an unconscious sense of drifting, drifting deeper . . . and how your right hand is heavier than your left . . . and deeper still . . . down . . . and down . . . but your right arm just stays comfortably still . . ."

My forearm was a warm brick of heaviness.

"That's it . . . and the muscles are stiff, immobile now, and there is no pain, only detachment . . ."

My arm grew rigid, but pleasantly so.

"And your arm is detached . . . but strong . . . right here, right now . . . an immovable iron bar . . . and you can find that strength, that numb detached strength, whenever you need it . . . you can generate that power, yes?"

"Yes." I started to laugh. "My arm," I said, and I pulled it out of the sling and waved it around.

"And you need to keep it safe in the sling for now," I heard.

"And five . . . and four . . . and three . . . that's it . . . feel the strength and healing move up and down your arm . . . and two . . . and . . ."

I came to, if that's the correct term for the mental shutters flying open.

My right arm felt odd. A little sore, but also stronger. I curled and flexed the fingers. "The catalepsy worked?"

"Yes," Eric said. "For quite some period of time, you were unable to feel or move your arm, but your unconscious was working on strengthening it nevertheless."

My body was pleasantly relaxed.

"Thanks, Eric. You're like some kind of magician."

"Don't thank me. You're the one with the facility. This could be a whole other calling for you."

I shook my head. "I've had my fill of callings."

Eric's eyes found the clock.

"We have a few minutes left. Anything else you want to discuss?"

Yes. No. "Not really."

"How are things with Julie?"

Busted.

"Here's what's upsetting," I said. "Every marriage I know has either fallen apart or is struggling not to."

"Maintaining long-term intimacy is perhaps our greatest challenge. Many fail."

"Exactly. I mean, my parents' marriage? You want to talk about failure?" I dialed back the tone of accusation. None of this was Eric's fault. "You and Adina have been together for, what, thirty years?"

"Thirty-five and change."

Longer than I'd lived.

"How do you commit to an entire lifetime with another person? How do you know?"

Eric's mouth was twitching at the corners.

"What's so funny?"

"You," Eric said. "This. Look, you don't know. At least, I didn't. How could I? But every morning I can and do wake up with Adina and think *Yes. I commit my heart to you, for today.* It's worked pretty well so far."

"That's it?"

"No, of course not. I also commit to riding out the rough patches. Last year Adina turned sixty-five. It hit her hard. All my quirks went from irresistible to unbearable. She almost left the marriage."

"What changed?"

"I'm not sure, to tell you the truth. Mostly I stayed put and gave her room to figure things out. Finding some like-minded seekers seemed to help her. Then this mandala tour

came up, and she felt engaged and passionate about her life again."

The pattern sounded familiar. My skin prickled.

"You think of commitment as rigid," Eric said. "Restrictive, like that splint on your arm. It's not. It's liberating. Worn loosely, marriage can be the most creative force in your life. Different every day, and the gateway to your greatest passion and fulfillment."

Julie's laughing face filled my vision.

I'd been thinking I *had* to marry her. What if I *chose* to marry her?

I wrote Eric a hefty check. My wallet might be lighter, but so was my heart.

I stopped on the landing outside Eric's office and gave Julie a call, watching the Buddha watching me. I got her voice mail.

"Hey, love. I miss you. Call me when you get this, okay? Lots to talk about."

I rubbed the Buddha on his topknot.

"Keep her safe, okay?" I said.

I was glad I'd taped the session. My head was whirling. But I no longer felt weak or powerless. A germ of a plan was forming. A strategy so crazy, it just might work.

CHAPTER 57

Why wasn't anyone texting me about the Maha Mudra event?

I'd stayed up half the night refining my idea. I needed to stop by Eric's one more time, not for therapy this time, for something else, but otherwise all that remained was learning the location of the full moon Saka Dawa Duchen.

I'd sent Martha home after one final eyeball check. She'd insisted I answer a few questions, like who was president, and what year was I born? I wanted to mess with her, but didn't. Martha's German. Teutonic humor is an oxymoron.

I took the burner phone outside to the deck. The sun was almost directly overhead. I was on indefinite hold, and acute restlessness was causing my brain to curdle.

Normally, the solution to this degree of agitation was an intense workout, but that was not possible.

I wandered back inside and stepped behind the screen to my meditation alcove. Tank knew something was up. He was close on my heels.

The state of disrepair resembled my own. No altar. No Buddha. Just an old Starlite suitcase and a hamper piled high with abandoned talismans.

Was it only eight days since I'd called on Green Tara for help? Executed fluid prostrations with ease?

The only meditative tool intact was hanging on the wall, the vibrant thangka given to me by Yeshe and Lobsang. The Wheel of Life.

I knelt clumsily on my cushion, arm pinned over my heart, a broken salute to this portrait of deluded existence. *Samsara*. Might as well go straight to the source.

I let my eyes focus lightly on the center of the thangka, a circle formed by a snout, a beak, and a tail. The pig, rooster, and snake represented the three afflictions of samsara—ignorance, greed, and aggression.

Allow.

Set in their core, the antidote: three powerful mantras, *om*, *ma*, and *hram*.

Hram hram hram, I thought, and my heart stuttered.

Allow.

Radiating outward, circles of suffering were gripped by the claws of the demon Yama, the god of impermanence and delusion.

Allow.

But hope was to be found as well. In Yama's third eye of wisdom. In the full moon in the left-hand corner. In the right arm of the Buddha sitting opposite, pointing to that same moon, reminding me that freedom from suffering was possible.

The full moon is the path. Allow.

I called upon the root mantras of our tradition, *Om mani padme hum.*

Om: May I be free of ego attachment. May I be generous.

Ma: May I be free of jealousy. May I be fair.

Ni: May I be free of desire. May I be patient.

Pad: May I be free of judgment. May I be resolute.

Me: May I be free of possessiveness. May I practice concentration.

Hum: May I be free of hatred. May I be wise.

I settled deeper, forming my own words: "Buddha, I need your help right now. Protect me from suffering and ignorance. Protect Julie and my friends. Protect us all and bring us to the inner wisdom of an awakened heart."

I don't know how long I sat after that, but at some point, my office phone rang. If it hadn't, I might be there still.

"*Hola*, Mr. Norbu. That means hello."

The transition from cushion to desk was dizzying. I had no idea who was calling.

"Who's calling please?"

"This is Kim Nordquist. Your assistant."

"Kim! Of course. Sorry, I was just . . . How are you?"

"I am fine, Mr. Norbu. I am having fun playing with my niece, Kimmy. She is teaching me to speak Spanish."

"That's great."

Si. Es bueno.

I waited: no need to encourage this particular direction.

"I am calling you because you need to drive up here. To Lemoore."

"Lemoore?"

"Yes."

May I be patient.

"We have a situation here."

"What kind of situation?"

"Oh. Bobby wants to talk to you."

"Hi. Lieutenant Smith here. Bobby. Thought I'd better jump in."

"What's going on?"

"Mpingo Draper's here with me. Also Commander Scott Pritchard. He's my squadron's ex oh."

"Your . . ."

"Executive officer. We need your help."

I reached for a pen without thinking, and my right arm screamed inside the sling. Luckily, a note pad was open and available.

"Commander Pritchard's daughter, Brittany, is missing." He covered the phone. "Correction, *may* be missing. She's taken off before—went to Los Angeles just last week, in fact. But she's always let them know where she is. It's been two days, and nothing."

"How old is she?"

Brittany, I wrote with my left hand. Or tried to.

"Seventeen. Just finished junior year at the high school up here. She was supposedly going camping with three of her classmates. One of those outdoor music festivals."

"What kind of music festival?"

- 310 -

"Not sure. You'll have to ask him. There's more. The commander checked her room. He found her iPad and cell phone all smashed up."

The skin around my temples tightened. More pain was on its way.

Mpingo must have muscled the phone from Bobby. "Ten? Mpingo here. I've known that child half her life. Brittany's a wild one, but there's a good heart in there. I told you about her before, remember?"

"Right. The chronic runaway."

"She just needs to find her own true north. This isn't like her."

"What about the classmates? Boys? Girls?"

"Girls. Their parents aren't military, so . . . but everyone's frantic. It's like they just dropped off the face of the earth."

"Can you put the father on, please?"

"This is Commander Pritchard." The natural authority couldn't hide his deep concern.

"Did your daughter say where this festival was?"

"Somewhere close, she said. Visalia, maybe? She was pretty vague. She said she'd call once they got there."

My left hand added *Visalia* to the note pad. It looked like my cat wrote it.

"What kind of vehicle?"

"Britt has a used VW Vanagon. We got it for her last year, in November. Early Christmas present."

"So no LoJack I assume, or GPS to track."

"No, but it's hard to miss. She hand-painted rainbows on both sides and a pair of red lips on the front."

"License plate?"

"Vanity plate." He gave it to me, and my hackles rose. "Initials JMM, followed by the numbers six one two one four."

I thought about the tox report on the vials of blood.

"Sir, is Brittany involved with recreational drugs?"

"She swears not, not anymore. She's all about purifying the body. Something else you should know. She's been

getting into some weird stuff. Chanting. This god-awful music. And she's obsessed with power spots. She even had me bring home my aeronautical charts so she could show me where these, uh, magnetic lines were."

"Ley lines?"

"That's it. Ley lines. Vortexes, she called them. She was worried I might crash if I flew through one." He cleared his throat. "Anyway, she seemed so happy about doing this, you know, with school friends for once, her mother and I didn't want to say no."

I fired up Google Images. Slowly typed in *vortex*, *ley lines*, *maps*, and *Visalia*. I pressed "return."

Boom, as Mike would say. Or was it bang? Either way, the California map that came up was most informative. Ley lines were indicated with curved parallel lines, as if drawn by a compass. They bisected the state, most notably between San Diego and Santa Cruz. And a pair of them converged in the town of Visalia.

A festival, a campsite, and a full moon tomorrow, June 12th. JMM, 6-12-14.

Maybe more than ley lines were converging.

"I'm on my way," I said.

Chapter 58

Should I call Bill?

Technically, nothing was confirmed. And technically, he had no jurisdiction that far north anyway.

I grabbed two gallon-size Ziploc bags from the kitchen and filled the first with a few toiletries—instant dopp kit. I used the second bag for the cat's-eye ring and TJ's discarded silk khata, items earmarked for my crazy plan. I bundled both inside a change of clothes. I pulled on a clean pair of jeans, a black T-shirt, thick socks, and my hiking boots—the ones that used Velcro instead of laces. Plus my Windbreaker. I kept things simple. The Starlite would only hold so much.

I stared at my gun safe, itching to retrieve my .38 Supergrade.

I resisted. My right hand was useless. I couldn't even grip a gun, much less shoot with it. The only thing stupider than leaving a loaded gun for a toddler to find was rushing into an unknown situation equipped with a firearm you were incapable of firing.

I carried the bundle of belongings into my meditation space and placed it inside the blue suitcase. I added my monk's robe. And last but not least, I returned the rewrapped silver bumpa to its side compartment, zipping it tight, peacock feathers and all.

What else? What else? What was I forgetting?

Of course. I ran to my desk and slid Sonam's sheaf of transcribed notes into a manila envelope. I laid the envelope on top of everything else, snapped both latches closed, and carried the case into the kitchen.

I called Julie and got her voice mail again.

"Jules. I'm headed for Lemoore. Something's come up." I paused. How much should I say? I settled for, "Call when you

get this message. I'm glad you're in Ojai. Stay there, okay? I love you."

Tank eyed the suitcase by the door, his expression baleful.

"I know, buddy. Sorry."

I poured a triple portion of kibble into his food dish. He refused to look at me or the bowl. I smoothed his blue-gray fur with my good hand.

"I'll be back," I said.

I was headed for the Mustang when I remembered my bum right arm. I not only couldn't shoot, I still couldn't shift.

The Neon it was.

Eric was waiting in his office. This time, our session only took 20 minutes. I was surprised at how smoothly it went. Maybe he was right, maybe I did have a second calling.

Afterward, he walked me down to the car.

"You're sure about this?" he asked.

"Yes."

The suitcase was lying on the backseat. I unsnapped the latches. Eric handed me the vajra hammer. Placed at a diagonal, the wooden handled tool just fit.

"I'd say break a leg, but that would be overkill," Eric said. "So . . . be well, my friend."

I stopped at an ARCO on Franklin, just before the freeway entrance. I filled the tank and topped up the radiator fluid, which was a little low. Soon I was cruising north on the 101. I merged onto the 170, which quickly became the 5. I was pushing the Neon hard. The drive was meant to take three and a half to four hours, but I planned on getting there in under three.

I buzzed passed Six Flags Magic Mountain, with its twisted metal thrills, and zipped through Valencia toward Castaic. The rumpled hills on either side of the freeway were a parched shade of brown, more burn victims of the recent heat wave. Up ahead lay the slow but brutal climb to Tejon Pass known as the Grapevine, a 6 percent grade.

I started the ascent. Cars began to pass me. I moved into the slow lane, my Neon and I dwarfed by the lumbering trucks loaded with nectarines, cattle, and who knows what else.

The engine began to labor.

"Come on," I said. "You can do this."

Just north of Gorman, at 4,000 feet, the "check engine" light came on.

I limped into the first available emergency bypass. White smoke was billowing out of my tailpipe, and steam leaked from under my hood. It took 20 minutes to cool things down, and another 15 to wrench the radiator cap off with my weak left hand.

Luckily I had a plastic gallon jug of water in my trunk. I filled the radiator, but before I could climb behind the wheel, Gatorade-green fluid was leaking onto the pavement.

This was not good.

My phone buzzed, a number I didn't recognize.

"Yes?"

"Is this some kind of joke?" His voice was both warm and gruff, like honey over gravel. He sounded on the far side of 60, but not by much.

"Excuse me?"

"You e-mailed about the orange-and-black Vyrus, right?"

"Yes, I did."

"And your name is Tenzing Norbu, and you live in Los Angeles?"

"That's correct."

"The same Tenzing Norbu who wired me a hundred grand for the only Vyrus I had in stock, and took delivery off a pallet ten days later?"

"What's this? What are you saying?"

"I'm saying according to my records, you're the guy who bought the bike."

There are 10,000 Tibetans with the name Tenzing Norbu. But something told me this didn't involve anyone but me.

"I'm confused," I said.

"You lay it down?" His voice was concerned.

"No. I . . . When did you deliver it?"

"Four months ago. You *sound* confused. You sure you didn't hit your head?"

"Not like that. And the payment was wired?"

"Yeah. Some kind of newfangled cyber transaction out of Los Angeles. But the money was good as gold, whoever the hell sent it."

"Thanks. That's all I needed to know."

The rest of the drive became its own endless cycle of suffering. My car was puffing white smoke, and every driver on the freeway felt compelled to let me know by honking and gesturing as he or she passed. Visalia was 130 miles up the road, and every 20 or so I had to pull off, find a working hose, struggle with the radiator cap, and refill the tank. And forget trying to rent a car on that empty, treacherous stretch of road. You can't, no matter how many times you ask the Internet. Turning back was not an option. So I just kept going.

By the time I pulled into the only campsite in Visalia, just off Avenue 308, it was dark. Thankfully, the entrance was brightly lit. I rolled past a small swimming pool, public restrooms, and a general store, closed for the night. I circled past maybe 30 occupied hook-up sites to my right, and another 20 down the other side, all occupied by campers and motor homes. But there was no VW van with red lips, and from the few people I saw, no one under the age of retirement. Worse, there wasn't a robe or sitar in sight.

This felt all wrong.

I parked near the front office and climbed out. The Neon gurgled, as if choking to death.

The office was closed as well.

I looked up. The light was too bright to find, much less follow, the moon.

Brittany and her friends weren't here, and neither was anyone else on my radar.

I leaned against the Neon's overheated flank. The last of the toxic water had pooled underneath the chassis. It spread across the pavement like poisoned ink.

Chapter 59

A white Dakota pickup pulled into the campground. The tall, fit man who climbed out wore a camouflage uniform. It was an odd color, more aqua than army green, although that might have been my eyes playing tricks on me.

"Lieutenant Smith?"

"Bobby, please." He started for my right hand, spotted the cast, and switched to my left. His grip was firm.

"Thanks for coming to the rescue. I think my radiator is cracked." I nodded toward the Neon, its hood popped.

"That's not good." Bobby eyed the pond of coolant. He ducked under the hood with a Maglite and reappeared with the oil dipstick. It was coated with gunk.

"Not just the radiator. Head gasket's blown. My opinion? She's a goner."

"I was afraid of that."

"There's a junk yard'll pick her up from here for free. I can call them in the morning."

"Sold." I'd never completely committed to the relationship, so the demise of my second beater car, unlike my first, was not painful.

Anyway, who needs a Neon when you own a Vyrus?

I went to retrieve the suitcase and almost dropped it.

"Let me take that," Bobby said. "Jesus, what have you got in here? Rocks?"

"One rock. A meteorite," I said. I left it at that.

Visalia was about half an hour from Lemoore. Enough time to learn how special Kim's brother was. Every nation has its warriors, its Kshatriya class, but not every person is

right for the job. Bobby, as far as I could tell, had found his true dharma.

"So you enlisted right out of high school?"

"That's right."

"And while you were serving, you earned a college degree."

"Yup. Online, through SOCNAV. Took about seven years."

"And then, what, more training?"

"OCS. Officer candidate school. Hardest twelve weeks of my life, including my first tour in the Gulf of Oman. Then six weeks of air indoctrination in Pensacola, followed by flight training, flight training, and more flight training."

"Wow."

"I was motivated. No other way to get my hand on the throttle of a Super Hornet. Here we are. Home sweet home."

I was too exhausted to register much about getting onto the base, except that gates and guards were involved, and Bobby had to flash his ID more than once.

The pullout sofa in the living room was lumpy, but I fell into a hard and dreamless sleep, too tired to mind.

Then it was morning. I knew, because slanted squares of sunlight were warming up my face. I could smell coffee and hear voices in the kitchen, including a child's piping trill. I reached under the pillow for the burner phone to check.

No texts.

Panic licked at the edges of my brain. I treated it with a deep cooling breath.

Kim walked in.

"*Buenos días*, Mr. Norbu. I brought you coffee." She handed me a mug imprinted with a dashing top hat. I'd seen the same image on a patch on Bobby's shoulder. "It is nice to see you."

"Same here."

"*Hasta luego.*" She left the room.

I had slept fully dressed. I found a small bathroom, my anxiety mounting. Today, or rather tonight, was Saka Dawa

Duchen. I had no idea where to go. And on the off chance I was texted a location, no immediate way to get there.

Bobby, Kim, and three others were in the kitchen. I assumed the statuesque African American with the gray cloud of hair was Mpingo Draper, and I was right.

"Pleased to meet you," she said. "But sorry for the reason."

Bobby's wife, Ramona, was caramel skinned, her thick black hair braided into a twist. She wore a camouflage flight suit like Bobby's. In daylight it was still more blue than green. She caught me staring.

"Like the camo, do you? Around here, we call it aquaflage."

"Ramona's nurse's corps," Bobby said, putting his arm around her. "She works at the Hornet Health Clinic."

I tucked that information away.

A little girl in pink shorts and a pink shirt stared at me from the corner. Her hazel eyes and hair matched.

"Hola," I said. "I'm Ten."

She hid behind her mother.

"We're off." Ramona met my eyes. "I'm glad you came. Brittany is Kimmy's favorite babysitter, isn't she, Kimmy?"

Kimmy nodded.

Ramona's face clouded with concern. She took Kimmy's hand and led her away.

"Kimmy goes to Kindergarten," Kim announced. "Sometimes I walk her there."

I turned to Bobby. "I need to meet with Brittany's parents. As soon as possible. There's not much time."

"Her mother works in Hanford," he said. "But Commander Pritchard's waiting."

We drove across the naval base. Pink and white oleander bushes partially masked the barbed-wire fencing. We passed more military housing, a shopping center, offices, and decommissioned aircraft skewered on metal stands.

Bobby rattled off the base services. "Beauty salon, Starbucks, commissary." He motioned. "Lemoore's divided into two areas, admin and ops. We're heading into Air ops."

The security measures were tighter on this end, and I soon saw why. We had entered strike fighter territory. Gunmetal gray fighter jets peppered a tarmac ocean, tailfins raised. They were still and dangerous as sharks.

"F/A-eighteens," Bobby said.

A distant rumble grew loud, louder, until the roar took on a life of its own. It pummeled my hearing like a fist.

A pair of Super Hornets whooshed overhead in tandem, so close to each other their wings could kiss. The roar faded away. A bird chirped, brave again.

"That sound." I shook my head in awe.

"We call it the sound of freedom." Bobby looked away, suddenly shy.

Now a single F/A-18 flew over us, shadowed by its ghost below. It completed two slow 180-degree turns, then lowered wheels-first onto a narrow runway. The landing gear barely brushed the tarmac before the machine lifted off and sped away.

A second strike fighter followed the same path, and I saw more planes strung out behind.

"What are they doing?"

"Developing habit patterns," Bobby said. "Lemoore's in the boonies. That means we can actually fly low enough to mimic landing on an aircraft carrier. This fleet is practicing touch-and-gos."

"Looks tricky."

"As soon as you touch down you have two seconds to attach a tail hook to a three-inch-wide arresting cable, on a seesawing flight deck, while at max power, because if you miss, you have to take off immediately or bad things happen. So yes. Tricky."

He guided the Dakota between metal maintenance hangars, each bearing its own VFA number, squadron name, and insignia. Maybe 20 in all. *Bounty Hunters. Vigilantes. Black*

Knights. Their painted emblems—snarling dragons, red-eyed skulls—were not that different from gang symbols, only these warriors were better equipped, more skilled, and far more dangerous. I was glad they stood on the side of honor.

The Tophatter hangar was halfway down to the right. I spotted the same jaunty black hat.

"Your VFA-14 squadron symbol is different," I said.

"We're the original," he smiled. "Nineteen nineteen. The oldest and the boldest."

A door in the hangar opened, and a man strode in our direction, as if he'd been watching for us.

"Commander Pritchard," Bobby said. "This is Detective Tenzing Norbu."

"Commander." I waved awkwardly. "Sorry, I can't shake hands."

"Appreciate you coming, Detective," he said.

He was well over six feet. His eyes were blue steel, and his hands were compact, the fingers blunt and thick. He wore leather work boots, a peaked khaki cap, and a winged insignia on a patch over his heart, his name and rank embroidered in gold. He'd be the picture of calm competence, were it not for the bruises of worry under his eyes.

Inside the hangar, plane parts were spread out on plastic sheets, awaiting repair, perhaps. Pritchard led us upstairs to his office. An aeronautical chart was laid out on the desk. I could see purple Magic Marker lines hand drawn over the grids.

A framed picture showed a smiling lieutenant commander in full dress uniform, medals decorating his chest like confetti. One arm was wrapped around a pretty teenage girl in ripped jeans, her expression half-sullen, half-hopeful. She'd attempted to dye her hair blue, but the result was more like aquaflage.

I picked up the photograph. "Tell me about Brittany," I said.

"She's a pistol," Pritchard answered. "Always has been. Two older brothers, but she can hold her own. Complete

tomboy. Which was fine, until all her girlfriends changed, and she didn't. It's not that she's . . . she likes boys. She's just not that interested yet. Girls this age can be cruel. She was feeling pretty isolated by the end of last year." He shook his head. "All that early moving around didn't help."

So the pattern of vulnerability was there. Again.

"What is she interested in?"

He smiled. "Stargazing. Yoga. Rock climbing. Shooting. She's a crack shot."

My antennae went up. "Tell me more about that."

"Well, I started her off skeet shooting a couple years ago, here on the base. She was so good I took her to Rankin Field in Tulare for her sixteenth birthday. Gave her my granddad's rifle to try out."

"What kind of rifle?" The nape of my neck already knew.

"Hunting rifle. A bolt-action Browning. She took to it like a duck to water. She can shoot better than me now, and I'm a pretty good shot."

So Brittany hadn't been aiming to kill, she'd been aiming to scare. More gaslighting.

Bobby was poring over the charts. "Have you seen this?" he said to me. "The Mojave Desert's like a wasp's nest of these ley line things."

I was still focused on the rifle. "Commander, Bobby mentioned Brittany was in Los Angeles earlier this week."

"That's right. Britt's been testing us like crazy. She's gone AWOL a lot lately. We grounded her the minute she got home from L.A. But when the opportunity to be with these girls came up, we just thought . . ." He slammed the desk with his fist. "Damnit! Where is she?"

"Do you know where the Browning is?"

"Of course. I keep it in a gun locker in the garage." His eyes narrowed. "What are you suggesting?"

My iPhone vibrated and I pulled it out of my front pocket. Julie. We hadn't spoken in almost two days.

"I should take this," I said, but Pritchard was already making his own call. He walked outside, talking rapidly.

"Hi," I said.

"He . . . love," Julie said. "We . . . ing . . . to . . . tree."

"Sorry you're cutting out."

"'fic bad," she said. "Ther . . . three . . . s."

"Sweetheart, I can't hear you."

I lost the call.

I sent her a text: WHERE ARE YOU. I WILL CALL YOU LATER. MARRY ME.

My phone buzzed again, a London number.

"Hello?"

"DCI Garfield here. Thank goodness you answered. I'll make this short. My man at Customs and Immigration called. Several more groups like Colin's have been flying into LAX over the past few days. Not just from Heathrow—they're coming from all over Europe. I don't like it. I don't like it at all." A ringtone interrupted. Mike.

"Sorry, I just have to . . ." I switched lines. "Mike?"

"Boss, did you get the text?"

The throwaway phone in my left back pocket dinged. I tucked Mike's call between my shoulder and ear and lifted the burner to my eyes: RAJARAP FULL MOON BHAKTI SATSANG. MAHA MUDRA AND FRIENDS. SPECIAL GUEST.

In my ear, Mike said. "It's in Joshua Tree. I'll come pick you up."

"Don't. I'm not home." I kept reading: FREE ADMISSION. GANACHAKRA CAMP GROUND. RAINSHADOW LANE. JOSHUA TREE.

"Shit, you're not? Where are you, man?"

My throat closed as I read the final few words of the text: 9PM UNTIL FOREVER. IT'S TIME.

"Call Bill and tell him. You're in charge of Tank," I said, and ended the call.

I switched back to DCI Garfield, but he was long gone.

Pritchard hurried back in, his face white. "Detective, the rifle's not there. Brittany must have taken it."

Ding. A text landed from Julie: DRIVING BOYS TO JOSHUA TREE FOR CEREMONY. TRAFFIC TERRIBLE. AND THE ANSWER IS STILL YES.

I groaned out loud.

"What's going on?" Bobby asked.

"Hold on." I texted Julie back: DO NOT GO TO JOSHUA TREE!!! TURN AROUND. GO HOME.

I pressed "send" and felt better.

"I need to get to Joshua Tree," I said to Pritchard. "As soon as humanly possible."

Pritchard's eyes narrowed as he ran scenarios. He'd switched from concerned father to pure tactician.

"Bobby, you're FAA certified, right?" he asked.

Bobby nodded.

"Who do you rent from usually? Chip?"

Bobby nodded again. "Chip Lancaster," he explained to me. "He's a vet. He runs Eagle Air, a flying school out of the FBO airport in Visalia. I rent his Cessna one fifty-two."

"Two-seater, or three?" Pritchard said.

"Two."

Pritchard's face tightened in disappointment.

Bobby had his phone out and was scrolling contact numbers as he talked. "It's a two-hour flight to Joshua Tree, give or take. I've done it before. We should leave here within the hour, Ten—Chip likes his planes back before dark."

"Anything else you need?" Pritchard asked me.

I pointed to the framed photograph of Brittany and her father. "Can I take that, commander?"

Pritchard handed it over.

I mentally ran down the list.

"I also need a barber, a doctor, and some strong coffee."

He didn't blink.

"You're in the right place," Pritchard said.

CHAPTER 60

Eagle Air's headquarters was a corrugated shoebox. The outside awning barely shaded a metal picnic table and two plastic chairs.

I eyed the three banged-up prop planes parked nearby while Bobby finished the paperwork inside. We'd booked the Cessna 152 for four hours, at $135.00 an hour. It seemed like a bargain, until I saw the actual planes.

I should talk. My right arm was wilted and vulnerable without its fiberglass splint, and hung by my side like a limp rag. I ran my other palm over my hairless crown. I hadn't been this bald since Dharamshala. Or thin. I was an excellent candidate for ascetic training school.

Bobby marched into the shimmering heat, followed by Chip, a squat man with fierce eyes and a bushy white hermit's beard. He barely glanced at me, which I found impressive given my red robe, naked scalp, and suitcase from another century.

"Let's do this," Bobby said.

Though the Cessna was a two-seater, its propeller didn't look like it could lift much more than a newborn.

May I be safe and protected. Healthy and strong. May I be happy and peaceful.

May I survive.

As Bobby checked his instruments, I checked to see if Julie had texted me back.

There was a red exclamation point by my text to her.

It had never been sent. I tried to send it again.

I pulled out the burner phone and sent the same message.

I swore under my breath. The battery was running low on both phones, and we were about to take off.

"FYI," Bobby said, "we're landing at the F-22 airfield. It's privately owned. Very close to where you want to go. Recently closed, but it should be okay to land."

"Closed?" That didn't sound good.

"Also, we'll be cutting through strike fighter training areas en route. We'll be lower and slower, of course. Don't worry. It's not against regulations."

I put on my headset so he'd stop talking. Bobby adjusted his mic and exchanged codes and instructions with an anonymous air traffic controller.

We taxied onto a short runway, the propeller emitting a chopping sound of complaint. I kept telling myself that Bobby was a crack pilot—he could tailhook a cable with a killer machine while moving at 250 knots—but my nerve endings weren't buying it.

I closed my eyes and didn't open them until we were airborne.

The fields below were like scraps of old brown carpet.

I heard a roar overhead. Two strike fighters streaked by, three times as fast and five times as high.

I sank lower in my seat. Two hours. I could make it through anything for two hours.

I must have dozed off, which was shocking.

Bobby's voice roused me, urgent in my headset.

"Ten. Look."

The desert was vast and stark, a desolate plain pocked with rock piles and knotty vegetation. But he wasn't talking about the landscape.

"What road is that?"

"Twentynine Palms Highway," he said.

The four-lane highway divided the terrain like an asphalt scar. One side, the side that connected to a bigger freeway and the jeweled lights of civilization, was almost empty.

The opposite side, heading into bleak nothingness, was wall-to-wall with cars.

CHAPTER 61

I don't recommend landing on the unlit runway of a closed airfield in semidarkness, but if you're going to do it, have a Super Hornet pilot at the controls. The Cessna kicked up a storm of dust and bumped over a few potholes, but otherwise brought us safely to a halt.

"You sure you don't want me to come?"

"I'm sure," I said.

"Anything else I can do for you?"

I hesitated. But I might not get another chance to say this.

"Not for me," I said. "But maybe for someone else. I saw your father. It was because of him that I found you. He'd like to see you and Kim again."

Bobby's face darkened.

"He's in bad shape. Not just physically. His regrets are eating him alive."

Bobby worked his jaw. "I'll think about it," was all he said.

It was a start. And I'd kept my promise. "Thanks for your help, Bobby."

"Blue skies," he called over his shoulder, and climbed into the plane.

I turned on my phone. With a whoosh, my text finally took off. Too late by a long, long shot. My phone pinged. The text was from Heather, which was a surprise.

CALL ME ASAP.

I tried Julie first, but she didn't pick up.
Heather was next.

"Heather?"

"Quick update. The detailed tox report came back on the Kapoor kid, and it's a doozy. It changes everything."

"What do you mean?"

"Well, we expected to find alkaloids, and we did. But we also found scopolamine. Not just a little, a lot. A lot-a lot."

"Meaning what?"

"Meaning the datura at the scene wasn't the culprit. It was a brilliant attempt to mask something much more disturbing."

I squinted at the sky. The Cessna was a lonely speck, far in the distance.

"Ever heard of something called Devil's Breath?"

"No." My mouth was already dry. I'd bought a liter of bottled water on the base. I gulped some down.

"Super hard to get, ridiculously expensive. It's derived from a tree in Columbia. A kind of trumpet vine. It's tasteless. Odorless. It can cause hallucinations, and it wipes out any memory of your experience while under the influence. If you survive, that is. Hell, maybe that's a blessing."

"Why?"

"Because the other thing it does is eliminate free will. Once you're under, you'll do anything. Slice and stab yourself to death, for example."

"I have to go," I said.

This time, Julie answered. "Hi, love. Hi, hi, hi! We got here half an hour ago." I heard laughter and singing. Drumbeats. Clanging bells.

"Didn't you get my text?"

"Yeah! I said yes, remember?"

"Julie, this is really important. Where are you?"

"This crazy campsite in the middle of nowhere. They gave us our own deluxe tent. There must be a thousand people here already. It's so cool. It's like Woodstock. They're handing out free food to everybody—oh my goodness, so delicious. Not the lassi, that was nasty, but the curried wraps? Like a naan cone with two scoops of tikka masala."

I'd never heard her so wired.

"We barely made it. Bumper to bumper, the whole way. The guys are scheduled to go on in an hour. Main stage, can you believe it? They're doing an ancient Tibetan temple dance. You should see the masks they're wearing. Scare-ry."

"Julie, stop talking for a minute."

"Oh. Okay."

"You need to leave right now." The call cut off.

I checked the signal. There wasn't any. But I saw the second text, from an unknown sender: YOUR FRIENDS ARE HERE. WHERE ARE YOU?

I dug out the burner phone. The battery was dead.

I yelled into the night, but no one was listening.

The abandoned airfield was a mile north of Twentynine Palms Highway and a half mile west of Rainshadow Lane. On the aeronautical chart, Rainshadow had continued north until it dead-ended in a snarl of purple Magic Marker lines, drawn by Brittany. The vortex of vortexes.

I could hike back to the highway, or cut across to Rainshadow and hope to catch a ride. Either way, traffic was at a standstill.

Or I could take the raven's route, a straight shot across the Mojave.

I picked up the leaden suitcase. The bumpy vinyl handle felt familiar in my hand.

I had left my past wearing this same robe, carrying this same suitcase, my skull naked and my heart in my throat.

On the edge of the horizon, a huge milky eye was rising.

The full moon is the path.

I started to run.

CHAPTER 62

The drumbeat reached me first, a pounding pulse. *Thump, thump, thump, thump.* My pace had slowed to a hobbled jog, slowed by the crumbling soil.

A blister bubbled and broke on my left palm. My tongue was petrified wood, the liter of water I'd purchased at the base long since finished.

I hugged my right arm close as I ran by gnarled creosote bushes and spiky chollas. Joshua trees greeted me with misshapen limbs. The hot air was a pungent assault of sage and saltbush.

"Ow! Shit!" The suitcase bumped hard against my kneecap as I swerved to avoid a needled orb—a barrel cactus as red and round as a beach ball.

My lungs were screaming.

A giant rock pile loomed, an eroded collection of boulders. In the middle was a curled rocky fist with a jutting thumb. I took strength from its thumbs-up as I detoured around the timeworn barrier.

Now I could see a tower, but not of solid stone. The man-made tripod of steel girders had a wheel on top, like a windmill. Fluorescent green lights spiraled, a spinning neon mandala.

Thump thump thump.

The beat grew louder. A horn lobbed its mournful wail over the desolate landscape.

"*Hram hram hram,*" sang a woman, chanting the seed syllable of the Wheel of Time into a microphone.

"*Hram hram hram,*" a swollen chorus responded.

My right boot sent pebbles scattering. I had ploughed straight through a man-made spiral identical to the one at Bronson Caves, ruining the sacred helix.

Stone stupas started popping up like little tumors on the desert skin as I entered a sprawling encampment of tents and caravans—hundreds of them, occupying every square inch of sand bordering the central arena.

Hram hram hram hram.

Thousands of arms flickered and swayed, an ocean of human anemones. A second, horseshoe-shaped eruption of boulders created a kind of natural amphitheater.

A crush of cars waited to get in, headlights stretching back for miles. I wondered if a Vanagon was among them, or if Brittany and her friends had already pitched a tent somewhere.

I would have to choose my next moves with care.

A young woman in pigtails and cowboy boots crawled out of a nylon igloo. She spotted my robe and bowed, hands clasped.

"*Namasté,*" she murmured.

Her pupils were the size of dinner plates.

"Do you have any water?" I rasped.

She ducked inside the tent and returned with a metal canteen hanging from a strap. "It's warm. Is that okay?"

My left palm was bleeding and raw. "Can you please open it for me?"

She focused hard on unscrewing the top. She handed me the canteen.

I paused. "When and where did you fill this?"

"What? Oh, this morning, at home." She pressed it in my hand. "Take it. Water's free in there. Everything's free. I have enough. I am enough." Her head tipped slightly. "Do you see that?" Her voice was breathy. "The air. Like golden fireflies . . ."

I looked, but saw only Dawa, a lunar disc low on the horizon.

"Hram, hram, hram, hram . . ." The girl spread out her arms and whirled away, a desert dervish.

I followed my own moonlit path to the sea of celebrants and waded in. The smell was overpowering, a thick mixture of sweat and patchouli. Plus something else, something acrid and coppery—like blood, but less defined.

Madness. It was the scent of madness.

The fortress of bodies made forward movement impossible, especially for someone carrying a heavy suitcase.

I had to find Julie and the others. I visually divided up the crowd in quadrants and started to scan each section. Peppered throughout the crowd, Maha Mudra followers twirled and swayed in their by-now-familiar tunics and head scarves. I tried to do a rough head count, but there were far too many, and the number seemed to be growing.

The drumbeat became more frenzied, triggering a crescendo of ecstasy around me. Suddenly something brushed against my calf. Warm, animal, and alive. I recoiled instinctively.

I looked at the ground and saw the rump of a fleeing dog, his leash trailing behind him.

At first, my mind rejected what my eyes confirmed. It seemed impossible. But the squat shape was unmistakable. "Homer? Homer, come!"

Somehow my voice penetrated the chaos. Or maybe it was my scent. Homer looked around, his eyes red rimmed. I ran to his side and crouched.

"Homer. It's okay, it's okay." I laid my hand on his back. His thick torso was trembling, but the stub of a tail flicked, an almost wag.

I dribbled canteen water onto his coated tongue.

"Where's Julie? Where's your mistress?" He lapped at the dripping liquid, whimpering.

I looped the leash around my left wrist and stood.

Don't panic. Keep going.

The tidal swell of noise lessened slightly as a harmonium on stage took over the tempo, slowing things down. I

couldn't even see the musicians through the packed wall of people. There must have been 3,000 or 4,000, and growing. They undulated and flowed like lava.

Keep going.

"Jai Maha Mudra. Please help yourself. There is enough for everybody." The voice was British. An upper-crust mixture of clipped consonants and elongated vowels.

Colin.

He was dressed in an orange tunic and a white head scarf. He passed around a cardboard container of naan wraps and disposable cups of lassi.

"Colin Purdham-Coote." I raised my voice. "Collie!"

He wheeled to face me. His eyes were bright and clear, and also drug-free, judging by his pupils.

I took a step closer. "My name is Tenzing Norbu. Tell Maha Mudra I'm here. That I understand everything."

He dropped the container and took off.

"Jai Maha Mudra," I called out, but he'd melted into the crowd.

Maybe it would work. Maybe it wouldn't.

With Homer added to my burdens, I would never make it through this crush, so I opted to go around. I started moving sideways, keeping Homer on a short leash.

"Excuse me. Excuse me, please." The crowd was thick but docile—like children who had been overfed.

I had guessed right. On the far right, a dusty path ran alongside the massive herd. New age entrepreneurs had set up shop here, temporary displays of silk saris, crystals, dangling dream catchers. But they weren't really selling, and no one was buying either. Zombie-like, festival attendees and vendors collected in passive clumps, as if waiting for someone to tell them what to do.

I spotted a massive stage, elevated and bathed in blue light. I picked up the pace and drew within ten or twelve yards.

The leash jerked hard against my wrist and I almost fell. Homer had planted his paws. He was done.

I hunkered next to him.

"Homer, I can't carry you, you have to walk." He flattened into a pile of stubborn dog flesh. I tugged at the leash, but he'd somehow tripled his weight.

Maybe I could tie him to something and come back.

Still in a crouch, I looked around to assess. A long booth was set up deep in the shadows to my right, off the main path. My perspective gave me a clear view to the back of the booth and the orange-and-black Vyrus parked there.

Maha Mudra was already here.

Somewhere.

I stood to get a better look at the booth. My heart stopped.

I was looking at an arsenal. No one was manning the table, but its contents had been readied for later use: woven baskets in neat rows, filled with sacred Tibetan weaponry.

Wooden longbows bound in silk, their bamboo arrows tipped with bone. Wisdom swords, scorpion-hilted blades, shakti daggers, and curved scythes. Trident pikes and spears, harpoons with rope tethers. Skull clubs and skeleton clubs. Corpse clubs for impaling the wicked. Nooses, chains, and more than one eight-pointed hurling discus. And then I saw the three-bladed phurba. The kind Nawang had used to murder Bhim. I dropped Homer's leash, ran to the table and grabbed the dagger. I tucked it into a fold in my robe.

Wanhhh. Wanhhh, a longhorn wailed. Drums and cymbals joined in, setting off a fresh roar of approval. I recognized the rhythms of a Tibetan Buddhist *cham* dance.

I had to get to the stage, and fast.

"Homer, come!" Homer groaned and pushed to his feet. I picked up his leash and we struggled forward. Finally we reached the corner of a massive raised platform.

Three masked figures leaped and whirled above me, their clownlike skulls invoking the deities with dance. To one side, his features pinched, an exhausted Sonam kept jangled time with a pair of brass cymbals.

A lone woman twirled along the edge of the stage—the woman I loved, though nearly unrecognizable in her current state.

Julie's eyes were closed and her mouth hung open. She was soaked in sweat, her hair a mass of wet ringlets.

Homer started to howl.

"Julie. Julie!"

She looked down. For a moment she didn't know me either, but then her face cleared.

"Ten. You look funny. Where's your hair? Guess what? I'm enough. I am finally enough." She closed her eyes and drifted out of reach.

"Julie! Come back!" She spun to the back of the stage.

The temporary flooring was elevated at least five feet. I tried to pull myself up, but without a splint my right arm was worse than useless. I had no way to grip or get any purchase.

I needed to shift things, and fast. Flush out the enemy. Somehow create a distraction without causing a stampede.

I turned to face the swaying crowd. They were all so young. So very young.

"Ma ha Mu dra," I began to chant. "Ma ha Mu dra."

I gestured for others to follow as I raised my voice. "Ma ha Mu dra. Ma ha Mu dra."

Where were the tunics? Where were her followers?

"Ma ha Mu Dra! Ma Ha Mu Dra!"

The first to join in was a kid in a sarong, cheekbones striped with war paint. Next, a girl in an elk costume, her dreadlocks braided into arched horns, took up the chant.

"Ma ha Mu dra. Ma ha Mu dra."

More and more added their voices, a contagious build, until at last the scattered choruses tipped into one unified cry.

"MA HA MU DRA, MA HA MU DRA." Their swelling demand stopped the *cham* dance cold. As a female figure appeared at the back, the masked dancers stepped to one side. The chants of the crowd turned to loud cheers.

But the woman who stepped forward wasn't Maha Mudra. It was Adina.

I had so wanted to be wrong about this. The sight of her broke my heart.

She wore a luminous white caftan, but there was no head scarf to suppress the silvery cascade of hair. She seemed almost to float past the masked dancers. She stopped at the front of the stage, mic in hand, glowing with purpose.

"Are you ready?" Her amplified words were met with an answering roar.

A colorful skeleton leaped off the corner of the platform and landed in front of me. He pulled off the garish mask. It was Wangdue.

"Are you really ready?" Adina cried. The crowd's response gained in volume. The sound grew deafening.

I leaned close, almost shouting. "Wangdue, I need your help!" I checked his eyes. They were clear. "You're okay? You didn't eat or drink anything?"

"No."

"Good. How about the others?"

"No," he repeated. "They not eat or drink. Is Saka Dawa Duchen. We all fast. Except for Julie."

"I can't hear you, my children," Adina called, her voice teasing. Impossibly, the din grew even louder.

"Wangdue, get Julie and the others and go straight to the van. Lock yourself inside. Don't let anyone leave, not for any reason, understand?"

He nodded.

"Where is it parked?"

He pointed to a huge makeshift lot, to the left of the neon windmill.

"Okay. Good."

Adina raised her arms and then lowered them slowly. "Shhh," she said, "Shhh." Silence grew and spread.

I ducked low, pulling Wangdue with me. I didn't want Adina to see or hear me. Not until everyone was safe.

"Take Homer," I whispered, pressing the leash in his hand. "Julie will come if you have Homer." I hung the canteen around Wangdue's neck. "There's water in here. It's safe to drink. Give some to Julie, but only a little at a time. She's been drugged. Do you understand? Everyone here has been drugged."

Almost everyone.

"Patience, my beautiful ones," Adina now crooned. "Enjoy the sacred kirtans. Eat. Dance. Dawa is climbing the sky. It will all be over far too soon."

"You not come with us?" Wangdue said.

"I can't," I said. "I have to stop this."

Wangdue bowed slightly. "We chant for you."

I gripped his shoulders. *"Tashi deley." I honor the greatness in you.*

"Tashi deley, Lama Tenzing. You keep us safe."

He pulled on his skull mask, lifted Homer onto the stage, and climbed after him. I watched as Wangdue herded the others to the back of the platform. They descended an aluminum set of stairs. A docile Julie followed along quietly. Thankfully, Adina was too flush with her own power to notice.

"So get ready, because you won't believe what's coming, as soon as Dawa is overhead." She was working the crowd into a fresh frenzy. "The full moon is rising. And you know that that means . . ."

"It's time!" the ecstatic crowd cried.

The blue spotlight split into pulsing strobes of color, and a thumping electronic backbeat started up. Adina motioned a waiting group of musicians onto the stage. A young man in a knit beanie grabbed Adina's mic and began to rap a call and response as others took up bongos, sitars, and an electric bass guitar. "I bow at his feet, so sweet, my master, bring me there faster, hear me calling, help me I'm falling, Guru Brahma! Say it!"

"Guru Brahma!"

"Guru Vishnu!"

"Guru Vishnu!"

"Kala Chakra!"

"Kala Chakra!"

Adina gyrated backward, her hair a spinning disk of quicksilver.

I ran behind the raised stage and took cover in a jumble of fallen rocks.

"Jai Maha Mudra!"

"Jai Maha Mudra!"

"Jai Guru Vishnu!"

"Jai Guru Vishnu!"

Okay, Adina, I thought. *Lead me to her.*

CHAPTER 63

Adina materialized at the top of the aluminum staircase connecting the stage to the desert floor. She raced down the metal steps, her hair a rippling stream. I watched from my hiding place as she hurried to the far side of the curved rock. She glanced both ways and disappeared.

At first I couldn't find an opening—it was as if Adina had passed through solid stone. But my fingers discovered a dark cleft, camouflaged by surrounding folds of rock. I sidled through, holding my suitcase close.

I emerged into arid landscape. A footpath wound into the desert, first climbing, and then dropping steadily through scrub and dry growth. A small lizard scuttled by. In the growing dark, pink rockface took on the marbled lividity of morbid flesh.

Behind me, a didgeridoo yowled.

They couldn't be far—Adina had arrived quickly once my cheer for Maha Mudra became a group demand.

The trail veered left. Below, a copse of fan palms rose from yet another mineral outcropping.

Palm trees in the desert? Bizarre.

Under the palm trees' fanned tops, shaggy fronds formed thick beards, silvered by moonlight. They looked like ancient desert sages.

I cocked my head at an unexpected sound.

Water—only a trickle, but unmistakable. I was getting close. Earth. Water. Sky. Space. A desolate oasis; a barren grove. The ideal setting for the ganachakra ritual.

Fire, too. Inside a long, shallow pit, lined with stone, mesquite logs spat tongues of flame. Woven baskets were stacked in a nest nearby.

And then I saw it, just past the fire pit: a human mandala. The fan palm sentinels were watching over concentric circles of Maha Mudra followers dressed in jewel-colored robes. Six circles of ten, and a central quadrant of four.

Sixty-four.

Or maybe only 63.

The middle square was missing its fourth occupant. The three already there were familiar. TJ's caftan was canary yellow; Colin, still in bright orange; and Adina, as I'd already seen, in snowy white. The inner quadrant color scheme of the Kalachakra Mandala. Orange. Yellow. White.

Only maroon was absent.

They sat in lotus position on what looked like animal skins. Displayed inside the incomplete square was an exquisite namchuwangdan mosaic constructed out of colored glass, bottle caps, and broken tile. It was both crude and powerful.

And seated on a throne in its center, wrapped in cobalt blue silk and daubed with a blood red bindi, was a demon disguised as a saint.

A voice floated up to me: ". . . drink of the elixir of life . . ."

Low, clear, neutral.

". . . quicksilver and sulfur . . . blood of the woman, seed of the man . . ."

Neither male, nor female.

". . . sacred sukra . . . the Power of Ten . . ."

The voice of my nighttime terrors.

Palden Lhamo, protect me. Give me strength.

The throne was a stack of rocks draped in embroidered gold. Maha Mudra's dark curtain of hair was topped with a five-sectioned crown, each section bearing the mantra of a corresponding deity. Below the crown, midbrow, the bindi seemed to glow. Her left hand grasped a goblet of hammered silver, half-full of reddish liquid.

"I drink the highest immovable," Maha Mudra said. "Bodhicitta nectar. Mystic alchemy."

The chalice rose.

Don't.

The image wavered like water.

Can't breathe.

I clutched at my closing throat.

Can't . . .

A cold muzzle pressed against the nape of my neck.

"Do. Not. Move," said a young woman's voice.

My suitcase started to slide, setting loose a cascade of pebbles. As it tumbled to the bottom of the slope, the acolytes scrambled to their feet. They spun in place, searching until they had me located. And now I could see the brandished blades and spears, the chains, cleavers, skewers and clubs. My three-bladed dagger would be about as effective as a butter knife.

I cast off the clutch of panic with a fierce expulsion of breath. I had to commit to this, or die. I turned my head slightly. "Don't shoot me, Brittany," I said to my would-be huntress. I heard a quick intake of breath.

"Jai Maha Mudra!" I called to the faces below.

CHAPTER 64

Maha Mudra was motionless on her throne. I descended, my eyes locked on her features. But there wasn't enough light to be sure. I had to get closer. Brittany followed behind me, her Browning .22-250 trained.

My suitcase lay askew at the foot of the fire pit. I bent and grasped its handle.

"Jai Maha Mudra," I repeated to the group as I straightened. "I've journeyed long and hard to get here." I aimed the next words at Maha Mudra. "I am not a stranger. You know me. And I know you. I know who you are."

Maha Mudra said nothing.

I touched my robe. "I am here to be your empty vessel. I am here to prove myself worthy. I belong to you."

Maha Mudra motioned the crowd to sit. She nodded her chin slightly to Brittany. Brittany lowered the Browning and reclaimed her spot on the outermost rim.

"So. You have found me," Maha Mudra said.

"Yes."

"Come closer."

I stepped between the rows of followers until I reached the center, and the throne. I could feel their gazes attach like hooks.

I studied the striking face before me.

There were differences, of course. The thick fall of black hair. A softening around the jaw; a fullness to the lips. The synthetic progesterone had done its work.

But the eyes. The eyes were the same. Black pools, ringed with gold. Like luminous mirrors: in themselves, nothing, but reflecting everything.

Nawang, I thought.

"Adi Buddha," I said, and dropped to my knees.

Shock rippled through the surrounding group.

"You can stand, Lama Tenzing," my brother replied. If in fact Nawang was still my brother. Maybe brother-sister was a better description. The ganachakra path to the divine required the merging of both energies, the masculine and the feminine, in order to achieve the highest state—holy hermaphrodite; cosmic androgyne. A symbolic transformation, not a literal one.

But Nawang had never been one for half measures.

I rose. He raked my body with his gaze.

"You look almost the same," Nawang said. "I thought you'd be more changed."

"I have been fasting," I said. "I retook the vows. I wanted to be ready for you."

The gold in his eyes seemed to catch the light.

I mentally reviewed the translated texts, and my recorded therapy session, blessing Sonam for his eastern insight, and Eric for his western wisdom.

"But you, Nawang. I can see the shift. You walked the hero's path for so many years. And now you have untied the knots within, haven't you?"

Nawang's nod was barely perceptible. "It is true. The lotus circles flow freely. The fire is ready for a final unleashing."

I indicated the group.

"And these are your adepts?"

"Yes. We only await the ascent of the full moon."

"Who is to be your wisdom consort? Brittany?"

Nawang glanced in her direction. His smile was fond. "No. Brittany is still somewhat unskilled."

"Adina?"

"Adina. Dear dakini Adina. She's better suited as karma mudra, aren't you, beloved?"

Adina's face flushed with pleasure.

This surprised me. According to the texts the final initiations required young karma mudras, ideally none older than

19 or 20. By including Adina, Nawang had ventured off the proscribed map. Which was bad, but also good. It was time to play my first card.

"So you have not yet chosen your wisdom consort?"

"I have not," Nawang said.

"Choose me," I said.

The crowd murmured in protest. I pushed ahead.

"Think about it. You have integrated the polarity of the sexes. You have tasted nirvana. You have crossed the threshold. You do not need karma mudras as dakini crones, or yogis as observers. You need a member of your own tribe. One who shares your noble blood."

Nawang wavered, his ego doing battle with the desire to succeed on his own terms. I adjusted.

"You predicted this yourself, Nawang," I said. "You found me when I was lost. First, as a child. And again, as an adult. You let me know you had never left me. You drew me here to your side. *He is coming.* That's what you said. And now it's time, and I am here. Only I can help you achieve the final perfection."

"No!" This, from Adina. "Maha Mudra, Tenzing can't be trusted!"

Nawang's nostrils flared, his hostility at the interruption palpable. He collected himself.

"Adina, beloved, lead the others in chant."

Adina's features took on an uncharacteristic meekness. She closed her eyes. "*Hram hram hram hram,*" she murmured.

"*Hram hram hram hram hram hram,*" the others joined in. The chant provided a low, pulsing undercurrent of sound.

Nawang's eyes bore into mine. "Is this true, little brother? Are you not to be trusted? Still?"

I dropped to my knees again, but this time to open the suitcase. I slipped the cat's-eye ring on my right pinkie finger. Then I picked up the vajra hammer with my left hand and stood.

Adina's chanting faltered for a moment. Then she continued.

"I will prove my devotion." I hefted the hammer. "This tho-ba crushes any obstruction to liberation. It holds untold power. Its head is a meteorite, formed during the first Kali Yuga, millions of years ago."

My words had ignited lust. Nawang stared at the hammer, his gaze avid.

"Whoever holds this vajra hammer has power over all, and feels no pain. This is the true scepter of the Adi Buddha."

I put down the vajra hammer, slipped the ring off, and kissed the amber cat's-eye. "I purify myself for you, with earth, fire, air, water, and ether." With my left hand I pressed the ring against my right thigh, hip, upper arm, and shoulder, finishing at the crown of my head. I put the ring on, my left ring finger this time.

Could I do this next part? I had to.

"I offer you my skin . . ." I pulled the phurba still tucked in my robe and scraped the blade, lightly skinning the inside of my right forearm. Blood welled as I dropped the dagger. The blade clinked against the shards of the namchuwangdan mosaic. "I offer you my bone."

And your arm is rigid and detached . . .

That's it . . .

And the arm is numb . . .

An immovable iron bar.

I stretched out my right arm. Raised my left, hammer held high. The blow was swift and sure, a direct hit on the unhealed ulna bone.

Crack.

I felt the bone rebreak, but the pain was distant, a faint echo of the real thing. I didn't even flinch.

I held up my dangling arm, dripping blood. "Jai Adi Buddha."

The chanting sputtered into silence as bodies shifted. A few even squirmed, but Nawang was mesmerized by my wounded limb.

"Give me the tho-ba," Nawang said, reaching for it.

"Let me serve you," I replied. "And send the others away. You don't need them. You have me."

A smile played at the corners of his mouth.

"You heard him," he called out. "Go on then. Leave us. Join the others below."

No one moved a muscle. Adina laughed softly, as if at a private joke. Her pupils were dilated after the chanting. All of theirs were. They were held captive by some kind of loyalty deeper and more dangerous than any chemical could induce.

Nawang returned his attention to me. "What can I do? They need me too much. They are ready to make the sacrifice, to cut the cords of ignorance. They will suffer, maim, even kill for me. They know they cannot ever die, for I am their Adi Buddha." He leaned close. "Careful. Mystic love is explosive. And addictive, Tenzing."

So is hatred, I thought.

He held out his hand. "Give me the tho-ba," he commanded.

His followers stiffened, watching closely. Withholding was no longer wise. I handed over the vajra hammer. He touched the blue-black head.

"How auspicious that we should meet again on this night, on Saka Dawa Duchen." He caressed the meteorite. "Do you remember our last full moon together, Lama Tenzing?"

"I remember Bhim," I said.

Nawang chuckled, a dark sound.

"Poor Bhim. He was my first. A bit clumsy. I thought I knew everything back then, but I knew nothing. How naive, to think that practicing the law of inversion was enough to take me to the pinnacle."

"I was in awe," I said. "You dared to break every precept. Lying. Stealing. Smoking ganja."

"Copulation," he savored the word. "Taking the life of another. Of course, I hadn't yet learned that others could break the precepts for me."

I made my voice hushed. "You were like a king to me. Like Kalachakra. You still are."

Nawang stroked the shaft of the vajra hammer, visibly relaxing. I almost had him where I wanted him.

"Our father knew," I said. "Apa always knew you were the special one. Let me serve you, Nawang. Let me take on the role of Maha Mudra. Let me be your *candali*, your shakti flame."

Nawang motioned me close. He drew back his lips, more grimace than smile. His eyes were windows into pure evil.

"I have known many women," he said, his voice like a hiss. "Men, too. I have eaten uncooked flesh and drunk the sacred tantric fluids. But I have not yet broken the final taboo."

"We are brothers," I said. "Let me be your consort. But send the others away."

"No," he said. His eyes hardened. "They stay." He raised his voice. "Let us begin. It is time."

I had to recalibrate, and fast. Thankfully, I had not underestimated my foe, not this time. His talents might be prodigious, but I still had a few of my own to call on.

I knelt by the open suitcase and pulled out Sonam's sheaf of papers.

"Look. I have translated the sacred ganachakra ritual for you, so your adepts can understand."

Nawang seemed pleased by this. I pressed on.

"But first, we must purify the breath and silence the mind. We must meditate. Ready ourselves for your greatest gift."

Nawang cocked his head, amused.

"And what might that be, Lama Tenzing?"

"Power," I said. "Remember? You told me this, long ago. And you were right. You still are. We share this desire, for power. But it is yours to claim. The Power of Ten. I am only your vessel, your vase. I am your brother, and you are my god. Let me prepare the people."

He was mine. He set the vajra hammer on the ground beside his throne and spread his arms to include the human mandala of followers.

"My brother Tenzing will lead us in meditation. Let us begin."

I took a seat, just in front of the throne, my suitcase at my feet. I could feel brittle bits of the mosaic through my thin monk's robe. I laid the papers on top of the suitcase.

I was taking a huge risk. Nawang, at least, had a long history of spiritual practice, and his sensitivity, like mine, was extreme. I was banking on the fact that everyone else in this inner circle had at least some familiarity with meditative concentration. I knew they were willing and eager to taste other realms—they were here, weren't they?

"Let us close our eyes, and settle into a deep awareness of our bodies," I said.

Nawang's dark pupils flashed at me one last time before he lowered his eyelids. There was something almost reptilian about the move.

"That's it . . . that's it . . ." I glanced at the concentric circles of seekers. Eyes closed, they rustled and got comfortable.

May their hearts and minds be receptive.

"That's it, that's it . . . beautiful, Adina . . . Yes, Britt . . ."

A massive chant rose from the desert below us. *"Maha Mudra. Adi Buddha. Maha Mudra. Adi Buddha."*

And then, farther away, the faint wail of sirens.

For a moment I panicked. What if it didn't work? How could I stop this tidal wave?

You remember that you are not alone, Ten. You are never alone.

"Hram hram hram hram," I chanted, hoping this familiar trigger would further induce a trance state. *"Hram hram hram."*

I was not alone, or unprotected. In a darkened van nearby, my fiancée waited, the love of my life. I had Bill and Martha, there for me always. Mike. Kim. The noble Kshatriyas up in Lemoore. Sonam and Eric with their wise men's tools. And my friends, my best friends, who were chanting right now for my safety and my success. I could do this. I was not alone.

"Hram hram hram," my voice became a whisper, and then a memory of a whisper. I allowed the restless quiet to deepen into a hushed silence. I started to talk, my voice soothing:

"Everyone here has felt lost and broken, abandoned in some way."

Including Nawang. Including me.

"And settling deeper into this moment . . .

"We all have a strong desire to do good in the world . . . yes?

"That's it . . .

"We want companionship as we walk the path . . .

"And preparing to relax very deeply . . .

"We want to belong somewhere . . .

"Commit to something greater than ourselves . . .

"Relaxing into the present moment . . .

"That's it . . ."

And I reminded us that sometimes our desire to do good and commit can cause us to stray into places that do harm instead.

And I let us know that we should forgive ourselves for these choices.

And I invited us to remember what freedom tastes like.

And I reassured us that saying *yes* and saying *no* could both be wise choices.

"And I'm going to ask you each to picture something in your life, something from a happier time that reminds you who you really are, and that you belong, no matter what. And when you open your eyes, you will remember. You will remember that time when you felt steadfast and sure. When you felt loved."

They were all in a deep, deep trance.

"That's it . . ."

I opened the suitcase to retrieve two final items. I stepped to the outermost row and placed the photograph of Brittany and her father in her lap. I returned to the center and slipped Paresh Kapoor's cat's-eye ring onto Colin's finger. I transferred TJ's silk khata from my neck to his. I balanced the vajra hammer on Adina's crossed legs, her anniversary offering to her husband, and now my offering to her.

"And even more relaxed. That's it . . ."

Finally, I picked up the peacock-feathered bumpa. Nawang's parting gift two decades ago, when I was just a scared boy with no place to call home and he was searching for the truth with a broken compass.

I laid the tarnished silver vase in Nawang's lap. Was he under? I couldn't tell. I took my place at the center one final time and closed my eyes.

"And on the count of five . . .

"One . . . we are carving a new life, like a river carves its bed . . . May we be safe and protected . . .

"Two . . . we are choosing to be well . . . May we be healthy and strong . . .

"Three . . . we will open our eyes in the here and now, liberated from our painful past . . . May we be full of compassion for all sentient beings . . .

"Four . . . sound in mind and body. . . with an open but wise heart. . . may we be free . . .

"Five."

I opened my eyes. The grotto was drenched in silver light.

"Look, Ten," Adina said. "The moon is so full. Where's Eric? I have to tell him."

CHAPTER 65

Nawang was broken, at least temporarily. When he opened his eyes, I could see that any sanity remaining had finally splintered. His eyes found me.

"Apa?" he said. His voice was high-pitched, like a child's.

"No, I am Tenzing," I said. "Your brother." Nawang nodded. He clutched his feathered vase close. His expression curious, he watched his acolytes file away as if they had nothing to do with him.

The others had come out of the trance state in stages, like waking from deep sleep. They stretched and looked around, a little confused. I asked TJ and Colin to collect the weapons. They circled with the baskets, and everyone filled them without complaint.

Using my good arm, I hooked Nawang's right elbow and led him down the path to the campground, following the bemused parade of 63 former followers. Nawang prattled nonstop. His bindi and the kohl around his eyes had smeared, and his five-pointed crown now sat at an angle. He looked completely mad.

"I just met my apa," he said. "He is a special man. A holy man. He and some other monks came to our village. Because of me!"

"How do you know he's your father?" I had to ask, though his blood would offer the final proof.

"Because! My mother told me! He said she should send me to him, when I was older. I knew he'd come one day. I knew he'd find me!"

Of course. My father must have heard of Nawang's early spiritual prowess and brought the abbots to see the boy for

themselves. He must have felt vindicated, especially after I proved to be such a disappointment.

Until his firstborn—his dream child—was revealed to be a living nightmare.

We walked through the cleft of stone into a scene of controlled chaos.

At first I thought the strobing blue-and-red lights were still part of the stage show. Then I realized they belonged to a swarm of patrol cars and rescue vehicles, their LED bars flashing. Bill had marshaled an army of responders.

I was grateful I had disarmed Maha Mudra's personal troops. These days, the flash of even a single blade could unleash a torrent of gunfire.

EMTs tended to the recovering hordes. Later, the festival attendees would remember almost nothing, but brag about being there anyway.

Bill strode up. "You are in so much trouble," he barked. His eyes widened at the sight of me, robed and bleeding. "Where's your hair? What the hell did you do to yourself this time?"

"Whatever I had to," I said. I stood to one side. "Bill, this is my brother, Nawang."

Nawang's smile remained sweet, even when they handcuffed him.

I had assumed that we shared receptivity to suggestion, but I hadn't bargained on how intensely Nawang would respond. As Bill led him away, my heart couldn't help but ache. This childlike state was almost certainly temporary. The evil would return as surely as the pain in my freshly broken arm. He was looking at multiple years in prison, if he wasn't deported first for his earlier crimes. Or maybe he'd wind up shackled in a psychiatric ward. Either way, I was glad to have met the little boy who existed before the darkness took hold.

Pritchard arrived next. Bobby must have done a round-trip in the Cessna after all. The commander ran to his daughter Brittany and gathered her in his arms, their roles reversed. She was the soldier returning from war this time.

Colin stood to one side, looking a little lost. Bill had relayed a message to me from Bertie, and I walked over to deliver it.

"Your father's on his way. He took the red-eye."

"I guess there's a first time for everything," Colin said. He twisted the cat's-eye ring on his finger. "Do you think I can take Paresh back with me? His ashes, I mean?"

I smiled. "I'm sure that can be arranged."

I knew I'd have to give a statement, but I persuaded the local police to let me find my friends first. They were still in the parking lot, clustered around the van. Eric and Adina stood together nearby.

Adina's eyes were red. "We're going home," was all she said, and all I needed to hear.

Wangdue, Sonam, Yeshe, and Lobsang had TJ surrounded. He didn't seem to mind at all. They were his true circle of safety, and he knew it.

I found Julie wrapped in a blanket inside the van. Homer, too. I climbed in next to them with my broken wing.

CHAPTER 66

As wedding ceremonies go, ours was turning out to be pretty extemporaneous. Exactly the way I liked it. We'd take care of the official part later, but this wasn't about being official. This was about honoring our commitment in the company of loved ones.

The setting was pure magic. Julie and Homer had discovered Meditation Mount when the monks were in Ojai.

"I know it's the one," she'd said on our way to the hospital to yet again set and splint my arm. "Just like I knew you were the one the first time we met."

Who was I to argue with that? So she picked the place and I picked the date.

"Next Sunday," I had said. "While Yeshe and Lobsang are still here."

Including Bill, that gave me three best men. Sonam, complete with yellow rooster hat, would oversee our vows. For Julie, Martha and the twins would attend. And that was it. That was the wedding party. We even left Homer and Tank at home.

Simple. Meaningful. Makeshift.

The vows were tucked into the inside pocket of my new linen jacket. We'd spent much of last night composing them together, an intimate give-and-take that boded well for our future. I took them out to reread:

I commit to full and heartfelt union with you, and I commit to embracing my own creative expression.
I commit to learning something new with you every day.

I commit to telling you my absolute truth, and to listening to yours.

I commit to making agreements I know I can keep, and I commit to keeping them.

I commit to letting you know every day how much I love and appreciate you.

And I choose to love you, every day, as much as I can, from wherever I am.

After we'd finished writing our vows, I'd handed Julie an envelope, business-size.

"What's this?" she'd said.

"The wedding. Also my nest egg," I'd answered. "Martha helped."

Julie opened the envelope, mystified. She'd unfolded a colored printout of a custom food truck.

"Oh, Ten," she'd said.

"I figured a gourmet restaurant on wheels might be just the ticket." It had taken almost all my savings, but I considered it a sound investment.

"This is pure O. Henry," she'd said. "'The Gift of the Magi.'"

"I'm not sure I understand."

"You will." She'd handed me her own envelope. "Also the wedding. Also my nest egg. Also thanks to Martha. She's been very busy."

I'd opened my own envelope. Inside was a colored printout of a yurt, airy and spacious and completely private. A perfect haven for a man and his cat, should the need arise.

"There goes our safety net," I'd said.

"Safety nets are overrated," she'd replied. And after that, we'd stopped talking, so we could figure out how to make love with only three arms between us.

The Ojai Valley glowed pink and gold in the dusky sunset. Lavender and sage perfumed the air. A fountain somewhere nearby warbled.

I stood with my best friends, my heart at ease.

Maude and Lola, their striped sundresses and expressions of concentration identical, walked down the path clutching little baskets. Maude was carefully dropping tiny white blooms, one by one. She noticed Lola's full load.

"Lola," Maude whispered, her voice urgent. "Throw the flowers."

Lola grabbed a fistful and hurled them straight up. They showered down like stars.

Martha arrived next with a bouquet of wildflowers, laughing and weeping.

And finally, Julie. The girls had helped her braid daisies into a garland. Her dress was gauze layered over sage green silk. Nothing like a fat meringue, and just like her—sexy, romantic, spiritual, grounded, creative, and earthy. All that was missing was the humor, but I had that covered.

I winked at Bill, and he raised his phone after thumbing the screen.

"Goin' to the chapel and we're . . ." Julie threw back her head and roared.

ACKNOWLEDGMENTS

Gratitude from Gay Hendricks

After so many books we've written together, it's getting harder to think of wonderful things to say about Tinker Lindsay that I haven't said before! Suffice it to say that being friends and colleagues with Tinker has been one of the most joyful and illuminating relationships of my life. Her genius and kind heart are treasured in our household, and I hope to be in her creative sphere throughout my life.

I feel more grateful as the years go by for the great mystery writers of past generations. I wouldn't have ventured into the field had I not fallen in early love with Sir Arthur Conan Doyle and his creation, Sherlock Holmes. Later, when I read John D. MacDonald's Travis McGee series I began to appreciate the advantages of having a character that could change, learn, and mature over time. Although I'm now a mystery writer I'm still as enthusiastic a mystery reader as ever; I read every Michael Connelly, T. Jefferson Parker and Robert Crais mystery novel as soon as they're published, as well as any other good thriller I can get my hands on.

The team at Hay House is a writer's dream. Reid Tracy and Patty Gift are two of the finest people I've met in my 40 years in publishing. Sally Mason-Swaab's editorial touch made the book sing and dance, and Charles McStravick's cover art has done a beautiful job of expressing the feeling-tone of the books.

My deepest bow of gratitude goes always to my wife, Katie, for 36 years of love and good times. I am very blessed

to have a mate who serves as muse and first listener for everything I write. One of our sacred traditions is that I read aloud to her everything I write each day. Her generous listening and helpful suggestions make writing a daily joy.

Gratitude from Tinker Lindsay

Without the brilliant and prolific Gay Hendricks there would be no Tenzing Norbu. I'm grateful to him from the bottom of my heart for inventing this timely and irresistible detective, and for inviting me to join him in co-creating Ten's world. As co-writer and as dear friend, Gay has changed my life profoundly. Huge appreciation to Katie Hendricks as well—for her insight, humor, and fierce commitment to creativity and joy.

Big thanks to our Hay House dream team: to Patty Gift and Reid Tracy for saying *Yes* to Ten, and for leading the way by enthusiastic and expert example; to our editor, Sally Mason-Swaab, who somehow combines a light touch with deep wisdom and thorough professionalism; and to Charles McStravick for his artful and compelling cover designs. I'd also like to offer my deep appreciation to everyone at Hay House for their ongoing support of work that heals, unites, and inspires. Never has the world needed it more.

Writers would be lost without willing experts, and I relied on a slew for this book. All accuracies are theirs. Any mistakes, tiny or glaring, are mine.

I owe enormous thanks to Detective Inspector Lee Barnard and Detective Sergeant Lee Minnighan of the London Metropolitan Police for walking me through their thorough and complex missing-persons investigative protocols. DS Minnighan went above and beyond the call of duty, providing me with hours of invaluable advice and reams of materials concerning everything from risk assessments to Border Systems watchlists.

Deep appreciation to Mark Tyrrell, co-founder of Uncommon Knowledge, whose hypnotherapy "scripts" and

video demonstrations were invaluable research tools.
Thanks, as well, to Jerome Lewis, Ph.D., for his deep well
of psychological wisdom. Because of Bob Steinbugler, I now
know everything there is to know about the VYRUS motor-
cycle. I gratefully acknowledge the L.A. County Coroner De-
partment's K-9 detection team Karina Peck and her German
shepherd "Indie"—they served as inspiration for Fran Hoa-
gland and Shirley Bones. And thanks to Pacific Oaks School
parent and winning Spring Auction bidder Liesl Copland, for
providing me with the excellent name *Ezekiel Foss*.

I relied on a number of fascinating books in my insatia-
ble quest to better understand the phenomenon of religious
cults: *Malignant Pied Pipers of Our Time*, by Peter A. Olsson;
Prophetic Charisma, by Len Oakes; *Cartwheels in a Sari*, by Jay-
anti Tamm; and *Holy Hell*, by Gail Tredwell. I also mined *The
Shadow of the Dalai Lama*, by Victor and Victoria Trimondi,
for insights into a darker interpretation of Tibetan Buddhist
beliefs.

My gratitude to film composer Michael McCuistion
for verbally recreating the Griffith Park Observatory show
"Time's Up," after it proved impossible to find in any archives.

I salute my friend and hero Lieutenant Commander
Brian Emme, who carved out enough time from his busy life
to patiently field this neophyte's nonstop questions while
ferrying me around Lemoore Naval Air Station. Watching
a series of thundering F/A-18 super hornets practice touch-
and-gos was both thrilling and humbling, and I'll never
forget it.

I so appreciate Laura Chandler and the Sacred Stream
Foundation in Berkeley for inviting me to join the monks of
Gaden Shartse Dokhang Monastery during their Northern
California tour. Their sand mandala and Losar ceremonies
deeply moved me, and their openhearted practice forever
changed me. To these venerable lamas I bow in heartfelt
thanks: Lobsang Chophel, Lobsang Dhonye, Geshe Dorjee
Gyaltsin, Geshe Jangchup Thinlay, Tanzin Namgail, Nima
Dorje, and Wangdu. Special thanks to Spiritual Master Geshe
Thupten for patiently explaining dependent origination,

among other erudite topics, and to Lungrik Gyaltsin (LG) for serving as cheerful translator throughout. Thanks, as well, to driver extraordinaire Sherri Serino for providing me with loads of delightful "touring tales," and to Wendy Guglieri and Jeanne Marie Chesko for taking me under their welcoming wings.

I am eternally grateful to my Writers Group—the magnificent seven—Monique de Varennes, Beverly Baz, Kathryn Hagen, Emilie Small, Blossom Pidduck, Pat Stiles, and Barbara Sweeney. I gave them very little time, and a metric truckload of pages, and without a peep of complaint they dove right in. As usual, their in-depth critiques of the manuscript were as insightful as they were kind.

And finally I offer my love, ever and always, to my husband and best friend Cameron Keys. You accept my foibles, honor my passions, and listen to my crazy dreams, literally and figuratively. The way you weave words into gold dazzles me. The way your heart responds to the world inspires me. How fortunate I am, to walk with you by my side.

ABOUT THE AUTHORS

 Gay Hendricks PhD has served for more than 35 years as one of the major contributors to the fields of relationship transformation and body-mind therapies. He is the author of 36 books, including *The Corporate Mystic, Conscious Living* and *The Big Leap,* and with his wife, Kathlyn Hendricks PhD, has written many bestsellers, including *Conscious Loving* and *Five Wishes.* Gay Hendricks received his PhD in counselling psychology from Stanford University in 1974. After a 21-year career as a professor of counselling psychology at the University of Colorado, he and Kathlyn founded the Hendricks Institute, based in Ojai, California, which offers seminars worldwide. In recent years Gay Hendricks has also been active in creating new forms of conscious entertainment. In 2003, along with the movie producer Stephen Simon, he founded the Spiritual Cinema Circle, which distributes inspirational movies to subscribers in 70-plus countries around the world (www.spiritualcinemacircle.com). He has appeared on more than 500 radio and television shows, including *The Oprah Winfrey Show* and *48 Hours,* and on networks including CNN and CNBC.

www.hendricks.com

ABOUT THE AUTHORS

© Cameron Keys

Tinker Lindsay is an accomplished screenwriter, author and conceptual editor. A member of the Writers Guild of America (WGA), the Independent Writers of Southern California (IWOSC), Women in Film (WIF) and Mystery Writers of America (MWA), she has worked in the Hollywood entertainment industry for over three decades. Lindsay has written screenplays for major studios such as Disney and Warner Bros., collaborating with the award-winning film director Peter Chelsom. Lindsay wrote the screen adaptation of *Hector and the Search for Happiness, The Space Between Us* (co-written with Allan Loeb), *Buddha: The Warrior Within* (co-written with Pan Nalin), *Those Who Have Eyes* (co-written with Cameron Keys), and many others. In addition to the Tenzing Norbu detective series, Lindsay has written two books: *The Last Great Place* and a memoir, *The Sound of One Heart Breaking*.

Lindsay graduated with high honours from Harvard University with a degree in English and American literature and language. She studied and taught meditation for several years before moving to Los Angeles to live and work.

www.tinkerlindsay.com

HAY HOUSE

Look within

Join the conversation about latest products,
events, exclusive offers and more.

f Hay House UK

🐦 @HayHouseUK

📷 @hayhouseuk

🖤 healyourlife.com

We'd love to hear from you!